The End of Asquith

The Downing Street Coup – December 1916

Michael Byrne

▌▌▌ Clink
Street

London | New York

Published by Clink Street Publishing 2016

Copyright © 2016

First edition.

ISBN: Paperback: 978-1-911110-10-1
ISBN: E-Book: 978-1-911110-11-8

Again for Nick

The events described in this book follow the broad outline provided by Roy Jenkins in *Asquith* (London: Collins, 1964) and Lord Beaverbrook in *Politicians and the War, 1914-1916, Volume II* (London: Lane Publications, 1932). The dialogue is largely imagined and the motives attributed to the principal characters are also conjectural, but all the meetings took place much as I have described them here and the outcome was of course the same.

Gore Vidal began every book in his seven-volume *Narratives of Empire* with a reminder of Mary McCarthy's famous list of 'things that "serious" fiction cannot deal with'. The final impossible item was 'a Cabinet meeting where actual politics are alluded to.' Vidal quoted this warning only to show how wrong McCarthy was. I have tried to follow where Gore led.

'The life of the country depends on resolute action by you now.'

David Lloyd George to Andrew Bonar Law
Saturday 2 December 1916

'That is a question which I must reserve for myself to decide.'

Herbert Asquith to David Lloyd George
Monday 4 December 1916

'Unity without action is nothing but futile carnage, and I cannot be responsible for that. Vigour and vision are the supreme need at this hour.'

David Lloyd George to Herbert Asquith
Tuesday 5 December 1916

London, December 1916.

Herbert Asquith is exhausted. As leader of the Liberal Party, one of England's two great political movements, he has been Prime Minister for over eight years. The last two-and-a-half years have been spent directing the country's increasingly ineffective war effort. His eldest son was killed at the front ten weeks ago.

During his early years in Downing Street Asquith had worked closely with David Lloyd George, then Chancellor of the Exchequer, to guide the country through a period of unprecedented social and political change. The budget of 1909 was fiercely resisted by the House of Lords but after two general elections in 1910 Asquith had been able to force the Tory-dominated upper house to surrender its right to reject legislation passed by the Commons. During those years the Government also faced unprecedented industrial unrest at home, a rising suffragette movement, anarchist outbursts, and near civil war in Ireland. An Irish Home Rule Bill was passed in 1914 but the question of Ulster's exclusion was deferred until after the war.

England joined the war in August 1914. Although it was widely expected to be 'over by Christmas' the country instead found itself bogged down in an orgy of slaughter, the likes of which had not been seen in Europe for centuries. Asquith's Liberal Government came under increasing pressure following military failure on a number of fronts. In May 1915 it gave way to a Coalition Government in which the Liberals were joined by the Conservative Unionists led by Andrew Bonar Law. Asquith remained Prime Minister. Lloyd George became Minister of Munitions and, a year later, Secretary of State for War. Bonar Law became Secretary of State for the Colonies.

Asquith's leadership was called into question as the war moved from one stalemate to the next. In December 1916 Lloyd George acted with support from Bonar Law and the Unionists to undermine the Prime Minister's leadership and replace him. Herbert Asquith, the last leader of a Liberal Government in England, was deposed in a political coup three weeks before Christmas 1916.

This is the story of that coup.

Those who feature in this narrative are listed here together with the ministerial or other public appointments they held in December 1916.

Leading Characters

Sir Max **Aitken** MP (1879–1964). Conservative/Unionist. Confidante of both Lloyd George and Bonar Law. (Later Lord Beaverbrook).

Herbert Henry **Asquith** MP (1852–1928). Liberal. Prime Minister since 1908.

Andrew **Bonar Law** MP (1858–1923). Conservative/Unionist. Leader of the Conservative Party in the House of Commons. Colonial Secretary.

Sir Edward **Carson** MP (1854–1935). Conservative/Unionist. Resigned from the Cabinet in 1916. Thereafter informal leader of the Unionist opposition to the Coalition Government.

David **Lloyd George** MP (1863–1945). Liberal. Secretary of State for War.

Other Leading Liberals

Augustine **Birrell** MP (1805–1933). Resigned as Chief Secretary for Ireland in May 1916 following the Easter rebellion in Dublin that year.

Sir Henry **Campbell-Bannerman** MP (1836–1908). Asquith's predecessor as Prime Minister 1905–8. Died in Downing Street in April 1908.

Winston **Churchill** MP (1874–1965). Resigned from the Cabinet in 1915 to command a battalion in France.

Lord **Crewe** (1858–1945). Lord President of the Council.

Lord **Grey** of Fallodon (1862–1933). Foreign Secretary.

Reginald **McKenna** MP (1863–1943). Chancellor of the Exchequer.

Edwin **Montagu** MP (1879–1924). Minister of Munitions. His wife, Venetia Stanley, had been the object of Asquith's affections before her marriage to Montagu in 1915.

Other Leading Conservatives/Unionists

Arthur **Balfour** MP (1848–1930). First Lord of the Admiralty. Prime Minister 1902–05.

Lord Robert **Cecil** MP (1864–1958). Minister of Blockade.

Austen **Chamberlain** MP (1863–1937). Secretary of State for India.

Lord **Curzon** (1859–1925). Lord Privy Seal.

Lord **Lansdowne** (1845–1927). Minister without Portfolio. Unionist leader in the Lords.

Walter **Long** MP (1854–1924). President of the Local Government Board.

Lord **Milner** (1854-1925). Held no office in Asquith's Government but later joined Lloyd George's War Cabinet.

Sir Frederick Edwin (F. E.) **Smith** MP (1872–1930). Attorney General.

Others

Helen **Asquith** (née Melland), (1856–91). Asquith's first wife. Their children were **Raymond** (1878–1916), **Herbert** ('Beb') (1881–1947), **Arthur** ('Oc') (1883–1939), **Violet** (1887–1969) and **Cyril** ('Cys') (1890–1954).

Margot **Asquith** (née Tennant), (1864–1945). Asquith's second wife. Their children were **Elizabeth** (1897–1945) and **Anthony** ('Puffin') (1902–1968).

Maurice **Bonham Carter** (1870–1960). Asquith's Principal Private Secretary.

Colonel Maurice **Hankey** (1877–1963). Secretary of the War Committee.

Arthur **Henderson** MP (1863–1935). Labour. Cabinet member and Paymaster-General.

Colonel Edward M. **House** (1863–1938). Adviser on European affairs to US President Woodrow Wilson.

Lord **Kitchener** of Khartoum (1850–1916). War Secretary 1914–16. Drowned off the Orkney Islands en route to Russia in May 1916.

Major-General Sir Frederick **Maurice** (1871–1951). Director of Military Operations.

Lord **Northcliffe** (Alfred Harmsworth) (1865–1922). Newspaper magnate.

General Sir William **Robertson** (1860–1933). Chief of the Imperial General Staff.

Lord **Rothermere** (Harold Harmsworth) (1868–1940). Newspaper magnate.

Lord **Stamfordham** (Arthur Bigge) (1849-1931). Private Secretary to King George V.

Venetia **Stanley** (1887–1948). Wife of Edwin Montagu. The object of Asquith's affections and recipient of numerous letters from him, many written while he was chairing Cabinet meetings, in the period 1910–15.

General Sir Henry **Wilson** (1864–1922). Military leader and (later) Unionist politician.

Woodrow **Wilson** (1856–1924). President of the United States of America 1913-21.

Contents

Prologue

'Prime Minister?'

He knocks again, a second time.

Still no response. This is unusual.

Straining for any sound behind the green baize door, he presses his ear to the cloth. Nothing. Was the Old Man asleep? That morning he had looked suddenly ancient – pale and fleshy, the bags beneath his eyes a sickly shade of grey. Margot had turned him out fastidiously: the suit was pressed, a new wing collar, no dandruff on the shoulders, shoes gleaming. But still the hair was tousled and the waistcoat strained to contain his increasing girth.

He looked like the end of the world.

The week had been awful and was getting worse. The pressure on the PM was unprecedented, a full assault from both wings of the Cabinet. Lloyd George had sunk the knife in gently at first but he was pushing now – with a smiling face and eminent courtesy, but also with increasing firmness. The Conservative ministers were twisting Lloyd George's knife. Asquith had weathered all sorts of adversity before but this was different, a new pitch of intensity. It was a coup, the first he had faced in eight years at Downing Street. Could he survive? Drummond was beginning to doubt it.

'Prime Minister?'

A third time, slightly louder. If he hears no response this time he must enter and see what is happening inside. He holds his breath and listens.

1

A voice from within, faltering: 'Come.'

Drummond opens the door as quietly as he can. The PM sits in the central chair, his hands folded on the table, back straight. A glass of water by his right hand but nothing else: no papers, no pens, no boxes. Again this is unusual. Asquith is staring out to the left through the high windows over Horse Guards. As Drummond approaches he turns his head to acknowledge him. But says nothing.

'Prime Minister, the ministers are waiting outside. The Liberal ministers, sir. You asked to see them again at five o'clock?'

Asquith stares at him. Still nothing. For a long moment he looks at Drummond quizzically. Is he ill? Is it possible that he doesn't recognise him?

'Sir, you asked me to call the Liberal ministers to see you. They are here. Would you like them to join you now?'

At this Asquith awakens. The grey pallor of his face begins to colour; the waxwork dummy becomes human again. He reaches into his breast pocket and removes a letter, laying it on the table before him, and speaks.

'I fear we may be in greater difficulty than I had anticipated, Drummond.'

He pauses.

'Mr Balfour has written to me. For the second time today. It seems he is not quite as determined to stay at the Admiralty as I had expected. That is to say, he is happy that Lloyd George should determine these matters. Not the Prime Minister. Not me.' He pauses again. 'I had not expected this. Balfour is turning and his Unionist colleagues are also slipping away. They do not expect me to survive the week.'

A pause.

'I fear they may be correct in that assessment.'

This is the first time Drummond has heard the PM admitting the possibility of defeat.

'Is Lord Crewe in the building?'

'He is with your colleagues in the morning room, sir.'

'Who else is there?'

'All the Liberal ministers, sir. The former ministers, that is.' The

Prime Minister had transmitted the resignation of every member of the Cabinet to the King the previous day. The King had asked him to form a new Government.

'Except the Secretary of State for War,' Drummond adds.

Lloyd George.

The former Liberal ministers. McKenna, the Chancellor, one of Asquith's oldest political friends. Lord Chancellor Buckmaster. Herbert Samuel, the Home Secretary, and Viscount Grey, the Foreign Secretary. Also Mackinnon Wood, Pease, Montagu, Tennant, Runciman and Harcourt.

'Is Mr Henderson with them?'

'No, sir. Just your party colleagues.'

Arthur Henderson, the sole Labour member of the wartime Coalition Cabinet. Asquith likes him more than he likes most of his other colleagues. This is strange: Henderson is a working-class man, gruff and uneducated. But he is also honest, clear-thinking and true.

And of course he isn't Welsh.

'Please ask them to wait for ten minutes, Drummond, then send them in.'

'Yes, Prime Minister.'

Drummond closes the door to the Cabinet Room leaving Asquith alone. In the hall he senses a chill, some movement that he cannot name. He walks quietly to the morning room and asks the ministers to wait: the Prime Minister needs time to deal with some matters before he sees them.

Crewe catches McKenna's eye across the room. He nods to him slightly, almost imperceptibly. The Chancellor nods back before turning to gaze out the window at the early evening darkness falling on the street outside.

PART I

The coup begins:

Tuesday 7 November 1916 –
Sunday 26 November 1916

– 1 –

'Order! Order!' In the shadows off-stage he straightens his tie, closes his eyes, mutters a short prayer, and feels sick to his stomach. And then…

A tremendous wall of noise greets Bonar Law as he enters the chamber from behind the Speaker's chair. Four hundred men shouting, groaning, waving order papers above their heads. Some standing, others seated. One or two leaning forward, pointing mockingly across the aisle. Mostly red-faced, post-prandial, boisterous. Some quite plainly drunk.

'Order! Order!' The Speaker calling to be heard. They ignore him.

As leader of the Conservative and Unionist Party and now also a senior Government minister, Law thought he could readily identify the many moods of the House. He can recognise the cheers that greet victory in the division lobby or a rousing speech. He knows also the groans that follow some crawling interjection, a ministerial embarrassment or obvious evasion, or a backbencher making a fool of himself. And he can identify immediately the unmistakable sound of the Commons in full fury. He has never suffered that indignity himself, although he had been party to two famous demonstrations that forced the Prime Minister to resume his seat without being able to speak.

This evening's noise is different, however; partly a roar, partly a whoop of anticipation.

Government members cheer the Colonial Secretary as he shuffles along the front bench to the dispatch box. He is still unused to the experience of Liberal members cheering him, the second party leader in the now not-so-new coalition. When Asquith had been forced to reconstruct his ministry in May 1915, Law had led the Conservatives into government for the first time in ten years. This was Britain's first modern experiment in coalition; two parties burying their separate interests and prejudices to advance a common cause. In this case to win the war.

Although Asquith's Liberals could still command a Commons majority at that time, the mood of the country had turned against them. A general election in wartime was impossible. So the Prime Minister had decided calmly, even casually, on coalition. Law and the Unionists had joined him. But still the war continued, an exercise in butchery that even now, more than two years since its onset, showed no sign of resolution.

The Government carried on through this carnage and confusion with the strange result that Liberal backbenchers are this evening cheering a man who four years earlier they had accused of treason over Ireland. He finds it a curious and disturbing sensation. They were literally at his back, cheering him on, urging him forward, secretly willing him to fail.

But suddenly a more sinister noise rolls over from across the aisle. The concept of 'opposition' has little meaning now that all parties apart from the Irish are represented in the Government. Asquith had persuaded Henderson, the Labour leader, to accept appointment as President of the Board of Education and later as Paymaster-General. He had also appointed other Labour MPs to a number of junior ministries. Eight of his Liberal colleagues had been forced to leave the Cabinet to make way for Law and the Conservatives. Mostly they departed without rancour, understanding the political calculus that had sunk them, but some harboured grudges that would cause continuing problems for the new ministry.

The most spectacular casualty had been Winston Churchill, the one-time Conservative who had crossed the floor and become a Liberal minister, filling the position he most coveted, First Lord of the Admiralty, in Asquith's first wartime government. The Tories hated Churchill with a grand and spectacular passion. The cost of persuading them to join the Government had been Churchill's dispatch, which Asquith had accomplished with brutal efficiency. He remained in the new ministry as Chancellor of the Duchy of Lancaster, a Cabinet role in which he had precisely nothing to do, but was driven into disillusioned departure in the autumn of 1915. Like many other MPs from both sides of the House, Churchill chose to transfer to France and active service at the front.

The curious nature of the swollen coalition meant that the Opposition benches now served mainly as a home for the vast overflow of Government MPs. But a daily shift in sentiment brought to the Opposition front bench those who planned to resist the Government on whatever matter was for debate that day. As he entered the chamber Law knew who was to face him across the dispatch box that evening.

Sir Edward Carson. Dissident Unionist leader. Former Attorney General. Member for Dublin University. An old friend of Law's. But in this evening's debate a calculating and dangerous opponent.

'Order, order.'

Speaker Lowther. A man of unsurpassable pomposity and self-importance, Law reflected.

'The House will come to order.'

Some semblance of quiet descends, enough for the Speaker to be heard.

'The House will come to order. The motion is this: that, in the opinion of this House, where enemy properties and businesses in Crown colonies and protectorates are offered for sale, provision should be made for securing that such properties and businesses should be sold only to natural-born British subjects or companies wholly British. Proposed by the Member for Dublin University, Sir Edward Carson. The Secretary of State for the Colonies will respond for the Government.'

Law rises. But all at once he feels dizzy and weak, the blood draining completely from his head. An image of his boys, James and Charles, comes before him. He can no longer see Carson sitting opposite. His two boys...James already in France, Charles soon to follow. The Prime Minister's son had been killed only six weeks before. At that precise moment Law knows that both James and Charles will die before the war is finished. He knows it with the full force of conviction that comes when it is impossible to dispute a matter. They will both die. He sits down again. The Speaker looks at him, puzzled, unsympathetic.

'The Secretary of State.'

Now Law is aware of a hand reaching across from his left. Balfour has inched forward to pour a glass of water and passes it to Law who grasps it, grateful. Three sips. Then more, draining the glass. Removing the handkerchief from the breast pocket of his topcoat, he wipes his brow. And rises again. James and Charles shimmer into a haze and then disappear. Carson's outline becomes clear again.

What is his gaze? Sympathy? Perplexity? Determination? All three.

Carson is the clearest thinker Law has ever worked with. A rigid logicist. A clear-sighted man of principle. Also a fanatic. About Ireland he had been unbendable, and Law had joined with Carson in his determination not to abandon those in Ulster who had shown loyalty to the Crown and the Empire. Nor to abandon those in the South who resisted the hatred of the Catholic Irish for 'the planters'. But Law had changed. A new and more emollient approach was needed in Ireland following the rebellion that spring. He had worked with Carson and Lloyd George to try to effect this but they had failed. Now here was Carson again, staring fiercely at him across the dispatch box. He knows what that portends. But he must speak.

'Mr Speaker.' A little hoarse.

'Mr Speaker, I regret that the policy adopted by His Majesty's Government in relation to the disposal of enemy assets in the Protectorate of Nigeria has caused such confusion among a number of my honourable and right honourable friends. I regret that our effort to explain the proposal to colleagues has not helped them to understand the practicality of our proposals. And I particularly regret that a number of members, led by my right honourable friend the member for Dublin University, have seen fit to propose this evening's motion. Let me explain again what the Government is proposing, and hope, even at this late hour, that they will accept the wisdom of our plans.'

Then Law explains to the House, as he has explained at least half a dozen times already, the Government's policy in relation to the disposal of German assets seized in Nigeria.

The assets are to be sold on the open market but with legal protections to ensure they cannot remain in German hands or be acquired by Germans or by individuals who might return them to German owners. For Carson these legal protections are inadequate; indeed they miss the whole point. He insists that the assets should be sold solely to British citizens. The Government will not agree to this. If the purchasers had to be British, that would restrict the market and suppress the price that could be achieved at a time when funds were desperately needed. And so Carson must be resisted.

But what is really going on here?

Law knows that Carson is playing a much more devious game than anything to do with Nigerian assets. His motion is in fact an attack on Asquith, his ministry, and the conduct of the war.

Law had long since perfected the technique of thinking while he speaks. With the House not quite attentive but not yet dangerous, his mouth can speak the words of the policy while his brain sharpens his understanding of the game Carson is playing. Carson hates Asquith with a passion. That emotion had not prevented Carson from accepting appointment as Attorney General when Asquith formed his coalition the previous year. But to nobody's great surprise Carson's appointment had lasted less than six months: he resigned from the Government in the autumn of 1915.

Carson retired to the backbenches where his disdain for Asquith increased by the day. The man was a fraud, a drinker, a groper. Worse than this, he was not a leader. The greatest war that England ever faced was under the direction of a philandering drunk, a prig who had been in office for so long that he had lost touch with the world outside Whitehall. From the autumn of 1915 Carson had committed himself completely to the destruction of Asquith and his Government.

But here was the obstacle. Law, Carson's great friend and ally on the Irish question, his leader in the Unionist party, is now firmly embedded in Asquith's decrepit Government. Asquith could only be driven out if Law deserted him, and short of deposing Law as Unionist leader, which was not his intention, Carson could only aim to frighten him. A frightened Law, fearing that his own leadership of the Conservatives might be under threat, could surely no longer ignore the obvious shortcomings in Asquith's leadership.

So Law had to be destabilised if Asquith was to be removed.

And that is what this evening's debate is really all about.

A defeat on the Nigerian issue, in itself a matter of absolutely no consequence, would wreck the Government. That was not Carson's intention. If the Government failed to suppress Carson's motion a reconstruction would be necessary but almost certainly under Asquith's continuing leadership. If the Government won but more Tories voted for the motion than against it, Law would have to resign as Tory leader. Again, that was not Carson's intention.

But a healthy minority of Tories supporting Carson's motion would warn Law that his position as Unionist leader was no longer certain. Which would in turn encourage him to reflect on alternative arrangements for government under a new Prime Minister. And who would that be? Law himself? Lloyd George? Curzon? Crewe? Was Carson himself too radical to emerge as a candidate? Redmond's Irish Nationalists would certainly oppose him but they were no longer of any consequence. It was not an impossibility. But then in politics nothing ever was.

'And so, Mr Speaker, I oppose the motion and commend the Government's policy to the House.'

Law sits back. Carson rises. No water needed by him. No clearing of the throat. He launches.

Reasonable at first, Law thought. More in sorrow than in anger, that kind of thing. People 'anxious to know tomorrow whether the Government which is waging this terrible war at a dreadful cost to their kith and kin, not to talk of their fortunes, is waging it in order that whatever advantages may accrue shall accrue to this country and this Empire, and to no one else.'

Heads beside Carson nodding vigorously. Occasional hearhears. An interruption by a Liberal backbencher is swiftly batted away. And after ten minutes a relatively weak conclusion, at which

Carson resumes his seat. Law knows from long experience that Carson has reserved his harshest tone for whatever Law might say in response. He rises and starts to speak again. Time to get to the point.

'Mr Speaker, all honourable and right honourable members will know that our policy in disposing of enemy assets in Nigeria is not the real object of my right honourable friend this evening. His motion is in fact a motion of want of confidence in the Government, moved – and I must say I do regret this – with a violence which to my mind is hardly in keeping with the serious situation in which our country stands.'

Vigorous shaking of Carson's head when accused of verbal violence. The bully bullied. Only way to deal with him. So Law continues. 'There is, Mr Speaker, no question that any of this should weaken the bonds of my personal friendship with the right honourable member. But his case is built on sentiment, not reason, and it is reason and common sense that I must appeal to in responding.'

Carson interjects to disagree with Law, the colour now rising in his face. Law responds, calmly, refusing to be baited but keen to see how far he can push Carson by attacking his case as illogical. Time to adopt an even calmer tone, restate the policy, say again how difficult he finds it to understand why sensible men might oppose it, and see how Carson responds. Law argues that the country's French allies would surely feel slighted, and rightly so, if they were to be told, after much sacrifice, that the British did not trust them enough to allow them to purchase enemy assets. And at this Carson erupts.

'Mr Speaker, I never made any such statement. I never expressed any lack of trust in our French allies. I simply said that they should not be competing against Britishers for property that we Britishers had won from Germans in the war. This is exactly what the French do to us in comparable circumstances.'

How to bait him further? To push him 'over the top', as they now say? Law has the perfect response:

'Mr Speaker, I'm afraid that logic fails my right honourable friend in this response. We cannot both trust our allies and also treat them with ill-disguised contempt at the same time. I cannot imagine a surer way of compromising our energies in fighting this dreadful war.'

At this Carson grows visibly red in the face. Law remains sober, knowing the vote will be unpleasant but now enjoying this goading of his one-time ally. What Carson cannot abide is long-windedness so Law once again repeats the policy and his point about the French, with Carson now shouting in interruption 'Absolutely untrue'. The Speaker begins to raise his hand but Law gets there first: 'My right honourable friend's position remains both confused and illogical.' Law knows that the worst thing one could ever accuse Carson of is a lack of logic. He takes the bait: 'Mr Speaker, this is outrageous. My right honourable friend has no right to wilfully misinterpret me.'

At this Law allows himself a broad smile. He finds Carson 'mistaken' and again repeats the policy. Carson has had enough: 'This is nonsense.' To which Law emolliently replies, 'My right honourable friend is not very polite. On many questions I admit that I should bow to his opinion. But on this matter I think I am much less likely than he is to talk nonsense.'

Laughter from the Government benches. Laughter – the clearest confirmation of victory in a Commons debate.

But Law knows that this is a pyrrhic victory. He walks through the No lobby when the vote is called. Less than half the House is there to vote. Asquith is present but Lloyd George, who had dined earlier that evening with Carson, is not. The result itself is no surprise: Carson's motion is defeated, but of Law's 286 Unionist members only 73 vote for the Government, 65 vote against, and 148 abstain.

Asquith shakes Law's hand and congratulates him on his work.

Later in the lobby, on a procedural vote, Carson also comes up to shake Law's hand. Smiles. And winks.

As Law leaves the chamber he is startled to see a large rat scurrying from under the Opposition benches to take refuge behind the Speaker's rostrum. Despite his strict Scottish Presbyterianism, Law believes in portents, but this was a portent of…what?

Asquith sees it too from the corner of his eye.

– 2 –

Monday 13 November 1916 —
Lansdowne House, Berkeley Square, London

Lord Lansdowne's study is on the second floor overlooking the square. It opens directly onto the master bedroom, which leads in turn to a dressing room and then on to four or five further bedrooms and day-rooms. The house is too damn big. Eighteen rooms – why in hell does he need eighteen rooms in the centre of London? There are rooms in this house that he can't remember ever visiting. He never climbs the stairs to the third floor, hasn't seen it since the turn of the century. He lives in the drawing room or the study.

Outside he hears Horton climbing the staircase from the hall, wheezing. In half a minute the servant will knock on the door and enter bearing his lordship's mid-morning tea and toast. A habit formed many years ago: whatever his engagement Lord Lansdowne must stop every day at eleven for tea and toast. This morning he has been composing a memorandum for the Prime Minister. It is possibly the most important document he has ever written in what has already been a long and distinguished (his Liberal friends might disagree) public career.

Earlier that morning Lord Lansdowne had taken three turns around Green Park. South from Lansdowne House to Piccadilly, in by the north-east gate, then south along the path towards The Mall. Sharp right at the Palace (standard flying, HM was at home) then up the gentle slope to Hyde Park Corner and along the northern path paralleling Piccadilly (he liked the alliteration) to the north-east gate again. And twice more around. A bitterly cold early winter's morning, frost on the ground, the trees entirely naked, leaves still rotting on the grass. Lansdowne, now growing old, had wrapped up warm. At half past seven on a chilly morning he might pick up a cold, or worse. That was not to be tolerated. As he walked he reflected with some pain on the draft memorandum he had prepared yesterday.

Sunday had been an awful day. Writing his note had taken a full eight hours, starting after church (idiotic sermon at St George's in Hanover Square) and then on without a break until dinner. The whole business exhausted him. He had to speak honestly but if he spoke the truth what would they say? That he was a coward? Or just a realist? This war was endless. It would destroy them all. The carnage was beyond belief. Already a whole generation had been butchered and there was no end in sight. He was a senior politician, a former Foreign Secretary, and now once again a Cabinet minister. Not leader of the Government but a senior minister nonetheless. He had a responsibility, some responsibility, for this damn war. What was he to do?

Lansdowne was Minister without Portfolio in the Coalition Government. He led the Unionists in the Lords and so was responsible for the party's affairs in the Upper House. But the Lords was no longer the powerhouse it had once been. It was only five years (it felt like a lifetime) since Lansdowne had led the struggle to resist Asquith's attempts to neuter the House. After Lloyd George's socialist budget in 1909 the Lords had revolted. This would not pass. Asquith and his Government were outraged: the Commons must have its way on money matters. A particularly inflammatory speech from the little Welshman in the East End. The financial issue had ultimately been resolved when the Lords reluctantly accepted the budget, but the larger issue of the Lords' role was now unavoidable because of the Irish. Asquith's Government was propped up by the Irish Party. The Irish wanted Home Rule. The Lords would never agree to Home Rule. The calculus was increasingly straightforward: for Asquith to survive, the Lords' ability to reject Home Rule – indeed to reject *anything* – had to be destroyed.

Lansdowne had led the Unionist resistance almost to the bitter end. Through two general elections in 1910 Asquith and the Liberals had retained their hold on power with the support of the

Irish. Finally the old soak had blackmailed the new king into a promise to create three hundred Liberal peers if the Lords would not back down. The Commons must have its way. The Government must have its way. Asquith must have his way.

Common little man, raised far too high.

In the end Lansdowne had blinked. The Government's Parliament Bill squeezed its way through the Lords. The peers' ability to resist had been reduced to a temporary veto. Home Rule for Ireland had been vetoed twice but there was no third opportunity for the Lords. Just before the outbreak of war, Ireland had been lost.

Lord Lansdowne, Henry Charles Keith Petty-FitzMaurice, an English marquess, owned the larger part of County Kerry.

His eldest son and heir, who had never visited Ireland, was earl of that county.

But here he was now, years later, back in office. Government was the natural state of affairs for Lansdowne. In the last century he had been Governor-General of Canada. He had been Viceroy of India. He had been Secretary of State for War. He had been Foreign Secretary. In fact he had been almost everything, although he had not been Prime Minister. Nor would he ever be. He was too old and was considered too obstructive. Bonar Law was the coming man, although times had certainly changed when a dull and unimaginative Canadian could possibly hope to become the king's first minister.

But the dull Canadian had accepted Asquith's invitation in May 1915 to lead his party into government. The coalition ministry was formed. Asquith had outwitted Law at every step, giving him the Colonies, preserving all the senior positions for Asquith's own Liberals. As Minister without Portfolio Lansdowne was a member of the Cabinet with, frankly, nothing to do. It left him to brood. His current brooding was of a particularly painful kind.

The war was chaos, total carnage. Death and destruction on an industrial scale, although who could care much about the Germans who had started it all? The French were also being decimated. But the toll on the English, who might have stayed out of the conflict but for an exaggerated sensitivity to Belgium, was immense. The generals were incompetent. The Government could not direct the war. Asquith's firm belief that his role was to referee ministerial discussions rather than to lead the country meant that the war effort was without vigour or direction. And even if such vigour could be found with another leader, where would that take us? How was the war to be ended? And when?

At Cabinet the previous week Asquith had asked all his colleagues to reflect on the current direction of the war and advise him on how they ought to proceed. He had encouraged them all to think deeply, to range broadly, and to advise candidly. The advice would remain confidential to the Cabinet: no material would leak outside the team. But it was time for imagination and new thinking.

Lansdowne had listened to Asquith's speech with particular attention. It seemed to him that those Cabinet members who held no departmental responsibilities were most responsible for responding to the Prime Minister's invitation. He had been due to visit Dugdale in Hertfordshire that weekend. But walking home from Cabinet he composed a short note advising his cousin that ministerial duties required him to remain in London for the weekend. Dugdale would understand. On Friday he cancelled all his engagements in order to think. He continued thinking on Saturday. And then on Sunday he began to write. He knew what he wanted to say but was unsure about his language and tone.

He also knew that Asquith's guarantee of confidentiality would not be honoured. Whatever he wrote, he must expect to see it circulated widely, and almost certainly also to the press, within the next few days.

It was time to consider what had previously been unthinkable: that the country should make preparations to negotiate a peace. A peace with honour but without gain. A peace that would prevent further carnage but give no meaning or redemption to the slaughter that had already taken place. A peace that would quickly destroy the politicians who negotiated it. It would end Lansdowne's public career and destroy Asquith and his ministry. But it would also end the war.

On Saturday he walked to his office in Whitehall to retrieve the paper that had first alerted him to what needed to be done. Robertson had been appointed Chief of the Imperial General Staff the previous December. Asked for his thoughts on the conduct of the war, he had sent a confidential note to the Cabinet in August. It was an alarming paper, especially its conclusion: *We need therefore to decide without loss of time what our policy is to be, then place it before the Entente Powers, and ascertain in return what are their aims, and so endeavour to arrive at a clear understanding before we meet our enemies in conference.* This was quite the clearest indication the Cabinet had ever received from a military man that a negotiated end to the war needed to be considered.

Lansdowne re-read Robertson's minute as he sat behind the desk at his office. The desk had followed him through all his political and ministerial appointments. He had purchased it in Ottawa in 1883 on first arriving there as Governor-General. All his most important decisions had been made at this desk. He knew that Robertson was correct. The line that he himself must take in his memorandum for the Cabinet was clear. He walked home to Berkeley Square to adjust his draft.

Now on Monday morning the finished version lay before him. It was still in longhand: he would have his tea and toast and walk to the Cabinet Office, where it would be typed and copied in secret.

A knock on the door. Horton entered. He turned to retrieve the tray he had just placed on a low table outside the room and carried into the study, then laid it quietly by the side of Lord Lansdowne's desk.

'Thank you,' Lansdowne said in a low voice. 'I will be in Whitehall until one o'clock, Horton, and will lunch alone when I return.'

'Yes, my lord.'

Horton left the room. Pouring his tea and delicately biting into the toast (his dentures had been giving him trouble) Lansdowne re-read his memorandum. It made clear that the Government must explore the possibility of a negotiated end to the war.

Lansdowne recognised the parts of his note that would create the most anxiety when his colleagues read it. Should he tell Law what he proposed to say before delivering the note to Asquith? He thought not: Law might want him to reconsider. He might worry that a leak could taint the party as pacifist, without backbone, cowardly. Lansdowne thought the exact opposite was true: it would be cowardly *not* to recognise the situation and search, however indirectly, for an end to the slaughter.

What does the prolongation of the War mean? he had written. *We are slowly but surely killing off the best of the male population of these islands...The financial burden which we have already accumulated is almost incalculable...* And the conclusion: *We ought at any rate not to discourage any movement, no matter where originating, in favour of an interchange of views as to the possibility of a settlement.*

That should do it.

What he really wanted to say in the memorandum must remain unsaid, however. The little Welshman had given an interview to an American newspaper six weeks earlier. The 'knock-out blow' interview, as it had come to be known (much to Lloyd George's pleasure), had entirely discounted any possibility of a negotiated end to the war. Britain would fight on to the finish, he proclaimed. Lansdowne recognised the political motivation that lay behind Lloyd George's intervention. Facing re-election later that year, it was widely believed that President Wilson was searching for a peace overture to garland his reputation not just as The Man Who Kept America Out but now also as The Man Who Brokered The Peace. There was no doubt that the war would only end after the Americans intervened. But given the momentum in that country against intervention, any such American move would be many years away. In the meantime there would be more British and French slaughter. Lansdowne knew that all talk of a 'knock-out blow' was hopeless. That could not be said, not even in the semi-privacy of the Cabinet, and certainly not on paper. But he had said enough.

He finished his tea and walked downstairs to the hall. Overcoat, hat, walking stick, scarf and gloves. The manuscript in his breast pocket. A brisk walk from Berkeley Square to Whitehall would take twenty minutes.

At his office he asked the duty typist to prepare the memorandum and make copies for distribution to the Cabinet. It was to be marked 'Most Secret', although Lansdowne reflected that 'Most Secret' was now the clearest indication that a document was intended for leaking. But the Prime Minister had asked for written representations and, besides, the case was stronger on paper than Lansdowne would have been able to make by speaking it.

The copies were ready within the hour. The office was efficient and thorough: his small staff was really remarkably business-like. The printed memorandum ran to eight pages. He placed the copies in a satchel and asked the clerk to telephone Downing Street and request a brief meeting with the Prime Minister. The PM would see him in ten minutes' time, on his way to lunch. Lansdowne left the office and walked to the end of Whitehall to gaze at the Palace of Westminster. A weak winter sun was finally breaking through but it held no heat. The city would slip slowly back into darkness within a few brief hours. He retraced his steps, entered Downing Street, and was saluted by the policeman at Number 10. The door opened and Lansdowne entered the building to hand Asquith the memorandum that would destroy his ministry.

– 3 –

'Your car will be here in thirty minutes, Prime Minister. The train leaves Victoria at ten o'clock and you sail from Dover at half past twelve. You will be in Paris by four o'clock. Monsieur Briand will visit you at the embassy at five, then dinner at the Quai at seven. The first stage of the conference will take place over dinner. Your papers are in the box and Colonel Hankey and Mr Bonham Carter will give you further information on the train. Do you need anything else, sir?'

'Just one moment please, Drummond. If I sign these papers now please have them distributed once I've left. There is also a memorandum for the King which must go to the Palace immediately.'

'Sir.'

'David, read this. It's from Lansdowne. His response to my request for ideas. You won't enjoy it.'

Asquith pushed the memorandum across the table to Lloyd George and returned to the pile of papers before him. Lloyd George watched him work. Asquith was sitting in the central position at the Cabinet table, a position he had occupied for more than eight years. A fire burned in the grate behind him but gave little warmth. A limp light entered the room from the windows over Horse Guards.

Lloyd George was trying to remember the first time he had met Asquith. He found he was unable to fix on the date. It must surely have been in about 1890, but when? He couldn't be sure. The man had been his chief for almost a decade but they had never been close. Asquith thought that Lloyd George was impatient, both with the pace of the war and also with his own position. Lloyd George had stood aside as Chancellor of the Exchequer eighteen months earlier to become Minister of Munitions and then, last May, when Kitchener had drowned off the Orkneys, he became War Secretary. But Lloyd George felt he was tied down on every side and unable to run the war. He thought Asquith was old, tired, worn-out. But what to do about it?

As Asquith worked his way through the papers, amending items in the margins, signing the bottom of each file, Lloyd George glanced through Lansdowne's memorandum. He did not expect to enjoy it, knowing that Lansdowne was no supporter of the 'maximum push' policy that Lloyd George was now advocating to anyone who would listen. In fact this marked a sharp change in his own view about the war, a reminder of how fickle politics is, how quickly minds could change, and how completely. Lansdowne had always been a fighter. He had fought Lloyd George over the budget of 1909. He had fought him (almost to the death) about reforming the House of Lords. He had fought him, and Asquith, and the whole Liberal Government, over Home Rule for Ireland, siding with Carson and Bonar Law in their outrageous preparations for armed rebellion and civil war in Ulster in 1914. When the war broke out in Europe Lloyd George had at first been a forceful advocate of Britain staying out. Let the foreigners butcher themselves into oblivion. Why should Englishmen, Welsh, Scots and patriotic Irish fight to the death over a hopeless archduke, a collapsing eastern empire, and a non-country like Belgium? No, Britain must stay out. He had almost left the Cabinet over the issue in August 1914.

But now all this was changed. Britain had engaged the enemy and, having engaged, must fight fiercely to the finish. Effort must be redoubled, no expense spared, no challenge unmet. In this Lloyd George enjoyed the full confidence of Bonar Law, the Unionist leader. But Law's colleague in the Lords, Lansdowne, was equivocating. And as for Asquith: who know where he stood? A war leader who wrote private letters to women friends (one of them the wife of another minister, by all accounts) during Cabinet meetings. Who played bridge and drank freely in the evenings. Who was known at five o'clock on a wintry London afternoon to wrap up and walk to the Athenaeum where he might spend an hour or two reading cheap detective novels in the library. This was a war leader? Or was he beginning to veer towards the policy of withdrawal that Lansdowne was now proposing? It was impossible to read him: in fact it always had been. Asquith was a chairman, not a leader. And with Asquith at the helm England would lose the war. Lloyd George was sure of this now.

In fact Lansdowne's memorandum was even worse that he had expected. Lloyd George knew from long experience that all Cabinet memoranda were to be read at two levels. The surface level, the words, what they say, and how the message emerges from the text itself. But then one finds the hidden meaning, buried beneath the text, detectable only by those long versed in the art of political whistling.

Lansdowne had written: *We are slowly but surely killing off the best of the male population of these islands*. This, though true, was not just a lament over a horrifying truth. It was a direct and highly personal plea to Asquith. This war killed your eldest boy Raymond just six weeks ago. What do you owe to him? What do you owe to *all* the sons of all your friends and colleagues similarly butchered by the pointless war that you are directing?

Lansdowne had also written: *The financial burden which we have already accumulated is almost incalculable.* Here he was speaking directly to the Chancellor of the Exchequer, Reginald McKenna. Your predecessor presses for a continuation of this slaughter which will not only kill all our children but will also put us in hock to the Americans for a hundred years, Mr Chancellor. How can you support such a policy?

And when Lansdowne had written *We ought at any rate not to discourage any movement, no matter where originating, in favour of an interchange of views as to the possibility of a settlement* he meant......
Lloyd George paused. He meant: make peace now. Call it a peace with honour. But England will know that it means surrender.

The key question remained: where did Asquith stand in all this? Lloyd George was unsure. Certainly he seemed reluctant to endorse the kind of 'knock-out blow' that Lloyd George, with Law's persistent support, was advocating so strongly. The PM was obviously exhausted. He had carried the burden of the conflict for over two years now. It was an endless war, dreadful loss of life, nothing at all gained. And the Cabinet decided nothing. Even minor decisions required endless meetings, and every major military engagement sanctioned by the Cabinet had led to catastrophe. The Dardanelles had been a disaster but Asquith had been unable to restrain Churchill in his insistence that it would open up a path to Constantinople which would knock Turkey out of the war. Carnage, mayhem, total destruction. Asquith presided at Cabinet; he never led. Lloyd George could feel the urge to lead welling up within him like a hard, physical thing. Asquith must stand aside. And if Asquith shared the sentiments being advocated by Lansdowne in this note he must stand aside immediately. But did he?

Lloyd George tossed the paper onto the Cabinet table. Asquith signed his last document and rang for Drummond, who entered immediately and took them away. He left the room as quietly as he had entered, the table now clear except for the Lansdowne note that lay between them. The Prime Minister spoke.

'Am I correct?'

'In believing that I would disagree?'

'Yes.'

'Completely. It's a disgrace. Even by Lansdowne's low standards, it's beneath contempt.'

'No, David, that is unfair. I asked for opinions. I asked for *honest* opinions. I was – I am – afraid that we all spend so much time together dealing with the daily crises, and we spend so much time hearing from generals whose confidence in their recommendations is matched only by their incompetence in delivery, we can no longer even *imagine* that there may be a different view. Well, here at least is a different view.'

'Prime Minister, I understand the point. But this is not a different view. This is just Lansdowne's own contrarian view. We all knew that he held it even before you asked for written submissions. So we've been through another paper exercise, another consultation, and the Cabinet will now waste more precious time considering Lansdowne's view and all the other views that will be expressed to you. And, as you always do, you will try to find some middle path that adopts the "best" of all these representations and forge them into a compromise policy that reflects the lowest common denominator of the Cabinet's collective view on this matter of life and death. Of *life* and *death*, Prime Minister.'

Asquith stared at him. Said nothing.

The silence lasted a moment.

'Prime Minister, I must ask: is this your view too? Do you share Lansdowne's pessimism? His defeatism? Do you think we should be "encouraging" those "movements" that favour discussing the "possibility of a settlement"? Do you?'

Asquith looked away. He paused. Then answered.

'In my position, I must at least *allow* it to be considered. It is the role of the king's first minister to take account of the views of every member of the Cabinet and do what he can to...'

'It is *not* his role, Prime Minister.' Lloyd George banged his hand on the table. 'It is *not* his role, not in wartime. In peacetime, perhaps, but even then nothing that we accomplished before the war would have been achieved without you, *you* Prime Minister, being willing to lead. To express your own view, to inspire your colleagues in new and courageous directions. So now we are at war and your courage has deserted you. More than ever in a war you must be the leader, not the chairman.'

Asquith stiffened. Sat up straight. Reddened.

'I need no lectures from you or any other minister about courage. I have done everything that I can to carry us through this war. I have tried every initiative. I have dealt with politicians, generals, foreigners, *everyone*, to try to win this wretched war. I have the blood of all those men on my hands. Those young men...' He paused. Remembered Raymond, his son. 'Young men who have lost limbs and lives and *minds* because this Cabinet, which I lead, has sent them to war. I resent, I *deeply* resent, your accusation that I lack courage.'

He looked away. There was silence.

Lloyd George spoke.

'I'm sorry, Prime Minister. I apologise. That is not what I meant to say.'

'Then what did you mean?'

A further silence.

'I meant that we cannot go on this way. I am a Secretary of War who cannot, who is not *allowed to*, run the war. Everything I do and say is refracted through the War Committee, which is too big, too unwieldy, and then back to the full Cabinet for decision. In a war we must act *fiercely*, *energetically*, with *vigour*. We must act *now*. We cannot run a war by committee, Prime Minister. And we cannot run a war when men like Lansdowne have a voice in the deliberations. You chair the Cabinet more adroitly than any other man possibly could. You lead the Commons better than any parliamentary leader I have ever seen. But to run a war is a frightful thing. It needs energy, dedication, action. And it needs men of vision with the courage to see things through. To be willing to risk failure in order to succeed. To *lead*.'

Asquith paused. He stared at Lloyd George.

'Well you are at least consistent in your views. I accept your apology. I know you meant no personal slight. We must discuss this further, we must come to some conclusion. Let's talk on the train to Kent.'

At this Asquith reached forward and slid the copy of Lansdowne's paper into his lap.

'I need to meet Drummond now, and Margot. I will see you in the car outside.'

'Thank you, Prime Minister.' Lloyd George rose and walked towards the door. Without a sound, Drummond slid it open before Lloyd George reached for the knob and stood to one side as the War Secretary left the room.

Before Asquith and his party had reached Kent, Lansdowne's memorandum was already in the hands of Carson and Lord Northcliffe, proprietor of *The Times*, who hated Asquith. Actually, Northcliffe just *hated*. Asquith was merely the target of the moment. But word began to spread, quietly, in the corridors, among the backbenchers, and then more virulently among the front benchers, that Lansdowne had prepared his remarks not at Asquith's invitation but at his insistence. For Carson and Northcliffe, Asquith was now bent on negotiating an end to the war. The trip to Paris was merely one opportunity for the Prime Minister to begin moving in that direction.

* * *

And so the principal actors in the drama that was about to unfold in the early winter of 1916 have now been identified.

Bonar Law in the Commons resisting an attack by Carson on the ministry of which Law was a leading member.

Law's colleague Lord Lansdowne urging a radical change of direction in the conduct of the war.

David Lloyd George also urging change but in a direction wholly different from that advocated by Lansdowne.

And at the centre of these various disputes the Prime Minister, Herbert Asquith, haunted by the recent death of his eldest son, trying to manage the competing forces that were now beginning to assail him.

The stage is set for a showdown. It needs only a catalyst to turn these various intrigues and protestations into a true crisis.

The spark to Carson's flame was provided by a man who would later become known as Lord Beaverbrook, the greatest newspaperman of his age. But in 1916 Beaverbrook was merely a backbench MP and a meddler. Later he wrote an account of these events, drawing on his own diary entries or (his critics charged) on newly-invented recollections that helped to bend the historical record in his own preferred direction. His role in the drama began on the day that Asquith left for the conference in Paris.

– 4 –

Tuesday 14 November 1916 — Hyde Park Hotel

How to begin this account? With the obvious I suppose – who, where, when, what and why. The key questions for any journalist, even a novice one.

I am Max Aitken, a Canadian now living in England. Actually *Sir* Max Aitken, but titles mean nothing to me. I serve my country as Canada's military representative to the Allied forces in France, working from London. I am also a Member of Parliament in the Unionist interest and a close colleague of Bonar Law but not yet a member of the Government. (I was offered a minor position last year but I declined.) My friends call me energetic, my enemies an intriguer. But in fact my interests are straightforward: I am for Britain in the war and for Bonar Law in politics. The two goals may not be wholly compatible, however. Law plays a key role and will soon play an even more central role in the reconstruction that now seems inevitable. But even then he may not be the leader. The man to lead us may be Lloyd George.

These notes are written to provide a shorthand record of the events of the coming weeks. If I fail as a politician I may at least become a journalist again. Sources are everything for a journalist: if you keep a clear record of events as they happen, particularly if you are yourself a party to those events (as I wholly intend to be), then you can craft the record to create a reality that may not quite have been the *actualité* of the time. If I am to write about Asquith's last days (as I earnestly hope these are, though one never knows with Squiff) I will need these notes.

I live at the Hyde Park Hotel in Knightsbridge. A brisk twenty minutes' walk to Whitehall through St James's Park. The rooms are modest but the hotel is both comfortable and homely, even in wartime. Parties of officers on leave from the front throng the bar every evening. My rooms are on the fourth floor with a view to the back that avoids the noisy thoroughfare in front. They are quiet and airy, wholly suitable for planning (plotting?) at the start of a day and calm reflection (further plotting?) at its end. My wife lives in the country, in my constituency in Lancashire. She rarely comes to London.

Yesterday I saw Lloyd George at the War Office. This morning I felt ill but Law came to see me here in my rooms at ten o'clock. He telephoned to say he was coming so I had an opportunity to wash and shave before he arrived. (Law is a stickler for hygiene and cleanliness.) I wanted to discuss the Lloyd George question with him, how far we should accommodate the War Secretary in his obvious desire to push Asquith aside, but I still felt ill and a touch light-headed. In any event all Law wanted to discuss was Nigeria. He asked for my help in ensuring that a particular foreign firm with ambition to buy certain Nigerian assets should be prevented from so doing. After he left I rose, unsteady, and communicated with my solicitors, my bankers, and certain officials at the Colonial Office to avert any such outcome.

In the evening Law returned, this time with Lord Rothermere. I was only marginally improved since the morning but by now it was even more important for me to advise Law of my most recent conversation with Lloyd George. But Rothermere stayed until nearly 11. He finally left to 'look in on tomorrow's edition' before retiring for the evening. I know he sensed there was something on my mind. He stayed until he could clearly see that I was unwilling to mention it in his presence.

Once Rothermere left I took his place by the fire, now low in the grate, opposite Law.

'Well?' he asked.

'He will. I am sure of it.' I hesitated. 'And we should support him.'

Law grunted. 'He will, will he? Damn sure he will. Lloyd George's ambition is exceeded only by his instinct for weakness. He knows Asquith is wounded so of course he will. This is his moment. But I'll be damned if I support him.'

Bonar Law is a curious man. Slow to engage his mind on a topic, his preference is to 'go away and think it through'. Any decision one requires of him is invariably deferred to the following day until he has had an opportunity to worry about it, usually in the privacy of his own home that evening. His sister lives with him, his wife being dead: does he ask her advice at home over his simple supper? (Law is a teetotaller and keeps the worst table in London: his food is quite awful.) Is Miss Law the secret power behind the Conservative throne? I sometimes wonder. Is she to Bonar what John Brown was to Queen Victoria – the humble footman who ran the Empire? It makes for an entertaining fantasy.

But once his mind is made up Bonar Law can be as firm as granite and all but impossible to reverse. On Lloyd George his mind was made up. He thought he was a man of energy and vision but dangerous: his immense ambition, sometimes nakedly on display, more often concealed behind an entertaining exterior, was permanently engaged. Lloyd George's primary interest in politics and life itself was always Lloyd George.

There was also an additional complication. Law had developed a surprising personal loyalty to Asquith. Or perhaps not so surprising. Law's unshakable sense of patriotism and duty convinced him that a Prime Minister in wartime deserved total support from his colleagues even if they were colleagues from another party. A reluctant convert to coalition, Law had grown used to his role as second man in the Government and believed that his support for the Prime Minister should be solid and unambiguous. Any disagreements were to be aired between the two men behind closed doors. And in truth there were few disagreements.

'I think you should reconsider, Bonar. You and he agree on so many issues, it would be foolish of you not to give him a hearing.'

'What is he proposing now?'

'The War Committee.'

'It's always the War Committee.'

Here we were on difficult ground. Everyone agrees that the present War Committee is hopeless. As a committee of the Cabinet it can take no decisions by itself. It has no executive authority. It has a dozen *ex officio* members and others are asked to join its meetings as required.

And it is chaired by Asquith, the consummate chairman, the ultimate consensus-seeker. The meetings are interminable and the Cabinet quite frequently rejects its recommendations and decides on an alternative course of action. Or, not infrequently, a further review. Everyone agrees that it is no good. But how to reconstruct it?

Asquith had recently proposed quite a radical (for him) alternative arrangement: that the War Committee should be reduced to three members – himself as chairman, Law and Lloyd George. Lloyd George had agreed to this but only if Law would serve. But Curzon had protested against the Tory interest on the Committee being represented by Law alone, hinting that he would resign from the Government if the scheme was adopted. Asquith countered that Balfour might join instead of Law, Balfour being more acceptable to Curzon than Law was. If the Unionists then insisted on having their leader on the Committee in addition to Balfour, as they undoubtedly would, Asquith would almost certainly have to bring in Crewe to balance the membership from the Liberal side. The size of the Committee was therefore growing already, even before its creation, and would probably grow even more. It was already a casualty. Law could not serve under these terms so Lloyd George could not serve either. Asquith's scheme was stillborn.

In fact, of course, Law was perfectly right to reject Asquith's scheme. His position as Unionist leader was a fragile one. George Curzon, that great pompous fraud, had never reconciled himself to the fact that a 'common little man like Law' had ascended to the Unionist leadership. Law was torn between his patriotic duty (as he saw it) to support the Prime Minister in wartime and his political need to assert his position in order to see off his detractors. It was a difficult path for him to walk and I, for one, believe that he walked it with courage and intelligence.

'What do you think?'

'Here is what I think, Aitken. I think this. Lloyd George is quite right to be dissatisfied about the conduct of the war. You and I know it and the public knows it too. They know it even without our friends Rothermere and Northcliffe telling them so every day in their newspapers. Of course we need to find a better way of harnessing the energies of our best men, and George is undoubtedly one of our best men. But Asquith is the leader. Asquith holds the strands of this coalition together. Asquith holds Parliament together. Without Asquith there is every chance of finding ourselves faced with anarchy rather than the kind of energetic leadership we all know must be discovered. So we must find a way of boxing this circle.'

He paused.

'And here is the thing, Aitken. The Liberals will never face this on their own. They are waiting for the Unionists to provoke the crisis and then to resolve it. And the Unionists want me to take it on. So what are my options? I must either sustain this ministry, under Asquith, or destroy it. But we are at war. I will not destroy a ministry in wartime even if that means curtailing the ambitions of my own party. I will not destroy Asquith. We must find a way of using Lloyd George, certainly, but I will not destroy this Prime Minister.'

We spoke a little further and then, shortly after midnight, Law rose to go home. After he said goodnight I called for a messenger and dictated a telegram for immediate dispatch to France. It was addressed to Lloyd George and read as follows: *If possible highly advisable you return France soonest for dinner Friday with other interested parties as discussed.* I paid the boy and told him it was for immediate dispatch to the embassy in Paris via the War Office in Whitehall. Then I went to bed and slept the sleep of the dead.

The same day — Tuileries Garden, Paris

Dreadful conference. Complete waste of their time.

Lloyd George had travelled with the Prime Minister, Hankey, Bonham Carter, Robertson and Maurice. The crossing, though short, was rough. Both Hankey and Robertson were sick. The further discussion with the PM about Lansdowne's paper had been inconclusive. The speech which Lloyd George had drafted for Asquith's opening remarks had been toned down by the PM. Candid comments about the underperformance of Allied generals had been removed to avoid giving offence. The pessimism which Lloyd George had felt should ground the remarks – a pessimism that was needed to inspire fresh thinking, not resignation and hopeless – had been deleted by the PM. What resulted was a mess of half-baked nonsense. No insight, no challenges, no decisions. It was Asquith extending his consensus-building chairmanship to an international level. It was hopeless.

They returned to the Hôtel de Crillon in separate cars. Asquith then told the War Secretary he wanted time alone to read before dinner. Lloyd George, his mind still cranking through the day's events, proposed a walk and asked Hankey to accompany him. As secretary of the War Committee Hankey knew what this meant. A storm was brewing.

The two men crossed the Place de la Concorde (deep irony, Hankey thought) and headed to the Tuileries Garden. Yellow light shone on the paths in the early evening darkness. They wore coats, hats, and scarves against the cold, and Lloyd George smoked a cigar. They did not indulge in polite conversation: they knew each other too well for that. Lloyd George began.

'I can't carry on like this, Maurice. I'm a bloody War Secretary who cannot direct a war.'

Hankey said nothing.

'I mean, you saw all that today. He was asleep after lunch, I swear it. Briand went on and on and on; *his* generals, *his* men, *his* honour. His bloody country would be on the floor if we hadn't saved them. Briand would be eating Sauerkraut with the Kaiser by now if the Germans hadn't shot him instead. And what are our plans to take the fight to the Germans? We have none.

'The PM was asleep in the afternoon and tonight he'll be drunk. Bonham Carter will put him to bed at eleven. And then on Friday we'll end this pointless, useless conference and go back to London to report to the pointless, useless War Committee. And they'll send a minute to the bloody Cabinet and Asquith will sit there and pre-side over it and probably propose a vote of thanks to all those who helped make the conference such a success. And by this day next week we'll have another thousand British men dead of sniper fire and dysentery and rats in the trenches.'

They walked to the building at the end of the path in silence. Then Lloyd George wheeled to the right, towards the Seine.

'I think I must push for the War Council.'

Hankey stopped. 'As Donald proposed? In the *Chronicle?*'

'Yes. But without Asquith.'

They walked on in silence. Then Lloyd George continued: 'It's not that I dislike him, Maurice. There's a huge part of me that really loves the man. Nothing we did from '08 could have been done without him. No other leader could have seen us through that. If I'd've been in his place they'd have destroyed me – the press, the Tories, even the Palace. Only Asquith could have faced down the Lords and steered Home Rule through. Only he had the courage to take us into this war. I would have kept us out, you know that.

'But we're in the war now and consensus doesn't work in a war. Consensus will kill us. We have a settled majority in Parliament so we have to ignore Parliament now. Asquith is the supreme parliamentarian at a time when Parliament is a hopeless distraction. Asquith is the supreme consensus-builder at a time when we need to ignore the Cabinet. You can't run a war through a Cabinet or a Parliament. You need something like a dictatorship. For wartime only, but dictatorship. Three or four solid men, men of vision, energy and ambition. Younger men. We must have it, Maurice. I can't shackle myself to this any more.'

Hankey said nothing. He knew he wasn't expected to respond. And besides, he wasn't a politician: he was a civil servant, an administrator.

Like Lloyd George he also loved Asquith. But he loved him with a love that is not blind but which recognises when the loved one is flawed. In this case fatally flawed.

They walked on. Lloyd George took encouragement from the conversation, which was really just a monologue. A public servant who declines to respond sends a message no less clear than a politician who speaks. If Hankey had thought the idea was hopeless he would have told him so. Obliquely perhaps, in code. But he hadn't. So Hankey agreed.

They returned to the hotel. After dinner Lloyd George telegraphed Aitken in London. *Confirming dinner Friday evening meet first WO 6 o'clock.*

Then he went out for a second walk in search of further company.

– 5 –

Thursday 16 November 1916 — Whitehall

Aitken again.

A colleague of mine went to see Carson in an attempt to discover the extent to which Carson was acting with Lloyd George. With George returning from Paris tomorrow and a dinner arranged for him with Law that evening, I was anxious to know if we really did have a third man ready to act in the country's interests. My own role could only ever be an auxiliary one. My position as a backbencher kept me away from the centre of power, but I could nonetheless facilitate and give some assistance to others in effecting the necessary change. They needed cover and organisation and I could certainly provide that. They also needed the ability to claim, should their arrangements take an unpleasant turn, that they had acted only at the behest of others. Those 'others', of course, stood to be discarded if things turned ugly. I was the key 'other' in those arrangements.

But just as *they* needed cover to disguise their movements, so too did I. I therefore asked Harrison to see Carson on my behalf. Harrison understood the position in which I found myself. As an Ulster MP he had no affection for Asquith. Carson, however, he held in the highest regard for his leadership of the Ulster Unionists throughout the long crisis of the Home Rule. I am not at all sure that Carson held Harrison in the same esteem but he was at least willing to meet him and share his views about how the latest crisis might be resolved.

The news by return was only partly encouraging. Carson had indeed spoken with Lloyd George on more than one occasion and told him that he, Lloyd George, must lead the move against the Prime Minister. As a Unionist member Carson might have been expected to favour Law, his own party leader, for that role. But it seems that Carson holds Law only marginally less culpable than Asquith for the current state of affairs. Nonetheless Asquith must be removed and would only be removed if Law were to withdraw his support for him, a development which Carson's manoeuvring in last week's Nigeria debate had been designed to encourage. Law would only move if Lloyd George persuaded him to, but Law would never be sure whether pressure from Lloyd George was being applied genuinely to rectify a national calamity or merely to advance Lloyd George's own career. In fear of the latter, Law was unlikely to try to bring about the former. But act he must.

Armed with this intelligence I arranged to see Law that afternoon. I confirmed that Carson was willing to support a radical change but I also conveyed clearly his doubt that Law would act to move things forward. Law merely shrugged at this news. I also confirmed that Lloyd George was returning early from Paris, ahead of the PM, and had accepted Law's invitation (offered by me in his name) to dine with him tomorrow evening. At this Law told me that he had already invited Sir Henry Wilson to dine with him and thought it would be good to have Lloyd George along to hear Wilson's report on the conduct of the war.

My heart sank. The only living person despised with equal intensity by both Asquith and Lloyd George is Henry Wilson. They considered him, with undisguised contempt, to be a political general who only ever acted in the Unionist interest. Asquith had never forgiven Wilson for his part in the near-mutiny at the Curragh in 1914. Despised by the Irish Party, Wilson was now actively despised by the Liberal leadership too. Lloyd George could recognise a schemer and a plotter at a hundred yards – in Wilson's case even a mile might have been close enough. With the professional courtesy due from one intriguer to another, Lloyd George understood the motives that impelled Wilson onward whilst despising him for his lack of success. For Lloyd George there was no point in being a schemer if one wasn't a successful one. Wilson was not.

I tried to persuade Law to put Wilson off. Lloyd George was returning from Paris specifically to see him on a matter of national importance. He could dine with Wilson any time. But Law would not move. He proposed asking Wilson whether he would object to Lloyd George's joining them and if he did not then it would be a table for three. In my presence, and greatly against my advice, he telephoned Wilson about this. Wilson had no objection and Law asked me to extend the invitation to Lloyd George on those terms.

I did. But I knew that it would be declined. And it was.

Lloyd George had an acute sense of the danger of the company one kept. He certainly wanted Asquith (who would learn at once of any dinner with Law) to know that there was discontent in the ranks. But a dinner with both the Unionist leader and the general for whom Asquith felt more contempt than for any other man alive would send a message to the PM that was too strong and too soon. Better to keep one's powder dry.

So Lloyd George dined at home and promised to see me at my hotel the following morning.

Saturday 18 November 1916 — Hyde Park Hotel

A long interview with Lloyd George at my rooms this morning. We breakfasted at nine and he stayed until just after midday. Last evening's abortive diner with Law had left Lloyd George in a state of dejection, almost despair. Was he genuinely distressed or was he dissimilating, wanting me to believe he was more agitated than he really was? With Lloyd George one never knew.

'What choice do I have, Max?'

'Don't resign. That would finish everything. Resigning is what he wants you to do? Don't give him what he wants.'

'If I thought there was the slightest chance of effecting a change by staying on then of course I'd stay. But it's hopeless. Asquith is hopeless, we all know that, but Bonar is just as bad. Asquith won't remove himself voluntarily, he'll only go if he's pushed. And *I* can't push him. He'll only listen to Law.'

'You must give Law time. I know him better than you do. He hates change, he despises it, thinks it's weakness. He thinks change only ever means you were wrong in the first place. And he hates being wrong. But he will change. Believe me, I know him.'

'So I must wait? Until when?'

'It won't be that long. I know he's ruminating. I've seen this before – he's beginning to turn. You must be more subtle: apply pressure, yes, but nothing dramatic. If you resign now you'll only bolt him onto Asquith.'

Lloyd George rose and walked to the window. He stared out. I sensed the tension in his back and the frustration rising from his shoulders.

'If I resign the country will understand why I went. I can explain it to them – I can make things clear in a way that Asquith never could. I'll talk about the Cabinet's indecision, the hopelessness of the War Committee, and my impotence at the War Office. They know I'm a man of energy, Max; they know what I've achieved in the past. If I tell them the current arrangements are hopeless they'll believe me, I know they will. Asquith and Law could never resist that. I'll resign and join Carson on the Opposition benches and fight for a new ministry to win this war.'

'A ministry headed by you?'

He turned quickly and responded with unexpected force. 'I don't give a *damn* who heads the ministry, Max. Don't you see that? I don't give a *damn* who the Prime Minster is. Law, Carson, Curzon. Even Crewe would be better than this. The point is, any Prime Minister can manage the Government and Parliament, but only a *leader* can win the war. The role of Prime Minister is irrelevant now. If I could make Asquith understand that and give me the War Committee this would all come to an end.'

'If you resign now there's no guarantee there will be a dissolution. And even if there is, Law will embrace Asquith, the Government will increase its majority, and you and Carson will be cast out as opportunists who forced an election in the middle of a war. Resignation would be hopeless. Keep calm and keep on pushing for change from within. Work on Law – he's the key. Law will get Asquith out for you. I know he will. He just needs proper handling.'

He sat down again.

'Monday, Max. We must resolve this by Monday. Otherwise I have to go.'

The same day — Mayfair

When Lloyd George departed I immediately telephoned Law and said that I had to meet him straight away. Against his habit of dining simply and privately he agreed to meet me at Claridge's. I asked for a table near the back, away from the windows and half-curtained off from the other lunchtime diners. It was time to be frank with Law if Lloyd George was not to take drastic action the following Monday. I held nothing back.

'I must speak candidly, Bonar.'

He smiled. 'I've never known you to speak in any other way, Max.'

'I saw Lloyd George this morning.'

'I thought you might. Wilson was full of compliments about him last night. Dangerous.'

'You know how Lloyd George feels about the current arrangements.'

'Yes. But he changes his approach every week. What does he suggest now?'

'The War Committee to be wound up. Instead there should be a War Council.'

'Members?'

'You, Lloyd George, Carson.'

'Chairman?'

'Lloyd George.'

'No Asquith?'

'No Asquith.'

'I see.'

We ate in silence for a minute or two. Law took small bites and chewed methodically before swallowing. Ginger beer only, no wine. I drank the claret, trying to gauge his response. There was none.

'Bonar, you must consider this. More than that, you must *accept* it. You are the Unionist leader in the Government: you bear as much responsibility as Asquith for our disasters. It cannot go on.'

'I cannot destroy a Prime Minister while the country is at war, Max. I cannot do that.'

'He doesn't need to be destroyed. He can stay as PM. Lloyd George wants him to stay as PM.'

'But not leading the war effort? Can a man be Prime Minister in wartime and not lead the war?'

'He must accept this, Bonar. Asquith knows about duty. He will accept it if he sees it's the only way forward, a matter of duty for him.'

'Umm.'

'And you must convince him.'

Another silence as he digested this. Then he responded.

'Let me be clear, Max. I understand the position. I understand the need to change our arrangements. But I am not at all ready to demote the PM, still less to stand him down completely. I admire Lloyd George's vigour but I am uncertain, really, whether his energy can be channelled into a style of leadership more effective than Asquith's. Honestly, I am unsure. He might be better. But he might be very much worse. And Carson – how do you expect me to propel a backbencher onto this War Council over the heads of men like Curzon and Chamberlain and Long?'

'We must have the best men for the job, Bonar. If Asquith is to stand aside then some of our own men must stand aside as well. Ask yourself how the Liberals will feel if their leader is to stay off the War Council and two of its three members are Unionists. We must have the best men for the job now, forget the politics. And you and Carson and Lloyd George are the best men for this job. We must have you, all three of you. The country must have you.'

A long silence. I knew better than to interrupt. Then he spoke.

'Ask George to meet me on Monday evening. We need to discuss matter, all matters, not just personalities. An open discussion, assuming nothing. And tell him not to mention it to anyone else yet. No Liberals, no Unionists. And not Henderson either. I don't want anyone to know about these discussions just yet. You understand?'

'What about Carson?'

Another silence.

'If George wants him there, then, yes. Check with George.'

'I will.'

'But no one else, Max. No one. You understand?'
'I understand.'

The same day — Prime Minister's Study, 10 Downing Street

As soon as Aitken left the dining room Law retrieved his hat, coat and stick and headed to Downing Street. The afternoon had ended and the yellow light of the streetlamps opened pools of brightness through which he walked. Just off Piccadilly a young man lit a cigarette and asked him for the time. Law walked on oblivious.

In the study at Downing Street he met Asquith, just returned from Paris. The PM looked tired. Law gave him a full account of Lloyd George's latest proposals. Asquith listened closely and responded frankly. In his opinion Lloyd George was unlikely to view the chairmanship of the War Council as anything other than a step in his progress towards total power. He wanted to run the war but he also wanted to run the country and the Empire. And Carson was an absurd idea. A man of talent and energy, no doubt, but the Prime Minister had formed no high opinion of his 'constructive abilities' during his few months in government. He might have had some experience with local paramilitaries in Ulster (Law stayed silent) but nothing prepared him for running a European war. Did Law not realise what pressure he would face if Lloyd George and Carson attempted to direct the war themselves with only Law to restrain them? And Asquith a tame Prime Minister on the side, reporting to Cabinet and Parliament about everything other than the thing that mattered most, the war? And who would report to the King about the war? No, it was impossible.

As always in Asquith's presence Law found it impossible to disagree with him. Asquith thanked Law for briefing him but advised him to proceed with caution in his discussions with Carson and Lloyd George.

'By the way, Bonar, I know you value him but Aitken is a viper. We need these people to practise the dark arts for us, certainly, but Aitken is a particularly slippery specimen. Are you sure you know who else will be receiving what I'm sure he would term his "impartial advice"? Be careful.'

Law returned to Pembroke Lodge and, his sister being away for the weekend, a quiet evening alone. He was sound asleep by nine o'clock.

Sunday 19 November 1916 — Walton Heath

Aitken again.

I saw Lloyd George at Walton Heath this morning. He remains pessimistic about Law despite Law's willingness to meet him tomorrow. I told him I believed Carson should join that meeting and he agreed. I telephoned Carson to confirm his attendance. Thus was established, and I must in all truthfulness claim that its establishment was by my own hand, the triumvirate that would bring down the Government.

– 6 –

Monday morning. Early.

I had been summoned to a daybreak meeting with Law. On my way to his office I prayed that he hadn't changed his mind overnight. He hadn't; but this was worse. I found it almost impossible to believe what he told me.

'I'm sorry, Bonar. I don't quite understand. You told Asquith? What were you thinking?'

Law rose from behind his desk and walked over to the fire. Only now was some real morning light beginning to penetrate the darkness outside. Law was an early riser and invariably arrived at his office before seven. He had received me with his usual bluff courtesy and asked me to take a seat by the fire, which had been set by a servant at six to be ready for the Secretary of State's arrival. As I settled myself he told me from behind the desk, quite casually, that he had seen Asquith on Saturday and advised him of Lloyd George's thinking. I was completely taken aback: we had agreed that neither of us would allow the discussions to become widely known at this stage, least of all to the man most closely affected by them.

'Max, how long have you known me?'

'Ten years, I suppose. But what has that to do with anything? I can't believe that you told him. Why on earth did you do that?'

'After ten years you will undoubtedly have gathered that the aspect of character I value most in a man is frankness. Whenever we can be direct with one another, we ought to be. When we don't have to resort to subterfuge, we shouldn't. I have always preferred men who work out their differences by plain and honest dealings.

I wanted to be frank with him. He alone can resolve this problem. Hence he must know what his ministers are thinking.'

A servant knocked and entered with tea. He set it on a small table by Law's elbow and then withdrew.

'What exactly did you tell him?'

'The truth. That George is driven to distraction by the inefficiency of the War Committee. That he wants it reformed as a War Council under his own chairmanship, with two or three other members, principally Carson and myself. That it should be separated from the Cabinet and have executive authority in managing the war. And that the Prime Minister should not be a member.'

'And how did he react?'

'Exactly as I expected him to. He believes this represents Lloyd George positioning himself for ultimate power. Which of course it does. He said that George had never been loyal. Not to him, not to his party, not to the coalition. Lloyd George is in public life for the advancement of Lloyd George alone.'

'And you replied?'

Law remained silent for a moment, as if trying to recall the details of his interview with Asquith. 'I told him that I share his views as to Lloyd George's character but we need to find a better way of harnessing his quite extraordinary energy. We must consider his proposal carefully, if only to find ways of effecting the policy without being captured by the personality. We must find ways of utilising his energy while minimising the risk that he poses.'

'The risk?'

'Yes.'

'To whom?'

Law smiled. 'David Lloyd George is a risk to everyone he encounters, Max. He had three Liberal colleagues, Cabinet ministers, with whom he firmly joined in opposing this country's entry into the war two years ago. All three ministers resigned from the Government believing that Lloyd George would also resign and rally the country to the pacifist cause. And did he? Our now most belligerent minister? Of course he didn't. And Churchill: they were as thick as thieves in the early years of the war. And then they fell out over the direction of the conflict. And now Churchill has no place in the Government.'

'Some would say that was at the Unionists' insistence, nothing to do with Lloyd George.'

'And that would be true as far as it goes. But did Lloyd George make the slightest attempt to save Churchill when Asquith cast him out from the Admiralty because our party insisted on it? He did not.'

'And the current threat that Lloyd George poses. To Asquith?'

'If and when the country finally tires of Asquith as leader of the Liberals, Lloyd George is his obvious successor. At least for the Radical wing of that party. Not for the Whigs, but then Crewe is the only Whig left in the Liberal Party these days. And frankly, Max, Lloyd George is as great a danger to me and my leadership of *this* party as he is to Asquith in his.'

Law was no fool. He understood completely that the agitation being created by Lloyd George against Asquith was very much the same as the agitation being created by Carson against Law. Whether this was because Carson craved Law's position as leader of the Unionists or because he sought to undermine Law in order to weaken Asquith's position as leader of the country remained unclear. But either way it created a dilemma for Law. His loyalty, patriotic rather than party-political, lay with Asquith. But politics moves quickly and today's allies can quickly become tomorrow's mortal enemies.

'You will also be interested is the PM's views about your friend Carson.'

'Carson is a colleague, Bonar, not a friend. One doesn't have friends in politics.'

'Of course one does, Max. And the most unlikely friends. It's a remarkable feature of this country that mortal party enemies can often be the very best of social friends. Consider Asquith's relationship with Balfour. Asquith's real political career began in 1906 when the Conservatives were destroyed and Balfour was ejected from Downing Street. But he and Asquith continued to see each other socially and on the most cordial of terms ever afterwards. If Margot had never married Asquith she might very well have married Balfour.'

46

'If anyone would have.'

'Well, yes, quite. I'm not wholly sure he's the marrying kind. But if Margot *had* married Balfour, where would that have left Asquith? Married to Mrs Montagu, perhaps?'

I laughed quietly. We all knew that Asquith had spent many Cabinet meetings writing to his daughter's friend Venetia Stanley... until Miss Stanley had suddenly broken the spell, and possibly also the PM's heart, by rushing off to marry Edwin Montagu, whose less than handsome features Asquith was now forced to stare at across the Cabinet table.

'So what did he say about Carson?'

'That Asquith and some of his friends, including Conservative friends, had not formed a high view of Carson's ministerial ability during his time as Attorney General. Of the three proposed candidates for the War Council I am sure that Carson is the one whose membership the PM would most strongly oppose.'

'And what about you as a member?'

'Oh no one has any problem with me, Max, on a War Council or a War Committee or even in Cabinet. I am the indispensable man, it seems.'

He laughed at his own reputation before continuing.

'Asquith is alive to the threat and has a plan to deal with Lloyd George. He told me that he proposes sending Robertson to Russia, in effect removing him from the War Office. With Robertson out of the way Lloyd George will no longer have to co-operate with a military man for whom he has no high regard. Our Welsh friend might then feel that he has finally attained real power within the War Office.'

'And that would be enough to have him withdraw his bid for a War Council under his own chairmanship?'

'Quite possibly.'

'Well, well. The old man shows political cunning even to the end.'

'I'm not sure this is "the end", Max. And Asquith is quite the most cunning politician of our age. He may be beaten up but Asquith has been around the ring a thousand times before. And he retains all the power permitted to a Prime Minister by the strange constitution we all work under. If Lloyd George thinks he can prise

Asquith out of Downing Street without a fight, he'll need to get out of bed even earlier than I do.'

He poured the tea, now a little cold, and we talked of other matters.

The same evening — Hyde Park Hotel

Lloyd George was lying again.

'Yes, Bonar. I had been dining with Carson. But we did not discuss the Nigeria business.'

'You did not?'

'No. Please believe me: we spoke only of other matters. Of course I knew that Carson was heading to the House after dinner to speak against you in the debate, but I assure you we did not discuss it. It would have been quite improper of me to have had a conversation of that kind.'

'That's the truth, Bonar,' Carson interjected. 'We dined at White's and then I came down to the House and Lloyd George returned to his office.'

'But you didn't vote at the division either.' Law pressed his case.

'I'm sorry, Bonar, I should have done. But the whips told me we had a clear majority and they assured me that I wasn't needed. I had a conference of the Supply Office that evening and thought I should attend that instead of adding to our numbers in the House. Had I known you wanted me to attend then of course I'd have been there.'

'You had the Prime Minister there anyway, Bonar.' Carson again. 'You weren't abandoned to the wolves all alone!'

And Lloyd George: 'Please say that you believe me, Bonar. I would be greatly upset if you felt there was any intention on my part to cause you a difficulty.'

Law did not believe him. On this matter Bonar Law felt sure that Lloyd George was lying. And Carson too. It was inconceivable that they could have dined together just before a debate that everyone knew would damage Law and not discussed the likely outcome. He did not believe their protestations of innocence. But Law also knew that he was not the main focus of their conspiracy. The real target was Asquith and his removal. About that they had most certainly conspired.

'Gentlemen, I accept your clarification. Let's leave it at that. Max, see, we're friends again. As you wished us to be.'

I smiled and walked to the sideboard to refresh Carson's glass. Law and George were drinking ginger ale. The necessary preliminaries having been observed, the meeting could begin.

'Gentlemen, if I may,' I began. 'I suggested this meeting because it has seemed to me for many weeks that the public concern about the way in which the Government is managing the war has reached a dangerous level. After so many reverses, so little progress, so many abortive initiatives, and so much human sacrifice and destruction, the country has grown weary of our efforts and cynical about our excuses.

'Carson's efforts in the House last week, however personally painful they were to you, Bonar, gave eloquent voice to that dissatisfaction. I know how difficult it is to admit these concerns in public but here among friends we may surely be frank. None of these conversations will be written down or recorded. And none of them', and here I looked at Law, 'will be communicated to the Prime Minister unless all three of you agree that should happen. Are we agreed that the matter can be discussed on this basis?'

Carson and Lloyd George both answered 'Yes.'

But Bonar Law said, 'This is not about Asquith. It's about the structures of government and our leadership in the war. Not personalities. Not the Prime Minister. I am willing to discuss these structures in confidence with you, gentlemen, but I am not willing to be a party to any conversation whose main purpose is, or could conceivably be considered to be, the removal of the Prime Minister. I must have your agreement on this point before we proceed. Do you agree?'

Again, though not without some obvious hesitation, both Lloyd George and Carson answered 'Yes.'

I turned to Lloyd George. 'It seems to me that the War Secretary should lead the discussion. Are you willing to begin?'

Lloyd George stood.

'It's not a bloody public meeting, George,' said Carson.

'I think better on my feet', he replied. 'The blood rushes from my head and I find I can converse more freely with Unionists when I'm calmer.'

Both men smiled. Lloyd George began.

'I want to say how much I agree with the last thing you said, Bonar, before we begin the hard conversation. Nothing that I say tonight is intended as a slight on my leader. I owe the full degree of whatever success I have enjoyed in public life to Asquith. I have followed him through difficult times for eight years now. He raised me to the Chancellorship and then he made me War Secretary. We fought many battles side-by-side against you and your colleagues. I owe my career to Herbert Asquith and he's the finest parliamentarian, the finest parliamentary leader, and the finest chairman of a Cabinet this country has enjoyed in the last half-century. My criticisms are directed at the structures, not the man, and my intentions are only to reform the structures and not to remove the man. I ask you to believe me in this from the outset.'

'We do,' said Carson, who did not.

'Yes,' said Bonar Law, meaning no.

The niceties had now been observed.

'Gentlemen, we all know that the war is at a stalemate. We have four hundred thousand British men dead and a further million wounded in the last two years. The French have lost six hundred thousand and their country is ravaged. Our other allies have lost half a million. And the Germans and their allies, about whom we do not especially care except that they are men too and are just as capable of feeling pain as we are, have lost over a million. None of us in this room, none of our colleagues in government, not even the oldest member of the Lords, has ever seen destruction and loss of life on this scale. It is quite unimaginable. And there is no sign of the war ending.

'Our political direction of the war is inept. Who is responsible for our strategic decisions about the campaign? The Cabinet? In principle perhaps, but not in fact. The War Committee? Of course not. It has no authority; it's merely a debating shop. The Secretary of State for War? I assure you, gentlemen, that if I say "charge" the generals will do nothing. If I say "retreat" they will do nothing. If

I ask for supplies nothing will happen. If I ask for an explanation none will be forthcoming.

'Why is this? It's simple, gentlemen. Two reasons.

'The first is that the Prime Minister will not decide. I have known him in peacetime and I have known him *decisive* in peacetime. He, and indeed I, led decisive battles against the Unionist party in peacetime. And we won those battles, let me remind you. So Asquith is not unable to make a decision. But he sees his role in the present Cabinet as requiring him to hear all sides, to let every member have his say, to request further clarification if he believes that another study is needed. One understands the desire for caution in peacetime. All the great political decisions that my party took six or seven years ago were taken slowly and with deliberation. We weighed the factors involved, the issues raised, the likely responses, the possible consequences. And then we made a decision.

'But now we are at war. We have no time for the luxury of such settled decision-making. We must act swiftly, decisively, energetically. And we must abolish those structures like the War Committee and even the Cabinet that hold us back from making bold decisions.'

'The Cabinet?' Bonar Law interjected.

'Gentlemen, I believe the only Cabinet we should have in England today is a War Cabinet. Three or four members. With executive authority to run the war. Chaired by a man who has responsibility only for the direction of our military affairs. The Prime Minister can manage Parliament and coordinate the work of our colleagues in the ministries, but neither his voice nor theirs should be heard in the highest councils of Government during a conflict as brutal as this one. Only the voice of the War Cabinet should matter if we are to win the war.'

'I am not in favour of deposing Asquith and I am not in favour of destroying the Cabinet.' Law again.

Lloyd George ignored him. 'The second reason why we cannot manage our war effort with any kind of effectiveness is because our leader, the Prime Minister, is mesmerised by military men. He feels himself incapable of questioning them, still less contradicting them. The generals are like gods to him. When, Bonar, have you ever seen the PM deal forcefully with a general? My predecessor Lord Kitchener was Asquith's greatest mistake and the country's greatest booby. He alone held us back by almost a year. I am sorry that he died, and that he died in that awful way, but, gentlemen, it was a blessing for the country that he went to his reward.'

From Carson: 'What are you suggesting about the generals, George?'

'None of them on the War Council. None of them even *near* the Council unless we send for them.'

'But how can you have a War Council without any generals?'

'That is precisely the issue, Bonar. These men must manage the *tactics* but as regards the broad thrust of the conflict they must act as we, their political leaders, instruct them. *We* must set the policy, not them.'

'But what do we know of strategy, of fighting a war?'

'We know at least as much as the military fools who have bogged us down in Flanders for twenty-four months and then as a distraction gave us the Dardanelles campaign.'

'The Dardanelles was Churchill's doing, not the military's.' This was Carson.

Lloyd George responded. 'It was the Admiralty and the generals between them who turned it into such a quagmire.'

I said nothing. Lloyd George stopped speaking. Both Law and Carson stayed silent at first. Then Law spoke.

'Carson, you have told me repeatedly that you would never join an Asquith ministry again.'

'If Asquith were Prime Minister and discharged that role by leading the Commons and co-ordinating the work of those ministries not engaged in the day-to-day war effort, and the direction of the war was left to a Council led by another man, then I could support such an arrangement,' he replied. And then to make it fully clear: 'If you asked me to re-join the Government as a member of this War Council I would accept.'

'I see', Bonar Law said. Carson's challenge to him, inchoate, unarticulated, had ratcheted up another notch.

'And you, Bonar?' Lloyd George asked. 'I respect your insistence that nothing should be done to humiliate Asquith. I support it. But the direction of the war must change. Would you support this kind of arrangement?'

Law sat in silence for a moment. 'I need time to reflect on what you have said. Any suppression of the role of the Cabinet would have to be a temporary expedient. For the duration of the war only. Not a precedent, and quite definitely to be abandoned after the war.'

'Of course.'

'Then I will give it some further consideration,' Law replied.

They spoke for a little longer about related matters but the gist of that first meeting of the triumvirate is as I have recorded it here. All-in-all it was not a particularly happy meeting. Bonar Law trusted neither of his fellow triumvirs. Carson might be more honourable but he was a greater and much more personal danger to Law. But Law was dazzled by the simplicity of Lloyd George's case, the persuasiveness of his argument, and the energy of his personality. Perhaps his proposal *did* offer some way of linking Asquith, George and himself in a better arrangement. And George was surely right to assert that things could not continue as they stood at present.

Carson and Lloyd George left together. Law followed shortly. I poured myself a whiskey and sat in Law's chair and wondered whether, in words that had grown bitter since some fool of a politician first uttered them two years ago, this would indeed all be 'over by Christmas'.

– 7 –

Tuesday 21 November 1916 — Westminster and Whitehall

Our discussions continued throughout the following day.

Carson saw Law at Law's room in the House of Commons at half past nine. Later that morning I arranged a further meeting of the three principals, this time at Lloyd George's office in Whitehall, a short walk from Parliament through a murky November morning. Little progress and no outcome, but at least they were talking.

At the end of that meeting I invited Law and Lloyd George to lunch with me in my rooms at the hotel. I thought it best to exclude Carson at this stage in order to focus on binding the two principals together. Our lunch followed what was by all accounts a spectacularly dull meeting of the Cabinet at which nothing was resolved.

Lloyd George arrived in a state of something like suppressed fury. Given the shambles of this morning's Cabinet, he argued, it was surely now clear that Asquith must not be a member of the War Council. He would dominate it simply by virtue of being Prime Minister and thereby destroy its effectiveness. Bonar Law then expressed the same concern he had expressed before: he would not be a party to any arrangement that humiliated the Prime Minister or reduced his role to a cipher. No progress was made. In fact I was myself for the first time annoyed by how Lloyd George behaved during the meeting. I had warned him that Law was unusually sensitive on this point. It would be better to try to reach agreement on other aspects of the arrangement before reverting to Asquith's ongoing role. But George had plunged straight in at the most delicate point. I knew that once Lloyd George had left Law would upbraid me for dealing so openly with him. As indeed he did. I bore the criticism stoically. The discussions were going to prove even more difficult than I had imagined at the outset.

The same day, earlier that morning —
Cabinet Room, 10 Downing Street

Herbert Asquith had been Prime Minister for longer than he could remember. Not that he couldn't remember his life before he entered Downing Street. Of course he could: he remembered his upbringing, his early days at the Bar, his first wife, Helen, and the tragedy of her early death, his marriage to Margot and then his rising political career, first as Home Secretary under Gladstone and Roseberry, and then later as Chancellor under Campbell-Bannerman until C.B.'s protracted illness and death in 1908. And travelling alone by boat and train to Biarritz to be appointed Prime Minister by the King when C.B. had entered his final decline.

Of course he remembered all these occasions; how could he not? But since he had become Prime Minister the earlier parts of his life had seemed to slip into a kind of restricted consciousness. Like the dream you remember when you awaken in the morning – vivid, colourful, strongly felt at that moment, but quickly fading away into nothingness. A dim memory by breakfast, a forgotten illusion by mid-morning. His early life had faded into something like that dreamlike state. He had assumed his true life only when he entered Number 10.

These thoughts came to him gently, unbidden, as he chaired that morning's Cabinet meeting. Ministers customarily assembled at Downing Street at half past ten. Asquith had risen at eight, washed and shaved and dressed. Breakfast with Margot at half past. Then at nine to the Cabinet Room, where he worked alone on his papers until the meeting. At twenty past ten Drummond knocked and entered. The Prime Minister gave him the papers with instructions written in his firm and steady hand at the top of each bundle. As he dealt with them Asquith had sorted the finished papers into discrete piles: for distribution to ministers, for his own files, for the Palace, or individual responses and instructions to various

Crown servants. Drummond recognised the different collections of papers and carried them away for distribution. The flow was endless. More files would await the PM's attention at the end of the meeting. Then through the afternoon and long into the evening.

'Your colleagues are assembling, Prime Minister. You will begin on time?'

'We will, Drummond, yes. But allow me ten minutes on my own first, please. I want to review the papers for our meeting before we begin. Lord Buckmaster is here?'

'Yes, Prime Minister.'

'And his paper was circulated yesterday?'

'Yes, sir.'

'Fine. We'll take that towards the end. Send Bush in to put some coal on the fire.'

'Sir.'

Drummond left the room.

As the clock in the hall chimed the half hour the door opened and twenty of Asquith's ministerial colleagues entered the room. All called or murmured 'Good morning, Prime Minister' as they took their allotted places. Lord Chancellor Buckmaster took the chair to Asquith's right. The Chancellor, McKenna, directly across the table from the Prime Minister. Lloyd George, War Secretary, to McKenna's left (they hated each other) and Grey, the Foreign Secretary, to his right. Bonar Law sat at Asquith's left-hand side. Samuel, the Home Secretary, flanked Buckmaster; Henderson, the Labour leader, flanked Lloyd George. Other ministers took the lesser places, one's power and influence being carefully calibrated by how far one sat away from the centre. Asquith could not see those at the distant ends of the table without leaning forward.

The meeting began and he guided ministers through the agenda. Much of it dealt with routine reports. Papers which had been read before the meeting were noted. Ministers provided further updates. McKenna wanted to talk about economic matters, particularly his dealings with the Bank of England in support of sterling. Lloyd George brooded, holding his fire for the War Committee meeting on Thursday, from which he would report back in detail to the subsequent Cabinet. Buckmaster's report dealt with a constitutional issue: the extent to which members of foreign royal families displaced by the war could take precedence in the United Kingdom during hostilities. It was a technical matter, in fact crushingly boring, but as it dealt with a 'royal' issue the Cabinet had to treat it with some pretence of seriousness. Asquith would prepare a written account of the meeting for the King after it ended. That would take him fifteen minutes: he would draft it just before going in to lunch.

As McKenna reported, Asquith wrote. He sat slightly back from the table, balanced a pad on the knee of his right leg, now crossed over his left, and wrote quickly and easily on a small yellow sheet.

Dear Cynthia – Another interminable Cabinet. McKenna is boring us with some technical report on the currency. Why is he telling us this? So far he requires no decisions from us, so why is he wasting our time? I wish I could cut him off – I would have no hesitation in terminating a more junior minister. But he is the Chancellor of the Exchequer and will claim he has a right to be heard by his colleagues on these issues. As I suppose he has. But in the middle of a war? Buckmaster has something to say to us later. It concerns The Family. Buckmaster will make McKenna sound concise and specific! I can see the WS glaring into the middle distance. He is in one of his moods today and will say nothing at all at this meeting, his own form of protest that anything other than the war should be discussed at these sessions. But we must try to maintain the semblance of 'normal government', the sense that life can go on and questions like these can be dealt with despite the horrors at the Front. I do hope your brothers are safe there. You must please tell me if I can find out anything about them for you. Shall we take a turn in the motor on Friday afternoon? I could collect you at 3 and have you back at home by 5. I do hope you will say yes – the thought of your lovely face and our plain honest conversation is all that sustains me through these dark hours. Ever yours my darling – H.

He folded the page and placed it in an envelope, writing her name and address – Miss Cynthia Sackville, Berkeley Square, West – on the front. McKenna was concluding.

'Thank you, Chancellor. Gentlemen, any questions for the Chancellor?'

There were indeed questions. Asquith allowed three of them before ending the discussion.

'Thank you again, Chancellor. We agree that you should proceed as you have outlined.'

McKenna nodded. Lloyd George glared.

'The next item. Lord Chancellor. Your report. Which we have read. Please summarise it, briefly if you can.'

Asquith knew that Buckmaster could no more summarise a report briefly than he, the Prime Minister, could sail to the moon. He reached forward for another yellow sheet as the Lord Chancellor cleared his throat. He had been meaning to write a lengthy reply to Miss Bowes-Creighton for some time. Now was his opportunity.

– 8 –

Lansdowne was due at seven o'clock. Asquith had invited him to stay on and dine with the family and a handful of other guests, mainly artistic types, friends of Margot. He knew that Lansdowne would decline even without hearing who the other guests were: when he knew their names he would show even less hesitation in making his apologies. As indeed he had. Asquith had never met a man quite as monomaniacal as Lord Lansdowne, except perhaps Bonar Law. The two leaders of the Unionist party were well-matched. Quite the most unclubbable pair of men he had ever encountered in his long career.

He gazed directly into the fire and allowed his mind to wander. He had come up from the Cabinet Room at six, asked for a brandy and soda in his study, and retired to relax before dinner. He had thought of walking to the Athenaeum to read in solitude there but the request from Lansdowne for a private meeting had come late in the afternoon and there was no time to get there and back before seven. He was reading a pot-boiler by Buchan, the Unionist author. *The Thirty-Nine Steps*. Buchan's hero Richard Hannay had many adventures, some more believable than others. But it took his mind away from the grim business of government and in fact was really rather good.

It had been a taxing day. No full Cabinet today but the War Committee had met at eleven for nearly three hours. Lloyd George at his most demanding: of political colleagues, of the generals, of the men, of suppliers to the army. It was all that Asquith could do to contain him and prevent an open rupture between the War Secretary and the military leaders. He had begun to find the War Committee almost impossible to control, still less to direct. Everyone's nerves were on edge. Most of the members were working long hours, which impaired their judgement and made it difficult for them to see alternative points of view. The Prime Minister's job as chairman was to bring the meetings to a consensus on the key points. But even Asquith, who prided himself on his skill in drawing any discussion to a clear and agreed conclusion, was finding it difficult work.

He knew, of course, that there was an underswell of movement against him in the country and the press. The two were quite obviously connected: the press was creating the discontent in the country, not reflecting any existing dissatisfaction. Lloyd George was leading the agitation and leaking to the press. And Carson was almost certainly involved as well. The discontented in both parties wanted a change in their leadership but the extent of the disquiet was, Asquith believed, not yet strong enough to constitute any real threat to his position.

Lloyd George wanted to take charge. He believed, quite understandably, that eight years was long enough for Asquith to have held the leading role in their party, and he saw the stalemate in the war as a golden opportunity to press his claims. But few others on the Liberal benches supported him: most, in fact, distrusted him, and quite a few openly despised him. And so while Asquith certainly felt the heat from Lloyd George intensifying, he did not believe there was as yet any need for him to act decisively to defend his position.

When that moment arrived he would have no hesitation in relieving Lloyd George of his position in the Government. And Lloyd George could then, in the kind of language usually despised by the Prime Minister but not without aptness in the present circumstances, bugger off back to Wales. Who knows, he might even meet his wife there, if he could remember what she looked like. Or introduce her to his mistress? He smiled as he imagined the scene. Perhaps, in the spirit of political irony that he relished, Asquith might recommend him for a peerage as Viscount Lloyd George of – say – Limehouse? He smiled again at the thought.

What was happening in the Unionist Party seemed even less of a danger to the Prime Minister's position. Law and Lansdowne were secure in their leadership, although Asquith was well aware that Carson was agitating on the Unionist benches in much the same way that Lloyd George was sowing instability on the Liberal side. But to what purpose? To displace Law? What would that achieve? The Unionists would never have Carson as their leader. So any successor to Law would have to be one of the 'three Cs' – Chamberlain, Curzon or Cecil – or perhaps at a stretch Walter Long. But Asquith could see no real appetite on the Unionist benches for any such change.

There was one other factor as well, a most important one. Bonar Law was loyal to Asquith. Not to the person but to the position. Asquith knew that to a Prime Minister in time of war, any Prime Minister, Law felt an overwhelming sense of obligation to show almost unconditional loyalty. Law had told him quite openly of his recent meeting with Lloyd George, Carson and Aitken. Held nothing back. Aitken was of little consequence, a semi-professional agitator. Lloyd George and Carson were more serious politicians but so long as the pressure came only from the two of them the threat to Asquith was minimal. Should Law ever engage with the two conspirators, however, that would change everything. But it seemed to the Prime Minister that this would never happen. So the irritation remained just that, an irritation. It was not a threat. Not yet, anyway.

He had other sources of information as well, of course. He knew that meetings had continued between Aitken, Carson and Lloyd George during the week and that some of those had also involved Bonar Law. He knew that Lloyd George had lunched with Hankey yesterday. For the Secretary of State for War to take lunch with the Secretary of the War Committee was no surprise, but he knew they had also had a private conversation in Paris last week. Hankey shared Lloyd George's concern about the ineffectiveness of the War Committee. But Asquith trusted Hankey implicitly and would have been astounded to hear that he was conspiring in any way.

He also knew that a further meeting of the four had taken place at the Colonial Office that very morning. He had asked to be advised by senior officials at the various ministries of any meetings that either

Carson or Aitken attended with their ministers. Whenever Aitken and Carson met together with both Law and Lloyd George, Asquith was particularly interested. He was sure he would hear from Law if anything of substance had been discussed that morning.

So something was afoot. But for now he did not feel that it merited any decisive response on his part. He was more troubled by the press. Just today the *Morning Post* had published an editorial which argued strongly for a Lloyd George premiership. Asquith found this somewhat confusing. The editor, Gwynne, had only last month written to him complaining bitterly that Lloyd George was intriguing against the generals. This was the same Lloyd George that Gwynne now wanted to make Prime Minister? It was deeply strange. No real threat just yet but he would have to watch how the situation developed.

The Lansdowne visit was unlikely to be connected with these movements. Asquith was aware that Lansdowne's recent memorandum, offered in good faith, had caused deep unease among other members of the Cabinet. Lloyd George's disdain for Lansdowne's views was unsurprising but Asquith detected a wider disquiet among his colleagues. Lord Robert Cecil had told him how furious he was at Lansdowne's defeatism and promised that he, Cecil, would offer the Prime Minister a rejoinder the following week. Once he had read that, Asquith decided, he would open a wider discussion among his colleagues.

At seven o'clock precisely there was a muffled knock on the study door.

'Come in.'

Drummond entered. 'Lord Lansdowne, Prime Minister.'

'Thank you, Drummond. Come in, Lord Lansdowne.'

Lansdowne entered. Head down, marching across to the PM's chair. Hand outstretched. Asquith rose to greet him. Shook hands.

'Thank you, Prime Minister. Good of you to see me at this hour. I know it's been a long day for you.'

Asquith gestured for him to sit in the easy chair on the other side of the fire.

'May I offer you something to drink? Tea, perhaps? Or something stronger?'

'Thank you, no, Prime Minister. I won't keep you long.' Asquith nodded to Drummond, a gesture that asked him to refresh his brandy. Drummond crossed to the drinks cabinet, poured a measure of brandy into a fresh glass, added soda and ice, and brought it to Asquith. He removed the earlier glass, now empty, and silently left the room, closing the door behind him. Asquith gave Lansdowne his full attention.

'You've read my memorandum?'

'I have.'

'And circulated it to our Cabinet colleagues?'

'Yes. Some days ago. I gave it first to the Secretary of State for War. Then to the others.'

'Have you heard their views?'

'I've had the War Secretary's views in some detail. One or two of the others have spoken briefly about it. But I asked them not to comment until they have read the other memoranda that colleagues are in the course of preparing.'

'What did Lloyd George think?'

'I doubt you need me to confirm what you already know about the Secretary's view of your case. He thought you were wholly wrong. He found it negative, defeatist, unduly pessimistic. And dangerous.'

'Dangerous?'

'In the sense that it would give comfort to our enemies should it become known that a senior member of the British Government, a party leader in one of our Houses of Parliament and a former Foreign Secretary, thought it expedient to advise his colleagues to seek terms with the enemy.'

'I did not say that we should seek terms.'

'You did not say so directly, I agree. But in suggesting that we must be willing to discuss any settlement proposals that might be forthcoming you were in effect advising us to seek terms.'

'With respect, Prime Minister, I disagree.'

'Of course you do. I understand. I would not expect you to claim otherwise.'

'There is a clear distinction between seeking terms and engaging in an exploratory discussion.'

'Perhaps to the professional diplomat there is. But I doubt that any intelligent member of the public would be capable of drawing such a distinction. Nor would any newspaperman wish to do so.'

Asquith could see where Lansdowne was taking the conversation. He, Lansdowne, was about to move (it seemed to the Prime Minister) into extraordinarily sensitive territory. Asquith debated mentally whether to end the conversation immediately or allow it to continue along the path upon which Lansdowne was about to strike out.

Lansdowne said nothing.

They sat in silence for a moment.

Then Lansdowne spoke.

'Prime Minister, may I speak in confidence?'

Treacherous.

'Every conversation between ministers of the Crown should be capable of being conducted confidentially, Lord Lansdowne. And yet I find myself reading accounts in the newspapers almost every day of deeply sensitive matters which were discussed between ministers on the most confidential terms. I can only say that I will of course preserve your confidence. But we are men of the world and we must weigh carefully the possibility that any of our exchanges may be reported by a third party and appear in the newspapers this week or next. If you are willing to open a conversation on that basis, please go ahead.'

More silence. Lansdowne cleared his throat.

'We must end this war. It is destroying us. We must end it now.'

'Are you advocating surrender, Lord Lansdowne?'

'Of course I'm not.'

'Well, what are you suggesting?'

'Colonel House will be in London in the middle of December.'

Colonel House. Woodrow Wilson's private emissary. The only man with immediate and direct access to the American president. His closest foreign advisor and confidante, his intermediary with the outside world. Wilson had just been re-elected president on a promise to keep the United States out of the war. But it was the settled policy of His Majesty's Government to turn Wilson around, to draw America into the war.

'Yes, he will. I am seeing him here before Christmas.'

'I suggest that I should see him too, Prime Minister.'

'I think Lord Grey and I can manage the meetings with Colonel House. Lloyd George too, perhaps.'

'I am suggesting that I see him in an unofficial capacity, Prime Minister.'

'You are a member of the Government, Lord Lansdowne. A minister without portfolio, without department responsibilities. But a member of the Government nonetheless.'

'I'm not suggesting that I see him on ministerial business, Prime Minister. I suggest that I should see him on your instructions with a secret message. To ask Wilson to ask you and the other belligerents to specify conditions under which they would be willing to end the war. I am asking you to appoint me – nothing official, nothing ever in writing – as your representative in opening a channel to Wilson that will bypass our embassy in Washington. You and Lord Grey will continue to communicate officially with him through our ambassador. The public line will continue to be that we intend to fight the war to the end, with or without American support, never surrendering. That we earnestly desire such support and want the Americans to come into the war on our side. As soon as possible. But you would also communicate more frankly with the president through House and me. And you would use us to find a way of opening a conversation with the Austrians and the Germans to end the war.'

Asquith stared across at Lansdowne. They had fought bitter political fights in the past. Fights that first one and then the other had won without destroying his opponent. This was different. This was an arrangement that could destroy them both. It was the highest risk that Asquith had been asked to take during the whole of his term as Prime Minister.

Lansdowne stared back at Asquith. He – Lansdowne – was horrified by the war. Whether the country emerged victorious or went down to ignominious defeat mattered little to him any more. The butchery of the next generation of Englishmen was already almost complete. Not only were their own sons dead but their whole way of life was ending too. Whatever certainty and stability their society, English society, even European society, had enjoyed before this Great War, it would never enjoy it again. Lansdowne saw only a shattered country, one in which he and his kind would no longer have any place. The military carnage could only lead to social disaster. By 1925, with or without a continuing war, England would be unrecognisable. Of that there could be no doubt now. Better then to end the war and spare at least some of his countrymen before the revolutions began.

Asquith also knew they were on the verge. If he lost the war his name would be debased forever. But even if he won, what then? Won at what price? A war that England had stumbled into almost accidentally would certainly mark the end of England regardless of whether they 'won' or 'lost'. In fact he was uncertain what either of those terms meant any more. This was a war that promised only a victory from which they would never recover.

For a long time he made no response to Lansdowne. Instead he stared at his old adversary and then shifted his gaze (they both did) into the glowing fire.

– 9 –

Bonar Law had invited Carson, Lloyd George and me to lunch at his home that Saturday. After the inconclusive meetings of the last few days we all felt the time for decisive action was now approaching. But how to proceed? My own strong sense was that we should go to Asquith with a definite proposal. But should we propose an arrangement that he could modify and accept, or would it be more effective to suggest something he would feel bound to reject? I was increasingly sure that, despite their protestations of loyalty, my colleagues would much prefer the Prime Minister to reject their proposal. That would put them on the path to high-principled resistance and I was in little doubt that this was indeed the road they longed to find themselves on.

My role was to help them onto that path.

Another bout of complaining about the hopelessness of the present situation would get us nowhere. This meeting needed to produce something solid. And so, after breakfast in my rooms at the hotel, I sat down with a fresh pot of tea and began to draft.

How does one structure such a document? In whose name should it be written? Certainly not Carson's: he had the least standing of all the conspirators. Bonar Law would never put his name to so divisive a memorandum. Lloyd George would, of course, but therein lay the difficulty. Another demand from Lloyd George might give the PM the opportunity of rejecting him completely, forcing him out of the Government. No, Lloyd George must continue to press verbally, informally.

But then the obvious solution presented itself to me. The triumvirate must send the Prime Minister a memorandum drafted in his own name. Asquith would then be asked by Law to review it, agree to it, and issue it. Only if the triumvirate acted in this way would Asquith come to know the seriousness of the opposition that now ranged against him. I had never written a document in the name of a Prime Minister before. It was an interesting exercise in composition.

How to begin? I decided to plunge straight in. Thank the existing members for their work but then candidly recognise the limitations of their efforts. I started to write:

> The War Council has, in my opinion, rendered devoted and invaluable service, but experience has convinced me that there are disadvantages in the present system that render a change necessary.

Asquith was never long-winded in his written output. This document must carry his voice and he would undoubtedly come straight to the point. Nothing would be gained by summarising the work of the present group or praising its members excessively. No; just say that good work has been done but the arrangement is no longer effective. Time for a change, to move on. I was pleased with my opening paragraph.

What were the essential points about the way in which a new body responsible for managing the war should operate? Daily meetings, certainly. Also the membership must exclude ministers charged with running large Government departments. Above all else the war chiefs must be politely but firmly removed as permanent members. And so I wrote:

> Some body doing the work of the War Council should meet every day. [*Including weekends? – no, that would be too much*]. It is impossible that the War Council can do this while its members have at the same time to fulfil the exacting duties of their Departments. At the War Council, also, we have felt it necessary to have the advantage regularly of the presence of the Chief of the Imperial General Staff and the First Sea Lord. Their time is in this way taken up sometimes unnecessarily when every moment is required for other work.

A good draft, I thought, although I knew that some of my colleagues held exactly the opposite view about the military men. A number of them would have created a war council made up *only* of the military. That would have been an appalling development in a democracy like ours. Let the military manage hostilities, of course, but overall guidance and direction of the war had to remain in the hands of elected politicians. But the *right* ones.

And so to the key point. How would Asquith deal with this? He would announce the establishment of a new body. Limited membership. No ministers with portfolios. And call it something without 'war' in the title, making it perfectly clear that while the military men were to run the campaign the new body was to run the country *at* war. I wasn't sure what Lloyd George would make of this: he would want to run the committee but would also insist that the word 'war' should feature in its title. Still, small steps.

> I have decided, therefore, to create what I regard as a civilian General Staff. This staff will consist of myself as President [*I could already hear Lloyd George's demurral*] and of three other members of the Cabinet who have no portfolio and who will devote their whole time to the consideration day by day of the problems which arise in connection with the prosecution of the war.

Had I struck the right balance here? Carson, Lloyd George and I all wanted Asquith gone, not just from his chairmanship of the War Committee but from Downing Street as well. But we had to reckon with Law's extreme reluctance to press Asquith on that point. He would never have brought Asquith any document that demanded his resignation, nor would Asquith ever have accepted it. So this draft had to hold Asquith formally in the key role whilst making the larger enterprise unpalatable to him. He would therefore reject the proposal. That would then allow Law to see that the Prime Minister had grown obstinate and unreasonable and cause him to rethink his absolute loyalty to him. It was a complicated exercise. Carson and Lloyd George would greatly dislike my draft, finding it too weak. Asquith would dislike it for being too strong, even if it didn't dispose of him completely. Law would – I hoped – find it just balanced enough for him to be willing to take it to Asquith. It was, I felt, as much as we could reasonably do as a first step.

The second key issue had to do with the names of those who were to become members of the new group and also the vexed question of its chairmanship. I had allowed Asquith to remain as 'President', a meaningless title which I felt sure he would find sufficiently insulting to cause him to reject the whole draft out of hand. But how to insert Lloyd George as the committee's key executive? I drafted as follows:

> As Prime Minister I will have little time for dedicated involvement in the work of the General Staff group. I have therefore invited Mr Lloyd George, and he has consented, to be its chairman, with full executive authority to bind both the Cabinet collectively and other ministers individually to executive action in pursuance of the General Staff's decisions. I have also asked Mr Bonar Law, Sir Edward Carson and Mr Arthur Henderson, and they have agreed, to constitute the members of the group. Mr Law and Mr Henderson have agreed to relinquish their roles as Colonial Secretary and President of the Board of Education respectively, and I will assign those positions to other colleagues in due course.

I felt less certain about this paragraph. It was in effect asking Asquith to exclude himself completely from the committee. It gave Lloyd George enormous executive powers, openly superior to those of other ministers and even of the Cabinet as a whole. It leap-frogged Carson over his more senior Unionist colleagues, an arrangement that would undoubtedly create tension in the Conservative ranks. Was this too strong?

I rose and walked around the room, opening the window for some fresh air and pouring more tea. Time was pressing on. I needed a draft that would give my colleagues no reason for declining to transmit it to Downing Street but which would also, while drawing the anticipated rejection from Asquith, not give *him* any grounds for claiming that those who had sent him the proposal were being unreasonable.

I needed to amend this paragraph.

I deleted it completely and started again.

Perhaps the details of the committee's membership should be left for consideration at a later stage once the principles of the arrangement had been agreed? And so I wrote:

> The three members who have undertaken to fulfil these duties are (   )

I left a blank space. No names.

But the issue of Lloyd George's role needed to be dealt with firmly in this opening communication and so I continued as follows:

> and I have invited Mr Lloyd George, and he has consented, to act as chairman and to preside [*the next few words were exquisitely important: how to detach Asquith from the group without seeming to remove him?*] at any meeting which, owing to the pressure of other duties, I find it impossible to attend.

I was delighted with this new wording. Asquith retained the right to preside at any meeting of the new committee, delegating the chairmanship only to Lloyd George on those occasions when, due to other pressures (exhaustion? drunkenness? a hangover? a letter that needed writing to a lady admirer?) he was unable to attend. And it would surely be recognised as soon as the group was established that Lloyd George was its presiding officer. Even if the Prime Minister *did* choose to attend Lloyd George would quickly wrest active management of the group away from him. And any attempt to take it back from Lloyd George would leave Asquith undone.

Asquith was too clever a politician not to recognise the extent to which real power was to be stripped away from him under this proposal. He would remain as Prime Minister, certainly, but how long would it be before the chorus of complaint resumed from the press that a tired and worn-out PM should be replaced by the younger man who had shown such extraordinary reserves of energy in his few brief months of running the war? Lloyd George would be Prime Minister by Easter if these arrangements were implemented. As such Asquith would have no choice but to reject the proposed arrangement. Law would then have no choice but to regret the Prime Minister's intransigence and allow himself to be persuaded to consider new arrangements. And, again, Lloyd George would be Prime Minister by Easter.

But perhaps even this attenuated draft was too harsh? Would other ministers see it too plainly as Lloyd George attempting a coup? Perhaps, I thought, I should add something further, some wording which on the face of it would seem to preserve for Asquith a central role in the new arrangement but which the Prime Minister himself would recognise as inconsequential, even insulting. The whole trick in this exercise was to craft a document which Asquith would *have* to reject while leaving him, the Prime Minister, clearly identifiable – and so blameable – as the unreasonable party. Suddenly the way forward became clear to me and in a final flourish I added a concluding paragraph:

> I propose that the body should have executive authority subject to this – that it shall rest with me to refer any questions to the decision of the Cabinet which I think should be brought before them.

Do you see the genius of this arrangement? It gives the man a veto. He can decide to refer any decision of Lloyd George's group to the full Cabinet for further consideration and review. Executive authority, although delegated to Lloyd George's group, still rests with the Cabinet. Asquith's decision as to which matters to take away from Lloyd George's War Committee would be definitive. And so on paper at least Asquith would remain the senior man.

Except that (and Asquith would recognise this sooner than any other politician) it would be an utterly self-destroying act on his part to exercise that authority. On the first occasion that Asquith moved to refer any matter from Lloyd George's War Committee to the full Cabinet Lloyd George would surely resign and appeal to the country. And from there he would certainly sweep to power. Any decision by Asquith to act against him would mark Asquith's own end.

It was the most perfect trap and I was immensely proud of my morning's work. I took my coat and hat and went downstairs in a mood of energetic optimism. Not waiting for the porter to step forward, I hailed a taxicab directly from the street and set off for Pembroke Lodge.

The same day — Pembroke Lodge

We met at Law's house and immediately took lunch in his dining room on the ground floor. It was a cold buffet but more substantial than Bonar's usual fare. Only Carson had alcohol, which may have fuelled his opening contribution. He inveighed mightily against the current arrangements: endless delays, endless policy reversals, endless bickering on the War Committee, hopeless chairmanship, always consensus or, if no consensus could be reached that day, deferral of decisions. And Lloyd George and Robertson locked in permanent conflict, minister against general, with no clarity about where final authority truly lay.

Carson was of course correct. But we had heard all this before.

On the way upstairs after lunch I was taken aback by a private conversation with him.

'What do you make of all this, Max? Really?' he asked me.

'Of all what?'

'Of this proposal to elevate George. To increase his powers. Even, depending on how Asquith responds, to make him Prime Minister?'

At that moment Law turned around and ushered us into the study before I could respond. But I had already formed the impression that Carson did not want a response from me. He was posing the question merely to put me on notice of his thinking. But what was that? Did he want us to consider an alternative to both Asquith *and* Lloyd George to run the war? Or an alternative Prime Minister to run the country? Who was he thinking of?

Law asked me to open the discussions.

'Gentlemen, we have been through the inadequacies of our current arrangements many times by now. We are all agreed that things cannot continue as they are at present. I suggest that the time for discussion is over and we must now begin to act.'

'What do you suggest?' This was Lloyd George. He had been waiting for this moment.

'I believe the time has now come to make the Prime Minister aware of our concerns. The man to do that is Bonar. The PM will no doubt ask him what he suggests should be done. I think it would therefore be helpful for Law to have in his possession a document for the Prime Minister setting out a proposed course of action. I prepared a draft of such a document this morning and, with your leave, would like to read it to you now.'

Carson and Lloyd George both invited me to read it. Law did not demur although his reluctance was obvious. But he did not forbid me so I unfolded my draft and read it to the meeting.

They responded in silence.

Carson spoke first. He saw the point immediately. In fact I was mildly disappointed that my attempt at subtlety had fallen so far short. But at least he agreed with what I was proposing.

'I agree with your draft in every particular, Aitken. I would much rather that Asquith stands aside but that will never happen as things stand. Your draft makes it perfectly clear that he is to be side-lined. He will never accept it, which is just as well, because if he *did* accept it I could not support the kind of confused arrangement you set out there. But I think your design is to appear reasonable and have the Prime Minister appear as the *un*reasonable party in opposing this initiative. He will reject it, as he must, and that will raise the stakes immensely. That is what we want. So I accept your draft.'

Bonar Law was, of course, more subtle in his response. 'The scheme proposed by Aitken is not as impractical as you characterise it, Carson. It could work. If any man could make it work it would be Asquith – it's merely another form of coalition within his existing coalition. Actually it's a third level of coalition: his own party is a coalition of Radicals and Whigs, his Government is a coalition with us Unionists, and now we ask him to form yet another coalition with Lloyd George. Asquith is skilled at coalitions so if anyone could manage this kind of arrangement *he* could. I will propose it to him and see what he says. If he accepts it voluntarily that could be an end to the present difficulty. But if acceptance has to be forced out of him that would of course be another matter entirely.'

'But you will tell him that he needs to accept this?'

'Yes. Of course. Or something very similar.'

I could see Lloyd George making mental preparations for his own contribution to the discussion. He spoke last of the three.

'Gentlemen, I won't bore you with false platitudes or another platform speech. Let me speak very bluntly. Asquith remains my chief and I am perfectly prepared to work with him. But Asquith will not work with me. His mind has been poisoned against me by McKenna and others. I am not sure that the structure proposed by Aitken will be acceptable to him – I greatly suspect it will not. But we must press the matter. We should put this to him, see how he responds, and consider then how to proceed further. One step at a time.'

Where did this leave us? I tried to be clear in my own mind. Here were three experienced and shrewd politicians, skilled beyond measure in hiding their true motives, saying what they did not believe, concealing what they really meant, and waiting always for someone else to make the first, dangerous move.

On the matter of reconstituting the War Committee as a smaller body with the PM as its 'President', all three were agreed that the proposal should be put to him.

On the membership of the Council there was likely to be less agreement, if only because the matter had not yet been debated extensively. They shared my view that this was a detail (albeit a most important one) that was best left until the fundamental principles of the scheme had been worked out.

But it was on the matter of how this new War Council was to relate to Asquith, or he to it, that we had no agreement.

Carson most definitely wanted Asquith out. Or at least relegated to a lesser role, perhaps as Lord Chancellor, if he proved willing to accept that semi-retirement with good grace.

Lloyd George wanted Asquith to relinquish completely any role in directing the war but, unlike Carson, could envisage him remaining as Prime Minister to manage the Government's other activities. Or so, at least, he said.

Law wanted Asquith to remain as Prime Minister with less authority than at present, although not with his authority curtailed in quite the dramatic fashion that Lloyd George was pressing for.

And so, while we had some measure of agreement as to our next step, all three members of the triumvirate recognised that the matter of Asquith's future role had not been settled.

But at least we now had an agreement on how to proceed. Lloyd George and Carson returned to the War Office. I set out for my house at Leatherhead.

Bonar Law set off for Downing Street to present my memorandum to the Prime Minister.

– 10 –

The political alliance between Herbert Asquith and Andrew Bonar Law was an extraordinary thing.

From 1908 until 1916 Asquith headed the most reforming Government for fifty years and challenged the Unionists on every front. On the budget of 1909, reform of the House of Lords, and Home Rule in particular, the urbane and unflappable Liberal leader had constantly outmanoeuvred the opposition party.

The landslide Liberal majority of 1906 had been greatly reduced in the two general elections held in 1910, but his continuing alliance with the Irish Party meant that Asquith's Commons majority remained unassailable. With the passage of Home Rule, however, Asquith knew that his hold on the Nationalists would never be as strong as before. They simply didn't need him any more and, being Irish, would show little continuing gratitude for what the Liberals had done in their cause.

But that would be for his successor to deal with. After the war.

At the height of the Home Rule crisis Bonar Law had come close to committing treason. At a monster rally at Blenheim in the spring of 1914 he announced that he could envisage no lengths to which those Irishmen who remained loyal to the union would go in defending it. Nor would he or his party hold back from joining them. More cautious members of his party were deeply shaken by Law's speech. This was surely treason. Asquith was of the same view but it suited his purpose to have the Unionist leader overplay his hand. Against mounting calls for the Government to take action against such extreme views, Asquith refused to respond.

His focus was on the next general election. A discredited Unionist party might allow his own Liberals to sweep back with an even greater majority.

Then the war came and changed everything.

When war was declared in August 1914 the Irish Home Rule Act, recently passed by the Commons despite a third attempt by the Lords to reject it, had been placed on the statute book but, by agreement between the parties, was held in abeyance until after the conflict. Some accommodation would then be reached for those counties in the north-east of Ireland with local Unionist majorities, but framing that compromise would have to await the return of peace in Europe. It was expected on all sides that the war would be short and in the circumstances it was time for loyalists to show loyalty to His Majesty's Government whatever its colour. Law and Lansdowne had promised no naked politics whilst the country was engaged in hostilities overseas. That *did* leave room for some less overt politics but those were to be conducted with subtlety. And Asquith was the master of subtlety.

The war did not come to an early end. Not only did it continue but it took on a character of stalemate and slaughter that statesmen across the Continent had never seen before. Tens of thousands and soon hundreds of thousands of men were annihilated. Every initiative for military breakthrough failed. After the catastrophe of Gallipoli and the Dardanelles it became clear that Asquith must reconstruct his ministry. In May 1915 the last Liberal Government gave way to the first wartime coalition. Bonar Law, who one year earlier had stood accused of treason, became Colonial Secretary.

It was widely felt, even by his own supporters, that Law had been outmanoeuvred by Asquith in the formation of the new government. All the leading positions were held by Liberals. Law himself, as Unionist leader, must surely have had a claim on the Treasury. But that was never pressed and instead Lloyd George yielded the Chancellorship to McKenna.

His position as leader of the second party in the coalition meant that Law had open access to Asquith. The two men met every day and something changed in their relationship. Both remained politicians, endlessly in search of party advantage in every new circumstance. But Law's sense that a minister owed deep loyalty to a Prime Minister in wartime tempered his political ambition. Some colleagues claimed that his failure in the distribution of ministries was just the first step in a losing hand that Law played consistently over the following 18 months. Asquith responded to his loyalty with great skill, never humiliating him and rarely contradicting him, even in private. The letters changed in their greetings from 'Dear Mr Bonar Law' to 'My dear Bonar', although Law's to Asquith remained 'Dear Prime Minister', as protocol required.

A further change had come over both men as well. Thrown together in the despairing circumstances of wartime, each began to find in the other not just an accidental political colleague but something of an associate as well. Law, in particular, grew to admire the skill with which Asquith, in his understated way, managed every situation with diplomacy and tact. It might be slow but it was certainly effective.

By the autumn of 1915 the Cabinet had grown weary of Lord Kitchener as War Secretary. Wildly popular in the country, he was hopeless in Cabinet and even worse in directing his ministry. Lloyd George, now Minister of Munitions, was particularly exasperated. No decision could ever be extracted from Kitchener. The war ground on but the War Office needed a total overhaul. Asquith took the initiative. Sending Kitchener to the eastern Mediterranean to assess the situation there, the Prime Minister himself stood in for the absent War Secretary for a month. He overhauled the workings of the ministry, replacing Sir John French as Commander-in-Chief in France by Sir Douglas Haig, and appointing Sir William Robertson to the newly-resurrected post of Chief of the Imperial General Staff. Kitchener was unimpressed by Asquith's work: he offered his resignation immediately upon his return but the Prime Minister persuaded him that remaining at his post was an absolute duty in wartime.

Only Asquith could have done this, Law thought.

And then in April 1916, after the Irish rebellion, Asquith accepted Birrell's resignation as Irish Secretary and went over to Dublin. The Unionists were demanding that Walter Long should be appointed Chief Secretary. But in fact Asquith appointed himself, a move designed to calm the nerves of the Irish Parliamentary Party. Based at the Viceregal Lodge, he visited some 400 Sinn Féin prisoners in Richmond Barracks as well as journeying to Cork and Belfast. He desperately wanted a new deal between Redmond and Carson which would allow the Irish Parliamentary Party to take over the government of the South. He persuaded Lloyd George to take on the job of mediation but the War Secretary would not accept a permanent appointment, nor would he take responsibility for the Irish administration.

Lloyd George had been right to insist on both points. His attempt at mediation failed but it was a noble effort. Again only Asquith could have dealt with the situation so adroitly.

In all these situations Law wondered how he himself might have reacted had *he* been Prime Minister rather than Asquith. Differently, of course. Perhaps more decisively. But it was beyond dispute that Asquith had held the Government together through two extraordinary wartime crises. For that he deserved praise and admiration. And some measure of loyalty.

For Law, of course, the dilemma was how to balance that loyalty against his position as leader of the main party opposed to all that Asquith's party stood for. Was he to postpone all opposition until peace was restored, an outcome that now looked infinitely far off? Or was some opposition required even in wartime?

A policeman saluted him as he turned into Downing Street on his way to Number 10. Another saluted at the door, which was quickly opened from inside. He handed his hat and coat to the servant who told him the Prime Minister was expecting him in the study. Law climbed the stairs past the portraits of prime ministers stretching back to Sir Robert Walpole. He had known the last five of Asquith's predecessors: Gladstone, Roseberry, Salisbury, Balfour, and Campbell-Bannerman.

He wondered how long it would be before Asquith's own portrait found its way onto the wall.

And after that? Lloyd George? Or even Law himself?

He knocked on the study door and entered when he heard 'Come' from within.

'Bonar.'

'Prime Minister.'

'Tea?'

'Thank you.'

The English ceremony. Prime Minister rings a small bell on his side table. Servant enters. 'Tea please, Chartres.' 'Sir.' Servant exits. Prime Minister takes a chair by the fire, gestures Law to the other chair. Pleasantries exchanged. A weekend in London. Unusual. Not very welcome. The Prime Minister would much prefer to be in Walmer or at The Wharf. Law would much prefer to be at home. Servant re-enters, places teapot, cups, saucers, milk jug and sugar bowl on table. Pours for both men. Exits. And then the interview begins. But obliquely.

'Are you and Miss Law free this evening, Bonar?'

'We have no plans, Prime Minister. A quiet evening at home I think.'

'Would you dine with us here? A small party. Crewe and Lady Crewe, the French ambassador and his wife, perhaps Lord and Lady Iveagh also. And some other friends of Margot. A dozen perhaps. Some bridge after dinner. The only condition is not to discuss politics and not to mention the war. We deserve at least one evening of respite each week. Will you join us?'

Law hated the idea. He hated society. His sister hated it also. But it would not do to say no.

'We would be delighted to, Prime Minister. Should we dress?'

'I would say no but the French ambassador will insist, I'm sure, so we probably should. Do you mind?'

He did mind.

'Not at all. I look forward to it.'

'I had thought of inviting Lloyd George as well but we probably need some time away from one another. We see each other too frequently these days. I think David needs an evening with his family.'

And Law, who had just come from Lloyd George, did not disagree. Though he did wonder what the Prime Minister meant when he referred to Lloyd George's 'family'. Surely they were all back in Wales?

'I find these weekends in London unsatisfactory. The sea air at

Walmer is so refreshing, and I feel closer to the men when we are on the coast. We hear the shells throughout the day and that makes the war more real than fighting it from a desk here in London.'

'I'm sure it does, Prime Minister.'

'And the King has asked me to lunch tomorrow. Same stipulation – no politics, no war talk. We shall see.'

Asquith was fencing. He knew that Law had requested the meeting for a purpose. He could guess what it was. He saw the paper bulging in his inside pocket.

'Prime Minister…I have, as I'm sure you know, been in further discussion with Lloyd George during the week.'

'And Carson too, I believe. And Aitken.'

'We have been reviewing the way our war organisation works.'

'Indeed.'

'You know about Lloyd George's concerns, Prime Minister. Which I share. We must reorganise the way we manage the war. Despite all our good work, yours especially, the situation is more and more hopeless. We need to form a new body charged with no departmental responsibilities. To focus without distraction on fighting the war.'

'I see.'

A silence.

'What do you propose?'

Law reached into his inner pocket and produced the paper.

'We have given the matter extensive thought, Prime Minister, and we want to suggest a new arrangement. The details are set out in this note. We have drafted it as a note to be issued by the Prime Minister should you approve of our suggested approach.'

Law hands the note to Asquith. Asquith glances at it. Asks Law if he could possibly pour more tea for both men while Asquith gives the note his attention. Reads it quickly, then starts reading again. Folds it over and returns the paper to Law. Who takes it, uncertain. Should he leave it here with the PM or take it away with him? He returns it to his inside pocket.

They sit in silence while Asquith digests the contents.

'Here are my thoughts, Bonar. Forgive me being straightforward. I will give you a considered response on Monday but my immediate sense is this. Yes, we must reorganise. Lloyd George must have a key role. Carson – if, as I suspect, Carson's name is to be inserted along with others in the blank space – is no good. The Prime Minister, I, must retain the chairmanship of any such group. I have no personal pride in the matter but a wartime Prime Minister cannot be excluded from the central body directing the war. And Lloyd George almost certainly agrees with me on this point. It's just that he envisages – perhaps not now, but sooner than you might think – another Prime Minister directing that war. And he does not mean you, Bonar.'

Silence.

Then Law speaks.

'I won't try to disagree with anything you say, Prime Minister. I won't disagree with you, but neither will I agree. All the points we make in the note need further consideration. I trust you will reflect on it and, as you say, let us have a fuller response as soon as you can.'

'I will. On Monday.'

Law rises to leave. The interview is over. His tea is suddenly cold.

'This evening, Bonar. Seven o'clock. I look forward to seeing you both then.'

Law leaves.

Asquith stares into the middle distance. Two thoughts assail him. First, how to respond to Law's note, which he could only characterise as impertinent and insulting? And, second, what would he do, what life he would have, if he ever ceased to be master of this house? He finds it a deeply depressing thought because in truth he sees nothing at all beyond his life in Downing Street. Just emptiness, hopelessness, and decline. And preparation for death and oblivion as Earl of Somewhere (Walmer perhaps?) in the House of Lords. The mausoleum.

It does not bear thinking about.

Law returns to the War Office where Carson and Lloyd George await his report. Later that evening he telephones Aitken to describe the meeting to him. The following day Aitken drives to Walton Heath to see Lloyd George. He finds him in an agitated state, worrying about the Prime Minister's response. Lloyd George is particularly concerned that Law did not convey the seriousness of the threat to the Prime Minister and that Asquith might yet prevail on Law to side with him in the coming struggle against Lloyd George. None of the principals sleeps easily that night as they await Asquith's response.

– 11 –

The King was the most boring man in his own kingdom. But monarchical boringness was sometimes a blessing: His Majesty's lunchtime monologue gave Asquith an almost perfect opportunity to reflect on his own position.

Long years of experience in dealing with bores had helped Asquith develop an unerring ability to anticipate quite accurately when a monologue would come to an end. A question would then be put to the listener, usually in the form 'Don't you agree, Prime Minister?' He had also developed the ability to know what the bore had been saying without actually listening to him and was therefore never caught out when his opinion was asked about a speech to which he had paid no attention. But with the King that second skill was unnecessary. The King's monologues only ever dealt with the reasons why things must never change. Not even in the slightest. The King was the most conservative man Asquith had ever met. And also one of the stupidest. Boring, conservative, and stupid. But he did his duty as he saw it and doing one's duty almost always forgives stupidity in a monarch.

He could also estimate how long the King would continue speaking before feeling the need for reassurance that his guest shared his concerns. Five minutes, probably, on this one.

So Asquith remembered.

He was sixty-two when the war started. Having been Prime Minister for so long he knew that most politicians saw him as the natural head of government, although he did speculate from time to time about who might succeed him. Grey, Lloyd George and (possibly) Crewe had topped that list before the war. Of those colleagues who might miss him if he was 'suddenly gone' he thought of McKenna and Montagu. Perhaps even Haldane, who had been his oldest political friend until Asquith removed him so bluntly from the Cabinet at the Unionists' insistence the previous May.

No serious thought of resignation had ever crossed Asquith's mind even though he sometimes found his duties burdensome, particularly in mediating between colleagues who disagreed with one another. Although vague yearnings for a more satisfying inner life occasionally came his way, he was in fact happier as Prime Minister than at any other time in his life.

Why was this? He felt he had been gifted with many skills that made him particularly suited to the role. But he also found himself consistently possessed of the single most important attribute required by any successful politician. Luck. He had recognised in one particularly introspective moment (which he had reduced to writing somewhere – where was that note?) that he had brains above the average, energy under the guise of lethargy, an ability to work quickly, patience, ambition, a clear mind, lucidity of speech, an ability to see an opponent's point of view, and a growing sense of proportion. But luck was the key.

He also recognised that although he was depicted as shy and reserved, even at times cold-blooded, he did in fact have a fondness for social pleasures and, in particular, a weakness for the companionship of clever and attractive young women. He knew that his family and many of his colleagues were fond of him and that he was capable of retaining the loyal attachment of a diverse group of people. In fact he also recognised that he had been blessed with a particular ability to get along with men of very different character and temperament. In this lay his skill as chairman of a body as complex as the Cabinet.

His greatest fear was that at some time in the future he would return (or be returned) to a life of dullness and obscurity. He despised those living at half-pressure. Neither Lloyd George nor Churchill, whatever their short-comings (and they were many), could ever have been accused of that failing. In fact Asquith had a reluctant admiration for both men, although in each case he noted a lack of consistency and judgement. Lloyd George lacked social compatibility and courage. Asquith admired his energy but lamented his indiscipline and unpredictability. A wonderful person in so many ways but totally devoid of any sense of broader perspective.

His views about Churchill were equally equivocal: tremendous fondness and fascination at the extravagance of his personality but also an abundance of exasperation as well. Before the war they had seen a good deal of one another at dinner parties and country house weekends. He found Churchill addicted to long monologues, just like the King (who was still in full flow), and indifferent to the views or reactions of his listeners. He had been an excellent First Lord until the war but the Dardanelles had destroyed him. He would never rise to the top in English politics although he would certainly return to the Cabinet if the Unionists were ever detached. In the later months of 1914 Asquith had thought about making him Viceroy of India after the war. Churchill needed a country – perhaps even a continent – to run.

He recalled a letter he had written to Venetia Stanley in 1915 in which he had rated his Liberal Cabinet colleagues. Crewe, Grey and McKenna were the top three, in that order. Equal fourth were Lloyd George and Churchill. Next came Harcourt and Simon, then Haldane and Runciman. Samuel, Pease, Beauchamp, Emmott, Lucas and Wood completed the field. Crewe impressed in the steadiness of his judgement and the fact that he never irritated Asquith. As the standard bearer of the party's Whig tradition he was also indispensable in finessing the Government's relations with the King. But he made little impact on the public and could never have run an effective Government.

Grey, his long-time Foreign Secretary, was an old and close political friend. But his growing blindness had led him to develop an increasingly doleful nature which sometimes irritated Asquith despite his great respect for Grey's integrity and determination. How long could he continue? He had given in his resignation half a dozen times since the war began. At some stage Asquith must accept it, if only to protect Grey's health. Who to appoint then? He wondered whether he could ensure Unionist support for himself against the latest push from Lloyd George by accepting Grey's resignation and appointing Curzon or Chamberlain to the Foreign Office. This was a matter he would have to consider in more detail that afternoon when composing his reply to Law's memorandum.

The pattern of Asquith's own life had not changed greatly during the early months of the war. Ireland, after a period of further recrimination and a violent attack on Asquith by Law in the Commons, had effectively been put into cold storage six weeks after the outbreak of hostilities. The Welsh Disestablishment Bill (what extraordinary matters had agitated the parties in the summer of 1914!) lingered longer. But by October of that year Asquith found himself needing to spend less and less time on parliamentary business.

The Cabinet at first met almost daily but in November 1914 it was decided to set up a War Council as a committee of the Cabinet. Asquith, Lloyd George, Churchill, Kitchener, Crewe and Grey were all members. Balfour (for the Unionists, but as a former Prime Minister as well) was also asked to join, and Haldane was added in January 1915. The service chiefs also attended and Hankey acted as Secretary. From then on the War Council met several times a week and the Cabinet reverted to less frequent meetings.

Although he could no longer be away from Downing Street for more than a few days at a time, Asquith continued with his pattern of regular dinner parties followed by bridge. He read voluminously and continued to engage in extensive written correspondence. The output to Venetia Stanley continued to grow. During the first three months of 1915 he had written 141 separate letters to her, four in one day alone. He saw her once a week when they went for a drive on Friday afternoons, after which he caught the five o'clock train from Victoria to Walmer, where he increasingly spent his weekends during the war.

Walmer Castle on the Dover coast was a perquisite of the Lord Warden of the Cinque Ports, an office Asquith had been tempted to take for himself when it fell vacant in the autumn of 1913. Unable to afford the expense, however, he had instead appointed Lord Beauchamp to the post. But he nonetheless spent many weekends there himself, having persuaded Beauchamp in December 1914 to let him have it for three or four months. On one weekend drive from Walmer he had encountered Lady Tree: he recalled with amusement her ridiculous question: 'Mr Asquith, do you take an interest in the war?' But he was aware that this was the same question which, in no less impertinent a form, he was now being asked by Lloyd George and his conspirators.

The King was looking at him. Still speaking, but winding down. Asquith gave him some attention as the monologue was coming to an end. It would soon be followed, as indeed it now was, by:

'Don't you agree, Prime Minister?'

He had been speaking of the war. Of the need to encourage even greater sacrifice at home in support of the men at the front. Extra effort in munitions. Growing vegetables on waste ground in the cities. The (to Asquith ridiculous) pledge against alcohol which Lloyd George had convinced the King to take for the duration of the conflict. Had he known it would last longer than six months the King would never have agreed. Did he drink on his own at the Palace, Asquith wondered?

'Of course, Sir. We must all make sacrifices. We owe it to the men who have volunteered.'

The King turned to Lady Daventry and resumed.

Asquith reflected on what he had just said. The glib and meaningless platitude he had just uttered. We owe it to the men at the front.

He remembered Raymond.

Dead.

Beb and Oc and Cys were also in the war. Would they die too? How long could it last? Puffin was fourteen. Could it last long enough to take him as well?

Suddenly Asquith was seized by an overwhelming sense of horror. Almost nausea. He could smell the stench of death in his nostrils. It was as if it had wafted all the way from France, across the Channel, past Walmer, up through Kent and along the river to find its way in through the chimneys and walls of the Palace. Into his nostrils.

The King's dining room smelt of death.

Lloyd George wanted to depose him and fight on.

Lansdowne wanted him to sue for peace.

Margot wanted him to resist in order to save their position.

How had he found himself transformed from a peacetime Prime Minister responsible for improving the lives of millions of his fellow Englishman into a wartime Prime Minister responsible for their deaths?

What was he to do?

– 12 –

Asquith began his response to Bonar Law with a test. He wrote:

> My dear Bonar Law,
> What follows is intended for your eyes only.

In politics no communication is ever private. In stating that the letter was for Bonar Law alone Asquith was not testing *whether* Law would show it to Carson and Lloyd George but *how soon*. If he showed it to them immediately Asquith would conclude that the conspiracy was well advanced. If he delayed, the conspiracy might still be in its infancy, or Law might not be as committed as he had indicated. That would give Asquith room to manoeuvre. But he suspected that the letter, which he intended to give to Law in person tomorrow, would be with Lloyd George later that morning.

He would start with a statement of thanks for Law's directness but would also immediately reject the proposal. It must be made clear from the outset that no Prime Minister could possibly accept the kind of challenge that was now being presented.

> I fully realise the frankness and loyalty with which you have put forward the proposal embodied in your paper note. But under present conditions, and in the form in which it is presented, I do not see my way to adopt it.

Asquith wrote quickly and without hesitation. His skill with words owed something to his career at the Bar but more to his long experience of dealing with other senior men. A face-to-face interview had more immediacy and could proceed more bluntly. Written correspondence was always for the record, and Asquith had no doubt that all his correspondence would eventually find its way into some archive where future historians would use it to reconstruct what had been going on in London on that dark November afternoon. Well, here it was.

He lifted his gaze to stare into the fire. This study had been the centre of his private political life for so many years. The Cabinet Room was used for more formal meetings. Those who found themselves speaking with the Prime Minister in his study knew they were at the centre of power. Lloyd George and Law had both spent many hours here. Carson never had. Aitken never would.

To continue. Some words of broad agreement with the sentiment that the War Committee needed reform, but not quite as much as Law was suggesting:

> I take a less disparaging view than you do of the War Committee. There is undoubtedly too much talk and consequent waste of time, but the Committee has done and is doing very valuable work; and is thrashing out difficult problems. I am quite open to suggestions for its improvement, whether in composition or in procedure.

But the idea that it might be composed only of politicians without any military men must be discounted immediately:

> I may say, however, that I do not see how anything of the kind can be really workable unless the heads of the War Office and Admiralty are members of it. Our recent practice of sitting a good deal without the experts is a change for the better and might perhaps be developed.

Not to exclude the military men completely would of course be unacceptable to the cabal. Well, so be it. It was for the Prime Minister alone to judge how Cabinet committees were to operate. Open to suggestions, certainly; but to have terms dictated to him by others, absolutely not. And so to deal with their central proposal:

> But the essence of your scheme is that the War Committee should disappear, and its place be taken by a body of four – myself, yourself, Carson, and Lloyd George.

This, of course, was not at all what they had proposed. The names of the intended members had not been written in the memorandum but his discussions with Law had left him in no doubt as to their identities. And the essence of the conspirators' demand was that Asquith, although remaining on as Prime Minister, should serve only as a semi-detached member of the new committee and not – as he wrote in his response – as its leading figure.

The memorandum drafted in his name had Asquith himself suggesting that although he would be the President (whatever that meant) of the committee, he expected to be so pressed for time that he would rarely attend and would therefore pass the chairmanship on to Lloyd George. This, of course, was the central thrust of their proposal. Well, Asquith would reject it, not by clearly stating how unacceptable it was but by deliberately 'misunderstanding' what was being suggested. There would be no ambiguity about the chairmanship of any reconstructed War Committee. Both Asquith and Lloyd George would be members but there was no possibility that any committee which included the Prime Minister would be chaired, directed or presided over (they could choose whatever weasel words they wanted) by anyone other than the Prime Minister.

So he would state the 'essence of their scheme' quite clearly in a manner they had not in fact proposed.

And then reject it.

Masterly.

And so to the question of personnel. To deal first with Carson, whom Asquith despised.

> As regards Carson, for whom, as you know, I have the greatest possible regard...

He smiled.

> …I do not see how it would be possible, in order to secure his services, to pass over Balfour, or Curzon, or McKenna, all of whom have the advantage of intimate knowledge of the secret history of the last twelve months.

The messages here were multiple. First, Carson is impossible. I appointed him Attorney General eighteen months ago. The irony of casting as the Government's chief law officer a man who only eighteen months earlier had been engaged in treason in Ireland, and for which he might well have been hanged, was supreme. But Carson left the Government after six months and spent the subsequent year harrying us at every turn. See the Nigeria debate in Parliament just ten days ago, Bonar. I have no intention of having that man in Government again, still less as a member of the inner Cabinet charged with directing the war. The language of 'securing his services' would bring a broad smile to Lloyd George's face when he read it.

Second, how do you propose (Bonar) selling Carson's promotion to your Unionist colleagues? Do you really think that Curzon, who considers you a dour, dull, middle-class Scottish upstart, and who wants your position with a hunger that is frankly embarrassing to observe, would allow you to promote a common Irish conspirer like Carson over him? Think again. Balfour might be less immediately offended by the proposal but he is a former Prime Minister who had been invited by the current Prime Minister to sit on the Committee of Imperial Defence for the last eight years. And he too is now to be relegated in place of Carson? Finally, McKenna. You would like to run the war without any reference to its paymaster, the Chancellor of the Exchequer? Ridiculous.

Asquith then proceeded to summarise his rejection of Carson with what was, for him, uncharacteristic frankness:

> That he should be admitted over their heads at this stage into the inner circle of the Government is a step which, I believe, would be deeply resented, not only by them and by my political friends, but by almost all your Unionist colleagues.

They might depose you, Bonar. Would you care to return to the backbenches? Or perhaps shuffle off to the Lords as Viscount Law of Nowhere?

And you would be also accused of the grossest political cowardice:

It would be universally believed to be the price paid for shutting the mouth of our most formidable parliamentary critic – a manifestation of weakness and cowardice.

He knew how sharply an accusation of cowardice would shake Law.

And then on to the central character in the drama, Lloyd George. For whom Asquith continued to feel admiration and, in fact, after all these years, something approaching affection even as Lloyd George now tried to destroy him. Asquith had never set down in writing anything so personally critical of Lloyd George as he now found himself required to do. It marked a break, both political and personal, in a relationship that had spanned a decade. He knew that what he wrote now would offend Lloyd George even after it was refracted through the prism of deception that characterised all political letters. He would read it and shrug it off, but it would offend him too.

Asquith had offended men before. He knew that political leadership at times demanded the despatching, often brutally, of once close colleagues. Haldane might never speak to him again. Winston would, but Winston was still a young man. It was time now to proceed against Lloyd George before Lloyd George proceeded against him.

The only way to do this was by warning Law and the other Unionists that Lloyd George was not to be trusted. If they sided with Lloyd George against Asquith on this occasion, Lloyd George would surely move against them in the future when political circumstances so required. At least with Asquith in charge the Unionists knew where they stood. Under Lloyd George they would never sleep soundly in their beds again.

As to Lloyd George, you know as well as I do both his qualities and his defects. He has many qualities that would fit him for the first place, but he lacks the one thing needful – he does not inspire trust.

And lest Law should think that Asquith did not fully understand the real movement now afoot, he would state it with total clarity:

Here, again, there is one construction, and only one, that could be put on the new arrangement – that it has been engineered by him with the purpose, not perhaps at the moment, but as soon as a fitting pretext could be found, of his displacing me.

The irony of this position struck Asquith with some force. He was, in effect, appealing to the Unionist party to help him dispel a challenge from within his own Liberal party. Had you told him in the summer of 1914 that it would ever come to this Asquith would have laughed aloud.

And so to conclude. Rejection of the proposal must be firm and clear:

In short, the plan could not, in my opinion, be carried out without fatally impairing the confidence of loyal and valued colleagues, and undermining my own authority.

And yours too, Bonar.

He re-read what he had written and was pleased with both the message and the tone. But he felt that some softening of the letter was called for and that he should also enter the usual protestation about not clinging to office. This was a political cliché, expected of every man holding high public office. It was, in truth, a total lie, but one required by convention. And so he wrote:

I have spoken to you with the same frankness that you used to me, and which I am glad to say has uniformly marked our relations ever since the Coalition was formed. Nor need I tell you that if I thought it right...

If *I* thought it right, Bonar. Not Lloyd George.

...I have every temptation (especially now) to seek relief from the intolerable daily burden of labour and anxiety.

Etc., etc.

Yours very sincerely, H. H. Asquith

There, it was done. He re-read it and was happy with it. He would give it to Law tomorrow and await developments.

And so the Prime Minister retired from his Sunday work and asked Chartres to prepare the motor and take him on a drive to Hampstead to help clear his mind for the week ahead.

INTERLUDE

Asquith dreams I

He woke before dawn the following morning bathed in sweat. He came up from sleep with a start, his head lifting suddenly off the pillow and rolling to his left side. Gasping for air, it took him a moment to realise where he was. Almost to realise *who* he was. Then, remembering, he lowered his head back onto the pillow. It was wet. The horror of the dream was still with him.

He had dreamed of his early life; his life as a child, as a student, as a young man.

He had dreamed of his first wife, Helen, and of their children.

Helen had been dead for twenty-five years now. And their first child, Raymond, his eldest son, had died ten weeks ago.

He had dreamed of the first years of their married life when there had been only three of them. Himself, Helen and Raymond. Just these three: a man, his wife, their child. And now two of the three were dead.

But the real horror of the dream was this. Asquith had been trying, desperately, to remember something. The effort had been wrenching and physical. He tried, he pushed, he twisted. But try as he might, he couldn't.

He couldn't remember.

He couldn't remember Helen's face.

In his dream he strained every muscle of his memory to call her to mind. He could see her walking towards him: her dress billowing in the wind, her hair falling over her shoulders, one arm raised to wave at him, the other holding Raymond's hand. Raymond's face full of excitement seeing his father approaching, breaking away from his mother, running to him. Helen's shoes, her dress, her hands, her hair. But not her face. Her face, in the dream, was a blank.

He had forgotten her face.

As his breathing became quieter Asquith remembered his early life. His father had died young but he could still remember what he looked like. Asquith's parents had five children. His older brother, William, was still alive, a schoolteacher, but he had never been strong. His sister Emily was also still alive but his mother had lost two other daughters at a young age.

He remembered the family leaving Yorkshire after his father's death and moving to St Leonard's in Sussex. The boys were lodged with an uncle and then a little later they became paying guests at another family's house in Canonbury, north London. He remembered the City of London School, his time in Oxford at Balliol, his early years at the Bar.

He had married Helen Maitland in 1877. He could clearly call to mind her father's face as he asked for permission to marry her.

But he could not see Helen's face.

They had had five children. Raymond, the oldest, was born in 1878, the year after they married. Then Herbert, whom they called Beb, in 1880; Arthur, called Oc, in 1883; Violet in 1887; and the youngest, Cyril, called Cys, in 1890. They lived in Hampstead while Asquith worked at his practice and, from 1886, as a Member of Parliament.

In August 1891 the family had taken the train north from London to Scotland, to the Isle of Arran. As a treat for his children and a respite for Helen, who hated to socialise with Asquith's legal and political friends, he had taken a holiday cottage by the coast for six weeks. The weather had been wonderful – long days of sunshine and clear, vibrant air. The children ran along the beach and played with their kites. Asquith walked behind them, hand-in-hand with Helen. They were perfectly happy. It was idyllic.

Helen had just promised that she would make more of an effort to help Herbert (not Henry: her husband was always 'Herbert' or 'Bertie' to Helen) with his political career when they returned to London. He knew that she hated it when he stayed away from the house late into the evening, but she knew this was his life. Now she said that she would come with him to the ceremonial dinners. He was deeply appreciative of her willingness to help.

In early September Beb fell ill. It seemed to be influenza. Helen confined him to her room and said that she would nurse him back to health. Henry looked after the other children – fishing in rock pools, climbing hills, playing pirates. The thirteen-year-old Raymond was almost too old for these games but Henry asked him to be his first officer in commanding the clan. He performed with energy and enthusiasm.

Some days later Helen herself came down with the flu. That was not unexpected because she had spent so much time with Beb. Asquith thought of sending for a doctor although it would mean a ride to the nearest town some twenty miles away. Helen told him she would recover soon.

Two days later as Beb began to recover Helen was much worse.

Asquith paid for one of the neighbouring farmer's sons to ride to the town to fetch a doctor.

The next few hours were hell. The children were distracted in the adjoining room while Asquith sat with Helen, holding her hand, soothing her forehead with cold towels. She was delirious and in great pain. There was nothing he could do.

Just as the doctor arrived and Asquith stood up to greet him, Helen died.

Asquith's whole world, his whole frame of reference, fell apart. The children couldn't be comforted. Beb, eleven years old, thought he had killed his mother. Asquith tried to calm him even as he himself was inconsolable. The neighbours came to take care of them, preparing meals, taking the children to see the farms, anything to distract them.

Helen was buried in the local churchyard the following Monday. It had not been influenza. It was typhoid, from the drains.

Herbert, now Henry, brought the children back to London and tried to rebuild his life.

He never visited Arran again, never saw her grave again. And now he had forgotten her face.

Helen.

PART II

The last full week:

Monday 27 November – Sunday 3 December 1916

– 13 –

Monday 27 November 1916 — Colonial Office, Whitehall

I spent Sunday night at my house in Leatherhead – 'Aitken Hall' as my critics have named it. Early on Monday morning I had a call from Law. He told me he was in some difficulty and asked me to come up to London straight away. He had received a response from Asquith which caused him some concern.

I motored up to London and met him at his office in Whitehall. Straight away he produced the letter from Asquith, I read it quickly and then took a seat by his desk to read it again more slowly. The words were one thing but the meaning was buried in the nuance. It was the meaning I was looking for.

I had not expected to be surprised by the Prime Minister's response. And I wasn't. He was going to fight.

Were *they*?

The comments on Carson were direct and straightforward, perhaps even more direct than I thought they might be. Law said he had visited the Prime Minister to say that despite the notice at the beginning of the document he must have his permission to show the letter to others, particularly those named in it. Asquith readily agreed. Given this, Law continued, would the Prime Minister wish to reconsider the words he had used about Carson? He must expect that Carson might re-join the Government at some stage and it would surely be unwise for the Prime Minister to have in circulation a document that commented so negatively about the man's abilities?

But the Prime Minister had refused to bend. 'I stand by what I have written and Carson will neither be surprised nor disturbed by it,' he said. 'I said as much to him directly when I accepted his resignation as Attorney General last year.'

As to the Prime Minister's observations about Lloyd George, Law had made no comment. This was a close colleague of Asquith's, the second man in his own party. Lloyd George would not have expected Asquith to equivocate and it would have been impertinent, Law felt, to have advised the PM about managing one of his own party colleagues.

With the Prime Minister's consent, copies of the letter had been despatched immediately to both Carson and Lloyd George. Law then left Downing Street and returned to his own office, from where he called me. The meeting with Asquith had taken place at half past seven and I received Law's call at eight. It was shortly after nine when I met him and reviewed the Prime Minister's reply.

'What do you think?'

'Exactly how I expected him to respond,' I said. 'He was never going to allow himself to be marginalised in this way. He knows that 'President' of the War Council means nothing and the country would see through it in a minute. We know he holds Carson in low esteem and he has decided to say so rather bluntly. On Lloyd George he is being slightly more direct than we thought he might, but is that any great surprise? He means to fight and is telling us so.'

'What does he think my role is in all this?'

I hesitated for a moment before responding.

'He thinks you are undecided, Bonar.'

'Well, I am.'

I decided to speak more boldly. 'He sees you, actually, as the actor around whom this whole issue will ultimately be resolved. He senses your unease and knows that you haven't decided how to proceed if no compromise is agreed.'

'I'm not playing a game on this, Max. My concerns are genuine and my motivation is clear. We have an impasse which I am trying to resolve. To the satisfaction of all parties.'

'But that won't do, Bonar.'

'It won't?'

'This dispute won't be resolved amicably, through compromise. Neither Asquith nor Lloyd George are looking at you as the man to effect a compromise that will satisfy both of them. George has thrown down a challenge to the PM. You were the messenger. Asquith has rejected that challenge and again you were the messenger. Now we have a dispute between both men – Carson is incidental to it all – which will never be resolved by compromise. The whole business is far beyond that now.'

I needed to make the matter clear.

'One of them will be gone by Christmas. Which one depends very largely on you.'

'On me?'

'On you, Bonar. You aren't a messenger any more. You're the catalyst. How this plays out depends entirely on the attitude you take to their quarrel.'

A silence.

'You need to take a side, Bonar.'

More silence.

'And that side can no longer be with Asquith.'

Law rose from his desk and turned to look out the window. It was another murky November morning with low cloud covering the sky.

'No. I will not "take sides". I will mediate. I will find a solution.'

He wasn't ready yet.

But that time would come.

We agreed to have a further meeting with Carson and Lloyd George that afternoon. I left to talk to both men and arrange the session.

The same day — Palace of Westminster

From Law's office I walked down Whitehall, across Parliament Square, and through the gates at Westminster. The House was due to sit that afternoon and Lloyd George had told me to join him at Carson's office after my meeting with Bonar Law. London was at its very greyest that morning. Late November, heavy cloud, drizzle, little light. Contrary to Edward Grey's famous aphorism, the lights *were* burning – at least along Whitehall and in the Palace of Westminster. The War Office seemed to linger under a more ominous cloud and the lights shone a little dimmer there. As I passed Downing Street I looked up to see if there was any movement. Nothing. The policemen outside Number 10 were soaked to the skin despite their mackintoshes.

Parliament Square was a sea of rain-soaked earth. A reminder of the mud in which so many men were living and dying in Flanders.

I could barely remember London before the war. Certainly it was brighter. Cleaner too, or was that a trick of memory? I remembered the summer of 1914 when the country seemed on the brink of civil war. The news from Ireland continued to alarm us all. Armed loyalist volunteers drilling in Ulster. Armed nationalist volunteers drilling in Dublin. Guns being run at Larne and Howth. Civilians shot dead in the streets of Dublin when the volunteers brought the guns into the city.

Redmond was barely in control of events in his own country any more. The Home Rule Bill had snaked through the Lords for a third time to become law. And then the summer saw the extraordinary conference at the Palace when eight men – two Liberals, two Unionists, two Ulster loyalists, and two Irish nationalist leaders – had attempted to find a way through the impasse by excluding the north of Ireland from Home Rule. But no compromise had been reached. Asquith and Law were in despair. Carson and Redmond had shaken hands as the meeting broke up. Both men expected a civil war to follow.

The European war had changed all that, however. Even before the Irish conference Grey had warned the Cabinet that the assassination in Sarajevo would have the most serious consequences. As Europe lurched towards war that July, the Irish question still dominated at home. But by the end of that month Ireland had been replaced by Belgium in the Government's attentions, and a possible civil war at home became a very real continental war in Europe.

Should England join?

England did.

And Scotland, Wales and Ireland too. And in time the wider Empire.

The war had already lasted almost thirty months. There was no end in sight.

I found Carson and Lloyd George in Carson's rooms. They talked and joked (I could hear Carson's booming laugh as I approached along the corridor) but the laughter fell away as I entered.

Both men wanted to know what Law had made of Asquith's response. I told them. I also recounted what I had said to Law about where his own duty now lay. And his rejection of my claim.

'Well', Lloyd George said, 'we shall see.'

We agreed to meet again in the early afternoon to continue the conversation (or as Asquith would have had it, the conspiracy) at Law's office.

The same day — Colonial Office, Whitehall

We assembled at three o'clock. Law asked us to wait outside his office for a few minutes as he completed some business with his officials. I could sense that Carson's mood had changed for the worse since the morning.

Genuinely? Or was this an act? One never knew with Carson.

When the clerk ushered us into the office we found Law already seated at the conference table. Hunched over, reading glasses on, Asquith's response in front of him.

'Well, gentlemen. Come in. Sit down. Tell me what you think. And then I will tell you what I think.'

My role in these meetings was never to speak unless I was specifically asked to. I was a backbench Unionist MP, albeit well-connected, particularly with the press, but these were the principals and it was for them to set the direction.

Lloyd George gestured expansively to Carson. Who began.

'It won't do, Bonar. We're not going to back down. At least I'm not.'

He stopped for a moment, then continued.

'Let me get the personal matter out of the way first and then we can deal with the issues. I resent…' He paused. 'I greatly resent that man writing about me in that tone.'

Law started to interrupt but Carson would not yield.

'I can forgive his lack of skill as a war leader. Nobody prepared him for this and who's to say that anyone else could have managed the first year of the war any better? But of course he's learned nothing at all since then. He's just got worse and worse with every passing month, which is why we must now move him aside...'

Again Law started to interject but Carson raised his voice.

'No, Bonar. I know. I know what you'll say. But hear me out. Asquith is incapable of leadership. He cannot unite the nation. He will not give the military men their head. He's an appeaser. We know that he wants to end the war and he'll do a deal with the Germans to achieve that. Lansdowne has told me so. But it's his personal qualities that make him so unfit for his office, and I resent his impugning *my* character and *my* capability when he himself is so wanting in both.'

In full flow now. 'A war leader? That man? *I* don't take motor rides around London in the afternoons to "relax". *I* don't read shockers at the Athenaeum at five o'clock in the afternoon and drink myself stupid in the evenings. *I* don't write letters to my lady admirers during Cabinet meetings and *I* don't guide their hands between my legs under the table at dinner...'

'Really, Carson. Enough.' Law had banged on the table and was now shouting.

'No, Bonar. Hear me out. You know it's true. He's a drunk and he's a lecher. Our leader, the hopeless "Squiff", a man who cannot make a decision after five o'clock and who swoons – and worse – in the presence of a good-looking woman. And then he says that *I* "will not do". It's an outrage. He must go.'

At which Law stood and shouted.

I had never seen him shout before. I had seen him angry and agitated. I had seen him bellow at public meetings to make himself heard from a platform. But I had never seen him shout at a colleague before.

'I will not have that said, Carson. I will not have that said in my presence, in this room. You are now without responsibility on the backbenches and free to shout out any insults you like from there. But not here. Not in the presence of two Cabinet colleagues of the Prime Minister. In wartime. I will not have Asquith's character blasted in this way. Withdraw what you have just said.'

'I will not.'

Lloyd George sat back and smiled. Even purred. Nothing amused him more than two Unionists indulging in a bout of sanctimonious *faux* outrage.

I felt it was time for me to break my vow of silence. 'Carson, Law, this is enough. Please. Calm down.'

Law walked to his desk and shuffled through some papers to compose himself. Carson glared at the table. But neither man spoke.

It was left to Lloyd George to break the silence.

'Law. Carson. Enough of this now. I understand your anger. Truly I do. But the country needs us to rise above these personal animosities. Let me tell you how I think we should proceed.'

After a brief pause Law returned to the table and resumed his seat. Carson, still furious, raised his gaze to look across at Lloyd George, who continued.

'The Prime Minister must cease to chair the War Committee. We have told him so. He has declined to agree. His comments about Carson and me are of no relevance. He made them for the record and they are on the record now and will remain so. May I suggest, Carson, that for the moment we simply ignore them? We can return to them later if we need to.'

Lloyd George looked across the table at Carson. He made no response at first but then nodded. Almost imperceptibly.

'Let us focus on the matter in dispute – the reconstruction of the War Committee and the reorganisation of its leadership. We need to decide, first, whether we agree that this matter must be pursued and then, second, how to proceed. Do you both still agree that the Committee must be reconstructed?'

'Yes.'

And then, simultaneously, from Law 'With Asquith' and from Carson 'Without Asquith'. Both men met each other's gaze.

'Well', Lloyd George continued, 'let us focus on the point on which we agree and ignore for the time being the issue about which we differ. There are now two things we must do.'

'And they are?' Carson asked.

'Let me start with the second. I think the time has come when

I must relieve Law of the unwelcome duty of intermediating between the Prime Minister and me. I think the time has come for me to speak directly to him.'

At this I lifted my head to see their reactions. Both Law and Carson stayed silent at first. It was Law who then spoke.

'A discussion, yes. But not an ultimatum. You have no authority from me or from my party to deliver an ultimatum to the Prime Minister on this matter.'

'I understand, Bonar. I have no intention of doing so. A discussion only. Premised on the proposals we put to him on Saturday and his response of this morning. To clarify, to explain, to seek common ground. Are you agreed that I may do this? He'll know that we have discussed his response but I give you my word that I won't approach him with any "agreed programme" but merely for a discussion. Do I have your consent?'

They both agreed.

I was elated but hid my feelings.

'The other matter is one with which I cannot assist you directly. We three, even four if we include Max, which we must...' He smiled in my direction. '... have met on a number of occasions in the last few weeks. My own party will be divided should events turn fractious, but that is a matter for the Prime Minister and me to take care of. But I am concerned about *your* party, gentlemen. Are they with you in this?'

Here Lloyd George was touching a raw nerve with Law. Nothing had been said to any of the other Unionist leaders about our recent meetings. We had deliberately excluded Lansdowne from the conversations, not wanting his growing pacifism to taint our reputations. And Law had held back from discussing them with the other Unionist members of the Cabinet. He was uncertain of the extent to which they would support him in these conversations, which, despite his endless pledges of support for the Prime Minister, were nonetheless beginning to attract the odour of conspiracy. But if we were to move forward Law was going to have to talk to his colleagues.

He knew it. But he was reluctant. Those conversations were just as likely lead to his own demise as to Asquith's. He stared at the table.

Lloyd George continued. 'I cannot have my conversation with the PM until your own party knows where things stand, Bonar, and I know in turn where you stand. Will you meet them?'

There were few things in life that made Law more bad-tempered than the prospect of meeting his colleagues. Nonetheless he knew that it had to be done.

'On Thursday. We will meet on Thursday. I will advise you of the sense of the meeting. And you can then arrange your audience with the PM.'

Lloyd George nodded and the meeting came to an end.

As they rose to leave the table I saw Carson wink at Lloyd George before stretching out his hand to Law to apologise for his outburst.

– 14 –

Sir Robert Donald, editor of the *Daily Chronicle*, re-read his editorial again over breakfast. Written the previous afternoon, it was the Liberal newspaper's most trenchant criticism yet of the conduct of the war. Donald was well-known to – indeed well-liked by – both Asquith and Lloyd George. But on this matter he had also been in touch with both Aitken and Law. He had determined to write an editorial that would leave his readers in no doubt about the need for a change in direction. Later he was to claim that his intention had been to help the Government, and Asquith in particular, rather than to bolster Lloyd George's plans to reconstruct the War Committee. But that was not the way his readers saw it.

Asquith read Donald's editorial in his study and was troubled by it.

Lloyd George read it in his office and was pleased.

Aitken read it in his hotel room and was delighted.

Carson didn't read it. He had long since given up reading the Liberal press.

Law read it and was unsure.

Lansdowne had it read to him and was disturbed. This would prolong the war.

At his house in Mayfair Lord Crewe read it and knew that Asquith's Government was approaching its end.

Donald had concluded his editorial with the following challenge:

Mr Asquith and his colleagues have directed the war through a committee: first the Committee for Imperial Defence, now the

War Committee. That Committee prepares for the Cabinet recommendations as to the conduct of the war which the Cabinet then considers. Our military leaders, whose skill and fighting spirit is needed at the front, are drawn into the meetings and regular affairs of the War Committee. By all accounts its deliberations are lengthy, its debates wide-ranging, and its recommendations to Cabinet most carefully formulated. The Cabinet then considers each proposal in detail before reaching a decision, a process that often requires extensive debate and many further meetings.

We suggest that in a time of total war this is not the most effective way for our leaders to proceed. The Cabinet should be willing to allow the War Committee to make its own decisions, binding on both our military leaders and also on the Cabinet itself without any further debate or review. Of course in our system of Government the Cabinet is the supreme decision-making body, subject only to the approval of Parliament and the assent of the Crown. But desperate times call for new approaches.

We urge Mr Asquith and Mr Bonar Law to agree to a new arrangement that would turn the War Committee into a more effective body. It should be reduced in size. No military men should be among its members, although they should attend its meetings as required. It should meet every day. Its reports to Cabinet should be advisory only. It should be granted by the Cabinet full executive authority to run the war. Its decisions should be binding on all other ministers and on our military men.

Mr Asquith and Mr Bonar Law should also consider carefully the constitution of the new War Committee. We are fortunate in having in our Parliament men of exemplary executive ability, energy, and foresight. These men must be released from their departmental responsibilities and charged with running the war. It is the war alone that matters now and all efforts should bend to its prosecution.

Mr Lloyd George is an excellent War Secretary and the War Committee should obviously be the core instrument for executive action and decision-making by his department. There are other parliamentary leaders, Liberal and Unionist alike, who share both his patriotism and his skills, and they must also be invited to serve. And respecting the labour interest, those ordinary men both at the front and here at home whose efforts are central to the war effort, a Labour minister should also be a member.

Mr Asquith and Mr Bonar Law have served the country nobly and well in directing the affairs of both Cabinet and Parliament throughout this conflict. They will both remain central to any new arrangements. But the time for action is now and both leaders must face their responsibility in ensuring that our machinery for decision-making in wartime is as perfect as it can be. Present arrangements do not meet this requirement. Success at the front depends now on an entirely new arrangement.

Donald was pleased. He folded his paper and left it on the breakfast table, rising quickly to go to his office in Fleet Street. He wondered how long it would be before Lloyd George was in touch.

The same day — Cabinet Room, 10 Downing Street

Herbert Asquith had chaired his first Cabinet meeting in the spring of 1908. Two years earlier he had become Chancellor of the Exchequer in Sir Henry Campbell-Bannerman's Government. The Prime Minister – known to all as 'C.B.' – was not a well man. Neither was his wife, to whom he was devoted. As his wife's health failed C.B. spent more and more time by her bedside. When she died in the summer of 1907 he was distraught and his own health then began to fail. He suffered a series of heart attacks and was increasingly unable to transact the business of government. Cabinet colleagues grew concerned, not just at the state of C.B.'s health but also at the lack of direction in the Government's affairs. The King grew concerned as well. Finally in the spring of 1908 C.B. was prevailed upon to resign as Prime Minister and Asquith was appointed in his place. Too unwell to leave Downing Street, Campbell-Bannerman lingered there for six weeks before dying of heart failure in his bedroom on the top floor.

Asquith was well aware of the sad circumstances of his old chief when he chaired his first Cabinet meeting. As he and the other members worked through the Government's business, his predecessor lay dying upstairs. It was a strange and melancholy experience.

Now, years later, Asquith had presided over so many of these meetings that he could no longer remember a time when meetings of the Cabinet were not a regular feature of his life. He had missed only a very few, either through illness or because he was out of the country. In the old days Lord Crewe would, by agreement with his Liberal colleagues, stand in for the Prime Minister when he was unable to attend. Since the formation of the Coalition, Bonar Law had taken on that role. By all accounts (he heard this from both Liberal and Unionist members) Law was a terrible chairman. Asquith was not only the natural head of the Government but also a most accomplished chairman of Cabinet. He was also recognised as the natural leader of the Commons; his command of the chamber was legendary. It was hard to imagine any other man who could take his place in either body.

The formal protocol for a Cabinet meeting was fixed. The Prime Minister entered the room first and took his place at the centre of the long mahogany table. Only the Prime Minister's chair had arms. Asquith hadn't sat in a chair without arms in this room for many years. When he wrote his letters during meetings it was easy to lean on the left arm and swivel in to write. He could not have written anything in a chair without arms.

A fire burned in the grate behind him. If it needed stoking he would ring a small bell by his right hand to summon a servant. To other members' great amusement (and, he suspected, to Lord Lansdowne's utter disdain) Arthur Henderson, the single Labour member of Cabinet, would from time to time leave his seat and stoke the fire himself if it showed signs of running down.

Once the Prime Minister had taken his seat the door was opened to admit the other members. They took their places with a series of 'Good morning, Prime Minister's and chatted briefly with their neighbours. Once the PM reached for the papers in front of him a silence descended on the room. Viscount Grey, the Foreign Secretary, had grown increasingly blind. He did not reach for his papers or consult them at all during the meetings. They had been read to him in advance by his staff at the Foreign Office. Lord Robert Cecil sat beside him and spoke to him in a low voice if he needed to be reminded of anything written in his notes.

'Gentlemen, thank you. A brief meeting today. War Committee tomorrow and I will advise you further of any matters we discuss there. You will all have seen this morning's suggestions in the *Chronicle* about how we should conduct our business. I will discuss this later with the War Secretary and the Colonial Secretary and we will let you have our views at next week's Cabinet.'

Lloyd George staring into the middle of the table. No reaction.

A series of brief matters for review. Notices of the King's issues: Crewe. An economic report: McKenna. News from Russia: Grey. A troop movement report: Lloyd George. Then the central business.

'Gentlemen, I asked you some weeks ago for your comments on the direction of the war. Thank you for your responses. You will all have read with interest Lord Lansdowne's proposals, either in his own briefing papers or, most regrettably, in the *Mail*. I will not speak again about the leaking of Cabinet papers to the newspapers except to say this. If I discover who was responsible for providing Lord Rothermere with Lord Lansdowne's paper I will relieve that member immediately of his responsibilities. He will be returned without delay to the backbenches, either in the Commons or the Lords, whichever House he hails from. And I will make no distinction as to which party the member belongs to. Do I make myself clear, gentlemen?'

A murmur of assent.

Still no eye contact from Lloyd George.

Of course it was Lansdowne himself who had leaked his own paper. The old fool. But Asquith's concern was not that Lansdowne had allowed his ideas to become public but that a number of newspapers had hinted that Lansdowne was acting on Asquith's behalf in advancing these proposals. In other words, that Asquith himself wanted to sue for peace but could never say so in his own name. And that he had therefore employed Lansdowne to publicise the Prime Minister's own views. That was a deeply dangerous exercise and Asquith must act immediately to counter it. But he was as yet uncertain quite how to do that.

At any rate, they had heard him.

'Lord Robert Cecil has presented a further paper which was circulated to you yesterday. You will all have read it. I invite Lord Robert to summarise his case and we will then discuss it.'

Gesturing to Cecil. Lloyd George sat back. Lord Lansdowne sat forward. Bonar Law remained ramrod straight in his chair. Asquith reclined, resting his arms, enjoying the fire behind him. Lord Robert Cecil spoke.

Asquith paid him no attention. He was elsewhere.

He chaired the subsequent discussion in slow motion. The usual, predictable comments. Lloyd George was restrained: he would obviously prefer a single effective committee to the creation of the second one that Cecil was proposing. But now was not the time to take a firm stand so he said little more. Nothing of consequence. To establish a second committee was, in Asquith's own view, a ridiculous idea. But like Lloyd George he knew that now was not the time for resisting. This was mere froth on top of a much deeper and more dangerous restructuring. He would face it later.

Lord Robert Cecil's proposal to establish a Civilian Organisation Committee was approved by the Cabinet *nem. con.* Terms of reference to follow. Membership to be decided by the Prime Minister in consultation with Bonar Law. Chairmanship not mentioned but the assumption was that Asquith himself would direct the committee.

The meeting broke up shortly after twelve. Members gathered their papers and wondered whether to return to their offices or head to their clubs for an early lunch.

Asquith was the last person to leave the room. He stopped at the door to look back. The fire was dying in the grate. Something held him back; he wasn't sure quite what it was.

In fact this was the last Cabinet meeting that Asquith would ever chair.

– 15 –

Thursday 30 November 1916 — Colonial Office, Whitehall

Bonar Law had spent much of the previous day's Cabinet meeting watching Asquith. He was mesmerised both by the indolence with which he chaired the meeting as well as the supreme efficiency with which he moved through the agenda. It was like a perfectly balanced machine, needing only the lightest of touches to turn it this way or that.

This was the man he was being asked to displace?

Looking around the meeting, he watched especially his Conservative colleagues. Lord Curzon, Austen Chamberlain, Walter Long, Arthur Balfour, Lord Robert Cecil, Lord Lansdowne, Lord Crawford, Henry Duke and F. E. Smith. Did they also believe that the direction of the war was inadequate? What did they believe should be done? Lansdowne wanted an overture that would lead to peace with honour but without victory. Cecil wanted to fight on. But what about the others? And what did they think of Asquith?

If Law moved against Asquith, a possibility against which his whole inclination recoiled, would his Unionist colleagues follow him or would they (and he imagined they well might) desert him and depose him? And yet if he did *not* move against Asquith would that prolong the war? Or, even worse, would Lloyd George find enough support to move against the Prime Minister independently and then remove Law from his post in a new coalition government?

It dawned on Law with sudden clarity that Lloyd George was right about one thing. In talking so openly with Carson and Lloyd George over the last two weeks, Law had moved too far in advance of his own colleagues. He needed to advise them of the conversa-

tions so far, tell them what had been proposed and how Asquith
had responded, and, as their leader, tell them also his own mind.
And so as Cecil was speaking he scribbled a note to Curzon and
sent it to him down the table. It passed unopened through the
hands of four Liberal ministers before reaching the Lord Privy
Seal.

C – most important that we and our Cab. colleagues meet
tomorrow morning. Please come to my rooms at the C.O. 10
o'clock. Vital you attend. I will advise the others.
BL

And so the meeting was arranged.

They gathered under another low London sky. Coats, hats and
walking sticks discarded. Places found around the table in Law's
office. The Colonial Secretary at its head. No tea. Straight to business.

'Gentlemen, I need to advise you of some recent conversations
I have had with Lloyd George and the Prime Minister. These conversations were informal and exploratory. They do not bind us or
our party but they will, I believe, eventually lead one way or the
other to important changes in the character and composition of
the Government. I wish you to know about them now in order to
advise me on how you think we should proceed. I have my own
views in this matter, which I will explain to you shortly. But first
this.'

There were two papers on the table in front of Law. He took the
first and read it to them, prefacing it by saying: 'This is a memorandum which I gave to the Prime Minister last Saturday. It was
prepared following a series of conversations I had with Lloyd
George, Carson and Aitken in recent weeks. We are concerned –
and I know you all share this concern – that the War Committee
is not functioning properly and needs to be reformed. We are not,
as you will understand from the wording of the note, in complete
agreement as to the scope of those reforms, but we are of one mind
as to the need for change. The document was drafted by us in the
Prime Minister's name as a memorandum which we proposed he

should issue publicly. We did not expect him necessarily to accept our recommendations, but we did want to impress upon him the need for some important changes. I will read it to you now.'

At this Law read the memorandum.

It was greeted with consternation. Almost all of those around the table started to speak at once. F. E. Smith spoke louder than most. Curzon was apoplectic. Only Balfour stayed silent.

He let them talk for a few moments to see if one voice would prevail and speak for all of them. It did not. So he eventually asked them, raising his own voice to be heard, to speak in turn. The voices subsided and Law turned to Curzon, seated on his left, and asked him to respond first. He would then proceed around the table and ask them to speak one by one. So Curzon spoke.

'This is an appalling development, Law. Absolutely outrageous. I'm shocked at what you've done.'

Murmurs of approval.

He continued.

'I resent greatly the fact that you have been treating with the enemy behind our backs. Let us leave Carson and Aitken to one side, they don't matter. But Lloyd George? You decided to present a note to the Prime Minister which in effect – cutting through all the weasel words of your drafting – requires him to stand aside as the head of the Government?'

More murmurs of agreement.

'And you expected him to agree? How did he respond?'

Law gestured to the paper in front of him. 'I have his response, which I will read to you in a moment. But first I must ask for your thoughts about the initial memorandum. I want to take this step by step. Do others agree with Lord Curzon?'

They voiced their assent (again only Balfour stayed silent) and then Walter Long spoke.

'Curzon is right, Law. Giving encouragement to Lloyd George in this way was, to say the very least, unwise. We don't doubt his energy but his ambition is to run everything – the war, the Cabinet, and the country. This is just a stepping stone. If Asquith were to make him chairman of the War Committee he would be PM by Easter. He has no intention of stopping with the War Committee. Don't you see?'

The conversation continued in this vein. Although he had expected resistance, Bonar Law was in fact greatly surprised at the intensity of their attacks on him and his part in the conversations. He proceeded around the table and listened as they voiced with increasing vehemence their opposition to Lloyd George and their support of Asquith. Only Balfour was measured in his comment. (In fact he felt quite unwell; he knew he was getting sick and that he should return home and take to his bed as quickly as he could.) When his turn to speak arrived he merely said:

'I don't think it was a wise move, Bonar. Too risky. But how did the PM reply?'

At this there was a renewed clamour to hear Asquith's response. Law picked up the second paper from the table and read it aloud. At the Prime Minister's comments about Carson there were murmurs of disapproval although this was in fact the part of Asquith's response that gave Law's listeners the most unalloyed pleasure. Carson was despised by his Unionist colleagues and to hear the Prime Minister disparage him in such measured tones was music to their ears. But with the rest of Asquith's response there was almost complete agreement.

Lansdowne spoke for them. 'How else did you think the PM was going to respond, Law? You bring him a paper saying, in his own words: the war effort is a failure; the machinery doesn't work; I'm going to appoint a small committee headed by a man whose ambition knows no bounds; it won't be answerable to Cabinet unless I, the now side-lined Prime Minister, think that one or two of its decisions might merit further review. How did you think Asquith would take it? Lying down? Certainly, Lloyd George, walk all over me. Shall I give you my seals now? I won't be needing them any more. Oh and here's the keys to Number 10 as well.'

They all agreed with Lansdowne.

And so it was now time for Law to push back.

'Gentlemen, thank you. I'm not surprised by your views. I thank you for your frankness and candour. But I must tell you why I acted as I did and outline also how this matter should, I believe, proceed.

'I am under no illusions about Lloyd George. Our party has been fighting this man for years. Many of his ideas are completely impossible. He is almost wholly animated by a deep hostility to our party, our supporters, and everything we stand for as Conservatives and Unionists. In ordinary times – as they were before the war – Lloyd George would be our clearest political enemy. Of that there can be no doubt.

'But these are not ordinary times. And Lloyd George hates Germans with far greater vehemence than he hates Unionists. In wartime the enemy of my enemy may well be my friend. I am convinced, gentlemen – and you have all worked with Lloyd George at close quarters too, so I know you understand this – I am convinced that this country, in the present war, needs Lloyd George's energy and enthusiasm as never before. Not only must we keep him within the Cabinet, we must also give him greater responsibility and scope for energetic action than we have done before. We must give him that scope even if it creates a level of political risk for us and our party.

'I have no intention, gentlemen – please hear me as I say this – I have no intention of being party to any enterprise that will damage or destroy this Government or cause Asquith to stand aside as Prime Minister. No intention whatsoever.' (As he said this the merest flicker of doubt, the tiniest shadow of uncertainty, crossed Law's mind. But he carried on). 'My participation in these discussions has not been premised, and *will* not be premised, on any move to depose Asquith. He brings a vital quality of leadership to our country at this time of peril. You have been in Cabinet, many of you, under his chairmanship for over two years now. You have seen the skill with which he leads the Commons. You know that he is a patriot and that he has sacrificed as much as any of the rest of us.

'So I will not be party to any plot to depose Asquith.

'Lloyd George is a politician of the common sort. He is a cunning man. He plots, he schemes, he plans, he acts. I want no part of his plotting. He is a Socialist Radical of the worst kind and in peacetime, gentlemen, we would and we will destroy him. But we are not at peace. We need his energy and we need his cunning, just as we need Asquith's continuing leadership. My role in this drama is to harness the best of both men, not to let Lloyd George take over nor to let Asquith go under. I am the mediator, gentlemen. I mediate on behalf of the country, not just on behalf of our Unionist party. And I need your support in that task.'

Cecil interjected. 'We set up a second committee yesterday to deal with this, Bonar. A Home Committee and a War Committee. We need to restructure the War Committee certainly but not to give anyone, and certainly not Lloyd George, supreme power on it.'

'No, Robert. I disagree. I've thought again about our decision of yesterday. It was a mistake.'

'A mistake?'

'When you reflect on it, the arrangement is absurd. Which of the two committees would be responsible for transporting troops to France, for example?'

Cecil replied, 'The Home Committee.'

'And suppose,' Law said, 'that the shipping authority on the Home Committee orders troops to be taken across in cement barges towed by tugs because the transports are wanted for other purposes. Do you suppose the War Council would agree to that?'

'It will need coordination of course,' Cecil responded.

'The last things we need in this war is another committee and more coordination. I'm sorry, Robert, I was wrong to support you yesterday. It was a mistake. We must not set up another committee. We are at war: the War Committee must run the war.'

The mood in the room had not lightened.

Law sensed that he was in dangerous territory. His core members, here in this room, wanted nothing to do with a stronger Lloyd George. On his other flank, however, were Carson and his disaffected Unionist supporters who wanted Asquith destroyed at all costs. But at least Law had stated his position. And he was determined to pursue it.

'Please give my proposal some thought. Twenty-four hours. Write to me with your views after that time. But please, not in haste. Think it through first.'

And then the meeting broke up. Balfour went home to bed where he would remain for the next week. Law took his hat and coat from the stand. He wrapped a scarf around his neck against the cold and walked with determination around St James's Park to clear his head and consider his position.

– 16 –

Thursday 30 November 1916 — St James's Park

In fact Law walked around the park seven times.

He started at the duck pond behind Horse Guards Parade and walked clockwise, parallel to Queen Anne's Gate, past the barracks, then down into the hollow where the park was at its nearest point to the Palace. From there the path rose again and tracked The Mall down to Admiralty Arch before turning back along Horse Guards and returning to the duck pond.

On his first circuit of the park Law thought of nothing. He felt drained by the meeting, by the events of the previous weeks. He found each day a new burden. Matters that required his attention in relation to the colonies were few, but the burden of Cabinet and War Committee was immense. Each time they took a decision he knew that hundreds or thousands of English lives would be lost even if the action proved successful. Each time the Prime Minister went around the table and asked for assent or dissent Law felt sick to his stomach. Even a brief 'I agree' sent more men to their death. The burden was awful.

Now he was faced by a new problem which added even more complexity to the situation. He tried to work through the issues methodically in his mind. Was reorganisation required? Absolutely. Did it need to be a radical change? He thought that it did. Must it involve personalities? Yes, it must. Would the Government have to be reconfigured? At some level, yes. Could the Prime Minister carry on? He thought so, but now he began to feel unsure. Should he continue to work with Lloyd George despite the opposition of his own colleagues? He thought so, yes, but again he was unsure. Would he himself survive the changes? He didn't give a damn.

He knew that he had to think this through, carefully, with focus, and understand what the meeting had just said to him. He knew they would resist and push back. The key decision for him now was how to respond to that resistance. If they pushed him hard should he abandon his conversations with Lloyd George and let the little man make his own case to the PM? Or should he stick with his instincts, ignore his colleagues' concerns, and attempt to direct the change that he now felt certain was coming?

He thought again of Asquith. He thought of all the Prime Minister had done, all the energy he had expended to keep the Government together and functioning effectively in these war years. Was no loyalty owed to him?

The afternoon's light faded into gloom as Law began yet another circuit of the park. He was recognised by one or two other walkers, junior men, who raised their hats to him. Law ignored them. He knew that he must form a settled view by the time he finished his walk, a view that would carry him through the renewed onslaught he could expect from his colleagues in the coming days. And also through the turmoil of the week ahead.

And then Bonar Law had an epiphany and the future was revealed to him.

This is how it happened.

He asked himself: what would it be like in, say, two weeks' time if Lloyd George was Prime Minister and Asquith was out of Downing Street? Never mind *how* it would happen. Ignore the twists and turns that must inevitably precede so momentous a change. What would it be like? What would it *feel* like? What would *he* feel like?

He imagined arriving at a War Council meeting. He imagined walking into the Cabinet Room in Downing Street to find not Asquith but Lloyd George sitting in the chair with the arms. Around him a small group of men. Henderson certainly. Perhaps Curzon. Perhaps Carson (though he thought probably not). Hankey of course. For the Liberals perhaps Montagu. But no generals, no admirals. All the others cleared away as well. And Asquith gone.

He could see Lloyd George with maps spread out in front of him, poring over the details. Questioning. Demanding. Instructing. The other members deferred to him (he had only been Prime

Minister for a week or so) and Lloyd George took care to ask Law for his views. Law offered his advice with enthusiasm and energy but knew that the new PM would form his own opinion and take his own decisions. He would not wait for consensus to emerge; he would listen to their views and then decide. No compromising. No committees. No referring back to Cabinet. Just action.

Where was Asquith in this fantasy? Asquith had become Earl of Walmer upon his resignation the previous week. The King had been more than ready to honour him in this way. He had also appointed him Warden of the Cinque Ports (Beauchamp having been given a step in his peerage and prevailed upon to stand down). Arrangements had been made to transfer financial responsibility for the upkeep of Walmer Castle from the incoming Warden to Parliament. Asquith had taken on the wardenship in tandem with a continuing role in the Government as Lord Chancellor. He now held the supreme role among the judiciary, chaired the House of Lords, and remained a member of the Cabinet. But he was no longer a member of the War Council. He had accepted this change in his status with good grace, not a little relief, and some satisfaction that his own financial affairs were now on a firm footing.

How did this fantasy feel to Law?

He had to be honest with himself: it felt invigorating. It felt as if new energy and vibrancy had been invested in running the war with no loss of dignity to Asquith. It felt as if it might work, as if they might after all survive and snatch victory from the current stalemate.

It felt correct.

It was at this moment that Bonar Law took the most important decision of his life.

He decided to lead.

His Unionist colleagues would write to him. They would warn him that he was reaching too far ahead of the party. That he was investing too much trust in Lloyd George in believing that the War Secretary would continue to serve under Asquith if Asquith made him chairman of the War Council. That Lloyd George wanted the premiership himself. Didn't Law see this?

Yes, Law did. He saw that now.

But Lloyd George was right to want it.

Of course he couldn't say this directly to his colleagues. There were certain political proprieties that needed to be observed even in wartime. But they were in the business of good government for England and of winning the war. And for that task leadership was paramount. In fact it was the *only* thing.

So Law decided – and felt almost overwhelmed with relief at his decision – that he would continue to work actively with Lloyd George. He would tell his party colleagues that he was convinced this was in the country's best interests. And he would also continue working with Asquith, pleading with him to accept the proposals being put to him. Knowing that he should. But knowing also that he wouldn't. And that, in the end, and very soon now, the situation would tip over and Asquith would no longer have the power to accept these proposals even if he wanted to. Because Asquith would by then have lost his footing and would be overthrown. Law's last role would be to convince Asquith to accept his demise with good grace and stay in the Cabinet as Lord Chancellor.

And then Law had his second epiphany that day.

In politics the currency of exchange is weakness. His Unionist colleagues were violent in their support of Asquith only because they thought he was strong. The PM had a majority in the Commons and controlled everything – appointments, positions, advancements, honours. Every other politician in the land – save only the radicals like Carson who no longer cared about advancement – supported Asquith because of his strength. But if Asquith began to bleed, even a little, then his support would quickly ebb away and soon become a roaring tide. No smell was more detectable to a politician than the smell of blood in the water. Asquith, despite the continuing press attacks on him, was not yet bleeding.

Law's role now was to make him bleed.

Not to cut him up. Not to injure him. But just to make him bleed a little, a few drops, into the political waters in which they all swam. And then all the noses would twitch in unison and the chorus would begin: Asquith is bleeding. Asquith is weakening. Asquith might not survive.

And after that initial sense that the Age of Asquith might be coming to an end, politicians of every party would immediately reassess their loyalties. The smallest surface wound could lead almost overnight to a haemorrhage from which he would never recover. Then they would look to the coming man. And that could only mean Lloyd George.

If this could be accomplished Law had no doubt that all of his ministerial colleagues (except Lansdowne, but he was yesterday's man) would willingly accept office in a Lloyd George government. By Christmas Asquith as Prime Minister would have been utterly forgotten. All power drained away. All influence gone. Enthroned in glory in the tomb of the Lords.

On his seventh round of the park Law stopped to sit on a bench in the hollow just across from the Palace. The dark had now drawn in and Law was alone except for an occasional other walker, his collar drawn up against the cold and the brim of his hat pulled down across his forehead, who slowed briefly as he passed by. One or two turned back to look at him after they had moved on. From the barracks across the road, behind the tall hedges, Law heard the sound of evening fallout as the guardsmen began to disperse. He was oblivious to the other world that was beginning to form in the gloom that surrounded him.

He thought on. Lansdowne would have to be ignored. Of all his Unionist colleagues, Lansdowne was the one most afraid of a Lloyd George premiership. It meant the continuation of the war with a new vigour, precisely the development that Lansdowne so opposed. He wanted to sue for peace. He was trying to associate Asquith with this view. Some sections of the press were hinting as much. Law knew it was part of his duty to Asquith to ensure that he was allowed to go with no stain of defeatism on his character. For this reason he would marginalise Lansdowne. Any letter of complaint from him would be responded to politely and then ignored.

The others would also complain and their concerns would be more substantial. They feared Lloyd George as the unknown. Asquith was the known, the obvious. They did not want to preserve Asquith out of any sense of loyalty to the man (privately

Long despised him, and neither Curzon nor Chamberlain thought well of him either). But they would cling to Asquith because Lloyd George was too erratic, too energetic, too unpredictable.

Well, Law thought, he would have to lead them along a path they did not want to travel. But lead them he would.

He would not, however, take Carson's path. There would be no open breach with Asquith, no demand that he should stand aside, nor any attempt to humiliate him. If Lansdowne was just defeatist, Carson was poison. Law would have no truck with his public campaigns. He would continue to resist him in any further meetings the two men were to have with Lloyd George.

So here was Law's decision. He would resist the pressure from his Unionist colleagues (which he knew would now become intense) and would continue mediating between Lloyd George and the Prime Minister. It was imperative that the Unionist Party should play a central role in the change that was now inevitable. Carson would step into the breach if he was allowed to. That must be resisted. So Law must continue to act as mediator.

He would advise the PM to accept the changes being put to him by Lloyd George, Carson and himself. He would impress upon him the need for new energy and the fact that the arrangement under which he, Asquith, would retain the presidency of the War Council with Lloyd George as its day-to-day chairman was the best of all possible arrangements. He would do all that he could to talk Asquith into accepting this.

Privately, however, he knew that Asquith would never consent. And now he knew that this lack of consent was for the best. It would allow the inevitable to happen: Asquith's hold on the premiership would be prised away and Lloyd George would take his place.

He also knew that the pivotal moment would be a Unionist one. Asquith would fall, not because the pressure from Lloyd George had become irresistible, but because Law's Unionist colleagues would come to the view that the sands had shifted, that Lloyd George was in the ascendant, and that they must perform the necessary dance to preserve their own positions after Asquith had fallen. It was the Unionists, therefore, who would bring him down.

And what was Law's role to be in all this? To lead the Unionists in bringing him down. And then to protect Asquith in his fall. To cushion the blow.

At last he knew the right thing to do.

In their fierce resistance to all that he had done, the Unionist ministers had helped Bonar Law to understand that all his actions so far had been correct but insufficient. Now it was time to lead.

– 17 –

Friday 1 December 1916 — Cabinet Room, 10 Downing Street

'Prime Minister, the Secretary of State for War.'

'Thank you, Drummond. Show him in.'

Lloyd George enters. Drummond withdraws and closes the door behind him. Asquith gestures Lloyd George to the seat opposite. Finishes working on the papers in front of him. Then looks up at his visitor.

'David.'

'Prime Minister.'

'You wanted to see me.'

'I did.'

'About the War Committee?'

'Yes, Prime Minister.'

Asquith pauses. Feels the warmth of the fire behind him. Make Lloyd George sweat a little. But then he remembers: Lloyd George doesn't sweat. So Asquith continues.

'I sent you a copy of the response I gave Law about your memorandum of last weekend. You've seen it?'

'I have.'

'And discussed it with Law and Carson?'

'Yes. And Aitken too. We've been discussing the matter for more than a fortnight now. This isn't just another Cabinet matter, PM. It's a life-and-death matter. We need to resolve it.'

'And my response is not acceptable?'

'No, Prime Minister. With respect – genuinely, with the very greatest of respect – it isn't.'

Asquith sits back in his chair and stares at Lloyd George. They have met together hundreds of times in this room over the last eight years and more. Now for the first time Asquith senses a new electricity in the air between them.

'David, I respect your opinion. I respect the fact that we have different views on how to deal with this. We'll continue to discuss it and I'm sure we can reach an accommodation.'

'It isn't a question of accommodation, PM. We have to make a fundamental change in the way we manage the war. Root and branch. Not just tinkering.'

He pauses. Then speaks again.

'I've given your response a great deal of thought and I want to propose an alternative arrangement. Slightly modified from last weekend. And I haven't discussed this with Law or Carson. It's my proposal to you. I'm sure I can get Law to agree for the Unionists if you're willing to agree for our side. It really is the only way we can settle this without difficulty.'

Without difficulty? Asquith stares across at him. He thinks… well, he thinks a thought that isn't a noble one. It does neither of them any great credit. But he thinks it anyway and although he doesn't articulate it openly it summarises the whole position for him neatly and concisely. He thinks: Lloyd George – you devious little shit.

'We have the War Committee in fifteen minutes. What's your suggestion?'

Lloyd George takes a paper from his inside pocket. Places it on the table in front of him. Then speaks.

'A three-man committee, PM. War Secretary one of the members. Also the First Lord of the Admiralty and one Minister without Portfolio.'

He pauses. Looks at Asquith.

Three members. The Prime Minister not one of them. So a direct repudiation of Asquith's previous response.

'The War Secretary and First Lord run extensive departments. I thought your last suggestion recommended members without departmental responsibilities?'

'I've reconsidered that, PM. I've thought about what you said to Law and you're right. But we can accommodate this. In each case I suggest we give them an Under-Secretary who is more than capable of running their department while the senior minister is absorbed in War Committee work.'

'So you and the First Lord. And the third?'

'Not yet decided, PM. To be appointed. But with no departmental responsibilities.'

So he's not thinking of Law if Law stays on at the Colonial Office? I wonder what Law will make of that? Probably still thinking of Carson. Another spit in my eye.

'Chairman?'

'One of the three, Prime Minister. To be decided.'

'Probably the War Secretary?'

'Not necessarily, Prime Minister. Though I do think it would make most sense.'

Another lengthy pause before Asquith responds again.

'You will recall, David, that one of my key objections to last weekend's proposal was your suggestion that the Prime Minister should not be a member of the War Council. That you had, in effect, marginalised him.'

'That isn't the way I see it, PM.'

'You don't?'

'No, I don't.'

Here is where the whole battle is to be fought.

'Again with the greatest of respect, PM, I believe the role suggested for the Prime Minister last weekend was absolutely the correct one. The Prime Minister is – you are – hugely burdened with Cabinet and Parliament, overseeing the departments of government, running the country in wartime. He hasn't – you haven't – the capacity, the time, or the energy to manage the war on a daily basis together with your other responsibilities. It just isn't humanly possible. So what I'm suggesting in that regard is, I agree, the same as I suggested last weekend. We have to find a way in which day-to-day responsibility can be delegated by the Prime Minister while he nonetheless retains ultimate control of the direction of the war.'

'So the same as before? The Prime Minister can refer any decision of the War Council to the Cabinet for ratification?'

'Yes.'

'It won't do.'

Asquith sits back. Now it is Lloyd George who stares across at him.

'It won't do, David. Think about it. Put yourself in my position...'

As you want to. You little Welsh creep.

'...and think about it.

'War Secretary comes to see the Prime Minister. Brings a report on that day's proceedings at the War Committee. Five decisions. Prime Minister reviews them, finds he's happy with four of the five but concerned about the fifth. War Secretary stands his ground. Says it's been considered in detail by his group. Papers which the Prime Minister hasn't seen have been reviewed by the Committee. Advice which the Prime Minister hasn't heard has been tendered to the Committee. They've debated it and reached a decision. Now the PM wants to undermine that decision, call a Cabinet, and have the matter debated afresh. How long would you stay on as War Secretary, David, if I did that? A couple of weeks? Perhaps a month or two?

'So the point is this. And it isn't made out of any concern for personality, David, but purely on administrative grounds. The arrangement can only work to the disadvantage of the Prime Minister. Either he second-guesses, in which case the War Secretary resigns and the War Committee fails. Or else he acquiesces in every decision of the War Committee, in which case he might as well not be involved at all.

'And if the Prime Minister isn't involved in the war, he might as well not be Prime Minister.'

He pauses.

Lloyd George says nothing.

Asquith continues. 'Where are we going with this, David?'

'We have to reach a settlement, PM.'

'Or?'

'Or I shall have to stand aside as War Secretary.'

More silence.

'I can't carry on this way. I'm a War Secretary who isn't running a war. I'm a member of a committee that is too big, too unwieldy, useless. It moves in reverse if it moves at all.'

'Because...'

'Because it's the wrong group of men doing the wrong task in the wrong way. I know I can do it better, PM. I know I can bring the energy and direction it needs if you'll let me reconstruct it and lead it my way. I give you my word that you and I will never fall out over this. I will honour and respect your position as Prime Minister. You will never be compromised in front of the Cabinet. But you must accept this, PM. Otherwise it's hopeless. And I can't go on like that.'

Again a silence. Each stared at the other.

'I will consider it further, David. Leave your paper with me. I'll have a response with you later this afternoon.'

'Thank you.'

Lloyd George rises and prepares to leave.

'No, you should stay. We'll bring the others in and start the War Committee now. They might as well see that we're still on speaking terms.'

They smile at one another. Warily. Speaking terms indeed.

Asquith calls for Drummond and asks him to bring in the other members of the Committee. The meeting starts at a quarter to one and finishes at two. Then Asquith goes upstairs for lunch. He brings Lloyd George's paper with him and begins to draft a response on his way to the study.

– 18 –

Friday 1 December 1916 — Prime Minister's Study, 10 Downing Street

Lunch was a simple affair. Asquith dined alone. Margot was out, back later in the afternoon. She would pack for Walmer when she returned. Bonham Carter was around but Asquith didn't feel like discussing the latest developments with him just now.

Chartres served a thin minestrone, boiled fish, steamed vegetables and a suet pudding. Asquith asked for half a pint of champagne to accompany the meal. The alcohol would make him drowsy at first but he knew that half an hour of sleep after lunch would revive him. He would then be at his sharpest and ready to respond to Lloyd George's challenge.

He slept in his chair by the fire. Asked not to be disturbed. His staff knew what that meant and gave him the solitude he needed.

At half past three he began his letter of response to Lloyd George. He knew that the tone would be everything. Conciliatory and accommodating but unyielding on the main point, which was that he, Asquith, would remain in charge. And that would push Lloyd George to the brink, or even beyond.

So be it.

The crucial factor was how Law would respond when he saw both letters. Asquith understood Law's character now; his reluctance to act peremptorily and his essential, very personal, conservatism. The letter of response to Lloyd George would be in Law's hands by dinner time. Carson's too. But he trusted Law's judgement, his ability to see through Lloyd George's tilt for power, and his basic decency and patriotism. So Asquith would respond plainly: no code needed.

Time to launch in. He wrote with a bold, confident stroke.

My dear Lloyd George. I have now had time to reflect on our conversation this morning and to study your memorandum.

How many letters like this had Asquith written over the years? Hundreds certainly. Probably thousands. After each Cabinet meeting the Prime Minister was required to prepare a formal, hand-written report for the King. A short account of proceedings, key interventions, memorable speeches by colleagues (very rare) and decisions reached. The King questioned him at their weekly meetings about these notes. Asquith had had the closest of relationships with the old King. His reputation (the King's) as a drinker and a womaniser belied a sharp political intelligence. Asquith looked forward to those weekly encounters and to the King's incisive questioning. With the new King it was different. Even now, six years into his reign, George's understanding of the constitutional role of the monarch remained limited, to say the least. The weekly audiences were a chore. On one occasion Asquith, pressed for time but also bored beyond patience by the King, had written him a one-line report of studied rudeness: *His Majesty's Ministers discussed many matters of importance and considered a range of alternative actions before settling on appropriate courses of conduct.* The King, to paraphrase his late grandmother, had not been amused. Asquith had apologised.

But Lloyd George had the sharpest intelligence and certainly the best political instincts Asquith had ever seen in a public man. He could sense any weakness, any wavering or uncertainty. So every word that Asquith wrote needed careful consideration. Lloyd George would look through the words for the hidden meaning, the deeper language of back-and-forth that only a seasoned politician could ever translate. So Asquith must be bold and plain-speaking in his response. First, however, some agreement:

Though I do not altogether share your dark estimate and forecast of the situation, actual and prospective, I am in complete agreement that we have reached a critical situation in the war, and that our methods of procedure, with the experience that we have gained during the last three months, call for reconsideration and revision.

Fine. The opening preamble was quite clear. We agree on the broad picture if not on the details. More unites us than divides us. Let's focus on the positives. That kind of thing.

Now to identify the defects of the existing War Committee, the failings to be rectified. Here Lloyd George would scan the letter in search of those matters that Asquith had omitted. For if they were omitted, that meant the PM did not consider them to be problems. And Asquith had no intention of making reference to the chairmanship of the committee in his list of, what, three?...no, four problems.

> The main defects of the War Committee, which has done excellent work, are (1) that its numbers are too large, and (2) that there is delay, evasion, and often obstruction on the part of the Departments in giving effect to its decisions. I might with good reason add (3) that it is often kept in ignorance by the Departments of information, essential and even vital, of a technical kind, upon the problems that come before it; and (4) that it is overcharged with duties, many of which might well be delegated to subordinate bodies.

Good. Now a concise and uncontroversial summary of the key point on which we are agreed.

> The result is that I am clearly of opinion that the War Committee should be reconstituted, and its relations to and authority over the Departments be more clearly defined and more effectively asserted. I come now to your specific proposals.

Here Asquith paused.

It wasn't hesitation that animated Asquith at this stage. It was the knowledge that this letter was pivotal to his whole career as Prime Minister. This was the first time that any minister had challenged his authority in such a brazen way. Margot, to her great credit, had always known this day would come and that Lloyd George would be the one to challenge him. Asquith knew it too but he had suppressed it. He recalled her reaction when he told her that he was proposing to have Lloyd George succeed Kitchener as War Secretary. 'If you allow that man to fill that position we will be finished. Gone from here by the end of the year.'

Asquith's response to the first letter the previous weekend had been wholly pro forma. He knew the cabal had held back on that occasion and would almost certainly strike a second time. Now the real challenge had come in the form of Lloyd George's latest letter, even though he claimed on this occasion to be acting alone. So Asquith's response now was pivotal. Based on how the PM responded, Lloyd George would decide whether to fight or concede. And if Lloyd George decided to fight then Law would have to decide whether to support him or stay loyal to the Prime Minister. So this letter must be clear, forceful, fighting. He re-read what he had written and was happy. No change was needed. Now he must turn to his conclusions, the determinations that only he as Prime Minister was qualified to make. The first of those determinations would be abundantly clear.

In my opinion, whatever changes are made in the composition or functions of the War Committee the Prime Minister must be its chairman. He cannot be relegated to the position of an arbiter in the background or a referee to the Cabinet.

This was clear. I am not backing down, David. I will not allow you to marginalise me. I am the Prime Minister and I will chair the War Committee. I make that perfectly clear to you, Law, Carson and Aitken, and whoever else reads this letter. I have no intention of standing down.

Once this was established Asquith felt he could make some concessions that might bring the conspirators on board, or at least reduce their ability to complain (almost certainly in the press) that he was ignoring them.

In regard to its composition, I agree that the War Secretary and the First Lord of the Admiralty are necessary members. I am inclined to add to the same category the Minister of Munitions. There should be another member, either with or without portfolio, or charged with comparatively light departmental duties.

143

And just in case Lloyd George should resurrect the distinction between president (Asquith; team captain, non-playing) and chairman (Lloyd George; man of action) that had featured in his earlier proposal, Asquith decided to add a sentence of quite exquisite political malice.

One of the members should be appointed Vice Chairman.

You can be number two, David. If I appoint you. But the chairmanship is clear. It belongs to me.

In terms of the committee's membership, Asquith decided to draw on the conspirators' own precedent of preserving a blank.

I purposely in this letter do not discuss the delicate and difficult question of personnel.

To make clear the committee's relationship to both Cabinet and the ministries he wrote that

The committee should, as far as possible, sit *de die in diem*, and have full power to see that its decisions (subject to appeal to the Cabinet) are carried out promptly and effectively by the Departments.

As for Cecil's suggestion, we adopted it at Cabinet yesterday, so let me make it clear that I intend to implement it fully.

The reconstruction of the War Committee should be accompanied by the setting up of a Committee of National Organisation, to deal with the purely domestic side of our problems. It should have executive power within its own domain.

And in conclusion, just in case you missed the point, David, let me reiterate:

The Cabinet would in all cases have ultimate authority.

And then with a flourish and the most perfect insincerity:

Yours always sincerely, H. H. Asquith

He reviewed what he had written. It was perfectly clear. We agree on a reconstructed War Committee. I will remain as its chairman. It will meet more frequently. It will be small and have a defined membership. Its relationship to the Cabinet will be clear: subordinate but, within that understanding, powerful. It will (possibly) have a vice chairman. It will work in tandem with a domestic committee (which I – although I haven't said this to you yet, David – will also chair). The First Lord will be a member but I want Balfour to continue in that role while you, I am sure, want Carson.

He read the letter one last time, sealed it, and called on Drummond to have it delivered. Drummond told him that Mrs Asquith had returned and was awaiting him upstairs. He gathered his papers and returned to the sitting room to explain the latest developments to Margot. He was tired and looked forward to a quiet family dinner that evening and then a motor to Walmer tomorrow. Lloyd George and Law would consider his letter over the weekend and he would deal with their responses on Monday morning. And that, he hoped, would be that.

But that was not that.

Instead the wheels of the conspiracy now began to turn in deadly earnest.

It started that evening, and in a very public way.

– 19 –

Friday 1 December 1916 — The Berkeley Hotel, Mayfair

The entrance hall of the Berkeley Hotel, what we North Americans would refer to (to the great disdain of the English) as the lobby, retained its air of understated opulence despite the war. Men home on leave could take rooms there; men of a certain class at least. It was rumoured that the rooms were increasingly being taken for irregular purposes: indeed it was rumoured that the War Secretary had himself taken rooms at the Berkeley for purposes of which no bishop would ever approve. The downstairs bar was frequently crowded with men on leave, as it was again this Friday evening. But who could begrudge these men their moment of high spirits? They might all be dead by the following weekend.

I pushed through the crowd at the end of the lobby and made for the dining room. Here a quieter air prevailed. Perhaps forty diners, many in service uniforms, a number of the civilian men dressed formally and their women similarly turned out. Unlike in pre-war days, however, the women wore little if any jewellery. That would have been in poor taste at a time of austerity and sacrifice. The men who continued to dress for dinner looked like relics of another age. Certainly no man under the age of fifty would have thought of doing so.

I was on a peculiar mission. His Majesty's Secretary of State for the Colonies was waiting in a taxicab, its motor still running, outside the main door. I was his emissary in search of the Secretary of State for War. I saw him seated at the far corner of the dining room. He was with the Governor of the Bank of England, Lord Cunliffe; the Lord Chief Justice, Lord Reading; and the Minister of Munitions, Edwin Montagu. I had no doubt from the look on

Lord Cunliffe's face that they were discussing the inadequacies of the current Chancellor of the Exchequer, Reginald McKenna. It was Cunliffe's only topic of conversation these days, and Lloyd George was doubtless enjoying the tirade against his successor. He always did.

I had seen Lloyd George earlier that evening. He called me to his office to tell me of his interview with Asquith. He showed me the memorandum he had given to the PM and told me of his response. A written reply was awaited but Lloyd George knew that it would simply confirm the refusal he had received before that morning's meeting of the War Committee.

Lloyd George described the PM's reaction as 'entirely unsatisfactory'.

I knew at this point that he had decided to fight.

While Asquith was lunching, dozing, and then preparing his letter, Lloyd George had also seen Law. Again he told him of the meeting and the PM's reaction. Law had stayed uncharacteristically quiet as he heard of the meeting. Lloyd George knew that the 'cogs were whirring' (as he later put it to me) in Law's brain while Lloyd George described the exchange. Law could also see that Lloyd George was about to fight. He was trying (Lloyd George thought) to decide whether or not to support him. In fact Bonar Law had already made up his mind on the matter but was refraining from showing his hand until the next move became inevitable. He would, he thought, await Asquith's written response.

As expected, Law had received a number of forceful letters from his colleagues following yesterday's meeting of the Unionist ministers. All advised caution. Lloyd George was not to be trusted. Asquith remained the leader of the Government and Law should have nothing to do with any attempt to destabilise him. He should not run ahead of his colleagues as they might find themselves unable to come with him. In other words they might push him over. But Law had made up his mind during yesterday's walk in the park.

I had also received a message from Law that afternoon asking if he could dine with me at my hotel that evening. I said 'certainly' and then cancelled all my weekend plans. The game was on.

We sat down to eat at half past seven. A simple meal which the waiters had to carry to my rooms on the fourth floor as the wretched lift was still out of service. Law had entered, wheezing, with a voice like thunder. 'Get the bloody lift fixed, Aitken. Or move out.'

He told me of his meeting with Lloyd George as we ate. I told him of mine. I could sense that Law was uneasy. The old loyalty to Asquith was still there but there seemed to be a new readiness to move things on. If Lloyd George broke with Asquith would Law still side with the PM? I couldn't tell, but I decided that the time had come to do everything I could to persuade him of the need to act. I rehearsed all the old arguments and Law heard me in silence. The only new point I added was to say that the war would eventually end and men would then look back and ask whether politicians had taken every opportunity to end it as quickly as possible. If the judgement of history was that key men had hesitated they would never be forgiven.

'Spare me the 'judgement of history' claptrap, Aitken.'

I said nothing more.

'History can take care of itself. I don't care what the historians end up saying about us. I need to do the right thing, the dutiful thing. If I do my duty then history can paddle off if it doesn't like me. No more of that history nonsense, please.'

'I'm not going to lecture you about duty, Bonar. You know more about duty than I do. You did your duty in 1914 when the Irish were trying to tear the Union apart. I'm not going to lecture you about that.'

'Thank you.'

We continued our meal in silence. It is always a strange sensation watching a man as his mind churns. When Law's jaws moved I sensed they were tracking the movements in his brain: the same issues, over and over, trying to judge, trying to decide, churn, churn, churn. It became quite surreal.

And then he spoke again.

'I want to see Lloyd George. Now. I want to see him now.'

I knew where Lloyd George was. He had mentioned earlier that he was dining with the others at the Berkeley and I told Law as much. I asked him whether he wanted to remain in my rooms or return to the Colonial Office and meet us there.

'No. Not at my office. Too indiscreet. I'll meet him here but I don't want to mope around in your rooms while you're out. I'll come with you in a taxicab and wait while you bring him out.'

'And Carson?'

'To hell with Carson.'

We set off for the Berkeley.

* * *

Lloyd George had always been secretive about his movements. I knew that he hated going out in society and much preferred the company of other men of affairs. He disliked being recognised in the street or when dining out. The great man of the people was in fact extraordinarily shy in the company of those he did not know and he dreaded having strangers approach him. So I was surprised to hear that he had agreed to such a public dinner in so prominent a hotel. What did not surprise me, however, was the clarity with which he had let me know where he was going to be that evening. He wanted me to know where to find him. He knew that I was dining with Law. He must have suspected that I would need to see him afterwards.

It would have been wrong of me to approach his table directly. Although I was known to all those in Lloyd George's party I was not, as they say, 'in their league'. And a public request for a few moments of his time might have alerted them that something was afoot. So I stood at the other side of the dining room and attempted to catch his eye.

My attempts at discretion were unnecessary, however. Even farcical. As soon as he saw me I heard him say 'I think Aitken is gesturing to me. Not sure why the fellow won't come directly over. Let me see what he wants.'

He left the table and approached me with a broad smile.

News of our meeting would surely be with Asquith within the hour. Montagu, who was one of the dinner party, was playing both sides in this fencing match. His wife, the former Venetia Stanley, was known to have been Asquith's lover until she had married his ugliest colleague last year and converted to Judaism to seal the marriage. How did Montagu look Asquith in the eye after that? And yet Asquith had treated him fairly and even promoted him to the Cabinet. The even-handedness of the man was admirable in the circumstances.

'I have Law in a taxicab outside. He wants to speak.'

'Good, good.'

He returned to the table and asked his fellow diners to excuse him. 'Thank you, gentlemen. A pleasure as always. I'm sorry to leave you but a matter has arisen that needs my attention.'

We left the dining-room and joined Law in the car.

All three of us remained silent on the short journey back to my rooms. Again the slow climb to the fourth floor. Both men entered, removed their coats, and sat in adjacent armchairs by the fire. I called down for some drinks (Law wanted tea, Lloyd George some lemonade). I needed a whiskey. Law lit one of his filthy cigars. And then the trading began.

I later heard that Lloyd George had by this time received a written response from Asquith but decided not to allude to it in this conversation. He and Law simply covered the same ground they had mapped out earlier in the day. But there seemed to be a new sense of engagement in Law now. He again made the case to Lloyd George for retaining Asquith as head of the Government. But now Lloyd George demurred. In all his previous dealings with Law, Lloyd George had taken great care to emphasise that Asquith was to remain as Prime Minister under any new arrangement. But now for the first time he no longer pressed that point. In fact he had moved beyond it and was testing whether Law had too. In the hesitant tone of Law's continuing claim that Asquith must stay on as premier, Lloyd George could read the language of transition. Law's claim was no longer offered with sincerity. Lloyd George knew then that Law had abandoned Asquith. He respected the fact that Law could not say so openly, particularly given the messages he had received from his Unionist colleagues the previous day.

But if Law was not prepared to be open about his change of mind, why had he insisted on seeing Lloyd George so urgently?

He was, in fact, speaking the universal language of politics. Ignore my words. Read my gestures. Interpret my silences.

Lloyd George read him like a book.

They parted at midnight with Lloyd George promising to forward Asquith's response as soon as he received it. This was not quite a lie but not quite the truth either. He was biding his time with Law. Let him sleep on this, turn things over. Tomorrow was time enough to bring matters to a head.

Saturday 2 December 1916 — Colonial Office, Whitehall

Early that morning Law arrived at his department to find a letter from the War Office marked 'Urgent and Most Private'. Lloyd George's handwriting was on the envelope. He sat at his desk and hesitated before opening it. He was right to hesitate because his life would never be the same again after reading it. The envelope contained a copy of Asquith's response to Lloyd George with a simple covering letter which read:

> War Office
> Whitehall, SW
> December 2nd, 1916

My dear Bonar,

I enclose copy of PM's letter.

The life of the country depends on resolute action by you now.

> Yours ever,
> D. Lloyd George

– 20 –

Saturday 2 December 1916 — Hyde Park Hotel

Aitken wrote in his strange spidery longhand.

Late on Saturday evening. Writing this brief note to record the day's events. I will elaborate upon them later but for the moment just to record them. The plates are shifting and the end of the game is at hand. By this day next week I will have forgotten what this felt like minute-by-minute so these notes are important.

I saw Lloyd George first thing this morning. The Prime Minister's reply had arrived; in fact Lloyd George now told me that he had it with him the previous evening when he spoke to Law. He proposed sending to him now under a cover letter that would force Law's hand.

The press was particularly bad for the Government this morning. A leader in the *Daily Mail* attacking the Prime Minister directly. 'The Limpits: A National Danger'. 'Limpits' is an old nickname for Asquith and his allies that arose from a dispute about the naval estimates some years ago. But to call the PM a 'national danger' was taking matters very far indeed. The other papers were more restrained but no less critical. *The Morning Post* denounced not only Asquith for his conduct of the war but also Law for supporting him.

This would of course all be attributed to me, and not wholly unfairly. I had some influence with the *Daily Express* and had also briefed Sir Robert Donald of the *Daily Chronicle* about what was happening. Both the *Express* and the *Chronicle* suggested a new War Council and they both named Lloyd George, Bonar Law and Carson as the vital members of such a body. The Prime Minister would not enjoy reading this over his breakfast.

But the *Express* was more alarmist and nearer the mark. It was the first newspaper to indicate not only that major political change was necessary but also that it was in fact about to erupt:

A great political crisis has arisen in the last twenty-four hours. Nothing is certain except that the crisis which has been developing for some time is now upon us. The lack of unity which has characterised the deliberations of the Coalition Cabinet is no Cabinet secret. The war is the one thing that counts, and here it is generally felt that the Government has shown lack of initiative and courage. Here must be the change.

I couldn't have put this better myself even though, despite many rumours to the contrary, I had *not* in fact written the *Express's* editorial that day.

If the *Express* was bad for Asquith, the *Morning Post* was just as difficult for Law. That newspaper's leader accused the Colonial Secretary of co-operating with those Conservative ministers who supported Asquith and the existing (hopeless) system for managing the war. They also accused him of being a half-hearted and indecisive adherent of Lloyd George.

Of course the great panjandrum in all this newspaper activity is Lord Northcliffe, who controls both the *Daily Mail* and *The Times*. Where does he stand in all this? It remains something of a mystery to me. Certainly the *Mail* was unequivocal in its denunciation of the present arrangements. But *The Times* was the newspaper of record. And *The Times* did not pronounce.

Northcliffe holds all politicians in utter contempt but he holds Lloyd George in marginally less contempt than Asquith. Although I had urged Lloyd George to get closer to Northcliffe, he found this advice difficult to accept. He must have felt that for Northcliffe to support him would cause great problems with the Liberal press and, by extension, with Lloyd George's own party. So he had to tread very carefully in his dealings with Northcliffe on these matters.

I had therefore been greatly surprised the previous morning to see Northcliffe and Lloyd George together at the War Office. I passed them quite by chance in the corridor and nodded to them both but received nothing more than a cursory nod in return from Lloyd George. From Northcliffe I received no acknowledgement at all.

But by Saturday morning things had changed. After Lloyd George had sent his masterly 'life of the country' letter to Law he met with Northcliffe once again at the War Office. Whatever was said at that meeting remains a mystery, but two things arose directly from it. First it became clear that Lloyd George had not told Northcliffe that Law was now 'on side'. He must have felt that to reveal this and risk its publication might have pushed Law so far that he would bolt back and re-join his own Conservative ministers in support of Asquith. In this Lloyd George was playing Law to perfection. It was a most impressive exercise in balancing colleagues, press and enemies in complete equilibrium.

The second result of the meeting was an article in that day's *Evening News*, another newspaper controlled by Northcliffe. I passed a poster in the street as I left the office at about four o'clock: its headline said 'Lloyd George packing up'. The article indicated quite clearly that the War Secretary was contemplating resignation if the War Committee was not restructured as he had proposed.

What was Asquith to make of all this?

* * *

In fact Asquith was to make very little of it. He was at that moment motoring through the Kent countryside on his way to Walmer. Margot and Puffin had gone ahead of him by train but he had asked Daniels to prepare the motor and drive him down. It would take at least four hours by road and Asquith intended to use the time to think. But actually just outside the dreary suburb of Lewisham the Prime Minister had propped a cushion by the side of his head and fallen asleep. He awoke in the dark just as they reached Dover and set off for Deal.

He had lunched at Downing Street with Reading and Hankey. Lord Reading, Rufus Isaacs, the former Attorney General and one-time suspect (along with Lloyd George, no less) in the Marconi share-dealing scandal, was now Lord Chief Justice of England. He took his judicial duties seriously but had no reservations about maintaining his former political contacts. Reading was one of the men with whom Asquith felt most relaxed in company, although he refrained from referring to Reading's Jewishness in the easy way that he did about Montagu's. Montagu was always 'the Assyrian'.

Reading reacted with shock when Asquith told him of his plan to spend the weekend at Walmer.

'You can't be serious.'

'Of course I'm serious. Why wouldn't I be serious? I need to think and I think best on the coast.'

'In case you haven't noticed it, Prime Minister, you're in the middle of the biggest political crisis since the Lords business five years ago.'

'This is nothing like the Lords, Isaacs.'

'It bloody well is, PM.'

Asquith looked at him sharply. He did not like bad language. Particularly in this house.

'Asquith, I must be frank. This is deeply, deeply serious. And it is likely to reach a crisis point this weekend. Have you read the papers this morning?'

'Of course I have. I always read them. First thing.'

'You saw what they say?'

'I've really given up paying attention to them, Isaacs. It's been like this for two years now. They've criticised me every day since Christmas 1914. As soon as they knew the war wasn't going to end quickly they turned their fire on the Government. That's what newspapers do. I've always thought it best to ignore them.'

'But Christ Almighty, PM., you can't ignore them now.'

Again Asquith glared. He particularly disliked profanity. Although it always amused him that Isaacs used the Christian form of profanity so readily.

'Look, Henry, please listen to me.' Isaacs was one of the few men allowed very occasionally to address the PM by his Christian name.

'The newspapers aren't getting this from nowhere. It's obviously a campaign. It's Lloyd George at work and he's using that little shit Aitken to brief against you in the press. This is much worse than the stuff they get up to every week. You have to look behind and see the pattern. Lloyd George tried to push you. You pushed back. He pushed again, harder. You pushed back. It's clear that he has Law with him but he doesn't have the other Unionists – yet. So he works up the press to put pressure on the Tories to read the popular mood. Need for a new man, new vim, all that stuff. He's attacking you on multiple fronts now. You've got to shove back. And hard. If you go away for the weekend you can rest assured that you'll be in a much more dangerous situation when you get back here on Monday morning. If you actually get back here at all.'

Asquith continued to stare across the table.

Hankey held back.

'Isaacs. I'm going to Walmer. Carson is on the coast for the weekend and I want to speak to him about this.'

Carson? On the coast? What nonsense was this?

'And breaking my plans would be a sign of panic and that's exactly what Lloyd George wants to see. He wants to see me panic. He wants to be able to tell his friends and the newspapers that I'm panicking. In particular, he wants to show Law and Curzon and Cecil and Chamberlain that I'm panicking. The Liberal ranks are solid so David can only move against me if he gets the Unionists to think that I'm panicking. Well I'm not. And they won't. I'm going to Walmer and I'll be back on Monday.'

The Prime Minister stood up and both Reading and Hankey did the same. He removed his napkin, folded it neatly, and placed it on the table. Then he left the room.

Both Reading and Hankey resumed their seats as the door closed behind him.

'What do we do now?' Hankey asked.

'We go to see the principals. The main men. In this 'coup'.'

'Meaning?'

'I'm going to see Lloyd George. I'll call on Montagu and get him to come with me. I'll telephone you after I've seen him and then you must go and see Law.'

'And say what to him?'

'I'll tell you after I've seen Lloyd George. Go back to the War Office and wait for my call.'

The Lord Chief Justice rose and left the room.

Hankey folded his napkin and sat in silence for a few minutes. He felt numb. For the first time in his many years of managing the Government's military committees he was not only speechless but unable to think as well. Could this really be the end? As he walked through the front door of Number 10 he saw the Prime Minister's car leave Downing Street and turn right into Whitehall. From there it would turn left at Parliament Square, cross Westminster Bridge, and head for the country.

He walked back to the War Office.

* * *

Reading met Lloyd George together with Montagu. It was an exasperating meeting.

'You can't be serious, David?'

'Deadly serious, Rufus. Never been more serious in my life.'

'You know he agrees with you on virtually everything?'

Lloyd George smiled. 'He agrees with me on everything that doesn't matter. On the points that matter he agrees with nothing I say. So it has to change.'

'Where are you apart, David? Where do you disagree?'

'Come on, Rufus. You know this by now. I must be chairman of the War Council. Not just me in person, David Lloyd George, but me as War Secretary. The War Secretary has to direct the war. The War Council runs the war. The War Secretary has to direct the War Council in running the war. I am the War Secretary. I must chair the War Council.'

'And the PM?'

'We've been over this, Rufus. I'm weary of going over it. The PM runs the government, chairs the Cabinet, leads Parliament. The War Secretary runs the War Council with complete executive authority for running the war. If the PM or the Cabinet don't like what he's doing then they can appoint another War Secretary. But they can't appoint a man one day and then say on the next that he's not allowed to do what they appointed him to do. Hopeless.'

Isaacs stared across at Montagu. Montagu spoke.

'And the other point of difference between you?'

'Balfour cannot remain as First Lord. He's hopeless. We need a vigorous man there. A man of action. Not Balfour. Somewhere else in the Cabinet for him, fine. But not as First Lord.'

'Carson?'

'Possibly.'

'Churchill?'

'Absolutely not. Winston has shot himself in the foot over and over since the war began. No, not Winston.'

'Law?'

'No, he's needed elsewhere.'

'Curzon?'

'You must be joking.'

'So Carson then?'

'Perhaps.'

Then Isaacs spoke again, this time in a lower voice. 'David, are you trying to overthrow the PM?'

Lloyd George sank back into his chair. The smile had left his face. The twinkle was gone from his eyes. He stared directly back at Reading.

'No, Rufus, I am not trying to overthrow the PM.'

A pause.

'But the PM is on very thin ice here and he knows it. If he denies me the capacity to run the war he risks not only reversing my career but of annihilating his own.'

'Annihilating?' This was Montagu. 'A bit strong surely?'

'Not in my hands, Montagu. All in the PM's hands now.'

'And Law's.'

'No, not really. Law knows where he stands. The other Unionists need to do their own thinking. But Bonar knows where he stands.'

They all remained silent until Lloyd George spoke again.

'Where is the PM now?'

'Gone to Walmer.'

'Ah.'

Reading spoke again. 'David, in the absence of the PM from London may I have your word that you won't resign today? And that you will say nothing in public or take any irreversible action until you've met with Asquith again?'

Lloyd George paused for a moment and then replied 'Yes.'

'Thank you.'

'You know that the Unionists are meeting tomorrow.'

'I do.'

'I'll speak with Law after that and we can judge the best way of proceeding at that stage.'

'And you'll talk to Asquith again before taking any action?'

'I will. But I think you should advise him that it might be wiser for him to be in Downing Street rather than spending a weekend on the coast. At this stage.'

He rose and thanked them for calling on him and then showed them to the door.

* * *

Reading telephoned Hankey to tell him of his meeting with Lloyd George and the commitment he had extracted from him not to resign that day. But Reading was in no doubt now that Lloyd George would quite definitely resign if no agreement was reached with Asquith by the beginning of the following week.

Hankey told Law about the meeting.

Law responded, 'I'm seeing my own colleagues tomorrow. You know that?'

'I do.'

'They are very strongly of the opinion that the PM should stay and that Lloyd George's bluff must be called.'

'If his bluff is called he will resign.'

'Are you sure of that?'

'Reading and Montagu are sure. They've just seen him.'

'Well, I don't know. You can never tell with Lloyd George.'

A silence. Then Law spoke again.

'Where is the PM now?'

'On his way to Walmer.'

'Oh God. Out of London? At a time like this?'

'I know.'

'Get him back, Hankey. Get him back straight away. This will all be settled by tomorrow evening. Tell Asquith that I advise him most strongly to leave Walmer now and be back in Downing Street tomorrow once my party meeting is over. You'll do that?'

'I will, Secretary of State.'

'Good. Thank you.'

* * *

'Bonham Carter?'

'Speaking.'

'Montagu here. I need to see you straight away.'

'What is it?'

'The PM is in Walmer?'

'Yes, he is.'

'We need him back.'

A moment's hesitation.

'What is it? Something in France?'

'Much closer to home. We need him back straight away. Can you get a car and follow him down to Kent?'

'I'll try. I should be able to. What do you want me to say to him?'

'I'm writing a letter now. I'll have it with you in thirty minutes. You need to hand it to him in person.'

'I will.'

'This is vital, Maurice. We must have him back in London straight away.'

And then, the telephone back in its cradle, Montagu reached for a page of Downing Street notepaper and wrote:

10 Downing Street
London S.W.
Saturday 2 December 1916
5 o'clock

Dear Prime Minister,

Lord Reading and I met with the War Secretary this afternoon. He is intent upon resigning immediately if you do not reconsider his proposals to reconstruct the War Committee. We do not believe that this is an act of brinkmanship on his part. He had intended to resign today but we have persuaded him to take no action until he has spoken with you. Hankey saw Bonar Law this afternoon and, as you know, Law proposes to consult again with the Unionist ministers tomorrow morning. Lord Reading and I therefore believe it is MOST URGENT that you should return to London this evening or early tomorrow morning. I am taking the liberty of sending Bonham Carter in a car to Walmer to deliver this note to you in person.

Yours sincerely,
Edwin Montagu

– 21 –

Sunday 3 December 1916 — 10 Downing Street

Lord Crewe had breakfast alone on Sunday morning before setting out for church and then on to Number 10. He sat through Communion at the Grosvenor Chapel (the parson was dull beyond words; he really had to go) and then walked down to Whitehall. It was a beautiful winter's morning, bright sunshine, crisp, clean air. London at its very best, the capital of the world. But an early morning request from the Prime Minister, delivered to his door by a servant from Downing Street, had warned him that this would be a difficult day.

Robert Offley Ashburton Crewe-Milnes collected titles as promiscuously as he collected Cabinet appointments. Created Marquess of Crewe and Earl of Madeley in 1911, he had been Earl of Crewe since 1895 and merely Baron Crewe for a year before that. On his father's death in 1885 he had become Baron Houghton. He had served as Lord Lieutenant of Ireland, Lord President of the Council, Secretary of State for the Colonies, Leader of the House of Lords, Secretary of State for India, and was now, once again, Lord President of the Council. He was one of the last surviving Whigs in the modern Liberal party and a friend of the King's. He was also one of Asquith's closest and most discreet advisers and, in effect, the PM's private line to the Palace. He despised Lloyd George and everything he stood for.

He had rarely seen Asquith flustered but the man who greeted him at Number 10 was not in a calm frame of mind. Asquith greatly resented being summoned back from his weekend away. Bonham Carter had arrived in Walmer at nine the previous evening. The PM was not pleased to receive Montagu's note but agreed that he would return. Bonham Carter was fed and given a room for the night on the understanding that they would set out for London at nine the following morning. He had breakfast with the family at eight and found Margot more understanding than her husband of the need for him to return to London.

'Are we in difficulty, Bongie?' she asked.

'I fear we are, Margot, yes.'

'Will we prevail?'

He was silent. She knew then that it was serious.

'Every chance. But he needs to nip this in the bud. We must have him back in London.'

'I see.'

She turned away and returned to her bedroom. She and Puffin would stay until the afternoon. She didn't want the routine disturbed any more than was necessary.

At first Asquith had said little on the journey back to London. For thirty minutes he studied an editorial in that morning's *Reynold's* newspaper. It was even harsher than yesterday's press had been. Lloyd George, it said, was insisting on his changes. He was prepared to resign if they were not granted and would then appeal to the country against the Government for mismanaging the war. It was understood that he was in open alliance with Carson and that both Bonar Law and Lord Derby, Lloyd George's Unionist deputy at the War Office, were likely to resign with him.

It was the tone of the article rather than its content that disturbed Asquith. The content could be dismissed as speculation but the article almost read as a direct interview, with the newspaperman punting soft questions in his direction and Lloyd George responding with carefully prepared and planted answers.

'You've read it?' Asquith asked.

'I have, PM.'

'What do you think?'

'It's damaging.'

'Is it true?'

'About Lloyd George? I don't know. At the very least it's a tremendous bluff. But Montagu and Reading are convinced he is on the point of going if you…if…if he doesn't realise his objectives.'

'Just chairman or my job too?'

'I honestly don't know, PM.'

The policeman at the door saluted as Asquith stepped out of the car. The Prime Minister raised his hat and managed a smile for the sightseers who waited in Downing Street to watch ministers come and go. He went straight to the Cabinet room where Montagu awaited him. A servant took his coat and hat and Asquith asked for some tea in his study.

'Lord Crewe?'

'On his way. He'll join us for lunch. A little late.'

'Lunch in fifteen minutes. Please join us.'

'Yes, PM.'

The Prime Minister went upstairs to the residence where he washed and changed his clothes. The tea revived him only a little. Then along the narrow corridor to the family dining room where Montagu again waited for him. They sat to eat and Asquith asked him to recount again the events of yesterday. Montagu had just finished his account when there was a knock on the door and Lord Crewe was admitted.

'Prime Minister. Montagu. Good morning – no – good afternoon.'

'Robert, thank you for joining us. I apologise for dragging you away on a Sunday.'

'Not at all. You've travelled farther. What's going on? Lloyd George?'

'You've seen *Reynold's*?'

'I have. He's raising the stakes now.'

'Indeed. Edwin, I apologise for the repetition but would you mind telling Lord Crewe what you've just told me about yesterday's meetings.'

Montagu told the story again. As he did, Asquith sat back in his chair and thought. He had begun to feel crushingly tired. He needed to rest. But this was not the time.

'I see,' said Crewe. 'Well, he really is serious then.'

'What do you think, Robert?'

'It's a nasty bind, Prime Minister, but you really only have one option. You must carry on as you've been doing. I can't fault any part of the offer you made to him last Friday. It's quite the correct thing to do. It would be completely impossible for anyone other than the Prime Minister to chair the War Committee. Lloyd George isn't stupid. He knows that. He's just pushing you to get better terms for himself. And I don't think he's trying to topple you – he doesn't have the support. Law is with you despite all the nonsense in *Reynold's*. Carson is an irrelevance. And the other Unionists in the Cabinet are solidly behind you. So it's not possible for Lloyd George to unseat you. Stand your ground, firm but fair, accommodating but solid on the essentials.'

Montagu knew that Crewe was right. Asquith really had no choice if he wasn't to turn himself into some kind of political eunuch. But he also knew that Lloyd George was determined to push. Was he taking a monumental gamble? Or did he know something they didn't?

'I agree with you, Robert. I'll see him this evening – I know we can settle this. Although I'm not sure we can agree on personnel. Law would be sound on the committee but he has no imagination. Carson would be hopeless and would resign in a matter of months. Henderson, good man, but no fighting spirit. It will take us some time to agree on the personnel but the key issue is the Prime Minister's role on the committee. I must chair it, and if David cannot agree to that then he must go.'

A silence.

Then Asquith spoke again. 'Do you think it would help if you went to see him this afternoon before I meet him? To clear the air?'

Crewe would have done anything for Asquith but he had to advise against this. 'It's really a matter between you and him now, PM. Law too, but only as a messenger from the Unionists. This is you and Lloyd George. I'm sure you'll reach an accommodation with him but if you can't then I'm afraid that one of you will most certainly have to go. And of course that will be Lloyd George.'

The same day — Pembroke Lodge

The noise from downstairs was growing louder by the minute. The meeting was proving more heated than either of us had anticipated. A brief lull was followed by another series of shouts and the sound of chairs moving and a door slamming. Then the heavy tread of Bonar Law on the wooden stairs and his unannounced entry into the room in which I awaited him. As the room was his own study in his own house I could make no complaint about this. But I had been growing concerned for over half an hour now, and I awaited news of the meeting with mounting apprehension. It did not sound as if things had gone very well.

The Unionist ministers had gathered at Bonar Law's house at midday, all except Balfour and Lansdowne. The former prime minister was at home in his sickbed but Lansdowne was even more strangely detained. He was passing the weekend at, of all places, the country house of the Foreign Secretary, Edward Grey, recently translated to the Lords as Viscount Grey of Kedleston. And so, at a moment of high drama for his party and his country, the man who wanted to sue for peace was lunching outside London with the man who had taken us into the war. Truly this was a peculiar country.

Bonar Law fell heavily into his chair. He held out a piece of paper and asked me to read it. I did and all my anxieties were confirmed.

'This would be disastrous, Bonar.'

'I know.'

'And it is intended for Asquith? Now?'

'It is.'

'How did this happen?'

The Unionist ministers' meeting had begun in bad temper. I reached Law's house shortly after 11 and found him finishing breakfast with his sister. He asked me to stay while the meeting took place but to remain in his study while the ministers met in the drawing room downstairs. Given the chaos being created in the press he thought the presence of another press man – me – might ignite their tempers even more. They were all furious at what had appeared in *Reynold's* that morning.

It was Curzon who started the onslaught, Law told me. A continuation of Thursday. Didn't Law know the character of the man he was dealing with? Lloyd George was out for himself through and through. The *Reynold's* piece had obviously been enunciated directly by him to its Liberal proprietor, Lord Dalziel, who had written it down as straight dictation and then printed it *verbatim*. It was an outrage.

Chamberlain and Long joined in the chorus of condemnation. Cecil was apoplectic. It was time to put a stop to this whole damn nonsense. Men were fighting and dying and here was His Majesty's Government engaged in a shameful bout of infighting and naked politics. Time to get a grip. Time for Law to get a grip, and Asquith too.

Law listened in stony silence. He had undertaken to hear them out before responding. It was Cecil who proposed that a note should be sent to Asquith in their names. He took some paper and a pen and sat at a small writing table to compose it.

'Gentlemen, before I draft something, can I please make sure that we are all now absolutely clear about our intentions,' he said.

'Lloyd George must be stopped in his tracks.' This was Curzon.

'Asquith must get a grip.' Long.

'We need to call his bluff. Lloyd George's bluff. He has no support in our party and precious little in his own. Asquith has indulged him for far too long. Now he needs to act.'

Long again. 'Asquith needs to reconstruct. Call in the seals from all his Ministers and start again. Reconstruct his Cabinet. Without Lloyd George at the War Office.'

'No, Walter. Not enough. That won't do it.'

This was Chamberlain.

'He did that last year when he formed the coalition. He called in the resignations of all his ministers but stayed in office himself. Reconstructed without putting himself at risk.'

'But he wasn't at any risk then and he isn't at risk now either.'

'And that's the point, Walter. He's *not* at any risk from Lloyd George or anyone else. So if he's not at risk then he should *take* a risk. Or at least appear to.'

'What do you mean?'

Chamberlain explained. 'Asquith needs to give his resignation to the King. His own resignation. That brings down the Government. We need to show Lloyd George that he may have the press baying against the Coalition but he has no support in the Commons. He won't be able to form a Government and that's the very reason he must be invited to.

'Asquith resigns. The King calls for Lloyd George. Lloyd George fails. Asquith returns stronger than ever.'

'Exactly.'

Oh my God, thought Law. The very worst possible outcome.

So Cecil wrote:

We share the view expressed to you by Mr Bonar Law some time ago that the Government cannot continue as it is. It is evident that a change must be made, and, in our opinion, the publicity given to the intention of Mr Lloyd George makes reconstruction from within no longer possible. We therefore urge the Prime Minister to tender the resignation of the Government. If he feels unable to take that step, we authorise Mr Bonar Law to tender our resignations.

Then Law spoke.

'Gentlemen, if this is your consensus view then of course I will take it to the Prime Minister. You've drafted a very straightforward memorandum, Robert. I understand, indeed I share your frustration at the dangerous nonsense in *Reynold's* this morning, but I am very reluctant to personalise the matter on Lloyd George in writing and I urge you...'

'No, Bonar. No.'

This was Long.

'We *need* to deprecate Lloyd George. Our note will be released to the press by Asquith. We need to be seen to be tendering not just dry advice about reconstruction but very pointed political advice that deprecates Lloyd George. We need to say that Lloyd George has caused this crisis, that he must be tested and found wanting, and that Asquith has our full support in doing that.'

'I agree,' said Chamberlain.

'As do I.' Cecil.

'I too.' Curzon.

At which stage Law asked for five minutes to clear his head, left the room, and joined me in the study upstairs.

I was full of sympathy for the awful position he found himself in. Half of his party, the senior half, the ministers, wanted Lloyd George rejected and full support offered to Asquith. The radical half, the backbenchers under Carson, wanted Asquith destroyed and Lloyd George to head the Government. Law led from the middle. The need to stay close to his senior colleagues required him to continue supporting Asquith but I knew (although he hadn't yet told me this directly) that his centre of gravity had by now swung to Lloyd George. He wanted Asquith to go but in a cushioned and dignified way, with good grace, honourably. If Asquith didn't understand this then he, Law, would be prepared to apply firmer pressure. His heart was now with Lloyd George and he wanted no association with any statement that would insult and provoke the man he wanted to run both the country and the war. He knew that his Unionist colleagues would bolt to Lloyd George as soon as the political wind changed. All the memoranda, communiqués, letters and other correspondence would be forgotten as soon as a new premier had emerged. But now, today, Law wanted nothing to do with that kind of language. What was he to do?

I shared his horror at the draft, not only because I thought it was an insult to Lloyd George, but also because the tactic might just work. It might actually achieve what neither Law nor I wanted. It might embolden Asquith to resign and watch Lloyd George fail. Which he would do if the Unionists stuck to their public posturing in support of the Prime Minister. I wanted Asquith out as much as Carson and (less openly) Law did, but this memorandum might actually save him.

Law needed the meeting to end so that he could think about what to do next. He returned to the drawing room and told his colleagues that he would see the Prime Minister that afternoon and advise him of their sentiments. The meeting broke up and the ministers scattered to their Sunday lunches.

And so in order to support Asquith the Unionist ministers were now telling him bluntly that he must now resign. Never was a communiqué – even without the studied insult to Lloyd George – more likely to cause confusion and offence.

As indeed it did. But for an altogether different reason.

Law wanted to honour the memorandum as drafted despite his reservations about the offending sentence. I pleaded with him to remove the reference to Lloyd George. He resisted with some heat. I implored him to seek further advice and he eventually agreed to have F. E. Smith, the Attorney General, review the memorandum. Smith came to Pembroke Lodge after lunch and read it. His advice was quite clear: the sentence must stay. The communiqué must remain as drafted: Law had no power to alter it now. He must take it to the Prime Minister in the form in which the ministers had agreed it.

Law accepted this advice and Smith and I then left. Law was to see the Prime Minister in Downing Street at three o'clock.

He motored first to the Colonial Office and then walked the short distance to Number 10.

Just outside the Banqueting Hall he retrieved the memorandum from his inside pocket, folded it carefully, and tore it into a dozen pieces. The fragments were dropped quietly onto the pavement along Whitehall where they soon washed into the gutter.

– 22 –

Sunday 3 December 1916 — Cabinet Room, 10 Downing Street

'Bonar.'

'Prime Minister.'

'Please, come in.'

Asquith was seated in the chair with the arms. He gestured to Law to take the seat opposite him at the Cabinet table. No offer of tea or other refreshments then. Straight in.

'So, a productive weekend, Bonar?'

'I have other ways of describing it, Prime Minister.'

They both smiled.

Then Asquith. 'I had hoped for a quiet weekend on the coast but it was not to be. The newspapers are getting quite agitated. And you've met your colleagues this morning. A good meeting?'

Law hesitated. Cleared his throat. Tried to clear his mind.

'A difficult meeting, Prime Minister. I have a message for you from my colleagues. Let me tell you what it is as they dictated it and we can then discuss it.'

Asquith was perplexed although he restrained his bemusement. 'As they dictated it?' This man was the leader of the second party in the country. And he took dictation from his colleagues? It was most unusual. But very little surprised him any more about Law's circumambulatory style of leadership.

'Who attended the meeting, may I ask?'

'Curzon, Chamberlain and Cecil. Also Long, Crawford and Duke. Not Balfour – he's at home in his bed, sick. And not Lansdowne either. He's in the country with Edward Grey this weekend.'

'Neither Balfour nor Lansdowne sent any message to the meeting?'

'They did not.'

'And Derby?'

Lord Derby was Under-Secretary of State at the War Office. Known to admire Lloyd George. There had been some discussion of having Derby at the meeting: he was a powerful figure in the Unionist Party, widely known, widely respected. Lloyd George thought he was a hopeless buffoon. But a useful one. In the end Law had taken the view that it might be seen as favouring Lloyd George to have Derby attend the meeting. He decided against him also on the grounds that to have invited one minister who was not a member of the Cabinet would have required inviting all the other Unionist under-secretaries. Best to keep the meeting tight. So Derby had been excluded.

'No, Prime Minister. Not Lord Derby.'

'I see.'

Both men paused.

'Well you'd better tell me what your colleagues decided then, Bonar.'

'I'll put it as plainly as I can, PM. First, we are all agreed that the current arrangements are completely inadequate for any proper conduct of the war and require quite radical overhauling.'

'I agree.'

'We believe that the best way of resolving the matter is for the Government to resign.'

'For me to reconstruct?'

Law hesitated.

'No, Prime Minister. For the whole Government to resign. Including you.'

Asquith stared at him as he announced this conclusion. A faint ringing began in his ears, rising gently but steadily in volume so that when Law spoke again Asquith could no longer hear him. He saw the lips moving but could no longer hear what he was saying. The ringing in his ears grew louder and shriller as Law's lips moved without sound. He became aware as well of a creeping numbness in his arm, his left arm, anchoring it to the side of the chair. He tightened his grip and watched as Law's lips stopped moving. The ringing in his ears began slowly to subside. It grew fainter and fainter as the tingling in his arm receded too. Asquith returned to the room. He was aware that Law was staring at him, awaiting his response.

'I'm sorry Bonar. Would you mind saying that again? Your colleagues want me to resign? To return my seals to the King and invite him to find another Prime Minister?'

'Yes.'

'And then who? You?'

'Not me, PM. I don't want the damn job. Not up to it. Never will be.'

'So…Lloyd George?'

'Yes.'

Again Asquith said nothing. No more ringing or tingling, thank God. But he needed to think quickly now.

'Would you and your colleagues support him if he tried to form a ministry?'

Here Law hesitated. He looked at Asquith with a puzzled expression.

'Didn't you hear what I said just now?'

'If you would repeat it, please. This is unexpected.'

'I said that my colleagues have no expectation at all that he'll be able to form a ministry. They advise you to resign so that the King will send for Lloyd George. He will make an attempt and fail. If the King were then to send for me I assure you I would decline the commission. If – when – Lloyd George fails, the King will send for you. And you will then return as Prime Minister and could deal with Lloyd George and his allies exactly as you please.'

Asquith stared out the window. This was not what he had expected. There was a further question.

'If I were to do this and Lloyd George tried to form a ministry, would you agree to serve under him? Not your colleagues – you say they will decline and support me. But would *you* serve under Lloyd George?'

Damn the man, Law thought. There's never any way around him. He's too clever. Never any way around. Well then, the only way forward is straight through him.

'I would not support him if I thought he had no hope of forming

173

a ministry. If I felt he had then I would have to consider the position at that time.'

The knife went straight in through Asquith's side.

He paused before speaking again. Stared at Law. Then:

'Well, I appreciate your candour, Bonar. As always. But I think we can work this out by negotiation and compromise. Without reconstructing the Government.'

'I'm afraid that is no longer an option, Prime Minister. My colleagues have also instructed me to tell you that if you decline to resign I must give you the resignations of all the Unionist members of the Government.'

'But I would re-appoint you all immediately.'

'I think, Prime Minister, that if you try to call in the resignations of every minister except yourself and form a new Government as you did last year, my colleagues might not be as ready to serve under you as they would be if you follow the procedure we are suggesting.'

'Of resigning myself and letting Lloyd George try to form a ministry?'

'Indeed.'

Oh Christ, Asquith thought. That it has come to this.

He knew that in politics the truth is very often the absolute opposite of the facts as they present himself. Law was telling him that he, Law, might not in fact support him but that the Unionist ministers were solidly behind Asquith. In fact it had been Asquith's assessment that Law was his closest ally in the Unionist party but that Law's colleagues were far less solid in their support for him than was now being suggested. A Prime Minister must never resign in the kind of speculative way that Law was proposing. He must never, ever, relax his hold on the prime position. Law's colleagues were suggesting that he should ease his grip so that Lloyd George would try and fail. But Asquith knew with every instinct of his political being that while Lloyd George had absolutely no chance of success whilst Asquith sat in this chair he would quickly find himself having *every* chance of success if Asquith were ever to absent himself, however briefly and temporarily, from Number 10. No, a tactical resignation could only be fatal. Under no circumstances would he resign.

Resignation could only mean departure. And Asquith had no intention of departing. None whatsoever.

He needed to end the meeting now, and quickly.

'Thank you. That makes the position perfectly clear. I will see Lloyd George and discuss the matter further.'

'And what will I tell my colleagues?'

'My dear Bonar, tell them anything you like. You've conveyed their message to the Prime Minister. The Prime Minister is considering it. He will advise them and all of his ministerial colleagues of his decision in due course.'

'I am instructed to convey all our resignations to you if you decide not to resign yourself.'

'I understand the position, Bonar, but I think you might at least allow me the courtesy of considering my own position first. I do not decline to accept your resignations: I have merely not agreed to receive them yet. There will be time enough for that.'

He had been dismissed. Law rose and left. For the second time that day he was leaving a meeting unclear as to its outcome but with a mounting sense that he was no longer in control of events.

* * *

I stayed with Lloyd George at the War Office while Law saw the PM. Lloyd George had called me at lunchtime to ask what the Conservative ministers had decided and I told him as diplomatically as I could. I could not avoid mentioning the rebuke they had delivered to him in their memorandum but he laughed it off.

'Politics, Max. Dirty business.'

Lloyd George remained in infectiously good humour as we waited. It was a Sunday and therefore (he claimed) it was wholly appropriate for him to sing some Welsh hymns from the Valleys. The secretaries at work outside his office had heard it all before and paid us no attention.

When Law returned I told him that I had already briefed Lloyd George about the meeting of Unionist ministers. Law was not in a good mood.

'Not really your place to have done that, Max.'

'But you asked me to tell him, Bonar.'

'Yes, well, perhaps I did. Anyway, George, now you know.'

Lloyd George hated being referred to as George. Law was usually quite scrupulous about using both his names. It was a measure of the pressure he was under that he had dropped back to the single name.

'How did he take it?'

'I don't know. Seemed a bit shaken. Not sure that the prospect of resignation had ever crossed his mind before. Reconstruction, yes. But not resignation. I told him – as I've told you quite frankly as well – that my colleagues will support him. But I'm not sure he believes me.'

Clever man, thought Lloyd George. No fool, Asquith.

'I think he will want to compromise with you. Move away from his insistence on chairing the committee. He wants to see you later in the day.'

'Well, let's see what he says then.'

I asked Law whether he had told Carson about the interview. He stared at me with a look that advised withdrawal. I didn't press the point.

Then Law said, 'I have another meeting with my colleagues. I must go.' We said our farewells. As we parted a secretary came into the office and passed Lloyd George a note. He read it, smiled, and looked at both of us.

'Message from the Prime Minister. He would like to see me in his study at six o'clock this evening. Well then, gentlemen, the issue may resolve itself by bedtime.'

– 23 –

Given what happened at Lloyd George's meeting with Asquith that evening and the widespread surprise with which the end of the crisis (as we then thought it was) was greeted, it is important for me to be as clear as I can be about the motives of the principal actors. Let me write this down in order to clarify things.

Asquith had taken fright at Law's communication from the Conservative ministers. He was being assured that they were solidly behind him and would give him total support against Lloyd George. As such they were encouraging the Prime Minister to take a significant gamble: to resign and allow his rival to try to form a ministry in the certain (as they thought) knowledge that he would fail. Asquith would sweep back to power in the wake of Lloyd George's failure and would then deal with his challenger appropriately.

But Asquith was not a gambler. Nor was he a fool. He knew that if he relinquished his authority he would no longer be in control of events. And events were everything in politics. Things happened – unanticipated and unexpected things. No, he would not let go. He would reconstruct rather than resign. That meant reaching an accommodation with Lloyd George. Well, he was a skilled negotiator. He would have to concede more than he had given already but he had little doubt that an accommodation could be reached. He would do a deal.

And that is exactly what Asquith did.

And both Lloyd George and Law apparently agreed to the deal. Why was this?

Lloyd George went to the meeting with the calmest demeanour I have ever seen in a man on the brink of destroying his own career. Law left the War Office with him. I remained behind. What did they talk about as they walked up to Number 10? Neither man ever told me but I greatly suspect that by the time Law left Lloyd George at the gates of Downing Street they had reached an agreement. I was not a party to that agreement. Nor was Carson or indeed anybody else. Neither man ever talked about it afterwards so whatever they settled between them is lost to history. But I am certain that they reached an understanding about the way ahead.

The settlement agreed with Asquith that evening was not, and was never intended to be, the end of the crisis. As far as both Law and Lloyd George were concerned it was a manoeuvre. And, as matters turned out, a remarkably successful one.

Here is what I surmise. Law knew that his colleagues were not solid in their support for Asquith. They professed total loyalty to the Prime Minister but he knew these men. They would change sides as soon as the balance of opportunity moved their way. Law himself wanted Asquith out but could not say as much to the PM nor even hint at his preference to his colleagues. So if a deal was agreed between the principals he would have to accept it. But a deal might not last for more than twenty-four hours and any unravelling of the deal might offer him (and his colleagues also, perhaps?) the cover they needed to change their minds.

Of course Lloyd George also wanted Asquith out. But he could not be seen as the pretender who had murdered the prince. Asquith would have to destroy himself. If Lloyd George agreed to a deal and the PM subsequently repudiated it, Lloyd George would be the injured party. And then, with Unionist support, he could unseat the Prime Minister.

So he would offer Asquith a deal coated in poison. Asquith would accept it and swallow the poison. And then events would move quickly to their inevitable conclusion.

In this, as always, the press would be the key. Northcliffe and *The Times* would be the key.

I believe – but I cannot prove – that Lloyd George and Law agreed this arrangement as they walked towards Downing Street late that Sunday afternoon.

In any event, understanding or no understanding, deal or no deal, matters now moved forward very quickly.

The same day — Cabinet Room, 10 Downing Street

It was a remarkably friendly meeting. Asquith had seen Montagu before Lloyd George arrived and asked him to remain in an adjacent room and stand ready to record any agreement they might manage to reach.

This was the last occasion on which Asquith and Lloyd George would speak face-to-face and alone while Asquith was Prime Minister. Some fifteen minutes into the meeting Montagu heard laughter from the Cabinet Room. First Lloyd George, high-pitched and fast, followed immediately by Asquith, deeper and slower. Silence again. More talking. Then more laughter. Relief came flooding over Montagu in great waves of pleasure. He thought that he might cry.

Another fifteen minutes later and Montagu was asked to join them in the Cabinet Room. Both men were smiling broadly. Things had gone well.

'Well, Montagu. We have settled the matter.'

'Prime Minister, Lloyd George: I'm delighted to hear it. Delighted and, if I may say so, deeply relieved.'

'Well, yes. It has been a trying few days. But matters have ended well. Here is what we have agreed.'

'Shall I write this down, Prime Minister?'

Montagu turned to retrieve some paper from the side table.

'No, no. No need to write it down. Not at all. Gentlemen's agreement. Not a peace treaty.'

Lloyd George seemed to find this uproariously funny and broke out again into his infectious high-pitched laugh. Asquith laughed too. Montagu smiled.

'Here is what we've agreed. David, correct me if I misrepresent any of it.'

'Go ahead, Prime Minister.'

'I will reconstruct the War Committee. Now to be referred to as the War Council. Smaller membership. Names to be agreed. The War Secretary will be chairman of the War Council. He will exercise his chairmanship on the firm understanding that, while he and the Council are to have extensive authority in all matters relating to the conduct of the war, the matter of war *policy* will remain under the supreme and effective direction of the Prime Minister.'

'So the key distinction, Prime Minister, if I may just make sure that I understand it' (this was Montagu) 'is between matters of *conduct* and matters of *policy*?'

'Precisely. David and the War Council will have supreme authority in managing the war. The Prime Minister will retain supreme authority – obviously to be exercised in consultation with the Cabinet – in setting war policy.'

It was the classic politicians' compromise, Montagu thought. It was also an accommodation they might well have reached many weeks before and spared us all the drama of the last fortnight. But in the end, as in almost every political dispute, it wasn't the settlement that mattered but the process by which the settlement had been achieved. Shows of strength on both sides. Give and take. Threats and bluster. And finally an accommodation, two statesmen acting together in the best interests of the nation. Masterly.

'The agenda of each War Council meeting is to be submitted in advance to the Prime Minister. He can suggest further topics for the group to consider. The chairman is to report every day to the Prime Minister on the Council's meetings and decisions. All decisions of the Council will be subject to the Prime Minister's veto but obviously the chairman and I will work closely together to ensure that a veto never becomes necessary. We recognise that it would have drastic consequences for the work of the Council if the Prime Minister ever had to exercise a veto. As such we are committed to avoiding it come what may.'

'And the matter of your attendance, Prime Minister?' Montagu asked.

'The Prime Minister may, at his discretion, attend any meeting of the War Council that he chooses to.'

'But not to act as its chairman?'

'No. Any meeting attended by the Prime Minister will continue to be chaired by the War Secretary.'

Lloyd George added, 'That is as we've agreed it, Montagu. A good outcome, I think?'

Montagu hesitated before responding. 'One other point, Prime Minister. Membership?'

'We haven't been able to agree on the matter of membership just yet,' Asquith replied. 'Further discussion is needed on that point. We've each accepted the need to consider our respective views on this matter overnight and will discuss it further in the morning. However, let me say to you in confidence, Montagu, although I'm sure you know this already, that the main point of difference between us concerns the First Lord of the Admiralty. The War Secretary and I are agreed that the First Lord should be a member of the new War Council. I prefer to retain Mr Balfour in that role. David is pressing the claims of Sir Edward Carson.'

Lloyd George interjected. 'But we have agreed that membership of the Council should be extended from three to four and that Mr Henderson should be the fourth member.'

'We have indeed.'

A brief silence.

Then Asquith: 'Good. That's all, Montagu. Thank you. Bonar Law is joining us now to discuss some further matters. Thank you for attending and also for the invitation to Margot and me to dine with you this evening. We hope to be with you at about nine o'clock. Is that suitable?'

'Very much so, PM. I look forward to seeing you then.'

'And Mrs Montagu?'

Thin ice here. Lloyd George almost purred.

'I'm afraid she is with her sister in Hertfordshire this weekend, PM. Just me.'

Asquith smiled. 'I look forward to it. Thank you again.'

And with that Montagu departed and Law arrived. No record was kept of the discussion that followed between the three men.

* * *

But Law told me later what happened.

He claimed he was surprised to hear that a deal had been reached between them. I accepted his claim at the time but actually I no longer believe it to have been the case. It was not, he said, the outcome he had wanted, but given that Lloyd George had decided to compromise he was willing to accept the outcome. I no longer believe this either. In fact I am sure that he and Lloyd George had agreed that Lloyd George should strike a pose at his meeting with Asquith in order to be seen to be compromising, and that Law would support the deal when he was invited to join the meeting. What happened the following day bears out my view that Lloyd George's meeting with the Prime Minister that evening was a sham.

On being advised of the settlement Law then agreed that all ministers other than Asquith would resign and Asquith would reconstruct the Government on the basis of the agreement he had just reached with Lloyd George about the new War Council.

Law then left the meeting to attend a further gathering of the Unionist ministers at F. E. Smith's house. There he was roundly condemned by his colleagues for allowing such an appalling outcome to arise. Asquith still in power but Lloyd George now stronger than ever. And all the Unionist ministers to be compelled to resign their offices with no guarantee of reappointment. I was once again present in an adjacent room and listened to the verbal beating that Law received. He took it stoically enough. But by then he was playing a longer game.

Montagu told me later that he walked with Lloyd George back to the War Office when the meeting at Downing Street ended. There Lloyd George confirmed once again how delighted he was at the agreement they had reached. He urged Montagu to persuade Asquith to prepare a written note summarising their agreement that evening. But no such note was ever prepared.

As he left the Secretary's rooms Montagu passed by the inner clerical office. The War Department was quiet (it was now seven o'clock on a Sunday evening) so he was surprised to see out of the corner of his eye someone obviously waiting to meet with Lloyd George.

His surprise turned to shock when he recognised the man who waited there.

It was Lord Northcliffe.

Who owned *The Times*.

– 24 –

'We are agreed then, gentlemen?'

'We are, Prime Minister.'

The Asquiths had just spent the evening dining with Montagu. At the end of the meal they were joined by Crewe and Reading, and Margot returned early to Downing Street. The Prime Minister and his colleagues reviewed the week's events and the arrangement Asquith had concluded earlier that evening with Lloyd George. All were agreed that it was the best possible outcome and congratulated the PM on his skilful negotiations with the War Secretary.

A letter arrived while the four men continued their conversation after dinner. It was from Law, warning Asquith that if news of the reconstruction of the ministry were to leak out peremptorily it might be interpreted in the country at large as the Conservatives resigning unilaterally from the Government. The announcement of the reconstruction needed to be controlled and made that night.

Asquith asked one of Montagu's servants to telephone the Palace and ask for Lord Stamfordham, the King's private secretary. When Stamfordham came to the telephone Asquith told him of his plan and asked him to obtain the King's consent to an announcement. A phone call twenty minutes later confirmed the King's permission. It was then that Asquith asked for the agreement of his three colleagues to the statement which was issued to the press at 11.45 p.m. that evening:

The Prime Minister, with a view to the more active prosecution of the war, has decided to advise His Majesty the King to consent to a reconstruction of the Government.

Other than Montagu and Crewe, no Liberal minister had been consulted or advised in advance about this statement.

Other than Law, no Unionist minister had been consulted or advised.

Henderson, the single Labour member of the Government, had not been consulted or advised.

All these men learned of their immediate fate for the first time in the following morning's newspapers.

They also read of another matter in Monday morning's *Times*, a story that would unravel all the negotiations of the previous day and reduce Asquith and his Government to rubble by the middle of the week.

But Asquith himself was oblivious to the storm to follow. He returned to Downing Street at half past midnight (he had wanted to walk home but the policeman who accompanied him insisted on a car: he reported later that the Prime Minister was 'tired and unsteady on his feet and might well have fallen over had he attempted to walk'). Once at home he wrote a brief note to Mrs Crawford.

I drove down to Walmer yesterday afternoon hoping to find sunshine & peace. It was bitterly drab & cold, and for my sins (or other people's) I had to drive back soon after 11 this morning. I was forced back by Bonham-Carter & Montagu & Reading to grapple with a "Crisis" – this time with a very big C. The result was that I have spent much of the afternoon colloguing with Messrs. Lloyd George & Bonar Law & one or two minor worthies. The "Crisis" shows every sign of following its many predecessors to an early & unhonoured grave. But there were many wigs very nearly on the green.

He was exhausted.
He took to his bed.
And dreamed.

INTERLUDE

Asquith dreams II

He dreamed of the House of Lords.

The mausoleum.

In 1905 Asquith had engaged in a conspiracy with Haldane and Grey, who as Liberal Imperialists had little confidence in their leader Campbell-Bannerman. C.B. had accused the Conservative Government of employing 'methods of barbarism' during the Boer War. Meeting at Relugas in Scotland, where Grey had a fishing cottage, they agreed that when the next Liberal Government came to be formed they would refuse to serve under Campbell-Bannerman unless he agreed to take a seat in the Lords and leave the leadership of the party in the Commons to Asquith. That would clear the way for C.B.'s retirement as Prime Minister, an early advancement for Asquith, and significant ministerial office for both Haldane and Grey.

In his dream Asquith now found himself back at the cottage in Scotland that summer. He saw himself in his early fifties and could feel again the vitality and energy he had long since lost. Haldane was not yet stout. Grey could still see. It was all a lifetime ago. He sat at the kitchen table after a day's fishing and sketched out the arrangement with them.

The plot collapsed ignominiously and remained for Asquith the most embarrassing moment of his long and successful career. When Balfour's Government resigned in 1905, C.B. had called the conspirators' bluff. He laughed at the suggestion that he should go to the Lords. He offered Asquith the Exchequer and Asquith accepted immediately. Grey held out for longer but ultimately wavered and got the Foreign Office. Haldane also wavered and got the War Office. But it was Asquith who had blinked first. Haldane and Grey always remembered that he had faced the test and been found wanting.

When they received their seals from the King in 1905 the new ministers had to find their way back to their offices through the thickest London fog for many years. Staggering up The Mall, Asquith bumped into a lamppost and gashed his forehead. Haldane almost fell under a motor vehicle. It took Grey two hours to find the Foreign Office.

The King, seeing them off from the Palace, thought it was hilarious. The most wonderful metaphor. Liberals lost in the fog.

Now, in his dream, Asquith was there again, wandering through thick London fog.

Only this time he couldn't recall what his destination was. Where was he supposed to go?

He couldn't remember.

His dream moved on. To another House of Lords plot.

In the summer of 1910 the Government's conflict with the Lords was approaching its climax. The Tory-dominated upper house had rejected the budget of 1909. Asquith had called an election at the beginning of 1910: the Liberals lost seats (no surprise given the extraordinary majority they had won in 1906) but with their Labour and Irish Nationalist allies they still commanded a strong majority in the Commons. The Lords then passed the budget but stood fast when the Government published a Parliament Bill that proposed to restrict the Lords' ability to block legislation for more than three years. Their Lordships had a particular aversion to this proposal because it would break their veto on Home Rule for Ireland, a constitutional abhorrence to them. They dug in.

When King Edward died in May 1910 and his son succeeded as George V, the parties agreed to a conference to find a way around the problem. They met for many months but reached no agreement. But as the conference recessed for the summer a strange proposal found its way from Criccieth in Wales, where Lloyd George was spending a few weeks, to leading politicians scattered around the country.

Lloyd George was proposing the formation of a coalition government, a 'Ministry of All the Talents'. By the time Asquith received Lloyd George's paper it had already been seen and discussed by leading Unionists including their leader Balfour, F. E. Smith, and Bonar Law. Churchill, then Home Secretary, had also received a copy. Under Lloyd George's proposal Asquith was to remain as Prime Minister but he was to lead the Government from the Lords. The very chamber that he and his Government were at that moment emasculating. Lloyd George was proposing for Asquith in 1910 what Asquith had proposed for Campbell-Bannerman in 1905. But Asquith did not laugh it off in the same easy way that C.B. had.

He was saved from internment in the mausoleum only because the conference dealing with the Parliament Bill collapsed. An agreed solution to the Lords' veto would have been essential to the formation of a coalition government. But no agreement could be reached. Lloyd George's proposed coalition disappeared like a phantom.

But Asquith remembered. He understood then for the first time how dangerous Lloyd George was. And how expendable he, Asquith, was to Lloyd George's larger ambitions.

In his dream he floated over the Palace of Westminster and stared down at the Lords' chamber. The roof dissolved and he watched their lordships in their red ermine robes destroying another Liberal Bill. He floated away and down the Thames towards the City. It was a beautiful sunny day and his skin tingled in the July heat.

Then it clouded over.

He turned in mid-air and returned to Westminster. Now the roof of the Commons dissolved and he stared down on the House in session. He saw himself standing at the dispatch box attempting to speak. Opposition backbenchers were baying at him and the Speaker could not bring the House to order.

Asquith knew which day this was.

The 24th of July, 1911.

The Prime Minister was reporting to the House on the Government's attitude to the amendments proposed by the Lords to the Parliament Bill. After months of division and strife the Government was now fully intent on having its way. Four days earlier Asquith had written to both Balfour and Lansdowne telling them that the Government would ask the House to disagree with the Lords' amendments. And then:

> ...should the necessity arise, the Government will advise the King to exercise his Prerogative to secure the passing into law of the Bill in substantially the same form in which it has left the House of Commons, and His Majesty has been pleased to signify that he will consider it his duty to accept and act on that advice.

In other words the King would create enough new Liberal peers to carry the Parliament Bill through the Lords against the Conservative peers' opposition. Only that morning, before coming to the Commons, Asquith had once again reviewed the list of 249 men he proposed to nominate as new peers. He was certain that the need to do this would never in fact arise: the Lords would blink first. In this he was proved right. But not yet.

He was cheered by crowds on his way to the Commons that morning. In the House, however, when he rose to speak, he had been shouted down. A tidal wave of noise was directed at him from the Opposition benches. Balfour, their leader, sat and examined his fingernails. The Speaker (useless man) appealed for order but they ignored him. For thirty minutes the Prime Minister stood at the dispatch box attempting to speak but was unable to make himself heard. It was a disgraceful scene, a deeply humiliating moment, a naked display of Tory bigotry and verbal violence. No Prime Minister in living memory had been refused a hearing by the House.

Asquith had savoured every moment of it.

He knew as he stood there braced against the verbal assault that he had won.

The memory of his triumph stayed with him forever.

His spirit, in the air over Parliament, watched as his car returned from Westminster to Downing Street. He stepped out of the car, exhausted but exhilarated. Telling Margot he needed half an hour's rest, he made his way to his bedroom at the top of Number 10. As he lay down on the bed his spirit re-joined him and together they slept.

Then Asquith awoke. Not quite refreshed. But alert and ready for the day.

It was the early hours of Monday the 4th of December, 1916.

The beginning of his last week in Downing Street.

PART III

The final days:

Monday 4 December – Saturday 9 December 1916

– 25 –

Later he remembered it as a glorious winter's morning. The sun peeped above the buildings to the east just as he left his dressing room to breakfast downstairs. A warm red glow in the sky had announced the coming sunrise. The streets and roofs were covered in mid-winter frost. London still seemed to be sleeping as Lord Crewe watched the first orange rays announce themselves over the City. He gazed at the emerging panorama for a few moments before turning to walk down the broad oak staircase and face the day.

As he lifted his knife and fork Crewe heard the faint tinkle of the telephone far away in his study. It rang for a few moments and then stopped. Hedley had answered it. For the telephone to ring at this hour was unusual and Crewe felt a moment of apprehension. It might be a death. Or an emergency. Something to do with the war? For a brief instant he was relieved that he had no son to offer to the killing machine in France.

A muffled knock and then Hedley opened the door.

'I'm terribly sorry, my Lord. The telephone.'

'I know, Hedley. I heard it. Who was it?'

'The Chancellor, sir. Of the Exchequer.'

'At this hour?'

A run on sterling? The Americans playing up?

'He apologises most sincerely, my Lord, but he says he needs to speak with you.'

'Now?'

'Most urgent, sir. He says.'

'I'm eating my bloody breakfast, Hedley.'

'I do apologise, my Lord. Shall I tell him that you are unavailable?'

Crewe thought for a moment. Damn the man. McKenna. Bloody useless.

'No, I'll speak to him.'

'My Lord.' Hedley left the room, the door slightly ajar. Crewe folded his napkin, rose and went to his study.

Telephone calls like this were happening all over London that morning. Buckmaster called Grey. Curzon called Law. Chamberlain called Balfour (but to no avail: Mr Balfour, he was told, did not receive telephone calls before lunch, and was anyway indisposed). Long called Cecil. Crawford called Runciman. It was the single greatest tangle of telephone calls between Cabinet ministers since the invention of the machine. Or actually of *ex*-Cabinet ministers. They were all now *ex*. Which is why they were calling one another.

'This is Lord Crewe.'

'This is McKenna. What's going on?'

'What's going on? I'm sorry, McKenna. What are you talking about?'

'You've seen *The Times*?'

It lay on Lord Crewe's breakfast table but was as yet unopened.

'No. Not yet. What is it?'

'He's re-constructing.'

'The Prime Minister?'

'No, Crewe. The bloody Archbishop of Canterbury. Yes of course it's the Prime Minister. Who else reconstructs the Government?'

'Calm down, McKenna', Crewe responded. 'Tell me more.'

'He issued a notice to the press at midnight last night saying that he's reconstructing the Government. Agreed with the Palace. All resignations in except his own.'

'All of us?'

'Yes.'

'The Unionists agree?'

'It would seem so. There's no word to the contrary.'

'And Lloyd George?'

'Nothing about him in the press announcement. But I know they met yesterday. And Law too. Have they agreed something?'

'I have no idea.'

'But you saw him yesterday too?' McKenna pressed.

'I did. And I advised him to stick to his guns and face down Lloyd George.'

'Curious way of doing that, I'd say.'

'Well, they may have reached an agreement. Let us hope.'

'Would have been nice if he'd told us what's going on.'

'I expect things moved too quickly for him to keep us informed directly. We'll hear this morning. Are you at your office?'

'Yes.'

'Let me finish my breakfast and I'll join you there at ten.'

'Fine. Good. Thank you. Sorry to have disturbed you.'

'No matter.'

'Oh, Crewe?'

'Yes.'

'You'd better read the editorial in *The Times* as well. It's pure poison.'

Oh God. Northcliffe.

'I will.'

Crewe put down the telephone. Well, well, well.

The call between Curzon and Law ran along similar if more volatile lines. Lord Curzon's servant waited until Bonar Law had been fetched. Then when the receiver was securely in Law's hands, the servant asked Law to await his lordship as he went to fetch him. This was the ritual of establishing the relative standing of those on the call. Peers did not wait on commoners, no matter how important. Or self-important, his lordship mused.

'Law.'

'Lord Curzon.'

'What the hell is going on?'

Law paused. This would be the pattern for the day.

'The Prime Minister is reconstructing the Government. It's in the newspapers. Announced last night.'

'I know it's in the bloody papers, Law. I've just read it in *The Times*. He's re-constructing?'

Law knew what was coming next. Had known it since they reached the agreement last night. Well, so be it. He would face them down.

'Yes. He's reached an agreement with Lloyd George. Crisis averted. But he needs to reconstruct to implement it.'

'An agreement?'

'A smaller War Committee. Four members. Lloyd George chairs. Asquith presides.'

'And you agreed to that?'

'I did.'

'On what authority?'

Law stopped. Drew a short breath and then exhaled.

I will not be treated like a servant by this pompous fool.

'On my own authority, Lord Curzon. My authority as leader of the Conservative and Unionist Party.'

'Leader in the Commons, Law. Lord Lansdowne leads us in the Lords.'

'Leader, Lord Curzon. Where it matters.'

Unlike you, you old fool.

'We spoke about this yesterday, Law. We specifically sent a message from our party's Cabinet ministers to the Prime Minister. We told him that he must resign, not reconstruct. Allow Lloyd George to try to form a Government and fail. To *resign*, Law. But as of this morning it would seem that Asquith is still Prime Minister and we are all out of office.'

'We hold our offices as caretakers until the new Government is formed.'

'Don't get clever with me, Law. I know how the damn constitution works. Point is, Asquith's still there. And so is the little Welsh weasel.'

'That's not how I would describe the War Secretary, Lord Curzon. But yes indeed. He is. They are.'

'Did you give Asquith our message yesterday?'

'I told him of our meeting and its conclusion.'

'Did you give him the memorandum?'

Law paused. Curzon pressed.

'Law, did you give him the memorandum?'

'I did not.'

Silence.

'You fool.'

And then Curzon returned the telephone to its cradle and the call was ended.

Away in Mayfair, Lord Crewe returned to his breakfast table. He read the notice in *The Times*. He was once again out of office though still a caretaker Lord President of the Council. Would he be back in office by the end of the week, he wondered? He was beginning to doubt it.

Downing Street — 9 a.m.

'Maurice?'

'Prime Minister.'

'The study please.'

The Prime Minister had breakfasted in the flat with Margot. There he read both the announcement of the Government's reconstruction, which, as he had written it himself, did not surprise him, and also the editorial in *The Times*, which did. Greatly. But even at this early hour, and despite the effect of too much wine the previous evening and his strange and exhausting dreams, the calculus of politics had already begun to run again in Asquith's brain. As with any development, the three burning questions. How had this happened? Where does it leave me? What should I do?

The Times's leader was deeply hostile to Asquith and his management of the war. That in itself was not news. He had been dealing with editorials like this for months now, even years. *The Times* was by no means the most vicious of the newspapers that opposed him. But this morning's leader was different. Not only did it excoriate the Prime Minister for his lack of leadership but it also indicated that senior-level changes, so desperately needed, had now been agreed and were about to be announced. It inferred that Asquith had been persuaded by his closest supporters that he was ineffective as a war leader. He had therefore agreed voluntarily to surrender day-to-day management of the war to Lloyd George. This new arrangement had been concluded that weekend and would be implemented immediately as part of the reconstruction of the Government announced late last night.

Asquith knew this was a leak that could only have come from Lloyd George.

He mused briefly on whether any of the others could have been behind it. Not Law: he didn't leak. Montagu? Possibly. But Asquith knew that Montagu was desperately attempting to reconcile him with Lloyd George and it would make no sense for Montagu, once agreement had been reached, to leak the outcome in a way that would destabilise the arrangement. No, not Montagu. It must be Lloyd George.

Asquith doubted that Lloyd George would have made the leak directly. Much more likely that the information was being fed to *The Times* by a third party. Probably Carson.

'You've seen *The Times*?'

'I have, Prime Minister.'

'I want you to make discreet enquiries. Your usual channels. Back door. Who did this? Who wrote the editorial and who fed him the information? You can find that out?'

'I can certainly try.'

'Good. Please do. Make some telephone calls. I have the Liberal ministers here at half past ten. Let me know what you discover before they arrive.'

'I'll do my best, PM.'

'Thank you.'

Bonham Carter left and Asquith tried to summarise his reflections. How had this happened? Almost certainly Lloyd George, either directly to Dawson, the editor, or to Northcliffe, the proprietor. Where does this leave me? In one sense weakened. The country now believes that I've surrendered to him. But actually in another sense stronger. It depends on how the Cabinet reacts. The Liberals will be apoplectic with rage. The Unionists? Not at all sure. They professed strong loyalty to me but wanted me to call Lloyd George's bluff. I didn't do that; I compromised with him instead. Will they accept the compromise or will they want my head because I didn't resign? Curious logic but there you are. Politics. Strange business.

And what should I do? Meet them all, see where things stand. The Liberals this morning. The Unionists this afternoon. If all is well then I'll reconstruct this evening, appoint the key ministers, get this over by tonight. Speed is of the essence once I know where people stand. But I need more time to discover that. So, today, explore. Decide how to react to Lloyd George's leak. A new Government tonight if the compromise still works. Sack him tomorrow if it doesn't.

In the meantime, wait and see.

A message was delivered from Lloyd George. Could he see the Prime Minister urgently?

No, Asquith thought. Not now. Not convenient. The Prime Minister is busy and will revert to the War Secretary later in the day when he has dealt with some urgent matters.

Back in your box, David.

Downing Street — 10.20 a.m.

Ten minutes before Asquith's meeting with the Liberal ministers Bonham Carter returned. He had made his discreet enquiries. The leader had been written by Geoffrey Dawson, *The Times's* editor. Apparently Dawson had stayed as Lord Astor's guest at Cliveden on Saturday night. The first half of the editorial had been written there. The remaining section was written in London on the Sunday. Dawson had met with Sir Edward Carson that afternoon.

'Thank you. That explains a good deal.'

'Oh and one other thing, Prime Minister. Even more tangled I'm afraid.'

'Yes?'

'Mr Montagu came to see me a few moments ago. He asked me to make you aware that he returned to the War Office with the War Secretary after the meeting here yesterday afternoon.'

'I know that.'

'As he was leaving he saw another man waiting to meet Mr Lloyd George.'

'And that was?'

A brief pause. Almost imperceptible. But politics is the language of the brief pause.

'Lord Northcliffe, sir.'

'Ah.'

I see, thought Asquith. I see.

So David is leaking in two directions at once. To the editor through Carson. But also to the proprietor himself. Belt and braces then, what?

Fine. Let's see where this leaves us with our colleagues.

Downing Street — 10.30 a.m.

'Gentlemen, come in.'

The Liberal ministers gathered in the Cabinet Room. They were not a happy group. In the absence of both the Unionists and Lloyd George the usual seating plan was awry. They sat randomly. But Asquith retained the chair with the arms.

'Thank you for coming. First I must apologise that news of the reconstruction reached you through the press rather than directly from here. As you will understand when I explain the matter to you, speed was of the essence yesterday. It was a very difficult day. But I'm pleased to let you know that the boil has now been lanced. The War Secretary and I met yesterday afternoon and we were able to agree on a way through the present *impasse*. The crisis is largely over. Although I must assure you that the interpretation of what happened is not at all as outlined by Mr Dawson in this morning's *Times*.'

At this Asquith explained the compromise they had reached yesterday. The new arrangements for the War Committee. Lloyd George chairing, Asquith presiding. And also the need, prompted by Law (which Asquith fully understood), to announce the reconstruction of the Government late on Sunday evening in case the Unionist ministers should act peremptorily.

'So you announced it at midnight to keep the Unionists on board but you didn't think to advise your own party colleagues first?' This was McKenna.

'I'm deeply sorry that it wasn't possible to discuss this with you in advance, Chancellor. But you have all been pressing me to resolve the issue and I know you understood that any resolution was almost certainly going to require a reconstruction. It is inconvenient, temporarily inconvenient, and certainly not the way I would have wished to advise you of it. But at least the matter is now resolved.'

'No it isn't, PM.'

McKenna again.

'It isn't resolved.'

Asquith stared across the table at him.

'You've surrendered to the War Secretary. And then he spits in your eye in *The Times* this morning.'

'We don't know for a fact that he had anything to do with the editorial this morning,' Asquith lied.

Montagu stared at the table.

'Of course he did, PM.' This was Crewe. 'Of course he did. One way of the other. This was David's way of telling the world that he won.' Asquith grew uncomfortable.

Then Lord Grey spoke. 'Prime Minister, it pains me to say that this is not a happy situation we find ourselves in. You reached a compromise with the War Secretary yesterday. We appreciate your negotiating skills and your determination to keep the Government intact while the country is at war. But the arrangement you reached with him is plainly unworkable.'

'Why is that, Edward?'

'Because it raises one member of the Cabinet to a rank above his colleagues and that should never be allowed to happen when the Cabinet member concerned is not the Prime Minister.'

Inelegantly phrased, Asquith thought, but accurate. And dangerous too. They were accusing him of throwing in the towel when he should have fought on. Of surrendering.

'Is this the opinion of you all?'

They replied one by one, all of them unhappy, all discontent.

'And you would like me to do – what?'

Crewe spoke. 'The arrangement is untenable, PM. It leaves the Liberal ministers unhappy and I suspect the Unionists are equally discontent.'

'Bonar Law will bring the Unionists onside.'

'I'm not sure that he will, Prime Minister. I'm not sure that he can.'

Then silence. Asquith stared at this group of men that he had led for so many years. It was the first time that his colleagues, without exception, had declined to support a decision he had made. A depressing development.

But politicians' minds are nothing if not flexible, and even as Asquith was facing a harsh and unwelcome truth his mind was re-calibrating the political calculus. The Liberals, though disappointed, were still behind him. To a man (although he wondered about Montagu) they would support him if he decided to push back against Lloyd George. They would support him.

So the key question then was where the Unionists stood. Would they support him too if he repudiated the agreement he had reached yesterday, or would they insist that he went even further and resigned himself in order to destroy Lloyd George?

He needed more time to think.

He brought the meeting to an end.

Shortly after they left the room another message arrived from Lloyd George in the form of a scribbled note from Montagu. Imperative that the arrangements agreed between them yesterday should now be committed to writing to prevent any further confusion of the kind that had arisen in that morning's *Times*.

No, Asquith thought. Not just yet.

– 26 –

'Prime Minister. I'm sorry to interrupt you but a number of ministers are asking to see you.'

Asquith pushes back from the table and moves the papers to one side.

'Who?'

'Lord Curzon, Sir Austen Chamberlain, and Lord Robert Cecil, sir.'

Interesting. Wanting to see me without Law. Well, well.

'Thank you, Drummond. Please show them in.'

Drummond exits soundlessly. A most remarkable skill, Asquith had always thought. He feels the warm fire behind him. Drinking tea although God knows he'd like something stronger. Still, bad impression. Too early. Needs to be on his guard. This one is crucial.

The Unionist ministers are shown in and take their seats opposite him. Curzon, Chamberlain and Cecil. The three Cs.

He likes Cecil although he finds him too much of a war zealot. Admires Chamberlain. Sound man, sticks to his principles. A man you can do business with. But he always thought Curzon was a creep.

Anyway, let's hear them.

'Gentlemen. What can I do for you?'

'We've spoken to Bonar Law, Prime Minister, and decided to see you directly ourselves. I should say that we also speak for Mr Long, who is detained elsewhere at the moment.'

Asquith responds. 'Mr Law will have explained the circumstances under which the press announcement was issued last night. I'm sorry you weren't notified in advance but I hope he told you why we felt it was necessary to act so quickly.'

'Correct degree of haste, Prime Minister. But the wrong decision.' This is Curzon.

Asquith responds sharply. 'You'll understand that any decision in a matter such as this has to be mine, Lord Curzon. But please tell me why you think I should have acted differently.'

'We – the Unionist ministers – met yesterday, Prime Minister.'

'I know you did.'

'Mr Law came to see you after our meeting.'

'Yes, he did.'

'But he did not tell you about the decisions we took at our meeting.'

'I was under the impression that he told me most carefully. You insisted that our arrangements to manage the war need to be changed. I agreed. In order you achieved that you advised me to resign and said that you yourselves would resign from the Government if I did not resign and allow others to try to form an administration.'

'We also deprecated the way Lloyd George has been behaving in the last few weeks, Prime Minister. I'm not sure you were told that plainly enough.'

'Well, let's leave that to one side, Lord Curzon, shall we? You'll appreciate my unwillingness to discuss the behaviour of one colleague in front of others. But I understand the strength of your feeling on this point.'

'But you didn't resign, Prime Minister.'

'No.'

'May I ask why not?'

'You may, Lord Curzon. Because the War Secretary and I were able to reach an accommodation – with which I should say your own leader, Mr Law, is in complete agreement – which meets your objections about the management of the war and requires only a reconstruction of the ministry.'

'With the very greatest of respect, Prime Minister, I fear you have been misled. And as a consequence you may have missed the point.'

Asquith stares across the table at Curzon. The depth of his contempt for this silly little man is beyond expression. Curzon still thinks he's Viceroy of India, master of all he surveys. Well, no brown faces in the room today, Asquith thinks. Englishmen only. Not all of us dangling earldoms and garters, but all senior politicians, Lord Curzon. And one of us sitting in the chair you so desperately want to plant your broad backside in.

'Those are, if I may say so, strong charges.'

'Prime Minister, we – the Unionist ministers – want you to meet Lloyd George's challenge head-on. His challenge to you, and the extent to which he destabilises the ministry, is a disgrace. He poisons everything he touches...'

'Too strong, Lord Curzon.'

'No, Prime Minister.' This is Chamberlain. 'You need to face him down. If you compromise with Lloyd George you'll have exactly the same instability every other month. He needs to be retired to the backbenches. And what Law does not seem to have told you is that you'll have our full support if you do this.'

Cecil next. 'Step back, Prime Minister. Resign. For the moment. Allow Lloyd George the chance to form a ministry. He has precious little support on your own benches, even less on ours. He'll fail. You'll resume your ministry with the principal threat to your authority on the side-lines.'

Asquith stares at the three men, one after the other. Considers carefully. How far can he trust them? Either their judgement or their sincerity. Then speaks.

'This is not quite the perspective I received from your party leader.'

Curzon again. 'Law has gone over to Lloyd George, Prime Minister.'

'I'm not sure that...'

'No, Prime Minister. Honestly.' Cecil again. 'Law wants Lloyd George to form a ministry. A successful ministry. He believes that he can take the Unionist Party with him in that plan. We are here to tell you that he cannot. You have a majority, Prime Minister, and we guarantee to help you hold that majority. But you must grasp the nettle now. You are presented with this kind of opportunity only very rarely. Grasp it now.'

'You will have our full support, Prime Minister. And Long's too.' This was Chamberlain.

'But only if you act decisively,' Curzon says.

He stares at them again. They control at least half of the Unionist Party. They also seem certain that Law cannot muster a majority of Unionist votes for Lloyd George. And Asquith knows from this morning's meeting that the Liberal ministers back him completely.

Where does this leave him? Here is the calculus as he computes it.

The Liberal ministers want him to repudiate yesterday's agreement, sack Lloyd George, and reconstruct the Government.

The three Unionists sitting before him want him to go further: to resign himself in order to sweep back into office once Lloyd George tries and fails to form a ministry. Then sack Lloyd George.

What about Law? Uncertain. Would he support Lloyd George? Has he gone over? Possibly.

What about Lansdowne? He would side with Asquith, surely?

What about Balfour? He could not imagine him supporting Lloyd George.

But would the Liberals continue to support him if he took the kind of gamble the Unionists are now demanding of him?

He sits and considers. Even after they leave the room. Then decides.

No.

Not yet.

For today, repudiation and reconstruction only. Not resignation. Wait and see.

* * *

Asquith leaves the meeting to go to the Palace. He speaks briefly with the King as he hands in the resignation of every member of the Government other than himself. The King commissions him to form a new ministry. Asquith thanks him and returns to Downing Street for lunch. After this he sets out for the House of Commons to take questions.

Prime Minister's Rooms, House of Commons — 1.30 p.m.

'I have to go, Law.'

'Prime Minister, this is extremely important.'

'I know. But later. I have questions in the House. I must go.'

'Are you standing by your agreement of yesterday?'

Asquith pauses. Stares Law straight in the eye.

'Lloyd George has been trafficking in the press. This morning's *Times.*'

'You must stand by the agreement. The press is nothing.'

'I'm not as keen on the plan as I was. Given the fact that he briefed Northcliffe as soon as our meeting ended.'

'Prime Minister...'

'I'm needed in the House, Law. We'll speak later.'

Cabinet Room, 10 Downing Street — 2 p.m.

Bonar Law had followed Asquith into the chamber. He sat beside him as he dealt with the usual round of self-serving enquiries from members. Once the Speaker indicated that the House would move on to other business, the Prime Minister left. Law followed. He was detained by a group of backbenchers as he walked through the lobby and by the time he disengaged himself Asquith had left, walking briskly back to Downing Street. Law followed as quickly as he could. Raised his hat to a number of ladies in the street who caught his eye and murmured hello. Ignored the men. He crossed Parliament Square and walked up Whitehall. The front door closed behind Asquith as Law turned into Downing Street. He followed him into Number 10.

Asquith had gone to the Cabinet Room.

Grey, Harcourt and Runciman stood in the outer room waiting to be called in to see the Prime Minister. Law saw Bonham Carter and gestured him to one side.

'I need to see the Prime Minister.'

'Lord Grey and his colleagues are about to go in, Secretary of State.'

'It's urgent. I'm sorry to appear rude but I must see him straight away. In advance of his colleagues.'

Bonham Carter went into the Cabinet Room. He emerged a moment later and asked Lord Grey and his colleagues if they could wait for another ten minutes. Mr Law needed to see the Prime Minister urgently.

'Excuse me,' Law said, as he passed them by. 'I apologise for the inconvenience. I won't detain him for long.'

'Of course,' Grey said.

Then Law walked into the Cabinet Room for the most important conversation of his life. It was short and direct. It was hateful. But it was essential.

'I need to know if you're standing by yesterday's agreement.'

Asquith stared straight back at him.

'I'm considering the position.'

'What does that mean? Considering the position?'

'In light of Lloyd George's leaking of our agreement to *The Times,* I'm considering where that leaves us.'

It was Law's turn to stare. Then to speak.

'Prime Minister, let me be frank. It gives me no pleasure at all to say this. But if the scheme you agreed with Lloyd George yesterday is to be repudiated, then I can no longer support you.'

'No longer support me?'

'No.'

'What does that mean?'

'It means what it says, Prime Minister. You must know where I stand. Now you do. I cannot support you if you repudiate yesterday's agreement.'

'I see.'

Silence.

'Anything else?'

'No.'

'Fine. Well, thank you for telling me. I'll let you know of my decision later.'

Asquith sat in silence as Law left the room.

Prime Minister's Study, 10 Downing Street — 2.15 p.m.

So Law had decided to fight. Well, Asquith would too. When Grey and his colleagues had left (after urging to the Prime Minister to fight on) Asquith sat down to write to Lloyd George. He knew that this letter would be the first in a series of exchanges that would force Lloyd George to resign. Asquith would not repudiate their agreement just yet but he would make it clear to Lloyd George how strongly he felt about the leak, which, he would imply, had been Lloyd George's doing. He wrote quickly and confidently without correcting any part of his draft:

> 10 Downing Street, S.W.
> December 4, 1916

My dear Lloyd George

Such productions as the first leading article in today's "Times", showing the infinite possibilities for misunderstanding and misrepresentation of such an arrangement as we considered yesterday, make me at least doubtful as to its feasibility. Unless the impression is at once corrected that I am being relegated to the position of an irresponsible spectator of the war, I cannot possibly go on.

The suggested arrangement was to the following effect: The Prime Minister to have supreme and effective control of war policy. The agenda of the War Committee will be submitted to him; its chairman will report to him daily; he can direct it to consider particular topics or proposals; and all its conclusions will be subject to his approval or veto. He can, of course, at his own discretion attend meetings of the Committee.

> Yours sincerely,
> H. H. Asquith

He knew that Lloyd George's response would arrive quickly. It would also determine his own next move. If Asquith himself was to be driven to resign then the process was important. He must not be seen as the aggressor. So they would first go through an exchange of friendly letters (well, semi-friendly: Lloyd George couldn't fail to notice the admonition in the PM's letter) before the full battle was joined.

– 27 –

And here it was. Lloyd George must have been waiting at his desk for Asquith's letter. And then dashed off an immediate response.

It was a fine protest of loyalty and affection. Asquith read it with admiration. To have such a man as an opponent! Really, he was extraordinary.

> War Office
> Whitehall, S.W.
> December 4, 1916

My dear Prime Minister

I have not seen "The Times" article. But I hope you will not attach undue importance to these effusions. I have had these misrepresentations to put up with for months. Northcliffe frankly wants a smash. Derby and I do not. Northcliffe would like to make this and any other rearrangement under your Premiership impossible. Derby and I attach great importance to your retaining your present position – effectively. I cannot restrain or, I fear, influence Northcliffe. I fully accept in letter and in spirit your summary of the suggested arrangement – subject, of course, to personnel.

> Ever sincerely,
> D. Lloyd George

.

It was a beautiful response: brief, elegant, emollient. And every sentence, every statement, every suggestion in it was a lie. It was masterly.

My dear Prime Minister. Whom I am trying to destroy. *I have not seen "The Times".* Of course you have, David. Or perhaps, having dictated it, you didn't feel the need to check that the subs had captured your tone quite correctly? *Do not attach undue importance.* I am trying to destroy you but, my dear Prime Minister, please don't let that disturb you. *I have had this for months.* I have directed this for months. *Northcliffe wants a smash.* Well that at least was true. *Derby and I do not.* Lie. Of course you do. And you mention Derby just to warn me that whatever Curzon and his lackeys are saying, you too have Conservative supporters. When this comes to a push Derby will deliver his Tories for you.

And how gracious. Both Derby and you would like me to retain my present position. How generous. But only if I am 'effective'. Which of course is precisely what you have accused me of *not* being for many months now. So I am not effective. And thus ineligible to retain my present position. The logic was so pure, so persuasive.

I cannot restrain Northcliffe. But why would you need to? He does exactly as you wish. And then of course you fully accept the arrangement we came to yesterday. But subject to personnel. Which we will never agree about because one of us wants Carson at the Admiralty while the other wants Balfour. So you do *not*, in fact, accept the arrangement we came to yesterday.

Ever sincerely. Indeed.

Asquith laid the letter in front of him and smiled. The initial exchange had now been concluded satisfactorily. Asquith serves, Lloyd George returns his serve.

Now it was time for the PM to volley.

Downing Street — 4.15 p.m.

His second meeting of the day with his Liberal colleagues.

'Gentlemen, please, come in.'

Buckmaster. McKenna. Runciman. Grey. Montagu (did he trust

him?). And the others. Henderson, the Labour member of Cabinet, would join them shortly.

Asquith recounted the events of the day since their meeting that morning. He had been to the Palace to complete the formalities. Crewe was still there in discussion with the King. Asquith had since then seen three Unionist ministers who pledged complete loyalty to him. But they had also urged him – with great force – to resign rather than to reconstruct. Law was to have emphasised that necessity to him on Sunday and Asquith inferred from their tone that their continuing support depended critically on his accepting and acting on that advice.

Law was also to have conveyed to the Prime Minister the Unionists' utter contempt for Lloyd George in his trafficking with the press. But Law had held back from delivering that message because, they told him, Law was now backing Lloyd George to form a ministry. Law himself had seen Asquith and told him that his preference was for Asquith to accept the agreement reached with Lloyd George yesterday. If Asquith could not do that – and based on the advice he had received from both Liberal and Unionist colleagues during the day it was clear that there was no longer any real support for the arrangement – then he, Law, could no longer support him. So Law wanted a compromise. Failing that he would pull away. Asquith told his colleagues that after the leak to *The Times* his preference had moved from compromise towards a more sweeping reconstruction and probably (although he hadn't quite made his mind up on this yet) consigning Lloyd George to the backbenches. But colleagues were now telling him that he should resign and run the risk (a minimal one, they assured him) of letting Lloyd George try to form a ministry. Which Law and at least some of the Unionists would support.

If the Prime Minister was to run that risk then it became a matter of parliamentary numbers. He needed to know his numbers. What did they have to say?

'Complete support for you if you decide to resign, Prime Minister.' This was McKenna.

Nods of assent from around the table. No voice raised in protest. No equivocation.

'Let me ask the question in another way, if I may, Prime Minister.' Buckmaster, the Lord Chancellor.

'Please,' Asquith said.

'Let us say that you resign as Prime Minister and the King then invites Lloyd George or Law to form a Government...'

The door opened and Henderson arrived.

'Good afternoon, Prime Minister. My apologies.'

'Mr Henderson, thank you for coming. Please, take a seat. We are looking at the option of my resigning and the King then asking Law or Lloyd George to form a Government.'

Buckmaster continued. 'If that happened, if Law or Lloyd George received the King's commission, would any of you gentlemen' – he looked around the room – 'serve with them?'

'Under no circumstances.' McKenna was resolute in his opposition.

Then Runciman, 'Absolutely not. My loyalty is to the Prime Minister and the leader of my party. I would follow him into Opposition if either of those two men formed a ministry.'

'I agree. I would too.' Buckmaster.

The others were firmly of the same mind. None of the Liberal ministers would serve under either Lloyd George or Law.

Then Henderson spoke.

'Gentlemen, I fear the situation is much less certain than you may imagine.'

Asquith felt a stab of pain in his side. Just above the hip bone. 'Why is that?'

'You seem to think that not many Conservatives could be persuaded to serve under Lloyd George. Law, yes, and also Carson and his die-hards. But not many others. I disagree. I think Law could carry many more of his colleagues than you might imagine into a Lloyd George Government.'

'But his colleagues were here this morning talking of their contempt for Lloyd George and giving the Prime Minister their full support.' McKenna.

'If he resigns. But not if he merely reconstructs.' Buckmaster.

Asquith interjected. 'But let us say that I do resign. Mr Henderson. Do you think that Lloyd George and Law could form a Government?'

'It's not certain, Prime Minister. But they'd get a damn sight closer to it than you all seem to be assuming.'

There was silence in the room. Then McKenna spoke.

'Arthur, honestly, I don't believe that. We've had Curzon, Chamberlain and Cecil here protesting their ability to carry their party against Law. Long agrees. And Balfour would never serve under Lloyd George.'

'Balfour's a busted flush.'

'Well, perhaps. But I cannot see that Law could deliver a large enough group of Unionists to join a rump group of Lloyd George's Liberals to get a majority in the House.'

'What about the Irish?' Runciman asked.

'Who knows?' Asquith responded. 'They'll wait to see which way the wind is blowing and then tack with it, I imagine.'

As he said this Asquith knew there was a question he needed to ask. Actually they all recognised the need to have the question raised, but only the Prime Minister could ask it. As he formed the words and started to speak he already knew what the answer would be.

'Mr Henderson. I apologise for putting you in this position. But you'll understand why I need to ask this now. If Law or Lloyd George tried to form a Government, would the Labour members support them?'

Henderson had no hesitation in responding. 'It would depend on the terms, Prime Minister. If the terms were favourable to the movement then we would join the new Government.'

And with Lloyd George in charge the terms would of course be favourable.

Asquith felt dizzy. His head was light, then heavy. He desperately needed some air. He thanked them and brought the meeting to an end. Buckmaster asked what was to happen next. Asquith responded that he needed to reflect on their advice before making a decision. But he would write again to Lloyd George and see what the response would be. He would see them again in the morning with a firm decision on how the matter was to proceed.

They left.

He remained.

He reached forward, removed a sheaf of Downing Street note-paper from the holder in front of him, and wrote his second letter of the day to the War Secretary. No excessive politeness now. It was time for Asquith to show that he was in charge of events and intended to remain so. He had no doubt that his letter would pre-cipitate Lloyd George's resignation and bring the crisis to a head.

Downing Street — 5.00 p.m.

10, Downing Street, S.W.
December 4, 1916

My dear Lloyd George

Thank you for your letter of this morning.

The King gave me today authority to ask for and accept the resignation of all my colleagues, and to form a new Govern-ment on such lines as I should submit to him. I start, therefore, with a clean slate.

After full consideration of the matter in all its aspects, I have come decidedly to the conclusion that it is not possible that such a Committee could be made workable and effective with-out the Prime Minister as its chairman. I quite agree that it will be necessary for him, in view of the other calls upon his time and energy, to delegate from time to time the chairmanship to another Minister as his representative and *locum tenens*, but (if he is to retain the authority which corresponds to his respon-sibility as Prime Minister) he must continue to be, as he always has been, its permanent president. I am satisfied, on reflection, that any other arrangement (such, for instance, as the one which I indicated to you in my letter of to-day) would be found in experience impracticable and incompatible with the retention of the Prime Minister's final and supreme control.

The other question, which you have raised, relates to the per-sonnel of the Committee. Here again, after deliberate consider-ation, I find myself unable to agree with some of your suggestions. I think we both agree that the First Lord of the Admiralty must, of necessity, be a member of the Committee. I cannot (as I told you yesterday) be a party to any suggestion that Mr Balfour should be displaced. The technical side of the Board of Admiralty has been reconstituted with Sir John Jellicoe as First Sea Lord. I believe Mr Balfour to be, under existing conditions, the necessary head for the Board.

I must add that Sir Edward Carson (for whom, personally, and in every other way, I have the greatest regard) is not, from the only point of view which is significant to me (namely, the most effective prosecution of the war), the man best qualified among my colleagues, present or past, to be a member of the War Committee.

I have only to say, in conclusion, that I am strongly of opinion that the War Committee (without any disparagement of the existing Committee, which, in my judgement, is a most efficient body, and has done, and is doing valuable work) ought to be reduced in number so that it can sit more frequently and undertake more easily the daily problems with which it has to deal. But in any reconstruction of the committee, such as I have, and have for some time past had, in view, the governing consideration, to my mind, is the special capacity of the men who are to sit on it for the work which it has to do.

That is a question which I must reserve for myself to decide.

Yours very sincerely
H. H. Asquith

He was exhausted. He went upstairs to lie down for an hour. And then, as he had the previous evening, which already felt like months ago, he walked to Queen Anne's Gate to dine with Montagu alone. He declined to discuss the day's events and did not tell him of his second letter to Lloyd George. They talked of Oxford, opera and the Levant.

– 28 –

Lloyd George's second letter to Asquith had taken much longer to prepare than the almost jaunty one he had sent earlier in the day. He finished it early on Tuesday morning and had it typed and delivered to Number 10 after breakfast. The delay had not been caused by any doubt in Lloyd George's mind. He had taken great care with it because he knew that he was now writing for the record. This was a letter that would soon be released to the press. He would then have to explain very closely why he was taking this action.

It was no surprise to Asquith to find that it was a letter of resignation. It left him with mixed feelings: a sense of some exhilaration that he, Asquith, had forced the pace and moved the matter towards a resolution, but also a sense of regret that his long-standing and often volatile partnership with Lloyd George had ended in this way. He read it with mixed emotions. But finally he felt relief that the issue had been addressed and the matter could now move to a resolution.

> War Office
> Whitehall, S.W.
> December 5, 1916

My dear Prime Minister

I have received your letter with some surprise.

On Friday I made proposals which involved not merely your retention of the Premiership, but the supreme control of the war, while the executive functions, subject to that supreme control, were left to others. I thought you then received these suggestions favourably. In fact, you yourself proposed that I should be the chairman of this Executive Committee, although, as you know, I never put forward that demand.

On Saturday you wrote me a letter in which you completely went back on that proposition. You sent for me on Sunday and put before me other proposals; these proposals you embodied in a letter to me written on Monday......

These proposals safeguarded your position and power as Prime Minister in every particular. I immediately wrote to you accepting them 'in letter and in spirit'. It is true that on Sunday I expressed views as to the constitution of the Committee, but these were for discussion.

Today you have gone back on your own proposals.

I have striven my utmost to cure the obvious defects of the War Committee without overthrowing the Government. As you are aware, on several occasions during the last two years I have deemed it my duty to express profound dissatisfaction with the Government's method of conducting the war. Many a time, with the road to victory open in front of us, we have delayed and hesitated while the enemy were erecting barriers that finally checked the approach. There has been delay, hesitation, lack of forethought and vision. I have endeavoured repeatedly to warn the Government of the dangers, both verbally and in written memoranda and letters, which I crave your leave to publish if my action is challenged; but I have either failed to secure decisions or I have secured them when it was too late to avert the evils...

I have more than once asked to be released from my responsibility for a policy with which I was in thorough disagreement, but at your urgent personal request I remained in the Government...

We have thrown away opportunity after opportunity, and I am convinced, after deep and anxious reflection, that it is my duty to leave the Government in order to inform the people of the real condition of affairs and to give them an opportunity, before it is too late, to save their native land from a disaster which is inevitable if the present methods are long persisted in. As all delay is fatal in war, I place my office without further parley at your disposal.

It is with great personal regret that I have come to this conclusion. In spite of mean and unworthy insinuations to the contrary – insinuations which I fear are always inevitable in the case of men who hold prominent but not primary positions in any Administration – I have felt a strong personal attachment to you as my chief. As you said yourself on Sunday, we have acted together for ten years and never had a quarrel, although we have had many a grave difference on questions of policy.

You have treated me with great courtesy and kindness; for all that I thank you. Nothing would have induced me to part now except an overwhelming sense that the course of action which has been pursued has put the country – and not merely the country, but throughout the world, the principles for which you and I have always stood throughout our political lives – in the greatest peril that has ever overtaken them.

As I am fully conscious of the importance of preserving national unity, I propose to give your Government complete support in the vigorous prosecution of the war; but unity without action is nothing but futile carnage, and I cannot be responsible for that. Vigour and vision are the supreme need at this hour.

> Yours sincerely,
> D. Lloyd George

Extraordinary man, Asquith thought. Quite extraordinary. He folded the letter and placed it on the table in front of him.

And then, after a few moments of further reflection, and to his very great surprise, he found that his eyes were damp with tears.

Tuesday 5 December 1916
War Office, Whitehall — Earlier that morning

Although Lloyd George was indeed an extraordinary man he was also an extraordinary politician. He had started his campaign entirely content to have Asquith remain in office provided that he, Lloyd George, was made chairman of the War Committee. But he soon decided that having Asquith continue as Prime Minister would make the whole enterprise hopeless. His written expressions of regret and gratitude to his chief were perfectly sincere but so too was his determination that Asquith should now be removed. On receiving the Prime Minister's second letter on Monday evening he arranged to see Bonar Law at half past seven the following morning. His letter of response to Asquith had already been drafted but before sending it he wanted to clarify Law's intentions. He felt certain that he knew how Law would respond but it would be wise to confirm this. After all, their next move would be definitive.

They met at the War Office early on Tuesday morning. Lloyd George showed Law the text of Asquith's letter. Law's face hardened as he read it.

'Well, he's finished then,' he responded.

'You mean...?'

'He's reneged on the deal he made with you on Sunday.'

'He says that circumstances have changed.'

'Circumstances always change, George. This is politics.'

'I have to respond.'

'Yes.'

'And I have to resign.'

'Yes, I see that.'

'We need to be clear, Bonar, about what happens next. May I propose a course of action that I believe can guide us both?'

'Go ahead.'

'I will resign. Asquith will try to reconstruct. I have over a hundred Liberals who will resist him. Your leading men are also insisting that he should resign and try to form a new Government, which the King will invite him to do. But he won't be able to form a ministry if both you and I stay out. Are you still content not to join him?'

Law hesitated. Not because he was in any way uncertain about what he ought to do, but because this was now irreversible. Then he spoke.

'I won't serve under him in any new ministry. His repudiation of the agreement he made on Sunday is definitive. I won't serve.'

'And your colleagues. Can you carry them?'

Once more Law hesitated. Again, not because he was uncertain. But because he knew what this second answer meant.

'Yes I can. I have the party behind me and the support of both the press and the country. And as for my colleagues, whatever their protestations of loyalty to Asquith they want to maintain their positions first. I can swing them. Balfour is key, we need to convince him first. But then the others can be carried.'

'So we can form a Government?'

'Yes we can.'

And then Lloyd George spoke with perfect sincerity, despite being a politician. And Law accepted his sincerity.

'If Asquith fails he'll advise the King to send for you, Bonar. Will you form a Government? I want you to. You are the man we need now. I would be more than prepared, I would be happy, to serve under you.'

Law was equally clear. 'I have no wish to be Prime Minister. None at all. If I'm needed to serve then I will. But I don't want to. And more to the point, I won't serve if Asquith declines to join the Cabinet.'

'As?'

'Actually I don't care what as. Not on the War Committee but certainly in the Cabinet. Maybe the Foreign Office.'

'Too important. And he'd never accept.'

'Well, perhaps best as Lord Chancellor.'

'I think that makes sense.'

'If the King asks me to form a Government', Law continued, 'I will accept his commission and do my duty. But I'll also explain to him that should Asquith decline to serve I would be unwilling to form a ministry.'

He paused.

'And I would then advise him to send for you.'

At that moment Lloyd George knew that he would be Prime Minister before the week was out.

– 29 –

Arthur Balfour had passed a troubled night. Laid low with influenza, he had taken to his bed in the middle of the previous week. By the weekend he was no better; in fact he was a little worse. On Saturday the doctor had visited again and pronounced him 'on the road to recovery' (dreadful phrase). Over the worst of it. Soon back to full strength and fitness. Why then did he feel so awful? His limbs ached, he ran a fever, and his sleep was interrupted by lurid and distressing dreams. They had changed his bed sheets twice during the day and again on Sunday morning. By then he felt only marginally better. He slept most of the day, a little easier now, and most of Monday as well. He woke early on Tuesday morning. He was still unable to rise and dress but rang for a servant to bring a basin of water to his bed. There, propped up on his pillows, he washed his hands, face and neck, and asked for some tea. He also asked the servant to bring him a pen and paper, to lift him up in the bed, to add two new pillows behind him, and to fetch his portable desk. He needed to write to the Prime Minister.

Balfour knew that he was much talked about behind his back in the way that enigmatic men are always talked about behind their backs. And he was indeed an enigma; perhaps even more than Asquith he was (and he knew it) a lingering relic of late Victorian England. 'Languid' was the adjective most frequently used about him. 'Languid Arthur'. It was better than the other names he occasionally heard, inspired no doubt by his lack of a wife. Well, let them read what they wanted into that.

And the famous epigram which he had contributed to English

letters, the phrase that captured a certain world-weariness stopping just short of outright cynicism, also attached itself to him irremovably. He could no longer quite remember when he had first launched the phrase into polite society. Sometime in the 1890s, he thought, now twenty years ago. But there it stood, in dictionaries of quotations, to follow him to the grave.

'Nothing matters very much, and very few things matter at all.'

Languid indeed.

Well, this languid man had achieved much in his career, an inspiration to diffident men everywhere. But few diffident men had started life with Balfour's advantages. His mother, Lady Blanche Cecil, was daughter of the 2nd Marquess of Salisbury and brother of the 3rd Marquess, Robert Gascoyne-Cecil. That uncle had become Prime Minister in 1885, served with a brief interruption until 1892, and returned again to Downing Street from 1895 until 1902. After Eton and Oxford Arthur had acted as his uncle's secretary before entering Parliament in 1874. He joined the Cabinet as Chief Secretary for Ireland, serving later as First Lord of the Treasury and finally as Leader of the House of Commons. In 1902 he became Prime Minister and remained in office until 1905. In his spare time (which, to his great surprise, he found he had much more of as Prime Minister than ever before) he had written two books of philosophy and played excellent tennis and golf.

During his time in Downing Street Balfour's Government had entered into the 'Entente Cordiale' with France, later extended to include Russia. The Entente had provided much of the momentum for England joining the war in 1914 and Asquith had invited Balfour to re-join the Cabinet in 1915 as First Lord of the Admiralty. This was the position in which Balfour still served. It was also the proximate reason why he needed now to write so urgently to the Prime Minister.

The real reason for his letter, however, was to tell Asquith, diplomatically but directly, that he, Asquith, was finished.

If ambiguity is the *lingua franca* of politics, there is an even more refined level of ambiguity in use whenever a former Prime Minister writes to a successor. Balfour couched his letter in that vein.

The code in which it was written needed to be decoded by the recipient, but Balfour was certain that Asquith was up to the task.

> Private
>
> > 4, Carlton Gardens
> > Pall Mall, S.W.
> > December 5ᵗʰ, 1916
>
> My dear Asquith
>
> I have been mostly in bed since the political crisis became acute, and can collect no very complete idea of what has been going on.

Balfour knows the importance of opening Asquith's eyes to the fact that what is happening is no mere irritation, no episode of political gamesmanship among his senior colleagues, but a true crisis. Asquith would certainly know that true crises only ever end with the departure of one or other of the protagonists. But Balfour was much less certain whether Asquith understood that the departing party in this case was likely to be – in fact was almost inevitably *bound* to be – Asquith himself. So, he thinks, let me call it what it plainly is: a crisis. And let me also tell you of my own position, Prime Minister:

> But one thing seems clear: that there is to be a new War Council of which Lloyd George is to be the working Chairman, and that, according to his ideas, this Council would work more satisfactorily if the Admiralty were not represented by me.

The key points here should be obvious, PM. Whatever hesitation you may have had, and almost certainly still have, about Lloyd George's proposals, actually his *demands* (let's be frank, they're always demands), the reconstruction of the War Committee as a new War *Council* is now inevitable. Please don't think you can avoid this by shuffling the personalities. Lloyd George must take charge of it, PM, not you. This is his show now and he wants me out, so:

In these circumstances I cannot consent to retain my office and must ask you to accept my resignation.

Political resignations are strange things. Balfour knows this as well as the next man. Sometimes they are meant to be taken literally. But not often. Usually they are an extended protest, a way of demanding attention, even a cry for help. Very rarely are they meant to be accepted without question. But Balfour is confident that Asquith will understand his intention here. And, more importantly, that he will be able to read between the lines.

I am well aware that you do not personally share Lloyd George's views in this connection. But…

And here is the central thrust of Balfour's letter:

…I am quite clear that the new system should have a trial and…

Read this next set of words most carefully, PM:

…under the most favourable possible circumstances…

There. You see my meaning? Yes?

…and the mere fact that the new Chairman of the War Council *did* prefer, and, so far as I know, *still* prefers, a different arrangement is, to my mind, quite conclusive, and leaves me in no doubt as to the manner in which I can best assist the Government which I desire to support. The fact that the first days of the reconstructed Administration find me more than half an invalid, is an additional reason (if additional reason were required) for adopting the course on which, after much consideration, I have determined.

Yours very sincerely,
Arthur James Balfour

He re-reads his letter briefly and calls for a servant to have it taken to Downing Street, where it arrives less than fifteen minutes later.

Downing Street — 10.30 a.m.

Balfour's letter reaches him just as Asquith is composing his response to Lloyd George. Still considering what tone to adopt in that reply, he scans Balfour's letter quickly and completely misses the point. He reads it as a letter about Balfour but it is in fact a letter about Asquith. Later Balfour was to reprimand himself for being so subtle. He should have written something much more unambiguous and direct.

That opportunity was to arise later in the day and this time Balfour took it. It came in response to Asquith's scribbled reply in which he asked Balfour to reconsider his resignation. Balfour's response later that afternoon was to propel Asquith out of office.

– 30 –

'Lord Crewe, Prime Minister.'

'Thank you. Show him in, please.'

When Crewe enters the Prime Minister's study he looks at Asquith and is immediately worried. The Prime Minister is dishevelled and unkempt. Also greatly tired. Papers strewn across his desk. This is out of character for a man who is usually so fastidious about his own appearance and paperwork.

'Are you feeling quite well, Prime Minister?'

Asquith looks up and attempts a smile.

'As well as I can in the circumstances. Which are trying, and getting worse by the hour. Our friend at the War Office has been in touch. Resigned. I took your advice and wrote him a stern note after yesterday's press. His response arrived this morning.' He passes Lloyd George's letter to Crewe.

'I'm writing to him now. Read his letter and tell me what you think. Then I'll tell you how I'm responding.' As Crewe reads, Asquith writes:

> 10, Downing Street, S.W.
> December 5, 1916

My dear Lloyd George,

I need not tell you that I have read your letter of to-day with much regret.

I do not comment on it for the moment, except to say that I

229

cannot wholly accept your account of what passed between us in regard to my connection with the War Committee.

In particular, you have omitted to quote the first and most material part of my letter of yesterday.

Yours very sincerely,
H. H. Asquith

This is a response of acknowledgement and protest, declining to discuss the details. Asquith wants to reserve his position: he plans to respond more fully to Lloyd George later in the day. This would have to do for now.

'What do you think?'

Crewe answers briskly. 'Exactly as we expected, really. You did a deal with him. He leaked the deal to puff himself up. You protested. He resigned in high dudgeon. As expected. Good riddance. He'll be history by the weekend.'

Asquith smiles. 'Your confidence always gives me new energy, Robert. God knows I need it now. This is all beginning to wear me out.'

And it shows, too, Crewe thinks.

'How was the King?'

Crewe has come from a meeting of the Privy Council at the Palace.

'As per usual. But he's a bit concerned about you.'

'About me or about the fate of his Government?'

'Both really. You underestimate him at times. He's a good man. I know you find him dull but he's dutiful and he does actually care about people. He's concerned about you. Hates to see you going through all this. Wants to see you come out the far side intact.'

'How would he cope with David in my place, do you think?'

'Initial horror, I'd imagine. Wouldn't have much good to say to the Queen about him. But his sense of duty would prevail and he'd work with him as best he could. Work with anybody, really, even the Socialists if he had to. That's what they're trained to do.'

'He's not a bad man, I agree. But I think he's about to have his mettle tested now.'

'Nonsense. It'll get tricky for a bit. But you'll bounce back.'

Asquith smiles, a smile of tiredness and grateful appreciation. The loneliness of his role sometimes wears him down. He needs people he can talk to in confidence. Crewe is one of those. No side. Always has Asquith's interests at heart.

Then Crewe continues, 'But you'll have to resign, you know.'

Asquith pauses. 'You really think so?'

'Depends on the Unionists. Do they know that George is gone yet?'

Asquith responds, 'Not from me, but I'm sure he briefed Law and Carson and they'll have spread the word. It'll be in the afternoon papers. If he's gone and I keep him out I wonder whether they'll press me to resign. Law will, but he wants me out for good. The others all protested that they want me out but only to have David try to form a ministry and fail. They've assured me they'd never serve under him. What do you think?'

'Don't know, PM. You're seeing them again this afternoon?'

'I am.'

'Well, as you'd say yourself, let's wait and see. And our own ministers are due at one?'

'They are.'

'Let's get some air before then. Come on, to the garden. I'll get them to bring out some tea.'

'It's bloody cold out there, Crewe.'

'Nonsense. Do you good. Get your coat and a scarf and we'll sit outside for twenty minutes. You look like you need some air. Come on, follow me.'

And so Lord Crewe leads the Prime Minister to the garden. Where they sit and talk trivia and drink their tea until Drummond comes to advise them that the Liberal ministers have now gathered in the Cabinet Room for their one o'clock meeting.

Downing Street, Cabinet Room — 1 p.m.

As Asquith stares around the room he mentally divides his colleagues into those who matter and those who don't. The colleague who matters most of all, Lloyd George, is not there. No invitation had been extended to him to attend the meeting. Montagu speaks at the start of the session to explain that Lloyd George is disappointed not to have been included: he wanted an opportunity to explain to his colleagues the action he had taken and the reasons why.

'Time enough for that,' Asquith says. There is no further discussion of Lloyd George's absence from the gathering.

The classification and ranking of his colleagues was an exercise that Asquith carried out quite frequently. He found it relaxed him and brought a sense of calm to the administrative chaos over which he often had to preside. Few colleagues had ever crossed the line from 'consequential' to 'less consequential', still less in the other direction, although there had been one or two exceptions. The top end of the 'consequentials' became 'important' colleagues; the bottom end of the 'less consequentials' headed towards exit and oblivion. But while he remembered the advice that Gladstone had given him in 1887 ('If ever you have to form a Government, Asquith, you must steel your nerves and act the butcher') he had rarely taken any pleasure in dispatching a colleague who proved inadequate to the task at hand. But there had been some.

In the category of colleagues who mattered there really were only four: Crewe, McKenna, Buckmaster and Grey.

Those who frankly did not matter much, the inconsequentials, included Samuel, the Home Secretary; McKinnon Wood, Chancellor of the Duchy of Lancaster; Pease, the postmaster general; Tennant, the Scottish Secretary, who was also Margot's brother; Runciman, President of the Board of Trade; and Harcourt, First Commissioner of Works.

He placed Montagu, Minister of Munitions and at one time Asquith's personal secretary, in a separate category. More than any other member of the Cabinet, Montagu had tried desperately to find a way of keeping Asquith and Lord George together in the same Government. For his efforts to reconcile the two men Asquith thought Montagu deserved respect. But for his lack of political judgement he thought he was a fool. He tried to convince himself that his low view of Montagu's judgement was in no way related to the fact that he had married Venetia Stanley eighteen months earlier.

Asquith opens the meeting.

'Gentlemen, since our gathering of yesterday afternoon I have written to Lloyd George explaining why it is no longer possible to implement the arrangement he and I discussed on Sunday afternoon. Lloyd George considered my letter overnight and responded to me this morning. I should tell you now that he has resigned from the Government and does not wish to be included in any new administration formed under my leadership unless the War Committee arrangements adopted by that new ministry are to his liking. As that would involve the Prime Minister relinquishing his chairmanship of the War Committee, and as I have now reached a settled view that such a course of action would be impossible, Lloyd George will not be a member of any new Government formed under my leadership.'

He pauses. Do they know already that Lloyd George has resigned? Of course they do. By now the dogs in the street know it too.

'Let me read you his response.'

At this Asquith reads the text of Lloyd George's letter of resignation. They listen in silence.

Asquith then reads the text of his own letter accepting Lloyd George's resignation.

'There has been one other development of which you should also be made aware. Mr Balfour has written to me resigning from the Admiralty. He understands that Lloyd George would prefer to have him replaced by Carson. I have written back to Balfour asking him to reconsider his resignation. But given that I must now reconstruct the Government without Lloyd George, or possibly give Lloyd George or Law a chance to form a Government first, the issue of Balfour's concern about Lloyd George's preference is no longer of any immediate relevance.'

He pauses.

'So, gentlemen, this evening I must either create a new Government or resign and allow someone else to make the attempt first. I am assured by Lord Curzon, Mr Chamberlain, Lord Robert Cecil and Mr Long that they would not accept office in any ministry formed by Bonar Law or Lloyd George. That renders the likelihood of any alternative Government being formed rather small, although we have heard that Mr Henderson thinks otherwise. For these and other reasons I am increasingly persuaded that I should take the advice you offered me earlier. If I reconstruct without Lloyd George or Law they will go on to lead a vocal and clamorous opposition in the House, in the press, and in the country. But if I form a new Government after they have tried and failed, they will then have no grounds for opposing the new ministry, given their own failure in that regard. In the middle of a great war the country must have a settled Government. So I am inclined' (he didn't pause, despite his distaste at having to say it) 'to resign. I would be grateful for your views in this matter.'

At which the Prime Minister sits back in his chair and awaits his colleagues' advice.

Crewe speaks first. 'It is a risk, Prime Minister. But on the whole it's a risk which I think you should take. This has gone on for too long and, as you say, the country needs clarity and settled leadership.'

'I agree with Crewe.' Lord Chancellor Buckmaster. 'The clamour would only intensify if we had them on the Opposition benches without the country having seen them for the failures they are.'

'I also agree.' Runciman.

Montagu, seated beside Runciman, speaks next. 'I must enter a dissenting voice, Prime Minister. Despite your exchange of letters I remain confident that an arrangement can still be constructed that would retain both you and Lloyd George, and also Law, in the Cabinet...'

'Under whose leadership?' Runciman asks.

Montagu hesitates and (was it possible, Asquith thought?) even appears to blush.

'Under Asquith,' he replies.

'Not a chance,' says Crewe. 'They've drawn too far apart now for reconciliation.'

The meeting murmurs its agreement.

Then Grey speaks. 'How sure are you about the four Conservatives, Prime Minister?'

'They came to see me yesterday, Edward. A vehement protest of loyalty. Denounced their own leader to me. They have assured me repeatedly that they would not serve under any Prime Minister other than me.'

'And you believe them?'

'Are you saying they might be lying?'

'Could be.'

'But why would they do that?' Asquith presses. 'Why would they lie to me about their own leader, whom they all plainly despise?'

'But Law has the support of most of his party. In the country. And in the press.'

'But not I think in the House. I don't think he has the numbers. I think we have.'

And again they murmur their agreement.

Asquith knows that he is taking a risk by contemplating resignation. But he also knows two other things as well. It would solve nothing if Lloyd George and Law were not seen very openly, very publicly, to have failed. They *must* be seen to fail. They must be seen to have been given every opportunity to put their grievances to the test. Otherwise their complaints would persist indefinitely.

He also knows that if he does not resign he will be the only person in the room who had not been forced to put his own career at risk in order to resolve the crisis. Many of them were not career-minded men, of course. But, nonetheless, he had pulled the rug out from under them, without any announcement, and forced each of them to yield up their ministries, however temporarily. He owes it to these men to take the same risk that he has himself imposed on them. And so he must resign.

They continue to discuss the matter for another thirty minutes. However they count the numbers they are certain that Asquith will prevail. The only thing that could impede their return to power was the possibility that the leading Unionists had been lying to Asquith.

He feels sure they had not been. He knows these men and he trusts them.

But Montagu knows otherwise.

– 31 –

Asquith took lunch with Margot after his colleagues had departed. They were joined by their daughter-in-law Cynthia, Beb's wife. Both women were aware that Asquith was tense and drained. Cynthia was staying with her parents-in-law and was due to dine with them again that evening. In the course of a simple lunch (no wine) she asked Asquith to explain the difference between *reshuffling* and *reconstructing* the Government. And also why (as Margot had already told her) he might, in fact, have to resign as Prime Minister.

'Reshuffling and reconstructing are much the same thing,' he explained. 'It's a matter of degree. Reshuffles usually just involve moving ministers around: A takes B's job, B takes C's, C takes A's. A kind of musical chairs. It gets more involved – becomes a more complicated reshuffle – when one or more ministers ask to leave the Government or the Prime Minister asks for their resignation. Then one can bring in new men to fill the places left vacant by the departing ministers, and one might also take the opportunity to move other ministers around as well.'

'You've done this a number of times?'

'I have. It's not part of the job that I greatly enjoy. But needs must. You remember last summer when Lord Kitchener drowned?'

'I do.'

'Lloyd George had been due to travel with Kitchener on the same ship to Russia. But he held back because I had asked him to try to find a settlement in Ireland. He might have drowned too had he gone to Russia.'

'Indeed.' This was Margot.

Asquith smiled.

'Anyway, I undertook a reshuffle after Kitchener died. I moved Lloyd George from Munitions to the War Office and I moved Montagu from the Treasury to Munitions. Harold, Margot's brother, came into the Cabinet at the Scottish Office. And others changed places as well. That was a reshuffle, quite a complicated one.'

'And a reconstruction?' Cynthia asked.

'Involves a much more complex process of negotiation and agreement. When we formed the Coalition Government last year I had to deal with the leader of another party, Bonar Law. For the first time I had to compromise in allocating men to ministries. Deciding how many places each party was to have and which ministries took time and negotiation.'

'But you got what you wanted, didn't you?' This was Margot.

'On the whole I did, yes.'

Cynthia had further questions. 'So what you're undertaking today is a reconstruction?'

'Well, yes. In principle. The King gave me authority on Sunday night to have every member of the Government resign. If I were to re-allocate them to new positions, possibly excluding some of them and bringing a number of new men into the Cabinet, that would require agreement with the Conservatives. So it would be a reconstruction, yes.'

'And why might you have to resign if the King has already commissioned you?'

Margot interjected. 'Cynthia, not now. Henry is tired. He'll explain this to us this evening.'

'No, my dear, let me explain. It's not all that complicated.' He placed his knife and fork on the table and spoke directly to Cynthia.

'You know that we've been having difficulty with Lloyd George recently. I thought last Sunday evening that he and I had been able to reach an agreement that would allow the Government to continue broadly in its present composition following a reconstruction. But that agreement has fallen apart. It's complicated; I won't say any more just now. But it's clear that Lloyd George is unwilling to serve in any new Government that I form. And Bonar Law is of the same mind. That makes forming a ministry more complicated, particularly with two major figures standing outside it. To address that difficulty I have, with the support of my Liberal and Unionist colleagues, more or less decided to resign. For the time being only, I hasten to add! The King will ask Lloyd George or Law, or possibly both of them, one after the other, to form a ministry. They don't have enough supporters in the House to carry that through so they will fail and the King will then ask me to form a ministry. I will succeed, leaving Law and Lloyd George out. And they won't be able to complain that they weren't given a fair opportunity to test how much support they have for their ideas.'

'But what if they *do* succeed?' Cynthia asked.

'My dear, they won't. Their numbers don't add up.'

Margot looked at him hard across the table. He could see the anxiety in her eyes. He looked away.

After lunch the Prime Minister took a short rest before returning downstairs for his three o'clock meeting.

Downing Street, Cabinet Room — 3 p.m.

In fact his job was one endless meeting. Or an endless series of meetings. They came in, they spoke, they agreed, he sent them away, they spoke again behind his back, they adjusted their positions, they returned and met again. And so the cycle continued. Rarely did they actually do anything from one meeting to the next. He found it infuriating. Meetings, meetings, meetings. Same process, different faces. And here he was again in the chair with the arms facing – again – the 'three Cs'. Curzon, Chamberlain and Cecil. They might have been a comedy troupe in a circus or an East End music hall.

In fact these three men had met together earlier in the day around the table in Chamberlain's room at the India Office. Walter Long had been with them, but not their leader, Bonar Law.

There they discussed Curzon's telephone call of yesterday morning with Law. Curzon was still apoplectic that Law had failed to give Asquith the resolution they had so carefully drafted on Sunday morning. He had not forgotten to do so; he had merely decided that he didn't wish to. Acting on his own authority as leader. Curzon found this outrageous.

Chamberlain, Cecil and Long were also unimpressed by Law's behaviour. It was quite unacceptable and he needed to be told as much. To that end Long had been dispatched to see Law and invite him to a further meeting with them at 4 o'clock that day. The invitation had been issued as an ultimatum, in effect requiring his presence at a court of enquiry. Long had been due to join them again after seeing Law but there had been no word from him since his departure to summon the leader. Things had obviously not gone quite as smoothly as planned.

When Lord Curzon had awoken that morning he decided that a fourth name must be added to the list of men who might find themselves Prime Minister by the weekend. His own. The likelihood was not very high but politics was all about taking chances whatever the odds. As he was shaved he thought of the two steps he needed to take in order to position himself for the summons to the Palace.

First he needed to get rid of Bonar Law.

Then he needed to get rid of Asquith.

That would leave him and Lloyd George. He thought, although he couldn't be completely certain about it, that he could probably persuade more Liberals to support him than Lloyd George could persuade Unionists to support *his* candidacy. It was all a little unclear, not at all certain, but certainly worth the attempt. Lord Curzon wanted to be Prime Minister more than anything else in his life. He wanted it even more than he wanted the delightful Elinor Glyn, his mistress of seven years, on her famous tiger skin. ('Would you like to sin, With Elinor Glyn, On a tiger skin? Or would you prefer, To err with her, On some other fur?' How he hated that rhyme. He heard passers-by reciting it in the street as he strode by them. Common people gave him the shivers.)

His strategy was clear. He would dispose of Asquith this afternoon. Law could be taken care of later in the day. Hence his meeting with Chamberlain, Cecil and Long, and their summoning of Law to see them at four o'clock.

Now for Asquith.

'Gentlemen, thank you for coming again,' the Prime Minister began. 'I can now give you some further information about my work in reconstructing the Government.'

Asquith paused to gain their attention.

'I have had a series of meetings with colleagues from both parties in the last two days, including Mr Law.'

'And Lloyd George?' This was Cecil.

'Lloyd George and I have exchanged letters. You will know that he has resigned from the Government.'

'We do.'

'Good. Well then, I have considered your advice very carefully, gentlemen, and that of my colleagues in the Liberal Party as well. I am minded to accept your recommendation and resign, allowing others to attempt to form a new Government. I will make up my mind by tea-time this afternoon but I want you to know that my instincts now tell me that you have been correct and this is the path I should now take.'

A silence around the table. No voices raised in agreement with his proposed course of action. No congratulations for doing as they had advised for many days now.

Asquith found this slightly disturbing. Nonetheless he pressed on with the two questions he needed to ask them.

Lord Curzon sat directly across the table from him. Now I have him, Curzon thought. All I need to do is ensure that I am the one to answer his questions before any of the others speak.

Asquith continued to summarise the position. 'You will know that Bonar Law has also indicated, together with Lloyd George, that he does not wish to participate in any new Government that I might form. I respect his views in this matter, as indeed I respect Lloyd George's views. But if either Law or Lloyd George were to attempt to form a ministry and assuming, as I think we must, that that endeavour would fail, the King would then be very likely to ask me to form a new coalition ministry. It would be difficult in the circumstances for me to ask either Law or Lloyd George to join in that enterprise. I would, however, wish to invite you all, and also Mr Long, to join the Government. But I must first know what your attitude would be to joining a Government from which Lloyd George and Bonar Law had excluded themselves.'

A brief silence. Curzon knew that he needed to time this very carefully. He must allow just enough silence so that Asquith will understand that the game is up, but he must also ensure that he himself is the one to break the silence. The timing was on a hair trigger.

The room continued in silence for a brief moment.

Asquith read the silence and knew that he was in difficulty.

Then Curzon stirred. Cleared his throat to establish that he would be the one to respond for his colleagues. And spoke.

'I'm afraid that, on reflection, Prime Minister, my colleagues and I are of the view that we could not serve in any Government that excluded both Law and Lloyd George.'

Asquith stared at him hard.

You treacherous little shit.

'When we spoke about this only yesterday, Lord Curzon, you indicated a different response.'

'We have discussed the matter again, Prime Minister, and we now take the view that no Government could properly serve the country at this critical hour if two of the three principal men were excluded from its affairs.'

The calculus was impeccable. We could possibly carry on without *one* of the three principal men but not without *two* of them. And as two of them, Lloyd George and Bonar Law, are now locked firmly together, that leaves only one man who is expendable. And that man is you.

Asquith sat back in his chair as a storm screamed across his brain. His eyes hurt and the whistling in his ears drowned out any other noise in the room.

Curzon watched him with curiosity. This is what a man looks like when he has been betrayed.

Asquith recovered enough of his poise (the storm in his brain abated) that he could ask his second question.

'And what, Lord Curzon, would be the attitude of you and your colleagues if Lloyd George attempted to form a Government?'

This time there was no hesitation.

'Given that Mr Law is now supporting Lloyd George, and given, as we hear, that the Labour members are likely to support him also, it seems that Lloyd George has an appreciably stronger chance of forming a ministry today than he had yesterday. As the country needs strong Government during the crisis of this war, then, if it seems that Lloyd George would succeed in forming a ministry, it would, we believe, be our duty to support him.'

Again Asquith sat back. The first punch to his left had been followed by a second to his right. He felt sick, nauseous, drained.

Again Curzon watched him with curiosity. This is what a man looks like when he has been destroyed.

They sat in silence for a few moments. Then Cecil spoke.

'Prime Minister, I – we – greatly regret that matters have come to this. But Lord Curzon is correct in saying that the country needs strong government. If Lloyd George looks as if he can provide that kind of stability with Unionist support then it would be essential to have you play your part in the new Government as well.'

'My part?' Asquith asked.

'Yes. In Cabinet. In an important office.'

'But not as Prime Minister?'

'No,' Curzon responded. The faintest flicker of a smile crossed his face. 'No, Mr Asquith, not as Prime Minister.'

And then the meeting came to an end. No concluding pleasantries were exchanged. Asquith didn't even rise to thank his guests for attending. The Unionists left and the Prime Minister sat in silence as Cecil closed the door behind them.

The end had come, in effect, at twenty minutes after three on Tuesday the 5th of December.

– 32 –

When he read the Prime Minister's reply to his letter of that morning, Arthur Balfour realised that Asquith had quite missed the point. This was uncharacteristic: Asquith was one of the most astute politicians he had ever dealt with. Nuance and subtlety were his stock-in-trade. Balfour concluded that he must be under truly immense pressure if he had failed to understand the message. Balfour resolved that his second letter must be much less opaque than the first one had been.

That further letter arrived just as Asquith was finishing his own review of where the volte-face by the Unionist ministers now left him. He was under no illusions. Having burnt his bridges with Lloyd George there was no longer any possibility of reaching an accommodation with him in relation to the War Committee. Simple reconstruction of the Government was no longer an option either given the immense pressure that both Liberal and Unionist ministers had imposed on him earlier in the day to resign. He could, in principle, ask the King for a dissolution, but to propel the country into a general election in wartime would be unconscionable. And in the circumstances there was no guarantee that the King would grant him a dissolution or, if he did, that the country would forgive him for taking such a step. It was obvious that his only option was to resign.

But he knew now that his resignation would not be a temporary affair. Lloyd George and Bonar Law would certainly be able to form an administration. His only hope, if 'hope' was the appropriate word to use in this context, was that the new Government would collapse in a matter of weeks and Asquith would then be asked to return.

But he would have to leave Downing Street this week.

The thought made him sick to his stomach.

He rose and was about to leave the Cabinet Room to break the news to Margot when a servant knocked and entered, bearing a letter. The handwriting on the envelope was Balfour's. Accepting the letter, he sat at the end of the table and read it. It confirmed his view that all was now over.

> 4, Carlton Gardens
> Pall Mall, S.W.
> Dec 5th, 1916
> 4 p.m.

My dear Asquith,

I am very grateful for your note and its enclosure. I highly value your appreciation.

I do not, however, feel much inclined to change my views. I still think (a) that the break-up of the Government by the retirement of Lloyd George would be a misfortune, (b) that the experiment of giving him a free hand with the day-to-day work of the War Committee is worth trying, and (c) that there is no use trying it except on terms that enable him to work under the conditions, which, in his own opinion, promise the best results. We cannot, I think, go on in the old way. And open breach with Lloyd George will not improve matters, and attempts to compel co-operation between him and fellow-workers with whom he is in but imperfect sympathy will only produce fresh trouble.

I am therefore still of opinion that my resignation should be accepted, and that a fair trial should be given to the new War Council à la George.

> Yours very sincerely
> Arthur James Balfour

The Liberals were due back in half an hour. Feeling exhausted and suddenly old beyond measure, he went upstairs to the residence to talk to his wife.

Downing Street, Cabinet Room — 5 p.m.

'Gentlemen, I have some difficult news for you. Let me come straight to the point. I have decided to resign and will see the King at half past six this evening to return my seals of office to him.'

A murmur from around the table greeted this news.

'I fear, however, that my resignation this evening will truly mark my resignation. For some time at least. I have already begun to make preparations for my family to leave Downing Street later in the week.'

'What?' This was McKenna. All of his colleagues now looked at Asquith with a mixture of surprise and distress. He held up his hand and continued.

'I saw Mr Chamberlain, Lord Robert Cecil and Lord Curzon earlier this afternoon. Those of you who suggested that their pro-testations of loyalty might have been overblown were, in fact, quite correct. They now plan to support Lloyd George if the King asks him to form a Government.'

'Jesus Christ.' McKenna again.

'McKenna, please.'

'I'm sorry, PM. But I can't believe they could be so two-faced. Are you sure?'

'I'm afraid so, yes. At least Chamberlain and Cecil had the grace to be sheepish about it. Curzon positively enjoyed himself. Never underestimate Lord Curzon, gentlemen. He is quite the most insincere and vain man I have ever encountered in public life. I'd also call him calculating but I am afraid – and in the circumstances I hope you will forgive me for being rather negative – he is too stupid to be an efficient calculator. Actually, let me speak frankly. And please excuse my language. Lord Curzon is a shit.'

'He wants to be Prime Minister himself.'

'Yes, he does,' Asquith replied. 'But Lloyd George won't have that. I'm afraid it's now very likely that David will be Prime Minister in a few days' time. Please do not feel under any obligation to me to decline an appointment if he asks you to join his ministry.'

A series of demurrals from around that table. 'Never.' 'No.' 'Not with that man.' And so on. Asquith was gratified by this display of loyalty from his colleagues.

'Oh, and by the way,' Asquith continued, 'Mr Balfour has written to me again reiterating his decision to resign. He believes that "Lloyd George's approach" is worth a try. So now the Unionists are peeling away one by one.'

A further silence until Crewe spoke.

'If this happens, Prime Minister – and I genuinely do mean *if* – what would you do?'

Asquith hesitated briefly. 'I would support the Government in the vigorous prosecution of the war and in any other commendable steps they take. But I would oppose them whenever that was required.'

'You would become Leader of the Opposition?'

No phrase fills a serving Prime Minister with quite as much nausea as 'Leader of the Opposition' when it is used in reference to himself.

'Yes, I would.'

From across the table he heard 'Forgive me for asking, PM, but would you serve in a Lloyd George administration?'

'No, Montagu, I would not. I would lead the Opposition and hold myself ready to return to this place if and when the new Government fails. Of which, I might say, there is every probability that it will, and at an early date too. So I will resign, gentlemen, and take my chances.'

'Are you sure it will be Lloyd George rather than Law?' This was Grey.

'Not quite, Edward. But I know Law and I'm sure he will defer to Lloyd George. So my wager would be on David. But what does it matter? Either way it won't be me. Or us.'

'Or Curzon?'

The question brought a smile to Asquith's face.

'The only satisfaction of this whole debacle is that it won't be Lord

Curzon. If it was, I wouldn't just resign: I'd throw myself off Westminster Bridge as well. And I'd recommend that you all do the same!'

At this they all laughed together. A little too heartily for Asquith's taste, but at least they ended on a happy note.

Downing Street, Prime Minister's Residence — 6.30 p.m.

'Lord Derby, Mrs Asquith.'

'Lord Derby?'

'Yes, madam.'

'What does he want?'

'To see the Prime Minister, madam.'

'Tell him the Prime Minister is occupied, Drummond.'

'He asked me to give him this note if the Prime Minister was unable to see him, madam.'

He hands her the note and Margot reads it.

Dear Asquith,

It is rumoured that you have determined to resign. Please, I implore you, do not take such a drastic and unnecessary step. There is still every possibility of reaching an accommodation with Lloyd George. The country needs both of you working together, not pulling apart. My Unionist colleagues have gone too far out on a limb with this. Please pause and make contact with L.G. before you take any more drastic action. I stand ready to assist in any way I can with such a conversation.

Yours ever,
Derby.

She pauses for a moment before rolling the note into a ball and throwing it into the fire.

'Please tell Lord Derby that the Prime Minister thanks him for his note, and for all his advice and counsel over the years, but he has already made up his mind to resolve the matter in a different way.'

'Thank you, Mrs Asquith.'
Drummond withdraws.

* * *

Ten minutes later Margot walks with Asquith down the staircase at Downing Street. Past the portraits of the former holders of his office. His own not yet among them. But not for long.

Asquith is dressed in a black frock coat with striped trousers, holding his top hat and gloves in his hands. Protocol requires the Prime Minister to appear in this outfit for any formal audience of the King. And resignations and appointments are the most formal of all such audiences.

As they wait in the hall for the motor to arrive the front door opens and Lord Curzon is admitted. Margot eyes him with open contempt, Asquith with a disinterested gaze. He approaches, paper in hand.

'Prime Minister, I've just come from a meeting of my Unionist colleagues. We have a resolution for you to consider.' He hands it to Asquith, who reads it briefly. And then hands it back.

'No longer of any relevance, Lord Curzon. I am on my way to the King to tender my resignation. But thank you for coming and please thank your colleagues for their, ah, advice. We will talk again tomorrow. And now, if you'll excuse me, I must go to the Palace.'

Curzon says his goodbyes and leaves.

Margot kisses her husband on the cheek. She is holding back tears.

Asquith puts on his hat and gloves and walks slowly to the front door without looking back. The servant opens it, the policeman salutes, the driver holds the door of the motor open for him. And then the Prime Minister begins his short journey towards the Palace, the King, and oblivion.

– 33 –

Tuesday 5 December 1916

Other meetings had taken place that same day, each of which contributed in turn to Asquith's evening journey to the Palace to return his seals of office to the King.

Pembroke Lodge — 6 a.m.

Bonar Law swam into consciousness after a night of deep and restful sleep. The room was still dark, the house quiet. His sister slept in her bedroom along the corridor. They were alone in the lodge.

Fragments of dreams fast disappearing merged with fragments of recollections from yesterday. A busy day. Meetings. The war. His dealings with other men.

From a far corner of his consciousness the most important reality of all drifted in and demanded his attention. This was Tuesday. Yesterday, Monday, he had broken with Asquith. Today Asquith would have to decide how to proceed, although it seemed to Law that the Prime Minister had now run out of options. It was therefore likely that at some stage today, probably in the evening, Law would be summoned to the Palace and commissioned by the King to form a Government. In other words he could this evening become, or at least be the primary candidate for becoming, Prime Minister of England.

He remembered Dr Johnson's aphorism about a man who was about to be hanged finding that his imminent death concentrated his mind wonderfully. To become Prime Minister wasn't quite the same as being hanged but the idea filled Law with a similar sense of dread. He did not feel competent to the task. Asquith, for all his faults (and they were many), was a superb manager of both business and men. He chaired Cabinet meetings with a deftness that Law could only marvel at. He managed Parliament with something approaching supreme skill. And until recently he had managed other men with a unique sensitivity and even cunning. Law knew that he himself possessed none of these abilities. He hated meetings. He despised Parliament. And his dealings with colleagues filled him with dread and an acute sense of his own inadequacy. But politics returns strange outcomes and the outcome of this latest crisis was likely to be an invitation to this inadequate man to form a Government. Really it was absurd.

He ought to have felt some sense of accomplishment, some pride that his career had carried him to the summit from which the affairs of the country and its Empire were directed. But he didn't have any sense of achievement at all, still less of triumph. He tried to understand and summarise how he felt. His life was in fact a vast sea of emptiness with fingers of dread and exhaustion attacking him from either side. But in twelve hours' time he would almost certainly be asked to take the lead. It turned his stomach. He rose from his bed, back aching, knees creaking, and turned on the bedside light. Then, wrapping himself in an old dressing gown, he made for the bathroom along the hall.

India Office — 11 a.m.

Later that morning, after a brisk walk across St James's Park, Curzon met with Chamberlain, Cecil and Long at the India Office. Balfour could not attend because he was ill, although this was actually a blessing because Balfour's attitude to Asquith was not something that Curzon completely understood. Neither Lansdowne nor Law were invited to attend; Lansdowne because of his growing reputation as a dangerous appeaser, Law because the meeting was in fact about him. Nor was F. E. Smith invited to attend either, again because Curzon was uncertain how he might react to the proposal that Curzon was about to put to the meeting.

The attendees discussed Law's recent dealings with Asquith. In particular his decision not to give Asquith the written resolution passed by the Unionist ministers at their Sunday morning meeting. This was unforgivable. Their leader in the Commons had, in effect, separated himself from the other leading members of his party. No leader who behaved in this way could possibly continue to enjoy their confidence.

Cecil, Chamberlain and Law all agreed with Curzon on this point, although they were astute enough to recognise Curzon's personal ambition in the matter. But with the political sands shifting furiously, now was the time to make sure that Law knew how they felt. They needed to meet with him to discuss the matter. Curzon had no doubt what that would mean.

This was why Walter Long had been dispatched from the meeting to advise Law that his colleagues wished to see him at four o'clock that afternoon at the India Office.

It was further agreed that even if Asquith did not summon them later today, the four Unionists would request a meeting with him that afternoon to clarify their position. Curzon agreed to arrange that meeting for three o'clock if no invitation arrived from the Prime Minister himself before then.

Colonial Office — 2.30 p.m.

When Law was told that Long had arrived and wished to see him he was immediately suspicious. The meeting had been requested before lunch but Law had put him off until early in the afternoon. Walter Long was a cunning man even by the standards of his senior colleagues. He did nothing without a purpose or a plan. To have him call at his leader's office for a chance conversation had never happened in the many years of Law's leadership. It put him on a high state of alert.

Long apologised for disturbing him. But he had come to see him on an important issue. When Law invited him to proceed Long said that he had just come from a meeting with Curzon, Chamberlain and Cecil.

'A meeting? Of Unionist ministers? Without me?'

'Well, yes. But why should that surprise you? We meet one another informally all the time.'

'Your meeting sounds slightly more than an informal gathering, particularly if they have dispatched you as an emissary after the event. No Balfour?'

'Still sick.'

'Smith?'

'No.'

'Lansdowne?'

'Not really appropriate.'

Law smiled. 'So, a cabal then?'

'I wouldn't quite put it that way.'

'Well how would you put it, Long?'

'We met to discuss recent developments. Asquith's intentions. And yours.'

'Mine? Really? And what would you say my intentions were?'

'It's increasingly hard to know, Law. We were particularly concerned that you didn't give Asquith the resolution we drafted last Sunday.'

'I've explained that before. It wasn't appropriate. Or necessary. I gave him a full account of our meeting.'

'We don't think that was a wise or proper way of proceeding. The resolution was drafted carefully. You omitted to convey to the PM the full extent of our criticisms of Lloyd George. Which gave Asquith room to negotiate a compromise with him later that evening. A compromise that has now unravelled, I agree, but he should never have been presented with the opportunity in the first place. And he acquired it only because you considered it expedient, for reasons that remain wholly opaque, to ignore a decision taken by the party's senior leaders.'

'Its senior leaders? Really? Let me remind you, Long, that our party has one senior leader in the Lords, Lord Lansdowne, and an even more senior leader in the Commons: myself. And that I am the more senior of the two "senior leaders". I'm happy to meet with colleagues to discuss their concerns at any time. But while I carry the burden of leadership then the final decision in all matters such as my meeting with the Prime Minister last Sunday rests with me. Alone.'

'We don't think that is the case, Law.'

'You what?' Law raised his voice.

'We need to review the position with you. We need you to meet us this afternoon. At four o'clock. At the India Office. In Lord Curzon's rooms.'

Law stared hard at his visitor. He was pausing, not to think, but to ensure that the full impact of what he was about to do was impressed on Long and carried back to his colleagues.

He rose. Long rose as well. Law approached him and brought his face close to Long's. Then he bellowed. So hard and so loud that spittle landed on Long's nose and he recoiled involuntarily.

'For as long as I am leader of this party, Mr Long – and I intend to remain its leader for a very long time indeed – I have no intention of responding to summonses from my colleagues to attend what would appear to be a court-martial. None whatsoever. So take that back to Lord Curzon, Mr Chamberlain and Lord Robert Cecil, and any other conspirators you may have in mind to add to your cabal. Do you understand me?'

Long hesitated. Then, in a lower voice, 'I do.'

'Now get out of my office.'

Long stared at him for a long moment before turning for the door. As he reached it Law spoke again. Slightly calmer, but the rage was still apparent.

'Actually, Long, please tell your friends that I am summoning *them* to a meeting. Here. At my office. At five o'clock today. You understand?'

'I do.'

'Good. Five o'clock then. I will look forward to seeing you all at that time.'

* * *

By five o'clock that afternoon Unionist tempers had calmed. Curzon realised on hearing Long's report of the meeting that his plan was no longer going to work. Law was not quite the coward he had imagined him to be. Well, good for him. At three o'clock they went to see Asquith and told him they would not support him. At their meeting at five o'clock the Unionist group, this time with their leader present, passed a resolution urging Asquith's immediate resignation. This was the paper that Curzon brought to Downing Street just as Asquith was leaving for the Palace.

Buckingham Palace — 7.30 p.m.

'Lord Crewe.'

'Your Majesty?'

'Please sit down.'

'Thank you, Sir.'

Crewe moved to a chair across from the King, who sat at the same time. The King removed his hat and placed it on the side table, then unbuckled his sword and placed it on the floor. He unfastened the top button of his tunic – it was biting into his neck. Asquith had just left, having returned his seals of office to the King. On being asked for his advice as to whom the King should now send for he replied that Bonar Law was leader of the second largest party in the Commons and as such it was his duty to advise the King to send for him. The King thanked him warmly for his service. He anticipated that they would meet again in the coming days and he looked forward to his further advice on resolving the current *impasse*. As Asquith withdrew the King asked Crewe, who had accompanied him, to remain behind.

'I have asked Lord Haldane for his advice.'

'His advice, Sir?'

'Constitutional advice. Given his experience as Lord Chancellor, I have asked him to advise me on a question which I believe may arise imminently.'

'May I ask what that is, Sir?'

'I must send for Law. If I ask him to form a ministry and he proves able to do that I will appoint him as Prime Minister. He may then, or shortly afterwards, ask for a dissolution. I am aware that a Prime Minister may ask for a dissolution at any time but given the fluid situation among the parties at present and also the fact that we are buried in a war, I need to know whether I am obliged to grant any such request. Or whether I have the option to commission another man to form a ministry without granting the Prime Minister a dissolution.'

'Haldane is the right man to advise you, Sir.'

'And your own view?'

'With respect, Your Majesty, as a minister in the outgoing Government and perhaps also a minister in a future one, it would be improper of me to advise you on such a matter.'

The King smiled. 'Indeed. Quite right. And that is also why I have asked the previous Lord Chancellor and not the current one to advise me. But you do agree that the question is a live one and that it is appropriate for me to ask for constitutional advice?'

'I do indeed, Sir. And Lord Haldane will advise you well.'

'Good. Well, thank you, Crewe. Look after Asquith, won't you? It's been a difficult time for him these last few weeks and I'm not sure it's going to get any better in the coming days.'

'Indeed, Sir. I will.'

Crewe rose and withdrew.

The King had not wanted Crewe's advice at all, of course. He had wanted him to tell Asquith what he was doing and, in particular, to get word to Law that he would be ill-advised to seek a dissolution if he were able to form a Government. Crewe knew what was being asked of him and attended to both matters as soon as the car arrived back at his office in Whitehall.

War Office — 8 p.m.

Bonar Law called me at half past seven and asked me to proceed immediately to the War Office to meet him there with Lloyd George. Curzon had returned from Downing Street somewhat out of breath. The meeting of Unionist ministers had by then descended into conviviality and wholly insincere expressions of goodwill over whiskey and cigars. Curzon told them that Asquith was already at the Palace resigning. The others shuffled away leaving Law to his thoughts. They knew what would happen next and thought it best to give him some privacy. He agreed to keep in touch with them throughout the evening and then telephoned me. I hurried to the War Office, waiting outside Lloyd George's rooms for Law to arrive.

'Well, Aitken. Interesting times', he said, as he came into the outer office.

With that we went in to see Lloyd George.

The War Secretary was sprawled on a sofa opposite his desk. As we entered he stood up and gave Law a mock salute.

'Prime Minister,' he smiled.

'Please, Lloyd George. Enough of that.' Law was not amused.

'Well we got him, Bonar. Well done. You too Max. This couldn't have happened without you. Well done to you both.'

Law sat and Lloyd George resumed his place on the sofa. I stood to one side of the two men.

'Let's review this now.' This was Lloyd George. 'The Government has fallen. The Prime Minister has resigned. He will certainly have advised the King to send for you, Law. By the way, does your office know where you are?'

'I told them I had gone to see you.'

'Last thing we want is the King trying to find you and being told that the next Prime Minister has gone to ground.' Lloyd George seemed to find this hilariously funny.

'Enough. Stop laughing. Enough of the levity. This is serious.' This was Law.

Lloyd George relaxed his laugh into a full smile. Eyes still beaming. But then the question.

'So, Bonar, what are you going to do?'

Law stared straight back at him.

'Exactly as we discussed.'

'Which is…?' I interjected.

Both men turned to look at me. In half a minute or so they had each forgotten that I was in the room.

'Lloyd George and I have agreed on how to take this forward, Max. I will advise the King that while I will attempt to form a Government I must have both Lloyd George and Asquith agreeing to serve.'

'He never will,' I said, meaning Asquith.

'If that is the case then I will tell the King that I am unable to form a Government and will advise him to send for Lloyd George.'

'But will our Unionist colleagues serve under Lloyd George?' I asked.

'Naïve, Max. Desperately naïve.' Law responded. 'Of course they will.'

It was at this point that they asked me, most courteously, to leave the room as they needed to discuss the disposition of offices in what was about to become the Second Wartime Coalition.

– 34 –

Once Aitken had left the room, Lloyd George showed Law the letter he had received from Asquith thirty minutes earlier. It was written just after Asquith returned to Downing Street following his meeting with the King:

> 10, Downing Street, S.W.
> December 5, 1916

My dear Lloyd George,

It may make a difference to you (in reply to your last letter) if I tell you at once that I have tendered my resignation to the King.

In any case, I should deprecate in the public interest the publication in its present form at this moment of your letters to me of this morning.

Of course, I have neither the power nor the wish to prevent you stating in some other form the causes which have led you to take the step which you have taken.

> Yours very sincerely,
> H. H. Asquith

Just as Law finished reading the letter the telephone rang on Lloyd George's desk. Both men looked at one another. They knew what it meant. Lloyd George answered.

'Yes?'

A pause.

'He is. Just one moment please.'

Lloyd George laid the receiver on his desk and turned to Law.

'For you. Lord Stamfordham. I think I should wait outside while you talk to him.'

'Nonsense,' Law replied. 'Wait here. It's your own bloody office.' He walked to the desk and lifted the receiver.

'Law here.'

'Mr Law, this is Lord Stamfordham. His Majesty commands your attendance at the Palace as soon as possible.'

Law paused and then replied, 'I will be there in twenty minutes.'

'Thank you.' Stamfordham ended the call. Law replaced the receiver in its cradle and turned to Lloyd George.

'Right. I'm summoned. I'll take your car and driver if I may. And I'll return here once it's over and we can discuss the arrangements in more detail then.'

Lloyd George smiled a broad smile. 'Indeed. Good luck. And listen, Law: try to enjoy it. It'll be an interesting experience. And see how you get on with him.'

'I'm afraid I know exactly how I'll get on with him. But I'll try to watch it as if it were happening to someone else. We'll talk later.'

As he reached the door Law turned and said,

'Oh, and one other thing. Send Aitken away, will you? I don't think we need him any more. Not directly anyway. I think we should just deal among the principals now. Don't you agree?'

Again Lloyd George smiled. 'Leave him to me.'

Buckingham Palace — 9 p.m.

The King had changed out of his ceremonial dress once Crewe had left. For his meeting with Law he wore less formal attire: a three-piece tweed suit and tie, his brogues polished until he could see the chandeliers in them. He was inviting Law to attempt to form a ministry. Only if Law returned later to confirm that he was able to discharge that commission would the King appoint him as Prime Minister. For that meeting the King would revert to ceremonial dress. He hoped that Stamfordham would explain to Law (or to Lloyd George if it came to it, which it probably would) that 'kissing hands' did not actually mean *kissing hands*. He expected the new Prime Minister to go down on one knee and place both his hands briefly in the monarch's own. No kissing would be involved, just a gentle inclination of the head towards the King's paws. He remembered his grandmother telling him how much this ceremony revolted her.

Stamfordham knocked and announced the visitor.

'Mr Law, Your Majesty.'

No response was required of the King. Stamfordham stepped to one side and the little Canadian came in. Approached the presence. Bowed briefly. And looked him full in the face.

'Mr Law.'

'Your Majesty.'

'Thank you for coming.' How long would this take, the King wondered? Not long, he hoped. All pretty straightforward. So let's remain standing, no seats.

'Mr Asquith has given me his resignation as Prime Minister.'

'Yes, Sir.'

'I thanked him for his service both to my father and to me, and I asked for his advice on who to send for. He advised me, quite properly, that I should send for you. Which I have now done.'

A silence. Law wondered whether he was expected to thank the King for doing his duty. Probably not. The King wondered whether any thanks would be offered to him for behaving so graciously. Probably not. The moment passed.

'And so, Mr Law, I am inviting you to form a ministry. If, following discussion with the members of your party and others, you find that you can compose a ministry that commands a majority in the House of Commons you will return and advise me of that fact. I will then appoint you as my Prime Minister.'

'I am greatly honoured, Sir, and I will do my best. But I must warn you that the prospects of success are not high.'

Damn the man, the King thought. Just bugger off and do what you can and let me know the outcome.

But Law did not bugger off. He continued.

'I'm not sure that I could form a stable ministry without both Asquith and Lloyd George agreeing to serve.'

'Asquith? In the Cabinet?'

'Yes, Sir. I think it is essential.'

'I won't meddle in this, Law: it's your responsibility now. But it strikes me that a Prime Minister who has just left office after eight years is unlikely to show much enthusiasm for serving in his successor's administration.'

'There is precedent for it, Sir. Lord Wellington served under Sir Robert Peel. Lord Palmerston under Lord John Russell. And of course, more recently, Mr Balfour has served under Mr Asquith.'

'Precedent, yes. But I'm not entirely sure the circumstances are equivalent. In any case I doubt you could persuade Asquith to serve. But I must leave that to you now, Law.'

'Indeed, Sir. And then of course...'

My God, he's going to go on.

The King had had a busy day. Deeply stressful, this business of changing Prime Ministers. He was tired and more to the point he had forgotten to visit the small room as he came upstairs. Law had arrived sooner than expected. Ordinarily the King would have let him wait. But in his haste to get the meeting completed, and in the expectation that Law would simply say 'yes' and 'thank you' and then go away, the King had neglected to 'do his duty' (as the family referred to it) on his way to the meeting. And so the inevitable had happened. He was increasingly aware of the pressure in his bladder. While Law wittered on, the King needed to pee.

'...there is the question of Lloyd George. It is essential that he should be a member of the Cabinet and in charge of our War Committee. I'm sure that Lloyd George would serve beside Asquith but I'm afraid I am equally certain that Asquith would decline to serve beside Lloyd George.'

'Even if I asked him to?' the King enquired. 'Or commanded him to, if necessary?'

'With respect, Sir, I don't believe that would be an appropriate course of conduct for you to follow.'

The King stared at him. You jumped-up little...pipsqueak. I haven't even appointed you Prime Minister yet and already you're telling me what I can and cannot do.

Law caught the King's stare and knew that he was angry. But Law stood his ground. Start as you mean to go on. Any ministry that I form will be formed by me alone without any pressure from the King.

'In any event I will of course make enquiries, Sir, and advise you promptly of the position.'

'Thank you.'

The King was about to dismiss him when Law spoke again.

Incredible. The pressure on his bladder had now become quite uncomfortable.

'If I do form a ministry, Sir, I must have your assurance that as Prime Minister I would continue to enjoy all the electoral prerogatives that have always accrued to a King's First Minister.'

Electoral prerogatives. Exactly what he had expected him to request. Law was a tremendous bore but he wasn't stupid. The King decided to act confused.

'I'm not quite sure that I follow you.'

'The right to request a dissolution, Sir. And an expectation that any such request would be granted.'

The King paused. Looked him in the eye. Remembered Haldane's advice. Then answered.

'I understand your request, Mr Law. And I understand why you are asking. You will also understand, I hope, that although a Prime Minister in peacetime can always expect to have any such request honoured by the King, things may be different in wartime. A general election could have a remarkably destabilising effect on military morale. Comfort to the enemy and all that. Germans seeing the English as leaderless and confused. It might encourage them to try for a knock-out blow whilst the country is electing a new Parliament.'

The King stopped and stared at him.

Law stared back.

'I'm afraid I am of the view, Sir, that any temporary instability in the administration during a brief election campaign would be far less damaging than if the instability which had prompted the Prime Minister to request the dissolution remained unresolved.'

Silence.

Law continued, 'And with the greatest of respect, Sir, I must ask for your assurance on this matter before I could accept your commission to form a ministry.'

The King stayed silent. But silence would not do. The pressure in his bladder had now turned to pain. The audience must end.

'Mr Law. Make your enquiries this evening and tomorrow morning. Let me know the position tomorrow. And…if you find yourself in a position to form a ministry I will give you a commitment to honour any request you may make for a dissolution. But I would ask you to consider matters very carefully before you ever make any such request.'

'Thank you, Sir.'

Law bowed and backed away. Stamfordham, who had been listening outside the door, came in and showed him out. He closed the door behind them.

The King sprinted for the stairs.

10 Downing Street — 9.45 p.m.

Asquith thought this might happen. As he dined with Crewe, Margot and Cynthia, a servant entered and passed him a note. He read it quickly. 'Five minutes, Cabinet Room,' he replied. The servant thanked him and left.

Asquith turned to his dinner companions. Crewe was attempting to keep their spirits up but the strain on Margot was obvious. They had talked about the crisis throughout the meal. Asquith told them that a Lloyd George Government was now all but inevitable: he knew Law would be asked first but was confident that he would fail to form a ministry. But he also suspected that the new Government would not last for more than a few months. Although they would have to leave Downing Street for the old house at Cavendish Square this week he was confident they would return soon. Probably not by Christmas, but perhaps by Easter?

Crewe suspected this was a fantasy but said nothing to deflate Asquith's optimism.

Margot knew it too but couldn't keep the desolation from her face.

Actually, deep down, buried beneath all the layers of political optimism, courage and imagination that had sustained him over so many years, Asquith knew it as well. He simply hadn't admitted it to himself yet.

'The note?' Margot asked.

'Law. Downstairs. Wants to see me.'

'I despise that man. That Judas.'

'Margot, please. That's unkind.'

She put her knife and fork on the table and burst into tears.

Asquith rose quickly and went to comfort her. He held her shoulders and kissed her hair. She regained her composure. He despised himself for not having prepared her for what was happening to them. He hated to see her suffering like this.

'I must go and see him. But it won't take long. I know what he wants and I know what my answer will be. Let's play a little bridge when I'm back. Robert, look after the ladies while I'm away.

Lord Crewe stood as Asquith left the room. He was no longer Prime Minister but the habits of a lifetime – or what seemed like a lifetime – died hard. Suddenly Crewe had an overwhelming sense that they were all growing old. An era was coming to an end. Handing over to other men. He was determined to retire even if – although he knew this wouldn't happen – Asquith returned to this house. It was time to set out on some new adventure in his life.

Asquith lit a cigar as he descended the staircase.

Law awaited him in the Cabinet Room.

Sheepish.

As well he might be.

He opened with what sounded to Asquith like a contrived statement prepared on his way back from the Palace. 'When a man has done another a serious injury, no good can come from explanations.'

Asquith smiled. Not so much at the clumsiness of the phrasing but at Law's obvious embarrassment and discomfort.

Asquith held out his hand to him. As they exchanged a firm handshake he replied, 'I have no feeling of hostility.'

They sat opposite one another at the Cabinet table. This time, however, Asquith avoided the chair with the arms. It would not have been appropriate.

Law began. 'I have just seen the King.'

'Yes.'

'He has asked me to see whether I can form a Government.'

'Congratulations, Bonar. You are one of the very few men in our history who has ever been asked that question. It's an extraordinary feeling, isn't it?'

Law smiled.

'I told the King that I would do my duty and make an attempt but I didn't believe I could succeed without you agreeing to serve.'

Asquith paused before responding. What he said now would shape the pattern of his future life.

'I have the greatest of respect for you, Bonar. You have all the skill and determination to be a fine Prime Minister. And I am grateful for your invitation. But I know you'll understand why that would be quite inappropriate, and, frankly, if Lloyd George is to be included, as I'm sure he is, impossible.'

Law paused.

'I won't press you, Asquith. I regret your reluctance but I understand.'

They sat in silence for a moment. Asquith had a number of suggestions that he might have made to help Law, who, for all his other virtues, was quite devoid of imagination and the ability to think in new directions. But he no longer felt obliged to assist. And so he stayed silent.

'I have another suggestion,' Law responded.

'Yes?'

'If I advised the King to send for Balfour, would you serve under him?'

Asquith smiled. 'It's an interesting suggestion, Bonar, and we could discuss it in some detail. But as my answer would again be no, let's not pursue it. If Balfour formed a Government I would decline to join his administration.'

'I see.'

They sat in silence for a few moments more. Then Law rose,

thanked Asquith for meeting him, and apologised for disturbing his dinner.

'Please give Mrs Asquith my good wishes and apologise to her on my behalf for all the distress I know this has caused her.'

Asquith rose and shook his hand again.

'That is very thoughtful of you, Bonar. Thank you. We'll speak again tomorrow.'

Asquith returned to his bridge.

Law went back to the War Office to meet Lloyd George. He then returned to Pembroke Lodge to reflect on how close he had been to becoming Prime Minister and yet how far away it now seemed. Law told Lloyd George that he would decline the King's commission and advise him to send for the War Secretary. Unsurprised but nonetheless deeply moved, Lloyd George thanked him before going on to dine with Aitken, Churchill and Smith at Smith's house. There they discussed the shape of the new Cabinet.

– 35 –

'I was surprised to see Aitken there this morning. I thought we agreed to side-line him?'

Law spoke to Lloyd George as they motored from Pembroke Lodge to Carlton Gardens. It was a beautiful winter's morning in London. The skies had cleared and crisp December sunshine flooded into their motor car. In the back seat, behind the glass wall that divided the passengers from the driver, they had placed a rug across their knees against the cold. Both men wore overcoats and scarves but their spirits were buoyed by the clear winter air. As they rounded each corner the sun changed its position: now in Law's eyes, now in Lloyd George's, sometimes behind, sometimes blinding them both from the front. They were on their way to see Balfour at his home.

'I know. But he rather insisted. And he is useful at times, isn't he?'

'At times I suppose. Have you thought about bringing him into the Government?'

'I have. But probably in a second-tier role. More useful to our work outside the main body than within it. Don't you think?'

Law grunted. Aitken was occasionally useful, he agreed. Not very trustworthy though. Law knew that he was keeping a journal. Newspaperman's instinct, he supposed. Aitken's account of recent days would be published some time. Long after they were all dead, he hoped.

The triumvirate had held its last meeting over breakfast at Pembroke Lodge that morning. Carson was brought back in from the cold and Aitken was also allowed to attend. There they agreed on a plan of campaign. Law had not wavered from his decision to tell the King that he was unable to form a Government. He would advise him to send for Lloyd George. If Balfour could be brought on board to support Lloyd George that might create the momentum to ensure that enough Unionists would support the War Secretary. Not to mention providing the cover needed by the three Cs to 'change their minds'. But they would almost certainly have to go through the motions one last time with Asquith to make absolutely certain that he ruled himself out. So, they agreed, four stages. Get Balfour on board. Law to say no. A conference of all the principals to clear the air. Then the King would commission Lloyd George.

Straightforward.

Except that it wasn't. Nothing in politics was ever straightforward. It was all personality and events. The two great unpredictables of public life.

But Lloyd George was nothing if not determined and Law was nothing if not methodical. With a plan in his hand he would pursue it doggedly to its completion. So, stage one. They set off after breakfast to see Balfour.

They found him still in his sickbed. The room smelled of winter flowers. Ghastly, Law thought.

'Balfour. Such a shame to see you laid so low. On the mend now though, I hope?'

Lloyd George was charm itself. Law scowled. He did not believe in illness.

Balfour thanked them for calling on them. Said he understood that Asquith had resigned and Law had been summoned. How interesting.

Lloyd George admired the old duffer's taciturnity. But he knew that a sharp political intelligence lay beneath the effete veneer. Lloyd George would never have described the current situation as 'interesting'. Deeply, deeply fascinating, perhaps. A surge of power at its most naked, its most raw. Energy pulsing through the arteries of the body politic like the vibrant blood of a young man in springtime. Through the arteries and the veins, one of which led directly to this house, this sickroom, this man. Balfour held the key.

'And how was your conversation at the Palace, Bonar?'

'Not quite a meeting of minds. The King seemed agitated, determined to get it over with as quickly as possible.'

'He hates ceremonial', Balfour responded.

'Maybe we should abolish it then? The whole Court thing – crowns and buckles, wigs and garters? Give the man a rest from all the trinkets and baubles?' This was Lloyd George.

Neither Balfour nor Law smiled at this observation.

'Anyway,' Law continued, 'I was very straight with him. Told him that I'd do my duty but couldn't possibly form a ministry without both Asquith and Lloyd George agreeing to serve.'

'Ah,' Balfour countered. 'Rather unlikely, though, I'd have thought?'

'Indeed. I saw Asquith later on. Put it to him. He said absolutely not.'

'I'm not surprised.'

'I did put one other option to him as well.' Law hesitated. This was important. 'I asked him whether, if I advised the King to send for you, Balfour, he would serve under you.'

Balfour's antennae twitched. Momentarily. Excitedly. But just as quickly drooped. It was the first time he had heard his name mentioned as a possible Prime Minister since resigning that office over ten years ago. For a brief moment it caused political electricity to surge along his nerves. But for a brief moment only. He knew that it was impossible: he was not the man to lead the country in a war like this. Law had mentioned it only to flatter him. Well, it had worked. He felt flattered. He stopped to inspect the sensation before responding.

'And I imagine he said no?'

'He did,' said Law.

Balfour smiled.

Throughout this exchange Lloyd George remained silent, watching the two Unionists fence. Soon the conversation would arrive at the point.

Balfour asked, 'So then, what next?'

'I will return to the Palace later today. Tell the King the situation appears deadlocked. Report on my conversation with Asquith.

And if no other option presents itself advise him to send for Lloyd George.'

Balfour turned his head to look at the War Secretary.

'So, David. Your time has come. Congratulations.'

'Thank you. But I'm not sure that I would be any more successful at putting together a ministry than Law.'

'Why not?'

'Numbers. I have a large group of Liberals. And I know the Irish and the Labour group will support me. But that's not enough. I need Unionist support as well.'

'But Law can bring that to you, surely?'

Law responded. 'I can. I'm sure we have the numbers to construct a ministry under Lloyd George. But we need the leading men to agree to it too, not just the backbenchers. All of Asquith's Liberals ministers will stay out, with the possible exception of Montagu.'

'Ah,' said Balfour, 'the Assyrian.'

Law ignored him. He didn't much like Jews but he didn't like anti-Jewish prejudice either. He continued, 'So without any leading Liberals we need to ensure that there are leading members of our own party willing to come in.'

'That surely shouldn't be a problem?'

Law answered, 'It seems that Curzon and Chamberlain and Cecil and Long gave Asquith quite an assurance of support in recent days.'

'Really? I wonder why. A rather foolish thing to have done.'

Lloyd George maintained his silence as the dance continued.

Law responded. 'They have, shall we say, seen the error of their ways and are rapidly travelling away from him. But they may need some further encouragement. My own relationship with them is rather fractious at the moment. But if you, Balfour, were to indicate your support for Lloyd George then I believe that nothing would stand in their way in terms of completing the journey away from Asquith.'

'I see.' Balfour stayed silent for a moment.

And then spoke. 'It would be rather an odd Government, wouldn't it? A Coalition led by the not-quite leader of the not-quite largest party?'

At which both Law and Lloyd George smiled. Balfour's answer was code for 'yes'.

'Well,' Lloyd George interjected, 'we have known stranger combinations.'

The soon-to-be Prime Minister knew that no further soliciting was required of the former Prime Minister. The motions would still have to be gone through but Balfour would cover them.

They stayed silent until Balfour spoke again. 'Good. Well, gentlemen, you are engaged on a fascinating exercise. May I make a suggestion?'

'Please.'

'Before you decline, Law, and before you accept a commission, Lloyd George, you need to ensure that Asquith is excluded and stays excluded. To achieve this he must remove himself from consideration once and for all. That can be engineered. At the moment he's standing back in the hope that your enterprise will fail. The way to exclude him permanently is to have a conference of all the principals and put it to him in front of everyone else. Force him to declare. Believe me, he will declare himself out.'

This was exactly what Law and Lloyd George had already planned to do. Death by conference. They all spoke the same language.

'The conference is essential. Law should suggest it when he sees the King this morning. Keep the attendance small. Both of you, Asquith, me if you want me' – they both nodded – 'and Henderson too. Have it meet this afternoon. The King will be nervous. I will see him privately before the conference and put his mind at ease. It will all resolve itself by tea-time.'

'Are you sure you're quite well enough to do this?'

'My dear Lloyd George, I wouldn't miss it for the world.'

They sat in silence for a moment. There was nothing more to say. Then both visitors rose and thanked Balfour for his counsel. They looked forward to meeting again later in the day.

After they left Balfour called a servant and asked him to run a bath. He wanted to scrub himself clean not only of the illness of the last week but also of the faint sense of filth he always felt after dealing with politicians.

Back in Whitehall the dance continued. Law went to the Palace to say that he feared he would be unable to form a Government. The King asked for his advice on how to proceed. Law told him that although Lloyd George was now the obvious candidate, in his opinion the air must be cleared before any progress could be made. He suggested a conference. The King agreed.

Telephone calls went out from Lord Stamfordham to all the principals commanding their attendance at three o'clock that day.

The afternoon newspapers spoke of a political crisis.

Asquith ate lunch in Downing Street and admired his view of the walled garden. It looked glorious in the winter sunshine.

– 36 –

Wednesday 6 December 1916
Buckingham Palace — 3 p.m.

He left for the Palace after a short rest in the upstairs bedroom. Once again Margot saw him off. Despite their many years of marriage she still couldn't tell whether her husband's cheerful demeanour was genuine, reflecting some relief that the worst was now over, or instead disguised a deeper sense of despair at the way things had turned out. She told him that she loved him and would speak with him when he returned. Some flicker of hope remained that he might emerge triumphant from the Palace, Lloyd George destroyed, Law banished, confidence restored. But in her heart she knew this would never happen.

While her husband attended the conference at the Palace Margot walked through the private rooms at Downing Street. Without asking her husband she had in great secrecy retained a firm of 'movers' earlier that morning. If they really did need to leave Downing Street this week she wanted to make some early preparations before they were forced out. It was a dismal task but it occupied her attention while her husband was away. She returned upstairs to begin.

Arthur Balfour arrived at the Palace at half past two. The King had asked him to arrive early in order to discuss the situation privately. He wanted Balfour – as a former Prime Minister – to chair the meeting. Balfour agreed to this arrangement and also that the King should attend without speaking and that Stamfordham should keep a record of proceedings.

On the substantive question of how to proceed, Balfour advised the King that an opportunity should first be given to the outgoing

273

Prime Minister, Asquith, to consider the practicability of forming a Government. If this failed then the meeting should turn to Law. If that in turn failed then Lloyd George should be given an opportunity. If all three men proved unable to form a ministry the King would then be entitled to ask another man to take on the task. In the circumstances that would probably be a peer: Curzon or even Lansdowne on the Unionist side, Grey or Crewe for the Liberals. Only if each of these options failed to produce a stable Government would the option of a dissolution require consideration. The King confirmed that he wanted to avoid a dissolution at almost any cost. Balfour assured him that matters would never reach that stage.

Henderson arrived first. He was followed by Law and Lloyd George, who arrived together. All three men were asked to wait in an ante-room. It was explained that Mr Balfour was with the King and they would be invited to join the meeting as soon as Mr Asquith arrived.

Lloyd George looked out the window into the inner courtyard in time to see Asquith's motor appear through the arch, turn a tight three-quarter circle, and come to a stop by the portico. Quite extraordinarily, Asquith had arrived by taxi. He stepped out alone and went to the driver's window to pay him. Having passed him the fare, Asquith tipped his hat at the cabbie, who then departed. A servant greeted Asquith at the steps and escorted him to meet his colleagues upstairs.

'Good afternoon, gentlemen.'

His greeting was jaunty. Cheeks a little flushed, Lloyd George thought, but no smell of booze off his breath. He shook hands first with Henderson, then Law, and finally Lloyd George. As he greeted him he reached out to grasp Lloyd George's right elbow with his left hand. It was a gesture that Lloyd George found very moving.

The double-doors were opened from within. Inside they saw the King as he waited for them, flanked by Balfour and Stamfordham. There was some momentary confusion about the order in which they should enter the room. In the end all deferred to Asquith, who entered first, followed by Law, then Lloyd George, and finally Henderson. Each man approached the King and bowed before turning to greet Balfour and Stamfordham. The King then directed them to an oval table in the corner of the room. They made their way across to it in silence.

The King's chair was at the half-way point of the oval. Stamford-ham would sit on his right, as always. The King gestured for Bal-four to sit opposite him. The others then filled the four remaining chairs. As they sat the King cleared his throat and began.

'Gentlemen, thank you for attending. We find ourselves in a dif-ficult situation and Mr Balfour has advised me, and I have accepted his advice, that a conference of the sort convened here might help us to find a way through.'

He paused to look around him. Heads nodding. So he continued.

'As you know, Mr Asquith gave me his resignation as Prime Minister yesterday. He advised me to send for Mr Law, which I did. Mr Law told me this morning that he would find it difficult to form a Government without both Mr Asquith and Mr Lloyd George being willing to serve. Mr Lloyd George is willing but, as I understand it, Mr Asquith is not. That leaves matters in some dif-ficulty; hence this meeting. I have asked Mr Balfour to act as chair-man. He served with distinction as Prime Minister in my father's time and is well aware of the problems that a situation like this can create. May I take it that you are all willing to have Mr Balfour chair the meeting?'

A chorus of 'Yes', 'Certainly' and 'We are'. No dissent.

'Good. Thank you. Lord Stamfordham will keep a record of the meeting and will circulate it to you all later in the day. I myself will take no part in the meeting other than to observe and hear what you decide. And so I will ask Mr Balfour to continue.'

'Thank you, Sir.' This was Balfour. 'Let me suggest that we might proceed in what I hope is some sort of logical sequence, gentle-men. Mr Asquith, as you are the outgoing Prime Minister...'

Asquith smiled. 'Out-gone, I think you'll find, Balfour.'

A murmur of laughter around the table.

Balfour smiled and continued. 'I am aware that Mr Law cur-rently holds the King's commission but I know he won't object if I begin by asking whether you believe it would be possible for you to construct another Government and continue in office?'

Law nodded his assent.

Asquith paused before answering. 'I think the very fact of my resignation indicates my sense that this would not be a practical possibility.'

Law interjected. 'I'm not sure it would be quite as impossible as you imagine, Asquith. There are certainly men on both sides of the House who would support you. Would you not make the attempt at least?'

Asquith recognised this for the trap that it was. And quite an infantile trap at that. Try, fail, actually fail ignominiously, and then be obliged to go away forever. No, not this.

'Would you support me if I did, Bonar? And you, David? Would you come into a Government under my Premiership? And I must add, to make matters perfectly clear, with me as Prime Minister remaining as chairman of the War Committee?'

It was Law who answered first. 'That isn't possible, Asquith. As you know. It's been the cause of all our recent controversy. We must have a change in the direction of the War Committee.'

Lloyd George stayed silent.

Then Asquith responded. 'In that case, gentlemen, and you know how much it pains me to say this, it remains the case that it would not be possible for me to form a ministry.'

A brief silence followed. It was fitting that it did for everyone around the table knew that this moment marked the end of Asquith.

'In that case,' Law asked, 'and without wishing to deviate from the agenda you've established for the meeting, Chairman, may I ask whether you yourself would be willing to attempt to form a Government?'

Balfour smiled. 'That's very kind of you, Law. A generous suggestion which I value very deeply. But no, that would not be possible. We are engaged in a great war and the country needs and deserves a Prime Minister who is more suited to national leadership in the circumstances of wartime. It is very kind of you to think of me but I must decline.'

A murmur of good wishes from around the table but no voice was raised asking Balfour to reconsider. Asked and answered, he thought. So now we must move on.

'Given these developments I believe we must now turn to the man who currently holds the King's commission to form a Government. Mr Law, you have said that you feel yourself unlikely to succeed in that task. Would you elaborate?'

Law spoke directly. He turned to Asquith and said, 'Would you serve in a ministry if I were to form one?'

Asquith paused before answering.

Then spoke.

'Gentlemen, we are all, as they say, "men of the world". We know that the business of politics and government is a rough one. We expect our opponents to attack us and force us to defend our every decision. We know that from time to time those attacks will turn quite vicious and we steel ourselves against those occasions.

'But I would be less than honest if I did not say that I feel myself to have endured the foulest campaign of vilification ever visited upon a political leader in modern times over the course of the last eighteen months. I had thought that by bringing my political opponents into the Government I would have been able to unite the country in our common war effort. But in fact, and to my very great distress, all that has happened is that an unconscionable degree of opprobrium and vilification has been heaped upon the Government and upon me personally during that time.

'The press, inspired I must say with regret, by some of those meeting here today, has been quite vicious and most unfair in its attacks upon me. I can bear this. I have been in public life long enough to shrug it off. But it has imposed a heavy and unfair burden on my family and I cannot have that continue.

'You discussed a moment ago, Bonar, your unwillingness to serve in my Government if I was unwilling to yield the chairmanship of the War Council to another Cabinet member. The press has made the same point repeatedly over the last many months. But this is a point on which I cannot and will not yield and neither, I suspect, would any new Prime Minister. I could not serve under you only to find myself contradicted on this point. In the end, if my country desperately needs me, I will do my duty. But to your direct question of whether I would serve under you, I very much regret that I would be unable to.'

The others greeted this speech in silence.

In part because they did not quite know what to make of it.

For Asquith to vent his spleen about the press and the leaking of information was not unexpected. He had every right to feel distressed and they knew it. They granted him that.

But what was he saying about serving under Law? It seemed at first to be a quite definite no. But then, had he veered? Was he saying there was some possibility that he might? It was unclear.

Law broke the silence. 'If Mr Asquith continues in his unwillingness to serve under me then I cannot see how I could form an administration.'

The King, a man to whom nuance was a stranger and subtlety a deeply foreign thing, then spoke.

'It would be improper for me to comment on Mr Asquith's observations, gentlemen. But this does seem to leave things no further forward than they were at the beginning of our meeting. Mr Balfour, can you guide us?'

So far Lloyd George had said nothing. It was one of the paradoxes of the situation that the most important meeting of his life was shortly to end without his having uttered a single word.

Balfour paused before speaking.

'Sir. Let me attempt to summarise and, gentlemen, please correct me if you disagree. First, Mr Asquith is unable to form a ministry because Mr Law declines to serve under him given their differing views on the chairmanship of the War Council.'

Both Asquith and Law nodded.

'Second, Mr Law would be willing to attempt to form a ministry if Mr Asquith would agree to serve under him. Mr Asquith is reluctant to do this but I have a sense that it represents a possibility which he might at least be willing to consider further.'

He looked at Law, who nodded. And then at Asquith, who did not.

'I think that while Mr Asquith and Mr Law should certainly be encouraged to discuss the matter further, we should also consider what His Majesty might be advised to do if Mr Law finds that he cannot proceed. If that turned out to be the case then I believe Mr Lloyd George should be invited to attempt to form a Government.'

Henderson spoke. 'I agree. That is the best way forward.'

Lloyd George stayed silent.

Law then said, 'I agree with your summary, Balfour. The initiative therefore rests with Mr Asquith. He should consider whether he would be willing to serve under me. If he would, then I will attempt to construct a ministry. If not then I will advise His Majesty to send for Lloyd George.'

On this point they were all in agreement.

Asquith then spoke directly to the King. 'Sir, I must consult my friends in this matter. Law, with your agreement, I will do that now, as soon as I return to Downing Street. And I will let you have my answer in the next few hours.'

'Of course.'

And then the meeting broke up. Stamfordham put his pen down on the table. The King thanked each man for attending. They all made for their motor cars.

Asquith was the last of the attendees to leave the Palace. He had decided to walk back to Downing Street across St James's Park. Two policemen from the Palace detail were told to accompany him. As he walked through the evening twilight he reflected on the position in which the conference had left him. His summary of the position was focused and concise.

I am out.

We will have a new Prime Minister by dinner time.

I wonder whether I can have Walmer for the weekend? I'm sure he'll say yes.

Would he serve under Law? Almost certainly not. It would be too much of a humiliation. Not even – although he was momentarily tempted – as Lord Chancellor.

And so the King will send for Lloyd George. I could block him by swallowing my pride and agreeing to serve under Law.

But then it was clear to him.

Law would be no good as Prime Minister. Lloyd George would.

So David it is, then. For the time being anyway.

I will return.

Won't I?

– 37 –

Asquith's walk through St James's Park helped to calm his mind even as he tried to decide what to do next. He needed to see his Liberal colleagues very quickly, one last meeting of that half of the outgoing Cabinet. He knew the questions he needed to put to them and he knew how they would respond. The outcome was now certain but he needed to observe the proprieties. It would be the final burial meeting of his long years in Government.

A small crowd had gathered outside the park entrance to Downing Street. A bit ghoulish, he thought. But then this was an important day in the life of the nation. They cheered as he walked past. He raised his hat to salute them and the police officers cleared a path to his front door. Well, not 'his' for much longer. Extraordinary building, Number 10. He had felt completely at home here almost from the moment they moved in. The upstairs residence was too small, of course, and extended family gatherings had to happen either at the Wharf or at Cavendish Square. But Asquith himself had felt that he truly belonged here from the beginning. Even as he chaired his early Cabinets with C.B. dying upstairs. He felt a moment of nostalgia in advance of leaving the house.

Inside Number 10 a servant took his hat, coat and walking stick. Margot stood half-way up the stairs. He caught her eye and slowly shook his head from side to side. Saying nothing, she turned to return upstairs.

Asquith went straight to the Cabinet Room. In the small ante-room his Liberal ministerial colleagues had already gathered. He was somewhat surprised: he had expected to have some time to gather his thoughts and write a letter whilst they were summoned. How did they know? He took Grey to one side and asked him.

'Stamfordham called us. Told us you were on your way back and needed to meet with us.'

'I see.'

It felt as if the Palace was already showing him the door. All a bit too urgent for his liking. Well, this is what life would be like now. Decisions taken behind his back, over his head. He was no longer in command.

He went into the Cabinet Room and took his chair, the one with the arms. One last time. The others entered and took their places around the table. Crewe, Grey, McKenna, Runciman, Buckmaster and McKinnon Wood. Also Harcourt, Samuel, Tennant and Montagu. And Henderson. All the Liberal ministers from his Government except Lloyd George. And the one Labour man too.

Crewe thought he looked exhausted. Perhaps they should have allowed him some time to rest after his walk from the Palace? But Stamfordham had been insistent. 'We need a decision now.'

Asquith stared around the room at his followers. Gathered his thoughts. Then spoke.

'Well, gentlemen. Here we are again. We seem to have been engaged in one long, endless meeting these last few days.'

A few murmurs of polite amusement. He continued.

'I have, as you know, just returned from a conference at the Palace. Mr Henderson was there too so he can correct me if he feels I misinterpret anything in reporting on our deliberations.'

Henderson smiled and nodded.

'The King and Lord Stamfordham attended the meeting without speaking. Balfour, Law and Lloyd George were the other attendees. Balfour chaired – actually rather well, I thought.'

Again Henderson nodded.

'We discussed how to proceed and I don't need to tell you the various options we considered. I promised that I would consult you on two matters and send an answer to Mr Law as soon as possible. Mr Law holds the King's commission and is willing to form a Government but only if both Lloyd George and I agree to join his administration. Lloyd George is willing. I indicated, subject to consultation with this group, that I was not.

'If I decide to stay out then Law will return his commission to the King who will send for Lloyd George. Law is willing to serve under Lloyd George and believes he has enough Unionist support to allow the formation of a Government. I accept that he almost certainly does, and that Lloyd George has enough support from among our own backbenchers to form a ministry.'

Silence. All eyes remained focused on Asquith.

'So, gentlemen, I must ask you two questions.

'First, given that neither Lloyd George nor Law will serve in any Government that I might form, are we all agreed that any attempt by me – even if the King's commission was returned to me, which is now highly unlikely – to form a Government without them would be futile and that I should not proceed to make any such attempt?'

The silence was momentary and then Crewe spoke.

'I think it would not only be impossible for you to form a Government on that basis but unwise even to try.'

Again, a murmur of assent from around the table.

Grey spoke. 'I agree with Crewe. I doubt it could be done. I think you might also look foolish and even petulant if you made the attempt. And also', and here Grey paused, 'it would make it much less likely that you would receive a similar invitation in the future should the new Government fall at an early date. As it almost certainly will.'

Asquith nodded.

'Yes, I agree. Well, let us dispose of that option then, gentlemen. I will make no attempt to regain the King's commission and form a new ministry.'

He continued. 'So we must face the second question, which is altogether more difficult. If Law repeats his invitation to me to join his Government, which, if I were to give any hint of being likely to accept he most certainly would, should I say yes?'

The silence that greeted the second question seemed deeper than before. No one spoke. There seemed to be an expectation that Asquith should speak further before any of his colleagues would comment.

And so he elaborated. 'The only position that Law would offer me, I imagine, is that of Lord Chancellor. Lloyd George would almost certainly stay on as War Secretary and chair the War Committee. It would, in effect, be a joint premiership of Law and Lloyd George. I would be a member of the Cabinet but not of the War Committee. The expectation would be that I would confine myself to managing the judiciary and chairing the Lords and that I would not involve myself in any wider Cabinet matters, and certainly none pertaining to the conduct of the war.'

Montagu asked, 'Would you consider it?'

Asquith replied, 'I am strongly minded *not* to, Montagu, for reasons that I will explain shortly. But I would value your advice before making a final determination.'

'I think you should consider it very carefully and very positively,' Montagu responded. 'We need a strong Government to conduct this war. We don't need our most able leaders sitting outside, maintaining silence or, worse still, trying to entangle the Government at every turn. Your presence in the administration would bring an end to the squabbles and show that all three of our principal statesmen can work together without rancour to win the war. So I believe you should indicate that you would consent to any such offer.'

Then Henderson spoke. 'I agree with Montagu. You asked Law to swallow his own political pride last year and come into your Government. He did just that. He accepted a subsidiary position when he might well have been entitled to the Chancellorship. He didn't demur and neither did any of his colleagues. If circumstances have now changed then your duty surely lies in doing exactly what you yourself asked Law to do eighteen months ago.'

Asquith stared hard at Henderson as he spoke. He really liked this man. He had grown to like him more and more over the last eighteen months.

But on this occasion he believed that Henderson was wholly wrong.

The discussion then swung in the other direction. Crewe, Grey and McKenna were resolute that Asquith should stay out. And that his colleagues gathered around the table should also stay out.

'Lloyd George's Government will be a dead letter by Easter. Don't associate yourself with it. You don't need to oppose them, just stand ready to form a new administration once his falls apart.' This was Crewe.

And then McKenna. 'I agree. It'll never survive. His coalition will be made up of a small group of disaffected Liberals and a larger group of Unionists constantly wondering why a Government in which their party has the majority should have a Liberal – and a pretty Socialist Liberal at that – as its leader.'

Montagu interjected. 'With the greatest of respect, McKenna, I believe you are entirely wrong about that. He'll survive. The country couldn't stand another change of leader in wartime. The Unionists will back Lloyd George and he'll survive. Any idea that we should stand out because we'll be back by Easter is just nonsense.'

'Rubbish.' This was Buckmaster. 'Even in wartime a country needs an Opposition. Some alternative must be available. Otherwise it's just a dictatorship. Asquith should stay out. It's the only way to stabilise the country and the only way we'll get back in the next year or so.'

And so the discussion continued. The weight of opinion seemed to be in favour of Asquith's saying no. Harcourt, Samuel and Tennant remained silent throughout the meeting. Montagu and Henderson urged him to serve. But all the others advised him to decline. He valued the judgement of Crewe and Grey more than any of the others. But the question that he couldn't ask the meeting was this: if I serve and he declines to invite you, as he surely will, where does that leave you all? And, indeed, our party?

As the conversation continued Asquith found himself, as so often before, attending to the argument with one half of his brain whilst assessing his own position with the other half. It seemed to him that there were two reasons for staying out. First, his own pride. How could he serve in a subordinate position under men he had commanded for so many years? He knew about the precedents. But he simply couldn't imagine taking directions from Lloyd George, still less from Law. It would be a bitter humiliation if he had to. And second, the argument that the country needed an Opposition was a good one. He looked around the table. Who would lead that Opposition if not Asquith? There was no candidate. And leading the Opposition was important not just for reasons of constitutional propriety. He believed that the chances of a Lloyd George ministry suffering an early collapse were not at all as high as some of his more bullish colleagues were suggesting. But events happen. Things change. Circumstances wander. If he stayed out there was every chance that he might be back in again at some stage, perhaps even stronger than ever. So, pride and possibility. Both reasons for saying no.

And the reasons for saying yes? Very straightforward. He needed the money. The Lord Chancellorship was the most lucrative position in the Government. He needed the income. But also he needed to be at the centre. After nine years in power he knew that he itched to be where the action was. He might feel humiliated at not being Prime Minister but how much more desolate would it feel not to have any position at all? To be truly on the fringes? He doubted that he could survive that.

So two reasons to say yes and two reasons to say no. And colleagues who seemed almost unanimous (those that mattered anyway) in counselling him to say no.

And then Asquith suddenly realised the third reason for staying out. The definitive one.

If he stayed within the Government all the external attacks on him would continue. He would remain a target – perhaps even the primary target – for press criticism. Northcliffe would never give in. With Asquith still in the Government, even if only as Lord Chancellor, all the newspapers would continue to attribute every reversal to him, blaming his 'lingering malign influence' on what would otherwise have been a fresh and energetic Government. And neither Law nor Lloyd George would have any reason to correct that misimpression.

And so for that reason, in conjunction with both of the others, he decided to stay out.

The conversation still continued around the Cabinet table. But nothing new had been said for the last ten minutes. It was time to bring this to an end.

'Gentlemen, please.'

Silence slowly descended.

'Thank you for your advice. As always, it has been very helpful.'

They waited.

'Having listened to your various recommendations, and having considered all the factors involved as fully as I can, I have decided that the interests of the country, of our party, and of myself and my family would be better served if I declined Mr Law's invitation to join his administration. The country needs its new Government to have a fresh start. It would not help that Government to have an outgoing Prime Minister among its members. I will therefore advise Mr Law that my answer is in the negative.'

They had all known that this would be the outcome but they were still surprised at the suddenness with which it all ended. Both for Asquith and for them. It was finished.

And then he stood. He moved behind his chair and pushed it square against the table.

'There will be time enough for expressions of gratitude, gentlemen, but let me offer just the briefest commentary now. We have served together for many years and have done our best to guide the country through difficult times. The country owes you an immense debt of gratitude and that will be recognised, I am sure, in due course. In the meantime the new Government will need our support in its efforts to win the war and our constructive challenge whenever it strays from that effort. It will have my support in this, and yours too I know. And so, for the time being, thank you. We will talk again soon.'

But he knew that they wouldn't. Certainly not in this room. The time for talking was over.

He broke with precedent by being the first person to leave the room because he did not think he could bear to hear them thank him and embark on a round of eulogies. It would all have been too much to bear. Anyway he wasn't Prime Minister any more. So there was no precedent left to break.

He turned to climb the stairs to his study. He needed to speak to Margot and then to write to Law. And then, my God, he needed to sleep.

– 38 –

Wednesday 6 December 1916
Prime Minister's Study, 10 Downing Street — 6 p.m.

His letter to Law was short. Composing it was an unhappy task
as it marked the definitive end to his time in Government and no
public man finds that easy to face. But he wrote it quickly nonetheless: his facility with words had not deserted him. As well as
making clear his own decision he also wanted to establish that
none of his senior Liberal colleagues would serve in the new Government either, nor would a majority of Liberal MPs support
it. But he knew that Lloyd George had the numbers so this was
merely a matter of clarification. And so he wrote:

> 10, Downing Street,
> Whitehall, S.W.
> December 6, 1916

My dear Bonar Law,

Since we separated I have discussed the matter with ten of my
late Liberal colleagues in the Cabinet.

They are unanimously of opinion that I ought not to join
your Government. They think, and I agree with them, that I,
and probably they can give more effective support from outside. They also think that we could not carry the support of the
Liberal party for any such arrangement. I have no personal feeling of *amour-propre* in the matter (as I believe you know), but I
am more convinced, the more I think of it, that it would be an
unworkable arrangement.

> Yours very sincerely,
> H. H. Asquith

He thought of having a messenger carry the letter to the Unionist ministers who were gathered in Law's rooms at the Colonial Office. There is no more pleasant activity for a senior politician than idly wondering what position he is to receive in a new Government. The Unionists were luxuriating in that speculation over their whiskies at Law's office.

But the matter was taken in another direction when Drummond knocked and entered the study. Lord Curzon was downstairs and wished to see Mr Asquith. Curzon again. Oh Christ, that bloody man.

'Tell him I'm engaged at present, Drummond. But please give him this.'

Asquith gave Drummond the letter.

Curzon could act as messenger boy. It had become his role in the whole affair. From Viceroy of India to post office courier. Suited the bugger.

And then Asquith, exhausted, told Drummond that he needed to lie down for an hour. He asked to be awakened in time for dinner at eight. As his head settled onto the pillow he fell into a deep and dreamless sleep.

Buckingham Palace — 7.30 p.m.

The transfer of power happened while Asquith slept. Law received the letter and read it without surprise. Told his colleagues what it said. Had Stamfordham telephoned and told him that he needed to see the King. He was asked to present himself at 7 p.m.

Law's final meeting of the day with the King was a brief one. He thanked His Majesty for commissioning him to form a ministry but regretted that he was unable to gather the necessary support. The King in turn thanked him for his efforts and asked who Law recommended he should consult next. Law advised him to send for Lloyd George.

The telephone rang in the War Office shortly before eight o'clock.

'Lloyd George here.'

'This is Stamfordham.'

'Yes, Lord Stamfordham.'

'I am asked by His Majesty to command your attendance at the Palace immediately.'

Lloyd George paused. His head swam and he felt very slightly dizzy. Then he composed himself.

'Thank you. I will be there in twenty minutes.'

Lloyd George's car passed Law's as they drove along The Mall. They were on opposite sides of the road, heading in opposite directions. Each was oblivious to the other.

Again, the meeting was brief. Lloyd George was shown into the same room in which that afternoon's conference had taken place. Stamfordham stood just behind the King. The War Secretary bowed, but not deeply.

'Mr Lloyd George. Thank you for coming. I have just seen Mr Law. He reported that he is unable to form an administration. On his advice I have sent for you. Do you think that you can form a Government?'

Again Lloyd George paused. This was the most glorious, the most wonderful question that any Briton could ever be asked.

'I am confident that I can, Your Majesty.' It was the answer the King wanted to hear although it wasn't quite true. Lloyd George still had work to do to confirm his majority.

'Then I commission you to undertake the necessary enquiries. Please report to me as soon as possible on your progress.'

The King wished him a good evening and left.

Stamfordham remained behind and shook his hand. 'Congratulations,' he said. 'Telephone me tomorrow when it's settled and I will arrange the formal session.'

And then he explained to Lloyd George what 'kissing hands' really meant.

Thursday 7 December 1916
Downing Street, Prime Minister's Private Residence — 2 p.m.

Asquith lunched alone with Margot the following day. Their conversation dealt with practical arrangements for vacating Downing Street: where they should live, how their belongings should be transported. He also touched on the practical question of money, explaining that she would have to reduce her expenditure quite dramatically under the new circumstances in which they now found themselves. They had little capital and no longer any regular income. Everything that was provided for them as a consequence of his office was about to be taken away. House, motor cars, servants, food and drink. All now fell to them to arrange. And to pay for.

Margot was taken aback by the news of their financial position. She was less surprised when he told her that any offer from the King of an earldom would be declined. It was accepted practice that an outgoing Prime Minister was offered a peerage but Asquith intended to stay in the Commons. He was still hopeful that a collapse in the new Government would call him back to the front lines.

He knew that the morning had seen immense political activity throughout Whitehall as Lloyd George and Law worked to construct the new Government. But few details had reached his ears. Downing Street was in fact an oasis of calm that morning. All the action was taking place elsewhere. He spent the morning in his study writing letters to friends.

Just after two o'clock Lord Crewe was announced. Margot greeted him with a kiss and then left the two men to discuss the position. Crewe had news.

'Well?' Asquith asked.

'They'll do it.'

'Of course.'

'And probably by later this afternoon.'

'Has he made any appointments yet?'

'Some made, others offered. But he'll get there.'

'I see.'

The strangest thing of all to Asquith was not that he was no longer Prime Minister but that a Cabinet was being constructed behind his back. This had not happened for many years. The business of constructing a Cabinet was his. But now another man was doing it. It was a peculiar and disorientating sensation. Not at all pleasant.

'Well, Robert, tell me what you know.'

'He met the Labour people last night and again this morning. Addressed their National Executive Committee. He spoke at length and persuaded them. Henderson is allowed to stay in and some other Labour men will have ministries as well.'

'That's hardly a surprise.'

'I know, but he's building the ship plank by plank. With Labour in and the Irish never in question he turned to our side next.'

'And how did he fare with them?' Asquith asked.

'Rather well I'm afraid. You know he uses Addison as his whip. Well, Addison has told him, or so Montagu tells me, that there are forty-nine Liberals who will definitely support him and up to a hundred and thirty who will back him when he's definitely in.'

'That many?' Asquith said. But he wasn't really surprised. Nor could he blame them. When power slid away, it slid rapidly. He would have his work cut out to win them back.

'And on the Unionist side?'

'Well, this is where it gets interesting,' Crewe responded. 'The first piece of news from there will surprise you.'

'Yes?'

'Balfour has joined the Government.'

Asquith felt as if someone had punched him in the face.

'Surely not?'

'He has, I'm afraid.'

'But Lloyd George spent weeks trying to persuade me that Balfour was no good and that I had to move him from the Admiralty?'

'Yes, well, Lloyd George has indeed moved him. From the Admiralty.'

'To where?'

'The Foreign Office.'

Oh my God. He felt another punch to his face. This was unbelievable.

'I see. Well, I'm astounded. I know Balfour wanted me to give Lloyd George's scheme a chance but I never thought he'd switch sides with such speed. I'm amazed.'

They sat in silence for a few moments. Then Asquith asked Crewe to continue.

'He's done something very strange with the War Committee.'

'I assume he's going to chair it himself?'

'Oh yes. But more than that. He's effectively abolished the Cabinet.'

And here again Asquith was taken aback.

'I'm sorry. He's done what?'

Crewe continued. 'He says that he plans to create a War Cabinet which will replace the full Cabinet. Five members only. All the others will be appointed to run ministries but they won't sit in Cabinet until the war is over. He says he wants to focus the whole attention of the Government on the war and he can't do that if the larger group continues to meet. So effectively the Cabinet is abolished.'

Asquith was amazed. Well, they wanted a change. They'd got it now.

'Who's in the War Cabinet?' he asked.

'Apparently he had the most trouble of all winning the Unionists over,' Crewe responded. 'Law was with him from the start: he gets the Exchequer and is in the War Cabinet. But the others proved harder to get.'

'He did a deal with them?'

'Of sorts. They asked him for guarantees. Three things. Churchill not to return to the Government. No ministry for Northcliffe. And Haig to stay on as C-in-C France and Flanders.'

He felt sorry for Winston but not surprised. The Conservatives hated a turncoat. He had no future with them.

'And he agreed?'

'Apparently yes, he did,' Crewe replied. 'So with the Unionists saying yes he has his majority. Henderson is the third man in the War Cabinet, and also Curzon and Milner.'

Ah, Curzon. So the little weasel got what he wanted after all.

'What about Carson?'

'First Lord of the Admiralty but outside the War Cabinet. And Derby's got the War Office but he's not in the War Cabinet either.'

What a strange way to run a war, Asquith thought.

'Oh and one other thing,' Crewe continued. 'This one will amuse you. Max Aitken.'

'I hear he wanted Trade or Paymaster-General.'

'Well he didn't get either of them.'

'He's left outside?'

'Well no, not quite. Lloyd George is giving him a peerage. He's off to the Lords.'

A broad grin crossed Asquith's face.

'Serves the little creep right.'

'But you haven't heard the best part yet. His title.'

Crewe was smiling broadly. Asquith had to ask.

'What?'

'You won't believe it. Of all the ridiculous names. Our friend Aitken is now…Lord *Beaver-brook*.'

At which the two men burst into uproarious laughter that ended only when Asquith withdrew the handkerchief from his top pocket and held it tight against his mouth.

Lord *Beaver-brook*!

Hilarious!

Only a Canadian.

– 39 –

Friday 8 December 1916
Reform Club, Pall Mall — 5 p.m.

Asquith rather liked the Reform Club. Beautiful exterior by Charles Barry resembling a Palladian villa. Extraordinary hall with that great open window to the roof. The sun had set by the time he arrived and the building was lit for the evening by candles and electric lamps. It wasn't by any means the grandest club in St James's. For rest and relaxation he much preferred the Athenaeum but as a Liberal club the Reform had a certain homely comfort. Although he hadn't set foot inside for over two years.

An enormous cheer could be heard from within the building as he left his taxicab. Accompanied by Grey he shook hands with the chairman and members of the committee on the steps of the club before ascending to the interior hall. What seemed like hundreds of men awaited him there, all cheering, waving papers in the air. It was like the House of Commons removed from Westminster but with a large throng of peers present as well. This was Asquith's first meeting of the Liberal Party in the years since he had succeeded C.B. as its leader.

He knew that among the cheering crowd was a large number of men who had already pledged their support to Lloyd George. Although every Liberal member of the outgoing Cabinet had declined to serve in the new administration, he knew that a number of the men now cheering him would soon accept more junior office in the new administration. So some of them were cheering his departure with regret whilst others cheered with relief. No matter. At least they were cheering.

The Cabinet had met in the Reform on a number of occasions in early 1914. While Downing Street was being redecorated the

Liberal ministers moved their meetings to a small room off the main dining room. He heard they had since named it the 'Cabinet Room'. Well, it served its purpose. It was secure and discreet and the bay window opened to the gardens allowing light and cool air to filter in during their proceedings. He remembered writing a number of his more extensive letters to Venetia Stanley whilst chairing meetings in that room.

He ascended the great staircase to the left of the hall, past the portraits of various Liberal grandees from the early days of the club. Also a rather striking portrait of Daniel O'Connell, the great Irish nationalist MP and author of Catholic emancipation. He remembered Redmond telling him that both he and O'Connell had sent their sons to a Jesuit boarding school outside Dublin, Clongowes Wood. Redmond had wanted Asquith to speak there on a visit to Ireland. He'd never had the time. He had now, of course, but would they still want to hear from him?

More men ringed the gallery and Asquith walked slowly, receiving their acclaim and stopping to talk to one or two of them. He recognised many of the peers and also the leading MPs. But so many of the other faces meant nothing to him. Were they really his backbenchers? Had he so lost touch that he failed to recognise many of them? He knew that Lloyd George would know their names, their histories, their finances and their failings.

He proceeded into the great room that ran the full length of the south side of the building. The crowd followed him in from the gallery, more men pouring up the stairs. They settled into their seats as Asquith was led to the rostrum. He was introduced as 'Prime Minister' by the chairman before the speaker turned bright red with embarrassment. Not Prime Minister now, just Asquith. The chairman corrected himself and introduced him by name. As Asquith rose there was a final great roar that lasted many minutes. He allowed them to roar their guilt away before raising his hands to ask for quiet. Then he addressed the meeting to explain the context of recent events.

He spoke in a clear and steady voice, telling them in detail what had happened in the last few weeks, making no criticism of the new Prime Minister. It was an enormous relief to be able to unburden himself in public in this way. He continued for forty minutes before thanking them fulsomely for their support and concluding his remarks.

As he turned to resume his seat another great round of applause arose from the crowd. Asquith was politician enough to know that applause must never be resisted. He turned to face them, not bowing, not waving, just receiving. It lasted several minutes and it reinvigorated him. The applause stopped only when Grey stood up and moved to the rostrum. Asquith resumed his seat. Then Grey spoke.

The final part of Grey's speech moved Asquith to tears.

'There is one subject and one person of whom I cannot speak as freely as I would like, because he is present – Mr Asquith, who is our leader. We are still together. Since the beginning of the war he has had to carry a burden heavier than that of anyone else. We know how bravely and steadily he has borne it, shouldering all responsibility, however great, bearing private anxieties and grief, however distressing, undaunted, dismayed and unshaken. The country does know something, but it will never know so fully as those of us who are his colleagues, how invaluable his presence as Prime Minister has been in days of crisis when no one else, by common consent, could have filled his place. Without him, no one can say what might have happened to the future of this country if he had not been there in that place in those times. He himself said that the strain and anxiety has been almost greater than anyone can conceive. Each one of us has felt that; but each one of us has felt also that the strain and anxiety upon him must have been greater than upon any one of us. That will come to be recognised in time, and I have no doubt in history, and even in the present generation, full justice will be done to what he has done.

'We, as his colleagues, today give him our tribute, our personal tribute, of admiration, of sympathy, and of affection.'

And then, to further cheers, Grey turned and resumed his seat.

As the applause died down the chairman proposed a vote of confidence in Asquith's continuing leadership of the Liberal Party.

It was carried by acclaim although the result was not confirmed until the chairman recognised one member who stood on his seat and raised his hand. This was Handel Booth, MP for Pontefract. When he was recognised he asked:

'Mr Chairman, may I enquire of Mr Asquith what role our party MPs are to take in relation to Lloyd George and his Government, and whether supporting that Government means crossing the floor of the House?'

Asquith stood to respond. 'Mr Chairman, as far as I myself am concerned, I shall sit on the Opposition front bench, and I invite those members who support me to do the same. But let me make this clear: I will not hesitate to provide organised support for the Government in so far as they continue to oversee the prosecution of the war with vigour and determination.'

A vast chorus of 'Hear, hear' greeted this reply.

And then it was over. The chairman declared the vote of confidence passed without dissent. Asquith and Grey left the rostrum and made their way through the meeting, along the gallery, down the stairs, and to the door. The vast throng followed and various onlookers cheered them along the way.

He knew as he left the building that this was the last occasion on which such a large group of Liberal MPs and peers would ever meet in a spirit of unity and common cause.

For the future it was only division, decay and despair.

– 40 –

Margot was relieved that he slept well on their last night in Downing Street. He also seemed revived by the party meeting that afternoon. Dinner was a quiet affair: Montagu, Bonham-Carter, Crewe and the family. She had watched him closely for any sign of distress but there was none. He was either genuinely calm or restraining himself with a great effort of will. She knew there would be a collapse and she watched for it. She knew that she herself was at breaking-point too. Together they would have to carry one another through.

After breakfast that Saturday morning they left Downing Street for the last time. There was a vague sense that they might return in the future but in their hearts they both knew how unlikely that was.

Drummond told her there was a tradition of the staff 'clapping out' the departing Prime Minister. She dreaded the thought of it. He did too but he respected the tradition. It also gave him the opportunity to thank the servants, whose presence and assistance in the house he had so often taken for granted.

They stopped at the return on the staircase so that Asquith could speak to them. He paused at the line of portraits and said jokingly that he hoped they would find a suitable photograph of him to hang beside C.B. 'Something from my younger days. Not the fat old man that I've become!' The servants laughed and Margot smiled at him.

His short speech of thanks was heartfelt and sincere. She was close to tears. 'You have made our stay in this house so happy. We could not have done this without you. From the bottom of our hearts, we thank you.'

The last thing he had done in his study upstairs was to prepare a note for Lloyd George. It was brief and friendly.

> 10, Downing Street
> London, S.W.
> 9th December, 1916

My dear Lloyd George

And so I turn this wonderful old house over to you. Take good care of it. The staff will do everything they can to make your stay here a comfortable one.

Your time as Prime Minister will be one of great challenge and difficulty. The war is at a critical stage. I offer you my full support and that of our party in your prosecution of it. And you know that such opposition as I offer will always be given in the best interests of the country.

God speed.

> Yours sincerely,
> H. H. Asquith

As they reached the front door he turned to take one last look at the house. Then a gentle wave to the servants and they were away.

To the small crowd gathered outside he raised his hat and smiled. They cheered him to the motor car.

They set off by road for Walmer. It was exactly the same journey he had taken just one brief week ago. But, my God, the changes since then.

She continued to watch him all the way to the coast and into the early evening. But he was robust and showed no sign of either grief or despair. From Lambeth he slept all the way to Deal.

As he climbed into bed that evening Asquith heard the dull thunder of the guns across the Channel as the war continued without him.

Epilogue

And afterwards? How did Asquith fare after Downing Street?

He spent his first Christmas out of office with the family on the Isle of Wight in a house loaned by Seely, the former War Secretary. It was also the first Christmas without Raymond. The memory of his son haunted him throughout the holiday.

New Year 1917 was spent at the Wharf. He read a great deal but his political role remained uncertain: he had not retired, he was still leader of the Liberal Party. But what that meant was uncertain. His former Liberal ministerial colleagues sat beside him on the Opposition front bench and constituted the main anti-Government voice in the House. Liberal backbenchers were more conflicted. Although Asquith had received a unanimous vote of confidence as their leader at the Reform Club, at least 126 of them had agreed to support Lloyd George's Government. Political activity was at something of a standstill, which, from Asquith's perspective, was probably a good thing as he was genuinely wary of pressing the new Government and damaging national unity. The press, still critical, would have attacked him with even greater ferocity.

In February 1917 he visited his Scottish constituency, the first such visit in a very long time. The family had been able to move back into 20 Cavendish Square but there were no more weekends at Walmer, although regular visits to the Wharf continued. He needed money, both to support his household and also to maintain Margot's lifestyle. In 1917 he was again offered the Lord Chancellorship, the highest-paid post in government, carrying £10,000 a year and a £5,000 pension. The former Chief Whip, Lord Murray of Elibank, and the Lord Chief Justice, Lord Reading, were used by Lloyd George as intermediaries. Asquith was not inclined to accept and was supported by Lord Crewe in his decision to decline.

He kept up a moderate level of political activity, visiting the western front at Haig's invitation and coming out in favour of proportional representation, the League of Nations, and (belatedly) women's suffrage. He had time to give the Romanes Lectures at Oxford, *On the Victorian Age*.

The definitive break-up of the old Liberal Party came with the so-called Maurice debate.

In May 1918 Major-General Sir Frederick Maurice wrote to a number of newspapers challenging the accuracy of various ministerial statements, including some made by the Prime Minister himself. Lloyd George had denied that in order to counter Haig's fondness for bloody offensives (Passchendaele had marked the high point of slaughter in the autumn of 1916) he – Lloyd George – had deliberately kept Haig short of troops. Maurice challenged this denial. When the Prime Minister repeated his claim in the House of Commons on 9 April 1918, Maurice, then Director of Military Operations at the War Office, wrote to the newspapers repeatedly employing the phrase 'that is not correct' after reciting Lloyd George's various claims on the matter, and also similar claims by Bonar Law.

Lloyd George was later to suggest in his *Memoirs* that Maurice's allegations were part of an Asquithian plot to destroy his Government. The result was a series of acrimonious exchanges between Asquith and the ministry about how the matter ought to be investigated and clarified. When the issue came up for debate on the floor of the Commons, Asquith, in a poor speech, moved that a select committee of the House be established to investigate it rather than (as Bonar Law, now Chancellor of the Exchequer, had suggested) a panel of judges.

Lloyd George replied to the debate with a passion and energy that Asquith had entirely lacked. He secured all his objectives: escaping from Law's earlier and rather dangerous offer of a judicial enquiry, forcing the House to consider the issue then and there, refuting and discrediting Maurice, accusing Asquith of having been party to a plot to bring down the Government, and procuring an overwhelming vote of vindication from the Commons. It was, in Roy Jenkins' judgement, 'a great parliamentary *tour de force'* and moreover 'an event from which Lloyd George would never allow the Liberal Party to recover'.

By this time the war was drawing to a close and Asquith had begun to understand that his party was unlikely to retain a dominant role in post-war politics. Lloyd George and Law had developed the idea of holding a quick election on a Coalition ticket. That meant a continuing alliance with the Conservatives rather than any attempt to present a united Liberal option to the electorate. On Armistice Day 1918 Asquith received a telegram of thanks from the King before motoring to the House of Commons to hear Lloyd George read out the terms of the agreement to end the war. The House then proceeded to St Margaret's Westminster for a service of thanksgiving. On the following day the Asquiths attended a further service at St Paul's and lunched with the King and Queen at Buckingham Palace.

At some stage in the next few days Asquith had a face-to-face meeting with Lloyd George. Accounts of the meeting vary but it seems that Lloyd George was unwilling to have Asquith involved in the peace negotiations in Paris unless Asquith agreed to accept a position in the Government. Asquith again declined to serve but was bitterly disappointed at not being allowed to play any part in settling the peace.

There followed the general election at which only those Liberals who had proved loyal to Lloyd George in the Maurice debate were unopposed by the Conservatives: this was the so-called 'coupon'. The election was a disaster for Asquith, who began to receive intimations of how dreadful the results would be as he sat only a few feet away from Lloyd George at a Lord Mayor's lunch in the Mansion House. He lost his seat in East Fife after thirty-two years and his party was turned into a rump: only 29 non-couponed Liberals survived the landslide.

The first year after the war was an empty one for Asquith. In the autumn he was invited to preside over a Royal Commission on the Universities of Oxford and Cambridge. Later in the year, however, public disillusionment with the post-war Coalition began to increase. A vacancy in Paisley offered him the opportunity to return to Parliament: he lodged for the duration of the campaign at the Central Station Hotel in Glasgow and, after days of election-eering with his daughter, Violet, retired in the evenings to read Trollope in solitude at the hotel. He succeeded in the by-election and was greeted on his return to Westminster by cheering crowds outside Parliament but almost complete silence within the chamber. He received many letters and telegrams of congratulations but there was none from Lloyd George or any other leading figure within the Coalition.

But Paisley was a false dawn, both for Asquith personally and for the Liberal Party in general. Although the party did enjoy a reunion of sorts and Asquith defended Paisley in two further elections, the fundamental disintegration of the party and its replacement by the Labour Party was now almost inevitable.

By now Asquith had developed a marked sense of failure about his later career. He was also worried about money: he had taken to writing to earn additional funds, having been forced in 1920 to abandon the family home in Cavendish Square for a smaller house, 44 Bedford Square in Bloomsbury.

The Coalition collapsed in October 1922 when Conservative MPs, meeting at the Carlton Club, effectively withdrew their support from Lloyd George. He immediately resigned, thinking (as Asquith himself had thought in 1916) that this would be but a temporary withdrawal from 10 Downing Street. Bonar Law returned from retirement to head a Conservative Government with Curzon as Foreign Secretary and Stanley Baldwin as Chancellor of the Exchequer. He also called an immediate general election. Asquith held his seat but the Labour Party took 138 seats while the combined Liberals took only 117 (60 Asquithians and 57 for Lloyd George). Although Asquith subsequently reconciled with many of his old foes (including Churchill, who had joined the Conservative Government) his reconciliation with Lloyd George was insincere and motivated only by the desire to avoid the political destruction that each seemed to herald for the other.

In the autumn of 1923 the new Prime Minister, Stanley Baldwin, went to the country advocating protectionism. This opened an opportunity for Liberals to unite around their commitment of twenty years earlier to free trade. The election resulted in significant Conservative losses (reduced to a total of 285 MPs) and moderate Liberal (158) and Labour (191) gains. For Asquith, there was no possibility of an alliance with the Conservatives on the protection issue. He also judged that the time was right for the country to have its first Labour Government. Lloyd George agreed with this judgement.

Ramsay MacDonald became the country's first Labour Prime Minister in January 1924. Lord Haldane, removed by Asquith as Lord Chancellor in 1915 because of Unionist allegations that he was pro-German, returned as Lord Chancellor in the new administration. The minority Labour Government relied for support on the Liberals but coordination between the two parties proved inadequate. Most Liberal MPs quickly grew tired of the arrangement. Following a Tory vote of censure the Government collapsed later in the year. Asquith's speech on the motion of censure was the last he was to make in the House of Commons.

By the time of the 1924 dissolution Asquith was seventy-two years old. Embroiled for some years in a dispute with Lloyd George about the party's right of access to the latter's political fund, he lost his seat in Paisley to the Labour candidate that year. The Liberal Party was decimated, reduced to just 40 members. In November the King again offered Asquith a peerage which he now accepted, asking to be styled Earl of Oxford. The King agreed but the family of Robert Harley, who had held the title two centuries earlier, objected, and Asquith eventually took the title Earl of Oxford and Asquith.

He found the standard of speech-making in the Lords deplorably low. He was also shaken by the death of his old adversary Curzon in March 1925, as he had been by Montagu's in November the previous year. Venetia Montagu wrote to him soon after her husband's death, the first letter they had exchanged for nearly ten years. In May he accepted the Garter from the new Conservative Prime Minister, Stanley Baldwin. But the appointment that he would have valued even more, as Chancellor of Oxford University, was denied to him. Despite fulsome support from (of all people) F. E. Smith, now Lord Birkenhead, he was defeated by the Tory candidate Lord Chancellor Cave. Two years later Lord Grey was elected unopposed to the position in succession to Cave.

The insincere rapprochement between Asquith and Lloyd George continued but money was still a stumbling block. In January 1925 Asquith had launched the 'Million Fund Appeal' for the party; it was not a success and further weakened his position vis-à-vis Lloyd George. A disagreement relating to the General Strike of 1926 led to Asquith writing Lloyd George a rare letter of rebuke, described by his biographer, Roy Jenkins, as 'long and portentous'. Refusing to back down, Lloyd George replied vigorously, further weakening Asquith's position as leader. But personal events were now to overtake his political life.

On the 12th of June 1926 he suffered a slight stroke and was incapacitated for nearly three months. In October 1926 he resigned as Liberal leader. As Jenkins comments, 'He had stayed too long in an impossible situation, believing, falsely, that the Liberal Party could be revived by its old leaders'. Early in 1927 there was a loss of power in one leg and he was confined to a wheelchair. In October he paid one last overnight visit to Venetia Montagu at Beccles. On his return to Sutton Courtenay he had to be helped from the car and was unable to climb the stairs to his bedroom. Thereafter he declined rapidly: a progressive hardening of the arteries caused him increasing confusion of mind and he suffered intermittent delusions that he was being held prisoner at the Wharf. He died on the evening of the 15th of February 1928 and was buried at Sutton Courtenay.

Paying tribute in the House of Lords (the mausoleum, as Asquith had it) the following day, Lord Haldane held back tears as he eulogised his old chief:

'He fought great controversies on which many of your Lordships may disagree with the course which he took, but none, I think, will refuse him a tribute to the power of mind and of character which he showed throughout; because, he was essentially a man of character. Having taken a decision, he did not ask whether it was popular, or whether he would get glory by it; he simply went on upon the lines of the conclusion to which he had come. And that was his character right through the course of his public life.

'The noble Marquess [of Salisbury] has alluded to the decision which Lord Oxford took to enter the War. I remember that decision well. My noble friend Lord Grey and I were with him on the night of Sunday, August 2, 1914. We saw him, and immediately, without hesitation, his mind was made up. He did not wish to consult anybody. He did not wish to look beyond his own surroundings. He simply decided that a situation had arisen in which, much as we hated war, war was inevitable if we were to be saved from war in a further form which might entail disaster to this nation. Then he pursued his course with dignity to the end, and he preserved unbroken the devoted personal attachment of his friends. He has gone from us and the nation is the poorer. His was a great figure, a figure that could, as others had before him, but few others, wield the House of Commons.'

The House of Lords then adjourned in tribute.

The Liberal Party was never to form a Government again.

CPSIA information can be obtained at www.ICGtesting.com
Printed in the USA
LVOW07s0916250216

476673LV00005B/302/P